An Expected End

Heart-Glow Volume VI

Prince Patrick de Valdavia

An Expected End
Heart-Glow Volume VI

SHEILAH R CRAFT

STARLIGHT BOOKS

STARLIGHT BOOKS

This novel is a work of fiction. Names, characters, places, and incidents either are products of the author's imagination or are used fictiously. Any resemblance to actual events, locales, or persons, living or dead, is entirely coincidental.

Cover photograph taken by Sheilah R Craft. The dolls in the cover photograph represents Eric and Marisol on their wedding day. The doll in the front piece photograph represents Patrick at age 19, also photographed by the suthor. Eric was customized by Laurie Lenz, and Patrick by Sheilah R. Craft. The dolls were manufactured by the Tonner Doll Company. The author does not have any business affiliations with Tonner Doll Company or ANGELS Doll Studio.

First Starlight Books edition August 2018

ISBN-13: 978-0615969114

ISBN-10: 0615969119

ACKNOWLEDGMENTS

The DeBruce Martineau family bless my life immeasurably. Eric, Angilia, and Patrick in particular remain priceless gifts from God, who gifted me with my imagination and my writing. These characters—people—likewise touch readers with their inner strength, faith, and love, as well as the manner in which they deal with and overcome the trials and heartbreak they encounter.

This family certainly reconfirms my faith and increases my strength. By living through traumatic moments with them, my ability to deal with similar events in my life has intensified and grown more faithful and hopeful. I am a far better person for living so intimately with them.

Watching young Eri and Patrick grow up during this novel remains bittersweet, because I always knew where their destinies led them. So do readers of the *Heart-Glow* series. While this novel was never difficult to write, parts of it were admittedly sad—even though I know the ultimate outcome.

This novel series is now at the halfway mark, with six volumes remaining. Readers will meet many other members of the DeBruce Martineau dynasty in some of these volumes, people who, like all of us, traverse life's peaks and valleys, joys and sorrows. Just because they are royalty and possess strong faith does not exempt them from malevolent events and heartbreak. Far from it, as Eric and Angilia attest: those whose faith is strongest often suffer the harshest. The test lies in how they respond to these incidents.

I am honored to have my life forevermore blessed by these remarkable people, and I truly look forward to writing the next six DeBruce Martineau family novels.

DEDICATED TO

SHARYN CRAFT MATRINEZ

AND

JOSE MARTINEZ

FOR I KNOW THE THOUGHTS THAT I THINK TOWARD YOU, SAITH THE LORD, THOUGHTS OF PEACE, AND NOT OF EVIL, TO GIVE YOU AN EXPECTED END.

--JEREMIAH 29:11

CHAPTER 1

"Where is Stefan?," Sabrina asked as her family gathered in the dining room for breakfast.

"I'll go get him!" Patrick eagerly volunteered and ran from the table.

"Walk, Patrick; don't run," his grandmother reprimanded.

"Yes, Ma'am," Patrick said as he slowed—until he was out of view. Then he ran up the marble staircase to the third floor. His grandparents' suite was next to his, so he ran down the hall and knocked on their door. No one answered. He called for his grandfather, but received no answer. "Maybe he's still in the shower," Patrick mused aloud.

The young boy shrugged his shoulders, opened the door, and stepped into the sitting room. Of course, it was vacant. After knocking on the bedroom door and not receiving an answer, Patrick entered. His grandfather sat in his chair. He had fallen back asleep!

Patrick nudged the older man's arm, practically yelled in his ear, and still got no response. "Grandfather? Why don't you wake up?" Patrick pulled on the man's arm, but it fell limp off the armrest.

Patrick wasn't sure what to do, so he just stared at his grandfather and willed him to move.

"Patrick, what are you two doing? Everyone's waiting."

"Eric!" Patrick ran to his older brother, who had been sent to rush Stefan and Patrick. "Something's wrong with Grandfather!"

"Wrong? What happened? Is he hurt?"

"I don't know. He won't move. He's in his chair." Patrick pointed to the bedroom.

Eric ran in, knowing what had happened before he touched his grandfather. "Patrick, go tell Father to come here. Tell him you need his help. Don't act upset or anything, though. Can you do that?"

Patrick ran downstairs and into the dining room, ignoring his grandmother's and mother's admonitions. He went to his father and motioned for him to lean close. Patrick softly said, "We need you upstairs. Something's wrong. Please hurry."

"Excuse me, please, but Patrick has a problem," Gerard calmly said to his family and took his son's hand.

"Please, Father, hurry!" Patrick urged as his father walked up the staircase. "It's Grandfather."

"I feared as much, Patrick. All right, hop on my back," Gerard said, and he ran up the stairs to his parents' suite.

Inside, he realized immediately that his father was dead. His oldest son stood staring at Stefan, his hand on the man's arm. "Eric, Patrick, wait in the sitting room, please. I want to be alone with Grandfather for a few moments."

"Do we have to? I want to know what's wrong," Patrick said, tears tinging his voice.

"Very well, but both of you stand over there," Gerard pointed a couple of feet away. He needed to check his father's pulse and breathing to make certain. Once he knew, he rang his father's assistant to telephone the coroner. He then turned to his sons, knelt before them, and said the hardest words he had yet uttered. "Boys, your Grandfather is dead."

"Dead?" Patrick asked.

"Yes, Patrick, my boy. Do you understand what that means?"

Patrick nodded. "He won't be here anymore. His soul left his body and is in Heaven with Jesus. His body will be buried. But he won't rise and come back to earth like Jesus, will he?"

"No, son, he won't. He will live the rest of all time in Heaven, just like you said. It's beautiful and peaceful there, we know that, right?"

Patrick and Eric nodded. Their grandfather's death was the first death they had personally experienced. "I'm going to miss him, though," Patrick admitted as a tear slid down his cheek. "He was so much fun."

"He sure was," Eric added. "I'm going to miss him, too. But what about Grandmother? What will happen to her?"

Gerard put his hand on Eric's cheek; his son constantly considered other people's feelings, even at his young age. The thought gave him some hope and comfort, given that this young boy was now the heir to the Valdavian throne.

"We will take care of Grandmother and love her, as we always have. She will be sad and lonely without Grandfather. After all, they were married for 62 years. Remember how I told you that I am their only child to live past your age, Eric? Grandmother has had a lot of sadness in her life, so we must be especially kind and loving with her. Do you both understand?"

Both boys nodded their heads. "Yes, Father," Eric said.

Gerard sent for his mother and his wife. When they arrived, Patrick ran to his grandmother and hugged her. Sabrina knew. She hugged her grandson close and breathed deeply for several minutes. She did not want to cry in front of the boys.

Matilda looked at her husband, and Gerard nodded once in answer to her unasked question. His father was dead, and he was the new King de Valdavia.

§§§§§

Royal Statement

31 January 1963

It is with the deepest sadness that I confirm the death of my father, King Stefan de Valdavia. He died peacefully in his suite this morning, the morning of his 83rd birthday.

My father's life was long and filled with love of God, family, Valdavia, and his job. He served this country with wisdom, courage, and compassion, keeping Valdavia out of the wars that plagued and plundered other nations. His faith in God remained his guiding force, and he never showed evidence that he supposed himself any better than any other citizen of this great country.

To honor his life and devotion, his funeral shall take place at Christ Church Valmondois on Saturday, 3 February 1963.

Valdavia is richer for King Stefan's service and tireless work.

§§§§§

"Eric? Are you awake?"

Eric tossed, turned, and opened his eyes. "I am now. What's wrong?"

"Can I sleep with you tonight?"

"Sure," Eric answered and flung back the sheets and blanket for his brother.

Patrick climbed onto the bed and snuggled beside Eric. "I really did think Grandfather was asleep. He looked asleep."

"I know."

"Is that what death is really like, Eric? One of our Sunday School teachers said death is the great sleep. I don't understand."

"Well, I don't think it is, but that's what a lot of people say," Eric said. "It doesn't make much sense to me that it's like sleep and that's all."

"I know. I mean, we go to Heaven, right? And we do things there, right? So how can we be asleep at the same time?" Patrick asked.

"We can't be both at the same time. I don't think we are. I think people probably mean that our bodies are asleep for eternity. That's the only thing that does make sense to me."

"Yeah, to me, too. Our bodies die. Our souls don't. But what do our souls live in when we get to Heaven?"

"New bodies, I suppose. Father told me that we get new bodies when we get to Heaven. Everyone still looks the same, but our bodies are made new and perfect," Eric explained.

"Oh. That makes sense. Thanks, Eric. Goodnight."

"Goodnight, Patrick." Eric watched his brother for a while, wondering what it had been like for him to find their Grandfather like that. Did it scare Patrick? After all, he was just a little boy, in pre-school, and that was a shocking thing to happen to anyone.

Eric looked up and silently prayed. *"Dear God, please take care of Patrick, and don't let Grandfather's death and finding him dead upset Patrick too much. And please take care of Grandmother now that she's without him. She must feel lost and alone and sad. And Father is the new king. He's in charge of the country now. Please help him. Goodnight, God, and thank you."*

§§§§§

Saturday morning, everyone prepared for Stefan's funeral. Matilda assisted her two sons, while Sabrina's lady-in-waiting helped her to dress. Everyone was quiet and somber, from the family to all of the servants. Stefan was exceedingly loved and respected, and even though Gerard had been an apt pupil of his father and had inherited his wisdom and kindness, everything had changed forever. Gerard understood that more than anyone else. He had deeply loved and

5

admired his father, and he prayed that he would be half the king his father had.

Matilda gathered her sons close before she returned to her husband. "Boys, you know that you and Father will walk behind Grandfather's casket on its way to the church. Walk slowly, and no matter how upset you may feel, please do not cry. That would only upset your father. I hope you understand, darlings. Yes, Father is the king now, and he must be strong for the people, but he is burying his own father today."

"I understand, Mother," Eric said. "I won't cry until I am alone in my room again."

"Neither will I, Mother, no matter how sad I feel," Patrick promised.

"You are the most perfect sons I could ever pray for. Thank you both for being such strong men today for your father." Sabrina kissed them, dried her own eyes, and went to aid her husband.

"I already want to cry," Patrick told Eric. "I miss Grandfather awful, and this is going to be the saddest day of my life. How do I not cry?"

"Well, think of the funny stories and jokes Grandfather told us, and just think of all the fun times you had with him. Mother always said you're incredibly like him. She called you two imps," Eric said and giggled.

"What's an imp?"

"An imp is like a fairy who plays pranks and gets in trouble. That's what Father told me when I asked him," Eric explained.

Patrick laughed. "I guess we are. I like being an imp. Thanks. Now I won't cry during the funeral."

"Good, but don't laugh either, for crying out loud," Eric said and rolled his eyes. Patrick laughed again and promised he wouldn't. Eric had his doubts. Imp indeed.

§§§§

Gerard kissed his mother and his wife before they entered a Rolls Royce for the drive to the church. The Palace servants had previously left in several cars and would enter before the family's arrival. Monarchs and heads of state were already seated in the church. Reverend Simmons greeted each guest, and personally escorted the King Mother Sabrina and Queen Consort Matilda to the Royal pew. People bowed their heads as they passed.

At that moment, Gerard put his hands on his sons' shoulders and walked out onto the courtyard to stand behind Stefan's cortege. The boys flanked their father, and both kept their heads bowed until the cortege began moving. Thousands of people filled the mall and lined the route to the church. Many more stood closely packed across from the church, all there to pay respects to their King Stefan.

At the sound of the first church bell, the cortege began its measured journey, and Gerard and the young princes looked straight ahead for the slow but relatively short walk to the church. Eric found himself staring at a gold star on the Valdavian flag that draped the casket in an attempt to restrain his emotions. The star, he thought, was just a depiction. It wasn't real. It couldn't feel, and it wasn't dead. That's all he allowed himself to think as he walked each excruciatingly slow step.

Patrick looked at the opposite corner of the flag. One tiny piece trembled and flopped with the movements of the carriage which bore the casket. Patrick grinned, thinking of how his grandfather had playfully mimicked the soldiers during a salute the year before. It seemed as if Grandfather once more aped the solemn ceremony. Patrick nearly laughed, but then remembered where he was and why. Grandfather was dead. He would never joke and act silly anymore. Patrick bit his cheeks to stop his tears. He couldn't upset Father. If he did, Mother would be disappointed.

Finally, they stopped in front of the church. Gerard, Eric, and Patrick stood at attention while the soldiers carried Stefan's casket to the foot of the church steps. All three of them heard people weeping and praying. Gerard and Eric stood rigid and straight. Patrick shuffled his right foot and glanced quickly behind him at the crowd. So many people, and all of them were sad. He wanted to run, because he was certain he, too, would cry. He wanted to cry so much, but he had promised his mother he wouldn't. He felt unexpectedly glad that he wasn't the oldest son, because if he were he would have to be the next king when Father died. That would be too hard, to always hide his emotions and feelings from people. He wouldn't be able to do that, Patrick feared.

Gerard and Eric took a couple of steps, and Patrick quickly fell into line alongside them. They followed the casket to the front of the church, where the soldiers placed it on a bier and Reverend Simmons made the sign of the cross. Then Reverend Simmons greeted them and bowed as they took their seats.

Matilda patted Eric's shoulder as he sat beside her. She glanced at Patrick and nodded once, as if to say he had done well so far. He sighed, glad he hadn't made a misstep. He then stared at the casket as the choir sang a hymn. Grandfather had been quite formal in public and at functions, but with Patrick he had been silly and fun. Patrick quietly giggled at the word imp. He and grandfather had played games and pranks, and Patrick especially enjoyed them.

Patrick never heard Reverend Simmons's sermon. He sat remembering the time he and Grandfather had dressed in old clothes they found in the attic and pretended to be pirates. Mother had found them after searching for Patrick for over one hour, and she looked horrified. Gerard had laughed at her reaction and insisted that he and Patrick be allowed to continue until all of the treasure was in their possession. "Well, I never," Mother had huffed and gone back to the dutiful Eric. They had such fun that day.

"My father became king when I was just six, one year older than my youngest son Patrick is now." Patrick heard his name and looked up. Father was speaking, so he better listen carefully. "I learned from watching him these past thirty-seven years. I have learned a tremendous amount about leading with faith and compassion, letting prayer guide me, and listening to my fellow citizens. Father was well-loved for a reason. He always put the needs of Valdavia's citizens above all else, and he did what was in our best interest at the time.

"I also learned how to be a husband and a father alongside the duties of kingship. Father always made time to talk with me, to help me with my homework, to play with me, and to do things with me, such as fishing and camping. I will do the same for my sons, Eric and Patrick, who are just eight and five. While duty is a priority, and will remain so, my top priority will always be my family. That is the greatest lesson I learned from my father, and I want my sons to learn the same from me.

"None of this," Gerard said as he waved his arm in a broad swipe, "would matter if I were to neglect the people most important in my life. I heard Father say that to the Prime Minister of England once. I never forgot hearing him say that, his voice tinged with emotion. He is right. So, I will carry on my father's work and create my own role as king, but I will do so while remaining devoted to my family above all else. All who knew my father at all will understand the importance of that."

Gerard returned to his seat as the choir once more sag a hymn, and then Reverend Simmons said the closing prayer. King Stefan would be interred in the Royal Vault with his ancestors, attended by his immediate family and close friends. Eric and Patrick walked behind their father and grandmother into the Vault, followed by Matilda and invited friends.

The soldiers held the casket above the tomb as Reverend Simmons prayed, and then they slowly lowered it into the tomb. Sabrina placed a red rose on her husband's casket and stood tall. She, too, refused to cry in public, Patrick realized. He wouldn't, either, despite the seeming finality of the lowering of the tomb lid. Grandfather was gone forever. Patrick squeezed his hands into tight fists to control himself. He couldn't cry until he was alone in his suite.

However, he would not return to his suite anytime soon. After the burial, the Royal Family thanked each guest for attending the funeral and honoring King Stefan. Patrick dutifully shook hands and thanked each person, all the while wondering how his grandmother was faring. He dared not look at anyone except the guests, although he stole a quick glance at his brother.

Eric did more than shake hands and offer thanks. He chatted with each guest briefly. About what, Patrick didn't know. He had no idea what he would say to any of them. He didn't know any of them, and all of them were as old as or older than his parents. He just wanted the funeral over with.

After all of the guests were thanked, Matilda kneeled and told her sons, "Now, stay on your best behavior, boys, because Father and I are hosting a luncheon for the guests. They are on the way to the Palace now to freshen and rest first. We will return shortly."

"All right, Mother," Eric said, and tugged his jacket sleeves as he had seen his father do many times. "Patrick and I are happy to help in any way. Aren't we?" Eric asked and looked at his brother.

Patrick just wanted to be alone, but he mustered, "Sure, we'll do whatever you want, Mother."

Matilda patted their heads and then spoke with Reverend Simmons briefly. She next linked her arm through her husband's, inadvertently leaving Sabrina alone. Patrick quickly noticed, and he went to his grandmother, took her hand, and gently squeezed it in reassurance. Sabrina nodded and gave Patrick a sad smile.

The family slowly walked down the aisle and through the double doors of the church. Outside, they noticed the thousands of mourners still gathered, many of them still crying and others holding flowers. As they went down the stairs, intending to enter their car, Sabrina stunned everyone.

"Come, Patrick. We must talk with everyone. They are here because they, too, love Stefan, and he would want us to think of them today."

"All right, Grandmother. I want to do what Grandfather would want."

Gerard looked at his wife and Eric and quietly said, "Mother is right. Father would not have ignored everyone. Let's go speak with them, too. The guests will understand." Matilda and Eric followed Gerard, and soon the entire Royal Family was speaking with and accepting condolences and flowers from the mourners.

Patrick stayed with his grandmother, while the others did the walkabout individually. Eric seemed mature for his young age, impressing people with his poise and ease. Many people told him this, including a gentleman who offered a floral arrangement of lilies to the young prince.

"Prince Eric, I loved King Stefan tremendously. He was a kind king, and he cared about us all. We knew that. We saw that. Valdavia has suffered a tremendous loss. I know your father learned well from Stefan, and he, too, will be a compassionate king."

"Thank you, Sir. That is kind of you to say. I love my grandfather, and I am going to miss him."

"I know, my boy. I know. Let me tell you, I am watching you, too, as the future King de Valdavia. I was outside the hospital when your parents took you home after your birth. I took one of the first pictures of you, and I keep it in my photograph album. You have all the makings of a great king. You are already so composed, dignified, and confident."

Eric felt his cheeks burn, and knew he was blushing. "Thank you, Mr. . . ."

"Brennan. Arthur Brennan. I hope to meet you again someday, God willing."

§§§§§

Late that afternoon, after all of the guests had left, the family could finally release their tensions. Gerard went to his father's office—his office—intending to sit in quiet solitude for a couple of hours. The day had been emotional and, yes, painful. Stefan hadn't just been the king; he had been Gerard's father, and the loss was immense. At that moment, he needed and wanted to finally cry; he had forced the tears to stay inside since Patrick had come for him on Wednesday morning.

Matilda went to her suite, changed into her dressing gown, and collapsed on the chaise. She knew this would eventually happen, but she had not not expected it yet. Gerard had been in excellent health at his last comprehensive physical examination just four months earlier. On Wednesday, she and Sabrina were planning to give him a surprise birthday party. After all, he had turned 83 that day. He had died on his birthday. Thankfully, she thought, his death seemed to be peaceful.

Eric had watched his parents ascend the stairs, and he noticed that Gerard's shoulders stooped. He realized that Father was sad. Eric trailed them, surprised that his father continued up the stairs while his mother went to their suite. Gerard stopped outside of Grandfather's office.

Gerard stood, unmoving, his head bowed for a few moments. Eric had remained quiet, walking on his tiptoes the whole way. Father was upset, and Eric was worried about him. He didn't know what he could do exactly, except to let Father know he understood and loved him.

"I want to be alone for a while, Eric. It's been a long day for you, so you can change and relax now."

"Yes, Father. I love you," Eric softly said and turned to go down the stairs.

Gerard turned the doorknob, then looked at his son, the boy who would one day be in this same position. "I know, son. Come in and keep me company. I'll like that much more than being alone."

Gerard and Eric sat at Stefan's desk, looking as the books, papers, files, and framed photographs. "I'm going to miss Grandfather. It will never be the same without him," Eric said as he held a photograph of Stefan, Patrick, and him.

"I will, too. It never is the same when people we love die. It can't be. Oh, their presence remains, as do the memories of them, but the everyday contact is gone forever."

"Not forever, Father." Gerard looked perplexed by Eric's comment. "We will reunite with Grandfather again someday when we die and go to Heaven. That's where he lives now, with his parents and God."

Gerard smiled and hugged his wise little boy. "Yes, he does, Eric. And if we remain obedient to God, we will, too, and yes, we will be with Grandfather again. How is my eight-year-old son smarter than his old father?"

"You aren't old, Father," Eric said and giggled.

"I don't feel old right now. Thank you for bringing joy back into my life. As I said in the church, you and Patrick are the most important people in the world to me. I love you both very much."

§§§§§

While the others went upstairs, Sabrina slowly walked through the foyer as Patrick stood watching her. She ran her finger over a chair, then a table, and stopped when her finger touched the edge of a picture frame. She carefully picked up the picture and held it to her chest. Patrick knew what the picture was; Grandfather had told him last Christmas: Gerard's and Sabrina's wedding portrait, taken on January 1, 1901.

Would Grandmother cry? Patrick wondered as he looked around. No one else was there, which meant he had to take care of Grandmother. As Patrick nervously watched her, Sabrina returned the picture to the table and walked extremely slowly up the staircase. Patrick followed her like a faithful puppy, to the east wing, down the hall, and to her suite. She closed the door, leaving him standing outside alone.

Patrick took a couple of steps toward his suite, but turned around at the sound of crying. Grandmother was crying! Patrick quietly opened the door and went to the sofa, where his grandmother sat heaving and crying. "Grandmother, I'll take care of you," he said and put his hand on her arm.

Sabrina looked at her grandson and motioned for him to sit beside her. "I know you will, Patrick. You are a good boy, even if you are a tad wild sometimes. You are a great comfort to me, darling boy." She ran her hand through his dark hair, which seemed always mussed. "You have your grandfather's slate blue eyes. It was his eyes that I first noticed, you know."

"No, I didn't know, Grandmother, but he would have liked to hear that. Mother said Grandfather and I are imps."

Sabrina laughed for several minutes, which made Patrick smile. He had made Grandmother happy. "You certainly are! Stefan was so formal and proper most of the time. In fact, I never heard him even utter a joke, let alone saw him cavorting around the Palace Oh, he played with your father, but their play was calm. That all changed when you were born. You awakened that in him, and it did him good to loosen up some. You brought him much joy, Patrick."

"I'm glad, Grandmother. I love him. I love you, too."

"We both love you, dear heart," Sabrina replied and kissed the top of his head.

Patrick sat with his grandmother until she yawned and said she would take a nap. Patrick kissed her cheek and went to his suite. Finally, after a seemingly-long day, he changed from his suit into jeans and a polo shirt. He stared out of a window for many minutes, and at last he cried. Patrick cried until he couldn't cry anymore, dried his face, and went to his desk.

He took a spiral-bound notebook from a drawer, picked up his pen, and wrote what he felt. He could never tell his family how he actually felt, because that would upset them. He couldn't do that.

Grandfather, I miss you so much. You were my best friend. I mean, Eric is a good friend, but he is always more serious. He doesn't dress up and pretend like we did. Playing with you was the best times I ever had. You always told me to not do what you did most of your life. You told me to have lots of fun, that life was too short to be so serious all the time. You told me to laugh lots, not frown or cry.

I try to, Grandfather, even today. I did think about that time we dressed up and played pirates. And I thought the corner of your flag was being naughty on the way to the church, like it was you who was making it flap around like that. That's the kind of thing you'd do.

But it's hard not to cry today. I'm sad that you're gone. I know you're in Heaven, but you're not here anymore. I miss you. I didn't cry during the funeral, because Mother said it would upset Father. Then, after the luncheon, Grandmother was crying. We have to take care of her now, so I couldn't cry in front of her, even though I wanted to at first. But I made her laugh, so I guess that's good. It's what you said people should do.

14

I'll do like you said, Grandfather. I'll have fun all the time. I'll make people happy so they're not sad. I'll do this, so no one knows how I really feel. I'll write it in this notebook. That way I get it out without anyone knowing. I'll keep this notebook hidden in the secret hiding place you made me.

§§§§§

No one wanted dinner; the day's events had exhausted each of them. Instead, they spent the late afternoon and early evening in their suites. Patrick wrote more in his journal; Sabrina looked through her photograph albums, remembering the moments of her shared life with Stefan; Matilda held her husband close as they sat on their sofa. Eric, still in his suit, stood on his balcony and stared up at the sky.

A knock on Eric's door roused his brain, and he told the person to enter. The main butler opened the door and said, "Prince Eric, Roger Rocard is in the foyer asking to visit with you."

"Send him up, Manley," Eric said. Roger had become his best friend a few years earlier when they had met at church one Sunday. Roger was the one person with whom he felt safe sharing his thoughts and feelings; he trusted Roger.

"Hi, Eric. I wanted to say something to you earlier, after the funeral, but my mother said that wasn't the time or place what with all of the important people and all. I hope you didn't think I don't care about what happened. I do."

Eric shook his head. "I'd never think that. I know you care. I know you liked Grandfather; he liked you, too."

"I'm glad. How are you, really?"

"Sad. Awfully sad. I know Grandfather isn't really dead. His soul is alive forever in Heaven. But we all miss him. I miss him, Roger." Tears filled Eric's eyes, and Roger noticed immediately.

"You haven't cried yet, have you?" Eric didn't respond. "Have you?" Eric shook his head. "You know you need to. You don't need to be strong in here with just the two of us. It's okay to cry. Heck, I cried like a baby when my uncle died two years ago. Remember?" Eric nodded. "So, go ahead. I'll leave you alone if you

15

want, but you can't hold the sadness in too long or it will only grow worse. That's what my mom told me."

"You don't have to go. Will you stay?"

"Of course, I will, Eric. That's what best friends are for. Good times and bad times. Talk to me, get mad at me, scream, cry, but get it out."

Eric couldn't help but smile. "I can't scream. Everyone will hear. But I've held it in since it happened. I can't do it anymore." Eric leaned against the wall, covered his face in his hands, and cried. Roger put his hands on his friend's shoulders and let him cry for nearly one hour. When Eric stopped, he took out his handkerchief, dried his face, blew his nose, and said, "I'm sorry, Roger. I didn't mean to be such a drag."

"Hey, man, no. You needed to do this. That's one reason I came. I figured you'd been the strong one."

"Patrick has, too. He found Grandfather. I don't know if he's cried yet, either. He's so young. I don't know what this will do to him. This is his first death."

"Well, now that you're dealing with your grief, you can help Patrick deal with his. He'll be okay. What about your father? How's he doing?"

"We had a nice talk in Grandfather's, I mean Father's, office after the luncheon. He had wanted to be alone, and I knew he was sad. He needed to cry, too, but instead we talked about our memories. I hope he's been able to cry now, too. I mean, it's his father, and that's got to be tough."

"I know," Roger said. "I'm sure he has. Your mother is great at dealing with him and helping him. Do you want something to drink? I could go get you something from the kitchen."

"Just water. Thanks. Get yourself something, too."

Soon Roger returned with the glasses of ice water, and the boys sat in Eric's sitting room. "You're still wearing your suit. Why don't you change? Want me to help you?"

"Sure." They went into the bedroom, and Eric took off his suit while Roger pulled slacks and a polo shirt from the wardrobe. While Eric dressed, Roger hung the suit on the wooden valet.

"When you become king, I'll be happy to be your valet," Roger said. He noticed Eric's expression. "I just mean, well, you are the heir to the throne, and you are my best friend. I wouldn't mind working for you."

Eric looked at Roger and smiled. "I'd like that, too. Friends are important in a job like Grandfather's and Father's. Grandfather had one of his good friends working for him for many years, and Father's assistant is his friend since university. They need people they know and can trust, like I trust you."

"Have you had time to think about your future yet? You are the next king now, and, well, you'll be in charge of Valdavia someday."

Eric sighed deeply and said, "I know. My life's role has been planned since my birth. Most people get to think about and choose what they want to do, but the oldest sons in my family are born knowing what we have to do."

"Does that ever scare you? I mean, you won't have a Prime Minister or a Parliament like the Queen of England. They have all of the real power. Everything will be in your hands, Eric. You'll be alone, really. I'd be terrified," Roger admitted.

"Scare me? No, not really. I've seen Grandfather do this all of my life, and now I'll watch Father and learn from him. He told me he began royal duties when he was 11, so in a few years I will, too. I'll probably also accompany him on some of his engagements, so I can learn from that, too. I'm not scared. It's what I was born to do. It's my duty and what I have to do. Father will teach me, and God will guide me. I know my life's purpose, Roger. I'll be a king like Grandfather and Father who cares about the people of Valdavia and does what is right and best for them. Anything less would be a disservice to Grandfather and to God, who created me to do this."

CHAPTER 2

Two days after their grandfather's funeral, Eric and Patrick returned to King Christophe Elementary School, accompanied as always by two body guards. Patrick looked sadly at Eric when they arrived at the pre-school classroom and Patrick had to enter. Eric's third grade classroom seemed far away, around the corner and at the end of the hall. The brothers would not meet again until after school. After all, Patrick attended only half of each day and was driven home by his body guard.

Patrick practiced his printing on the special lined paper, even though he knew how to write. Grandfather had begun teaching him before he started school. He could write his entire name and address on the first day of school. Still, the lesson was required, and it did occupy him. His mind lost interest when Mrs. Gilmer, the teacher, read a book about squirrels to the class. He stared at the book cover, but he heard his grandfather telling him a story about his first hunting trip and how he couldn't bring himself to shoot the rabbit. Patrick didn't like hunting, either. Why kill animals that weren't doing anything wrong?

Eric kept busy with multiplication, geography, science, art, and history. He refused to look at the center of the wall, above the chalkboard. Grandfather's portrait always hung there, and he had noticed a black mourning band over the portrait. He didn't was to cry in school, so he ignored the portrait and looked only at what Mrs. Galland had written on the board. Roger sat beside Eric, and he realized what had upset his friend. Roger, however, thought it best not to talk about King Stefan at all. Heck, his funeral had been just two days earlier.

Patrick arrived home at 12:20 that afternoon, dutifully did his homework, and then took out his notebook to write. In his childish printing, he wrote:

5 February 1963

I hate today. I had to go to school like nothing had happened, like Grandfather isn't gone. That's not right. It's not fair. Grandfather sometimes drove us to school and picked us up, too. I get out at noon. He sometimes took me to the candy store before we went home. I always got his favorites, sour lemon balls, because I could share them with him. Gosh, I miss Grandfather.

No one said anything, which I'm glad. I would have cried if they did. I don't want to cry in public. Grandfather wouldn't like that. But I couldn't stop looking at his portrait in our room. It has a black ribbon over it now. That made me very sad, and I wanted to run home. But Grandfather wouldn't like that, either. Instead, I stared at his face when I wasn't doing anything, like during nap time. I just put my head on my arms and stared at Grandfather. I could almost hear him telling me to do my best in school today, so I did.

Mother said life goes on. I'm not sure what that means. Except everyone acted like they do every day, and Eric and I returned to school. We'd been out since I found—since Wednesday. I guess we have to keep doing what we've always done. That doesn't seem right really. I mean, my life is different now. Father is the king now. Grandfather is gone. How can I be the same as I was before? But that's what Mother seems to want, so I'll go to school every day, and I'll do my best just like Grandfather told me to do. But I'll never let anyone know what I'm really thinking or feeling, never. I'm never going to talk about what happened last week, because then I won't cry and upset anyone. And I guess that's most important.

§§§§§

The two princes completed the school year, and life did go on. Gerard's assistant, Thomas Kruger, had been working with city and church officials in planning the King's coronation. Every minute detail had been planned, and Thomas did a run-through in early May with stand-ins for the Royal Family, making sure all went as planned.

That same week, a Royal Couturier arrived to take measurements for the Royal Family's robes. During the ceremony, Gerard would wear the coronation robe made for the first King de Valdavia, Christophe Martineau, in 1331. For all other formal occasions, he would wear the new robe, as would his wife and sons.

"Why do I need a robe?" Patrick asked his bother as the couturier measured their parents. "You're going to be the next king."

"You're still the King's son, Patrick. You were born a prince just as I was. And you are second in line to the throne, don't forget."

"What does that mean?"

"If something happens to me, you'll become king. So, you have an important place, too. And even if nothing happens to me, you will still perform duties on behalf of Father. You represent the Crown, just as we all do: Father, Mother, Grandmother, me, and you. We are the Valdavian Royal Family."

"Oh. I don't want to be king. You better not do what King Edward did years ago in England. I heard Grandfather talking about it once. It made Edward's younger brother have to be king, and he didn't want to, either. Promise me you won't do anything like that, Eric. Please."

"I won't abdicate, Patrick, I promise. I wouldn't do that to Father, Mother, Grandfather, and all of our ancestors. The oldest living son of each king is the heir. That's how it's always been, and that's how it will stay. I'll never change that. But why don't you want to be king?" Eric asked.

"Because it's too much work and resondability."

"Responability?" Eric looked confused. "Oh, I know. You mean responsibility."

"Yeah, that. I don't want that. It's heavy. Grandfather said so. It hurt him, I think, 'cause it's heavy. I hope it doesn't hurt Father."

Eric smiled affectionately at his little brother. "It doesn't hurt, not really. Heavy responsibility just means in Valdavia the king rules alone, not with a Prime Minister or a Parliament like in other countries. The king makes all of the laws, decisions, and even decides the court cases. It's a lot of work. That's what Grandfather meant, Patrick."

"Oh. I still don't want to be king. I don't want to grow up just to work all the time. That's no fun."

"All grown-ups work, or most of them do. But no matter how hard their jobs are, many of them find time for fun. Like Roger's father."

"I guess. And Grandfather did have fun with me, didn't he?"

"He sure did. Grandmother said you were the best thing that happened to him."

Patrick's eyes sparkled for the first time in months. "Really?"

"Yes, really. I've never told you a fib, and I never will. You're the only brother I have. I want you to help me when I'm king. Will you do that?

"You do? Sure, Eric, you can count on me. I'll always be with you, I promise," Patrick said and hugged his brother. Life might not ever be the same again, but with Eric beside him, he would feel loved, safe, and, well, important. His brother stood as his best friend now.

§§§§§

The day began extra early for Gerard on Tuesday, June 6, 1963, his coronation day. All meetings and other work had to be put on hold for the day, and although he understood the importance of the ceremony, he felt anxious for the day to be over and for work to resume.

Eric dressed, and then helped Patrick dress. New suits had been made just for the coronation, and new shoes ordered. They would not put on the robes until it was time to enter the carriage.

"I look stupid," Patrick said as he looked at himself in the full-length mirror. "This is old-fashioned, like in history books. I don't like it."

"I know it looks old-fashioned, but it's supposed to. It's based on the Victorian era, when Great-Grandfather Gerard was born. That's what Father and Mother wanted for us to wear today."

"I still feel silly. This lace color makes me look like a girl, and the pants are shorter. I don't like it," Patrick whined.

"I know you don't. I'm not thrilled about it, either, but it's what they want. And you don't look like a girl."

"You certainly do not, Patrick," Matilda said as she entered Patrick's suite. "In fact, you look like a little angel, just perfect and beautiful."

"I do? This is what angels wear?"

"Well, I don't really know, son, but you do look like an angel. Try to stay that way, please. We will go down soon. Both of you stay neat and clean, and don't wrinkle your suits. I am going to check on your grandmother." Matilda blew them a kiss and left in a billow of satin.

"If this is what angels wear, I don't ever want to be an angel," Patrick insisted.

Eric giggled. "Why not? Angels are pretty important, you know."

"Well, they might be, but I'm not wearing this for however long eternity is, and I mean it. I'm wearing jeans and a t-shirt."

"Mother wouldn't approve," Eric teased his brother.

"I don't care. Heaven is not where she's in charge, so I can wear what I want. Father Simmons said it's not the clothes that matter, it's the heart. So, God won't care what I wear."

"Good grief," Eric said and rolled his eyes.

§§§§§

Thirty minutes later, the boys were summoned downstairs, where manservants helped them put on and fasten their robes. Matilda's lady-in-waiting and Gerard's valet assisted them. Gerard wore the antique 1331 robe for the Christian Ceremony in the church, until he returned to the Palace for the Constitutional Ceremony in the Throne Room. The coronation throne, crown, scepter, and other jewels had been taken to the church that morning and were under armed guard. After the Christian Ceremony, they would remain locked in the Royal Vault until Eric's coronation.

Eric and Patrick sat across from their parents, alongside their grandmother, in the coach, which drove though the city of Valmondois so that as many people as possible could view the Royal Family on this historic day. Gerard and Matilda waved to well-wishers, who screamed and cheered as they passed. Sabrina, too, waved, and the respect for her touched Gerard's heart. Eric whispered to Patrick that they should wave, too, so Patrick shrugged his shoulder and waved. He noticed school friends in the crowd, and he smiled at them. None of them had ever seen him actually look like a prince before. One bowed rather than smile, and Patrick realized for the first time that people would treat him different because he just happened to be born a prince. He didn't like that; he didn't want to be different.

However, the ceremony proved interesting, and both princes watched closely. They were seated in specially made miniature thrones to the right of their father's throne. They both forgot that everyone saw them as they watched their parents state the oaths to serve Valdavia and God.

When the ceremony ended, they followed King Gerard and Queen Consort Matilda, as well as King Mother Sabrina, down the aisle. Sabrina wore the robe that had been made for her Constitutional Ceremony on August 4, 1926. Thirty-seven years. Her own coronation replayed in her mind throughout the day. How she loved Stefan so, enough to leave her home and family in Penobscot County, Maine to begin a new life in Valmondois, Valdavia—a place she had only seen in history book engravings. She never regretted her decision for one second of her life.

When the Royal Family left the church, the cheers and screams caused Patrick to cover his ears. Several spectators noticed, and were charmed by the little boy, many snapping photographs of the moment. The youngest member of the family momentarily stole the attention from his father, the King. Gerard noticed people pointing and taking pictures to his left, and he glanced over. When he saw his youngest son with a rather pained expression, hands over his ears, he smiled.

With the crown on his head and the scepter in his hand, Stefan bent to speak with Patrick. "Son, I know the cheers are loud, but everyone is excited and happy today. When you are older and go on engagements, these screams will be only for you. You are already quite popular with the people. Many of them are watching you, Patrick."

"They are? Why? I thought today was all about you, Father."

Gerard laughed. "No, not just me. It's about all of us, our family and the people of Valdavia, our friends and neighbors. Why don't you pose nicely for their pictures, my little man?"

"All right, but this noise makes my head hurt. I'll try to ignore it," Patrick promised, as Gerard stood and waved to the crowds. Patrick waved, albeit a quite unroyal wave, which always charmed people. Matilda, Sabrina, and Eric joined, and the family stood on the church steps for several minutes to allow people to take pictures.

Finally, their carriage pulled up, and they entered for the long drive home through the city streets. Eric noticed a familiar face and nodded to him. Arthur Brennan bowed in response, and then lifted his camera to take a picture of the young heir.

Throughout the slow carriage ride, the family continued to wave and to acknowledge peoples' well-wishes with nods. Eric sat straight and regal beside his grandmother, while Patrick leaned against the seat. "I'm tired," he thought, "and my head hurts. I just want to go home."

Sabrina, who sat between her grandsons, leaned over and told Patrick to sit up straight. "Shortly after we return home, your father has the Constitutional Ceremony, so you mustn't rumple your suit or robe too much." Patrick signed but obeyed and sat up. "That's a good boy. Make Grandfather proud as he watches you from Heaven, dear."

What? *"Grandfather can see me? How? I thought only God can see us. I'll ask Reverend Simmons about that. But I don't want to upset Grandfather. I'll be good, but there won't be time to sleep in tomorrow. I have to go to school. I'm sorry Eric has to be so respondable. He'll be miserable."* Patrick looked at his brother, who waved and nodded to people, smiling the whole time. *"Well, maybe he won't, but I would be. It's a lot of work to do anything in this family."*

The cheers continued until after the Royal Family's carriage pulled under the back veranda. Gerard went to the throne room and took off the crown and robe, placed the scepter on a table, and prepared for the Constitutional Ceremony, during which he would vow to uphold the laws and constitution of Valdavia.

Matilda would sit alongside him on the thrones as his Queen Consort, even though she did not have any powers herself. She, like all Queen Consorts before her, was a support to her husband as well as a hostess and companion. She would continue her patronages and Royal duties, however, now on behalf of her husband.

Eric and Patrick sat with Sabrina in three chairs near the thrones, while invited guests sat in rows of chairs. The ceremony took two hours, and Eric watched and listened with genuine interest. He would, after all, take these same vows one day, hopefully many years in the future. Patrick constantly swallowed his yawns, remembering that Grandfather expected him to be a proper prince in these situations. There was a time for work, and there was a time for play. Grandfather worked an awful lot, but he did have fun. Patrick supposed his life would continue the same even if he wasn't going to be king.

A reception followed the ceremony, and Patrick had to greet people, shake hands, and talk to them. About what, he had no idea, but he supposed weather was always a good subject if nothing else came up. Women, in particular, swarmed around the five-year-old, finding him lovely, sweet, and charming. "Just like an angel," Mrs. Hicks said. Mrs. Young and Miss Hiller gleefully agreed, and Miss

Hiller went so far as to bend and kiss his cheek. No one except his family members had ever kissed him before.

Eric noticed from across the ballroom, and he smiled. Patrick would become a wonderful prince, and Eric would feel ecstatic to have him as a helper. *"I know! When I become king, I'll give Patrick a title all his own, a knight or a duc. He can be my main assistant and help me rule Valdavia. That's exactly what I'll do!"* Eric thought as he watched his brother. They would become an awesome, strong team.

§§§§§

As soon as the reception ended, Patrick took off his robe and ran upstairs to his suite. He quickly changed into blue jeans, t-shirt, and sneakers, his favorite clothes. He promised himself he would never wear a suit like today's ever again. He ran his hands through is thick black hair, mussing it into curls and waves. "Those ladies and Mother might think I look like an angel, but I just want to be me," he softly mumbled to whoever was listening, be it God and Grandfather or anyone else.

"I just want to be me. I want to choose what I do," he continued to grumble as he pulled out his notebook from the secret hiding place in his baseboard, grabbed a pen, and plopped on the floor. He opened the notebook, but stared out of the window for several minutes, thinking, before he wrote.

6 June 1963

Father's coronation was today, and boy was it a long day. Only because I had to wear this uncomfortable suit, which Eric said was made like Great-Grandfather's time. I hated it. It felt tight around my neck, and it itched. I was miserable all day, but I couldn't do anything about it. Plus, it made me look stupid. If I had to wear a suit, why couldn't I wear one of mine? As soon as it all ended I ran upstairs and changed. Grandfather sometimes had to wear these special clothes and the robes and crown. Father will too, and so will Eric. I do feel sorry for Eric. He can't do whatever he wants. He has to be the next king even if he doesn't want to. I made him promise not to quit, or I'd be king. He did promise me. He also said I can help him. I will. Being king must be lonely a lot. There aren't a lot of friends around. Maybe I can get Eric to play sometimes, maybe that will help him, too. That will be fun!

But I can never let Eric know how I really feel about anything, 'cause it will upset him just like it will upset Father. So, there is no one I can talk to. I will just write everything in my notebook and keep it hidden. No one knows about that place, just me and Grandfather, and he is gone. So it's just me. I am all alone. That's how it has to be.

§§§§§

The next two years passed unexcitingly, with nothing extraordinary occurring for the family. On the last day of first grade, Patrick got in the Rolls Royce with Eric and smiled broadly. Eric misunderstood the smile.

"Are you happy that school is over for this term?"

"No, not really. I like school."

"Then why the huge smile?"

"Well, because I get to spend more time with Mother, Father, Grandmother, and you. School takes up a lot of time for stuff like that," Patrick said as he looked out of the car window.

Eric giggled. "I guess it does. People spend at least 18 years of their lives in school, more if they go to university."

"Wow. That's a lot of time we could do other things, more important things. Isn't life too short to waste that much of it?" Patrick asked, still looking out of the window.

"School isn't a waste, Patrick; it's important. It prepares us for the rest of our lives and helps us learn things. Everyone needs to learn."

"I know, but it still seems like way too much time to spend on one thing when there are so many more things to do. Besides, how can school help prepare you to be king? You'll learn from Father."

"Yes, I will, but school is still important. It helps with my socialization skills, for one thing, because a king has to meet and work with a lot of people. It also teaches me good communication, because I will have to talk to people, give speeches, and write letters and other documents. I also want to learn about history, geography, and government so I understand Valdivia and other countries better. Father and Grandfather both went to university after high school."

"Will you go to university, Eric?"

"Yes. Father and I have already talked about it, and it's the best thing for me to do."

"Oh. When will you go?" Patrick asked, looking at his brother for the first time. He hadn't expected Eric to leave home at all.

"After high school."

"How long is that? Very long?"

"Oh, seven years. I'll be 17."

"That doesn't seem very long at all."

"I won't be gone forever, and I'll come home on holidays and for summer vacations. Then we can do things together."

"You will?" Patrick smiled, then looked like he would cry. "But you'll make friends, and you won't have time for me. That's how it always is, I know. Some of the boys in school said so about their brothers."

"Well, I'm not their brothers. I'm your brother, and I don't lie to you, remember that. Sure, I'll make friends, and some might visit, but that won't stop me from doing things with you. You have to hear all about what I'm learning, because you are going to be my number one assistant, remember?"

"You still want me to? Does that mean I have to go to university, too, and spend even more time in school?"

Eric laughed again. "No, not unless you want to, Patrick. You're a smart kid, so you'll learn lots by the time you're finished with high school."

"Okay, good. I want to have some fun before you become king and I have to work all the time," Patrick said with a relieved smile.

At the Palace, the boys went upstairs together, still talking about how Patrick would be Eric's assistant and his most important help when he was king. Gerard heard from the landing above, and he smile/d broadly, wishing he had a brother to talk to all of these years. He knew how much Patrick would mean to Eric when that day came, and he was the new King de Valdavia. He knew Patrick would love, support, and protect his brother regardless what happened. Gerard closed his eyes and softly said, "Thank you for these two boys who will carry on when you decide my life is over."

§§§§§

"Patrick, dear, would you mind keeping me company for a while?" Sabrina asked her grandson from his open suite door.

Patrick looked up from his notebook and said, "No, Grandmother. Just let me put everything away. Patrick put the notebook in the bottom of a desk drawer, under papers and folders, and then went to his grandmother.

She took his hand and walked to the end of the hallway to the tall windows that overlooked the expansive back lawn. "I have lived here since my wedding day, 64 years. I was 22 years old, and I had never been out of the United States before. But I said goodbye to everyone and everything I loved and came here, because I loved your grandfather so very much, Patrick. So very much. And now I miss him just as much, I admit it. My life feels empty without my Stefan." Sabrina began crying and pulled an embroidered handkerchief from her sleeve.

"I miss him, too, Grandmother. I do, and nothing feels the same without him. But he wouldn't want us to cry, so please don't cry. I'm here, and so is Eric, and Mother, and Father. He's your son. We love you, Grandmother. We don't want you sad. But I guess you can't help it. I think the more you love someone, the more it hurts when they die, because you loved Grandfather a whole lot and you hurt a whole lot. I loved him a lot, too, and I still hurt a lot."

Sabrina sat on a window seat and pulled Patrick to her in an embrace. "Oh, my wise little boy," she said and sobbed. "Yes, I think so, too. I doubt my pain will ever go away until I am reunited with Grandfather."

"Reunited?" Patrick slowly pronounced the new word. "What does that mean?"

"It means to meet loved ones again."

"Oh. You mean in Heaven, don't you? That's the only place you could see Grandfather again, because that's where he lives. You're not going to Heaven now, are you, Grandmother? Please don't go yet." Patrick felt tears fill his eyes.

Sabrina smiled and put her wrinkled hands on his cheeks. "No, darling, not now. I don't know when I will go to Heaven. Only God knows. But I can't say I will be sad to go. I will miss you, though, and Eric, Mother, and of course Father. But I have had a good life despite everything that happened that broke my heart. God has a reason for such things, and it's not our place to doubt or to question why people die when they do. When I do die, don't be sad for me, Patrick, please. Know that it's what I want, to be with Grandfather again. Promise me that?"

Patrick nodded. "Okay, if you want me to. I understand you wanting to be with Grandfather, because if Mommy died, I would want to be with her again. But you know, Grandmother, you can talk to me when you feel lonely or sad, okay?."

"I know, Patrick. I do love you so, my sweet angel." Sabrina kissed the top of his head, and then put her fingers on her temples.

Patrick looked confused. "What's wrong, Grandmother? Are you sick?"

Sabrina closed her eyes for a few moments, and then said, "No, I don't think so. It's just a terrible headache."

"Should I tell Mother and Father?"

"No, darling, just let me sit here for a while and feel if it eases up some."

"Okay. I won't talk," Patrick said and stared at his grandmother for what felt like days. She just sat there with her hands pressed to her head and a dreadful expression on her face like when a bee stinger is removed. She was in a lot of pain, and Patrick wasn't sure what to do. Should he run and tell Father? *No. I can't leave Grandmother alone. Something bad might happen while I'm gone. But what if something bad happens while I'm here? I don't know what to do,*" he thought as he nervously twisted his fingers.

"Patrick, are you still here?" Sabrina asked after more than 20 minutes.

"Sure, Grandmother. I haven't moved, see." He held his hand out to her, but she looked to his left rather than at his face. "I'm right here, Grandmother, right in front of you."

"Patrick, please help me to my sofa. I need to rest my head. This headache is getting worse, and my eyes are blurry. I can't see very well right now."

"Okay, Grandmother, I'll lead you and walk slow. Just come with me." Patrick took her hands and walked backwards into her sitting room as slowly as he could. His heart pounded, and he felt scared. But he couldn't leave Grandmother for one second now. What was he supposed to do? He could always shout for Father or Mother or one of the servants. He would do that when he got her on the sofa.

"Where am I?" Sabrina suddenly asked.

"We just got to your suite door."

"Why are we here? I was tending my rose bushes in the garden. Why on earth did you bring me up here?"

"Grandmother? We were talking, and you got a bad headache. You wanted to rest on your sofa."

"Did I? I don't remember. But I am so tired. Let me stop for a minute," she said and held tightly to Patrick's hands.

Her eyes were open, but she never looked at Patrick. Why? What was she looking at? Patrick's fear increased with every beat of his heart.

"Where are you, Patrick? I feel your hands, but I can't see you. I can't see anything." Patrick was on the verge of screaming for his father when Sabrina nearly fell on him. "What is happening to me? Oh, Patrick, don't leave me, please don't leave me. I can't see, and my head hurts so horribly."

"I-I won't," Patrick managed to say. As he held his grandmother's hands, Sabrina did fall, puling Patrick down with her. What had happened? She wasn't moving, and her eyes were closed. "Grandmother? Can you hear me?" Grandmother?" No! Not Grandmother, too!

"Father! Mother! Someone! Come quick!" Patrick screamed as loud as he could.

Gerard and Thomas heard from the fourth-floor office, and both ran quickly to the third floor. "Patrick! Where are you?" Gerard shouted when they got the top of the stairs.

"Grandmother's room. Hurry!"

"Dear God, no, not Mother!' Gerard barely said as he ran as fast as he could, stopping cold when he saw Patrick on his knees beside his mother. "Call an ambulance, Thomas, hurry."

While Thomas ran to the telephone in the sitting room, Gerard knelt beside his mother and felt the carotid artery in her neck. There was no pulse. He put his ear close to her nose, but neither heard nor felt any breath. He immediately began performing cardiopulmonary resuscitation. He didn't stop until the doctor arrived with the ambulance.

The doctor removed the defibrillator and told everyone to stand clear. Gerard held Patrick close to him, tightening his hold when the young boy jumped as his grandmother's heart was shocked.

Gerard kept praying, even though heartbeat was not restored. After 25 minutes, he whispered, "That's enough. Let her be. Mother is gone."

"Grandmother is gone? She's gone to Heaven with Grandfather?"

"Yes, Patrick, she has."

"Oh. Well, we were talking about that a few minutes ago before she got the headache. She said she was ready to go to him, and for us not to be sad when it happened. I mean, not sad for her, because she wants to be with Grandfather."

"She told you she was dying?" Gerard asked in disbelief. "Why didn't you yell for me then?"

"No, I asked her if she was going to die soon, and she told me she didn't know when, that only God knows. We talked some more, and she kissed me and put her hands on her head. She said she had a bad headache."

"What kind of headache, Prince Patrick? Did Her Majesty say?" the doctor asked.

Patrick shook her head. "Just a terrible headache. I asked if I should get Mother or Father, but she said she wanted me to stay with her while she sat on the window seat out there," Patrick explained and pointed to the end of the hallway.

"All right. Thank you, Prince Patrick. Your Majesty, we will transport King Mother Sabrina to the morgue when you and your family are ready." The doctor and the emergency medical team left the suite until word that the body was ready.

"Thomas, please go find Matilda and Eric, and ask them to please come to Mother's suite." Thomas nodded and left, at which time Gerard kneeled beside his mother once more. Gerard placed a hand over hers, bowed his head, and prayed.

Patrick saw tears fall down his father's cheeks. Patrick wished he could cry, too, but he remembered what mother had said before

Grandfather's funeral. Patrick's tears would upset Father. *"I don't really understand why. Most people cry when others die. But that's what Mother said, so I will never cry in front of Father. He must want me to be a strong man, so I will be. For him, I will be,"* Patrick thought as he stood beside his father.

Patrick put his arm around his Father's back as far as it would reach. *"I can be strong for Father, and I can help him when he feels sad or upset. That's what I can do. I can help Father and Eric. Father is the king now, and Eric will be the king when. . . when Father dies. I don't want Father to die. Please, God, don't let Father die ever. We need him. Mother, Eric, and I need him."* Patrick's hand tightened on Gerard's suit jacket as he fought to hold his tears.

"Patrick? Son? What's wrong?"

Patrick swallowed hard and managed to say, "Nothing, Father. I just know how sad you are, and I want you to know I love you."

"I love you, too, son, very much. You are a great source of strength for me. You give me hope and faith in the future."

"Me?" Patrick asked. Gerard nodded. "I'm glad. That's what I want to be for you, Father, always."

"You will be. You are growing into a strong, compassionate young man, and you will be a comfort and a help to me," Gerard said and kissed his son's cheek.

"Grandmother?" Eric asked in a tear-filled voice when he and Matilda entered the suite. "Father? Is Grandmother. . . . ? Is Grandmother gone?"

Gerard put an arm around Eric and said, "Yes, Eric, she is. She has gone to Heaven."

"She is with Grandfather now, so don't be sad about that. It's what she wanted. She told me so," Patrick added when he saw Father looked like he would cry again.

"Oh. But it is sad that she's gone," Eric said. "Really sad."

"I know, boys, it is. We will miss Grandmother dreadfully. But please remember what God tells us. His children never die; we live forever in Heaven. Patrick is right; Grandmother and Grandfather are together again, in Heaven rather than here on earth. That's the only difference," Matilda explained as she, too, knelt beside them.

"I know, Mother," Eric said, "I do, and I believe everything the Bible says about Heaven. I know Grandfather and Grandmother are happy and safe. But I do miss Grandfather still, and I'll miss Grandmother, too. That's not wrong, I know it's not."

"No, it's not, son. It's natural to miss people we love when they go away or die. God understands that. I miss them, too. We all will for as long as we each live," Gerard softly said and looked at his mother's body. "Boys, say your goodbyes to Grandmother, and then the ambulance will take her."

"Take her where?" Eric asked.

"To get her ready for her funeral." Gerard patted his sons' hacks. "Mother and I will leave you. Come tell us when you are done. We will be just down the hall."

"Yes, Father," Eric said. When their parents had gone, Eric could not hold his tears any longer, as much as he tried to. He pressed his hands over his eyes in an attempt to staunch the tears, to no avail.

"You cry, Eric. I'll stay with you. It's okay to cry." Patrick put his arm around Eric and patted his shoulder—just as Grandfather used to do.

Eric put his arms around Patrick and cried on his younger brother's shoulder. Patrick continued to pat Eric's back, comforting his brother as Father said he should. As the youngest son of the king, Patrick's job was to help and to console his father and his brother, the current and future kings. That's what Father said Patrick did, so that's what he would always do.

Patrick let his brother lean on him until Eric stopped crying, sat up, and dried his eyes. "Grandmother did tell me she didn't want us to be sad when she went to Heaven," Patrick told his brother.

Eric nodded. "I'm not sad about that. I just love her, and I'm going to miss having her here all the time."

"Me, too. But we all die. That's part of life. Father Simmons said so. He said death is nothing to be scared of. I don't understand what really happens, though, so I don't know if I should be scared or not."

"I'm not scared of death, Patrick. I just get sad when people I love die and leave. That's all. Life here changes without them, just like when Grandfather died."

"Yeah. I know. Why aren't you scared?" Patrick asked.

"Because I believe that Jesus died and lived again for my sins, so I will go to Heaven. There's nothing scary about Heaven, nothing at all. It's the most beautiful, perfect place ever."

Patrick nodded. "Yeah, you're right about that. Heaven isn't scary at all. I wonder if people in Heaven can have fun and stuff."

Eric laughed, which made Patrick smile. He didn't like it when Eric, Father, or Mother were sad or upset. "I can never be scared as long as you're around, you big goof ball."

Gerard allowed the boys to view their grandmother's body taken away. An autopsy would be performed to determine the cause of her death. Gerard wondered about the terrible headache Patrick had mentioned. Had his mother suffered a stroke? he wondered. He would find out, but in the end, it didn't matter. His mother was 86 years old and had been lonely without Stefan.

The doctor did rush the autopsy results, and he personally delivered them to King Gerard. His mother had suffered a ruptured brain aneurysm, which had proved fatal. Gerard felt pangs of regret that she had suffered, but he found solace in knowing that her pain was forever erased.

The family retired to their suites, but Patrick soon found himself at Eric's open door. His brother sat on his window seat, hugging his knees and staring at the sky. Patrick watched him for a long time before Eric noticed him there. "Are you all right, Eric? Do you need company, or do you want to be alone?"

"I'm okay, just sad like we talked about. What about you? Weren't you with Grandmother when it happened?"

Patrick nodded. "Yeah, I'm okay. She had a bad headache, and then she fell. That's all. It happened fast."

Eric worried, though. Patrick had found Grandfather two years earlier, and he had just been with Grandmother when she died. That was an awful lot for such a young child. Eric stared at his brother carefully. Patrick looked all right, not upset or scared or anything like that. Maybe Patrick was just stronger that way, Eric thought.

Just to make sure, he told Patrick to come in and sit with him for a while. Eric would keep an eye on him. Eric promised himself to always take care of and protect Patrick, no matter what. They were brothers, and after Father and Mother died, they would be the only family. Eric had to protect Patrick.

§§§§§

Three days later, on August 17, 1965, Valdavians prepared for King Mother Sabrina's funeral. The American girl had met, fallen in love with, and married Prince Stefan. The people of Valdavia, she frequently told her family, welcomed her as one of their own as soon as she disembarked the ship that had brought her from faraway Maine. She came to love them, too, and worked tirelessly on behalf of charities, women's groups, and schools. She adored children, and when her first three children died, she deeply grieved. So, too, did the citizens of Valdavia.

Sabrina and Gerard suffered much heartbreak, but they never forsook their duties and their vows. Both remained genuinely loved and respected. The grief shown for Gerard in 1963 and for Sabrina in 1965 was sincere and indisputable. When the family prepared for the short procession to the church, Eric squared his shoulders, straightened his tie, and took a deep breath. He could not, would not, let the weeping get to him. He would not cry. He was the heir, the next king, and he had to learn to restrain his emotions in public situations.

Patrick didn't have the same constraints as his brother, but he, too, had to fight back his tears. *"I can't cry, no matter how much it hurts. I have to be strong for Father and Eric. They depend on me. They expect me to be strong. I have to be strong. I have to be strong. I have to be strong."* Patrick repeated his mantra all the way to the church, up the aisle, throughout the service and burial, the ride home, and the luncheon that followed. He continuously, silently said, *"I have to be strong"* until his brain thought no other words. That evening, he printed the words in black crayon on a page in his notebook, large and bold: **I HAVE TO BE STRONG**. It became his life's motto and purpose.

§§§§§

The following day, Arthur Brennan—the regular postal carrier who delivered the Palace mail—appeared at the gates, where the guards greeted him. Along with the sack of mail for the Royal Family, Mr. Brennan delivered cards addressed to the four members of the family. The guard who took them promised to deliver them to the King's assistant, Mr. Kruger.

The cards were handed over to Mr. Kruger as promised, although they never made it past the inbox on Thomas's desk. Two days later, Patrick came in search of a piece of think paper for drawing, but no one was in Thomas's or Father's offices. Father wouldn't have that kind of paper in his office, so Patrick looked in Thomas's. He didn't move anything, just lifted papers to look underneath. *"Huh? This is mine?"* Patrick thought when he saw an envelope with his name on it. Another envelope had Eric's name. Patrick took the envelopes and ran downstairs to Eric's suite.

"Eric! We got letters!" Patrick exclaimed as he ran in breathlessly. "Here's yours."

"Thanks. I'll read it later. I want to finish this book first."

"Okay. What's it about? Anything good?"

"Sure. It's about the creation of Valdavia, how it came to be a country and separated from France."

"Oh, okay. I might need to read it when I'm older, so I can know more for my job as your assistant. Remind me when I'm a lot older," Patrick said.

Eric laughed. "Sure thing. It's from the Palace library, so it will always be here."

"Okay. Cool. See ya." Patrick ran to his suite, so he could open his letter. He tore the flap and pulled out a card. He couldn't read all of the words, though, so he went to his mother, who was on the patio.

"Hello, Patrick, darling. Do you want to sit with Mother a while?"

"Sure. I got something in the mail, but I don't know all of the words. Will you read it to me please?"

"Of course." Matilda took the card and smiled. "It's a sympathy card for you from a Mr. Arthur Brennan, who lives not too far from the Palace. He wrote, *Dear Prince Patrick, I am so very sorry at the loss of your grandmother, King Mother Sabrina. She was a lovely, kind woman, whom I had the honor to meet on several occasions. Her kindness, gentle demeanor, and genuine concern enshrined her in my heart for all time. I instantly saw why Prince Gerard fell in love with her in 1900.*

You descend from a long line of fine, noble people, my young Prince, and I have keenly watched you since your birth. I look forward with tremendous pleasure to watching you become a strong, solid, handsome man with sons of his own. You have my utmost sympathy and devotion. Your servant, Arthur Brennan' I must say, Patrick, that is quite a message for a seven year old boy. You must have made quite the impression of this Mr. Brennan."

"That's cool Mother. Thank you. I'll write Mr. Brennan a letter back. I'm going to my room now to write it. Thomas will mail it for me in the morning," Patrick said and flew off faster than a hummingbird.

Patrick got out some of the letter-writing paper Grandfather had given him once, more for making paper boats than writing letters, but it would work. In his childish print, Patrick wrote with a ballpoint pen:

18 August 1965

Dear Mr. Brennan,

Thank you for the card and the note. You are very kind to think of me. I love Grandmother very much and miss her very much. She was a neat lady. I'm glad you met her. She liked people. I hope I get to meet you sometime, too. I'd like that. I don't want to think about having children yet. Maybe in a lot of years I will, but not now. Thank you for writing.

Your friend,

Patrick

The following day, the guard handed Patrick's letter to Mr. Brennan, who beamed like a boy on his birthday, as if he had received the best present ever. He joyfully, carefully opened the letter right then and there, and actually shed a tear when he saw the young prince's handwriting and misspelled words. "I will treasure this all the days of my life," he told the guard. "This means the world to me. Thank you. Please give Prince Patrick my heartfelt thanks as well."

The guards smiled as the familiar postal man whistled as he set off on the rest of his daily route. "I guess the Royal Family really do make people happy," one of the guards said.

"Yes, they sure do. We see it every day, don't we? People out here all the time waiting for a glimpse of one of them. Sometimes, that's all it takes," another said.

"Sure. But that little Patrick writing that letter, that's just about the best thing anyone in this Palace has ever done," a third guard added. The others nodded, watching the happy Mr. Brennan making his way down the mall.

§§§§§

Once again, daily routines resumed, and soon the school year began, as it did each September. Patrick entered second grade and Eric sixth grade. Both boys earned excellent grades, although the notes on Patrick's report cards indicated that he tended to daydream and doodle often. Neither Gerard nor Matilda felt any great concern. After all, considering all that he had been through in recent years, his parents were astonished that the boy hadn't shown signs of trauma or depression. So, they let Patrick be Patrick, just as he desired, and he continued to excel in school even with his daydreams and doodles.

No one ever worried about Eric, the studious, responsible son. He always obeyed, followed orders, and remained neat, polite and well-behaved. As he progressed through elementary and middle school, Eric made friends easily, but kept a small, tight circle of close, trusted friends. He continued to learn about his country's history, including laws his ancestor kings had passed, and about the judicial, banking, and tax systems. He knew his future duty, and he wanted to know as much as possible and to be the most prepared he could be when the dreaded but inevitable day came that he inherited the throne of Valdavia.

Eric's close friends often came home with him after school, doing their homework together in the library or in Eric's sitting room. Then, when homework was done, they would go onto the expansive back lawn or the basement (formerly the dungeon) to play. Sometimes Patrick joined them, which Eric never minded.

Often, though, Patrick wandered off on his own, exploring the Palace grounds and enacting pirate scenes or cowboy gunfights— imaginary play taught him by his Grandfather Stefan. Patrick might have appeared alone to any observer, as he did to his mother as she viewed him through the watch tower telescope one October afternoon in 1970.

Patrick had a red bandana tied around his forehead and an old leather belt around his waist. He jumped from rocks to trees, causing Matilda to scream for her husband in fear of the boy's impending doom. Gerard rushed up the winding staircase, peered through the telescope while his wife hyperventilated, and burst out laughing.

"What is so funny?" she demanded. "Patrick is going to kill himself!"

"No, he's not. He's playing pirates. You know it was one of the favorite games he played with Father. Let him enjoy his childhood while it lasts." Gerard stared though the telescope for several minutes and then added, "In fact, I dare say he's not alone out there."

"Have you gone daft? There's no one else there."

"Oh, maybe no one we can see, dear, but there is someone there with him."

"An imaginary playmate at his age? Isn't 12 a bit old to suddenly create an invisible playmate?" Matilda asked, now wondering if Patrick needed therapy.

"Oh, this isn't new at all. He's had this playmate since 1963."

"So, your father's death did affect him. I knew it. We need to take him to a psychologist."

"Matilda, really, don't you see? Patrick is playing with Father. He's held onto the happy times they had together. Father was Patrick's best friend. Both of them told me so, and it was as clear as rain. Patrick has kept Father alive in the most delightful way." He noticed his wife's doubtful expression. "I overheard him in his suite one afternoon and peeked through the crack in the door. No one else lives in the east wing now, so Patrick was all alone. Except for his playmate, Grandfather. Can I ever tell you how that warmed my heart to see and to hear? Our little boy loves his Grandfather so, and enjoys his company so much, that Father visits him."

"V—Visits him?" Matilda turned pale. "Are you telling me that your father—that your father haunts this Palace?"

"No. He simply plays with his grandson. That's all."

"That's all? You and Patrick have both gone insane," Matilda said and went down the staircase on shaking legs. Ghosts, indeed. A pirate-playing ghost. What was next? She didn't want to know. She needed a tranquilizer, and quickly.

§§§§§

That September, Patrick began seventh grade, easily becoming friendly with most of his classmates. He and a group of boys ate lunch together, studied together, and played together during recess. Before long, Patrick became enormously popular among both the boys and the girls at King Stefan Middle School. The boys enjoyed playing, talking, and exploring with him, while the girls merely stood and watched him on the playground or sat at their classroom desks and stared at him. Patrick never noticed; he was always too busy and occupied.

His friends, however, noticed, and Bobby leaned close and whispered, "Hey, Patrick, all those girls are just standing there watching you."

"Why? I'm not doing anything important, just putting air in this basketball."

"I don't know, but they've been doing it for days now. Tons of them just standing there watching you do whatever it is you're doing."

"Well, they're going to be in the way and maybe get hit with the ball when we start playing. They better move," Patrick said as he pumped air into the ball.

When Patrick finished and threw the ball to Tom, Greg said, "They won't move."

"Then we will. Come on," Patrick said and led the boys to the other basketball hoop.

"Uh, they followed us," Steve said. "Now what?"

"Now we play. If they just want to stand there, that's their business."

Stand there they did. Every time Patrick made a basket, the girls squealed. When he jumped to make a shot, they screamed in delight. When he chased the ball to prevent Greg from stealing the shot, he brushed some of the girls, who began jumping and screaming.

"What are they doing? They're making too much noise, and they're crowding the court," Patrick said. "I mean, if they want to watch us play, fine, but they can do it from over there." Patrick pointed toward the benches against the school building.

"Yeah, really," Marty agreed. He made the next shot, and Patrick caught the ball. The girls screeched. "This is ridiculous. We can't play like this."

"Yeah. Let me handle this," Patrick said. He walked over to the girls, who looked as if Robert Redford had just appeared. "Hey, would you girls mind moving? You're kinda crowding the basketball court."

"Sure, but only if you give us your autograph, Patrick," Annie said with a huge smile.

"Huh? My what? What for?"

"Because you're just about the dreamiest prince in the whole world," Stephanie gushed.

"You sure are," Kimberly, Emma, Natalie, and several others added.

"What? What did I do?" Patrick asked, dumbfounded by the whole incident.

"You're just, well, you're just you, that's all, and you're dreamy," Tammy said with a blush.

"That's silly."

"Please, give us your autograph, Prince Patrick," Debbie pleaded. Several girls added their requests.

Patrick looked back at his friends, who shrugged. "This is silly, but if it means we can play basketball, then okay."

Patrick began signing slips of paper, notebooks, folders, shoes, arms, blouses, and anything else the girls had that he could write on. The mob scene did not go unnoticed by Patrick's body guard—or the other girls on the playground, who all screamed and ran toward him. The body guard rushed to Patrick, realized what was happening, and monitored the situation. His duty was to protect Prince Patrick, although he had never had to actually do anything on the schoolyard.

Before the boys could resume their game, the bell rang, and everyone had to return to their classrooms. The girls who still awaited Patrick's autograph protested, which brought the teachers and finally the principal to the scene. "Girls, you will return to your classrooms immediately," Mr. Hersall demanded. The girls moaned but obeyed. "Are you all right, Prince Patrick?" the principal asked.

"Yeah, sure, but they kept us from playing basketball over silly autographs. I don't get it," Patrick said and scratched his head.

"Well, I do, and I'm afraid you will need to be much more closely supervised."

"Why? Did I do something wrong?"

"No, Patrick, you didn't. But the most recent issue of *Teen Dream* magazine released over the weekend. You are on the cover, and full-page pictures of you fill the issue. It seems our young ladies have seen it."

"What? Me? Isn't that for people like David Cassidy? I don't understand." Patrick and his friends had not seen the magazine. But many of his friends had sisters who regularly bought the magazine.

"Usually, but they sometimes have other people in there too. My sister buys that thing at the pharmacy. One time, it had your brother Eric on the cover," Steve explained.

"Really? He never said anything. This is stupid," Patrick said and kicked the grass.

"That may be, Your Royal Highness, but your security is the school's number one priority," Mr. Hersall said. "I'm afraid in the future, you and your group of friends will have to spend recess in the school gymnasium. We cannot risk an incident."

"The gym? All to ourselves? Hey, that's cool! Then we can play basketball with no interruptions!" Patrick exclaimed and high-fived his friends.

Patrick's bodyguard, Devon Nance, sighed in relief, and thanked Mr. Hersall. "I think I'll stick closer to Prince Patrick from now on, if you don't mind."

"Not at all. Now, let's all return to our classrooms for next period."

The rest of the day went without incident. Patrick invited Greg and Steve to the Palace after school, so they rode with Patrick in the Rolls Royce.

As soon as they entered though the back patio, Matilda grabbed Patrick in a hug. "Are you all right, dear? Mr. Hersall telephoned and told me what happened this afternoon. How frightful."

"Gee whiz, Mother, nothing happened. Just some silly girls who held the basketball court hostage unless I signed autographs. How stupid is that?"

"You weren't hurt?"

"Of course not, just embarrassed. Can we go outside and play?"

"Yes, dear, but be careful."

After the boys left, Matilda spoke with Devon about Patrick's protection. "Something similar happened to Eric last year. I was told to expect more of this as the boys get older. I understand that people are interested in them as the heirs to the throne, but they aren't rock stars. They are little boys, my sons, and I will not let anything happen to them."

Gerard stepped into the foyer at that moment. "Nothing will happen to them, Matilda. They are handsome, intelligent boys, and young girls find them appealing. It's all innocent, really. There is nothing to worry about, believe me. The security staff are well aware of how to protect Eric and Patrick. We might as well get used to this. Eric is a teenager, after all, and he is a best-selling poster boy as I understand."

"I'm what?" Eric asked as he came in after school.

"Patrick is on the cover of that magazine this month, and the girls mobbed him at school today, just as they did you last year. And Thomas informed me that posters of you, my son, are outselling David Cassidy posters."

"That's ridiculous. I'm going upstairs to do my homework," Eric said and did just that.

"See, dear? Nothing to worry about. Tea tins at coronation time and posters at 15. It's all the same," Gerard said and kissed his wife's temple.

CHAPTER 3

The nation celebrated Prince Patrick's thirteenth birthday on January 6, 1971 and Prince Eric's 16th on November 17 later that year. "Where have the years gone?" Matilda asked after Eric's party ended. "It doesn't feel as if 16 years have come and gone since I gave birth to Eric. Our time with them is so short, isn't it.?"

Gerard sighed and said, "Life is too short, my dear. While I watched Eric open his presents, I remembered my own sixteenth birthday. And yet this year I turned 51. Time seems to speed by as we live life, and we realize that we are running out of time. Mortality has a way of skewing our attitude about so much, doesn't it?"

"Can we please end this morbid conversation before it further depresses me? Thinking about my death, your death, and our teenage sons' deaths is not something I care to do."

"I know dear, but it is part of the life cycle. No one is exempt. But let us celebrate our lives and every day we have here on earth rather than dwell on the end of our lives. Life is about love, adventure, joy, and living God's purpose for us. This life is but one part of our existence, dear, you know that. How we live here determines how we live in Heaven."

"I know, Gerard, of course I do. It's just that birthdays and anniversaries that mark the passing of years tend to make me reflect on life, death, and what it all means. I'm all right really, just in one of my sentimental moods. Eric is graduating high school in just a few months and then going off to university. My first baby is practically a man, and that makes me more sentimental than usual," Matilda admitted and sobbed into a tissue.

Gerard put his arms around her, held her close, and whispered in her ear, "Your sentimentality is one reason I love you so. You cried like a baby at the first movie we went to in 1937. I found that charming and sincere. I knew I had married the right woman for me. You feel things deeply and passionately, and I admire that."

"Oh, you silly fool," she protested as she blushed. "I love you for your tender side. You're not nearly as stern as you want people to think you are, you know. You're a teddy bear, not a wolf."

"Hush; don't let my secret out," Gerard said and dipped her into a kiss as she fought her giggles—just as she had done so long ago on their first date.

§§§§§

Sure enough, as May 1972 neared June, the interest in Prince Eric hit its zenith. He graduated in early June and would enter the University of Cambridge, where he would study government and political science. The daily newspapers reported every tidbit of information they could gather regarding the heir's life and plans. Eric remained oblivious, but his loving mother clipped every mention of her son and kept them in a scrapbook.

Matilda kept a scrapbook about Patrick, too, having long gotten over her fears of press coverage. She might have been the Queen Consort de Valdavia, but she was foremost a doting mother, and she delighted in the positive reports her sons garnered. Both Eric and Patrick maintained excellent grades, stayed active in school organizations, and performed Royal duties as well. She remained proud of and interested in her sons' lives.

"Mother, what are you doing?" Eric asked as he came upstairs after school one Tuesday and saw his mother pasting at her sitting room desk.

"Adding to my Prince Eric de Valdavia scrapbook," she said with a smile.

"Your what?"

"My scrapbook of clippings about you, Eric. I save as many as I can in this scrapbook. I have one for Patrick, too."

"Why?"

"What a silly question. I'm your mother and I'm proud of you both. It fills me with happiness to read all of these reports about the good things you and Patrick are doing. I want to save them to look back on when I am old and gray."

"Oh. All right, Mother. I'm going to do my homework now."

"See. You are such a perfect son, Eric, just perfect. Mother is so proud of you."

"Thank you," Eric said, blushing, as he went down the hall to his suite.

§§§§

Patrick and his friends chatted as they walked to their next class. They were weeks away from finishing middle school and just a few months away from beginning high school. Lately, that was all most of them talked about. "Well, we've gotta get through with this class, for one thing," Patrick said as they neared the music room. "This class makes me just want to laugh every day."

"Well, it makes me want to puke," Greg said and put a finger in his mouth to mimic the action. The boys giggled, and Greg asked, "How can you enjoy this, Patrick? It's goofy. I mean, we're in eighth grade, not third grade. It's stupid."

"Naw, not really. I think it's kinda fun. Yeah, it's a bit goofy, but it's fun. It's good to laugh and have some fun. Life needs more of it."

"Yeah, maybe," Steve agreed. "But you sure do get into these songs. You sing louder than anyone in class."

"Why not? Most people just mouth the words or barely sing. If she wasn't signing so loud, she wouldn't hear anybody except me. I think she thinks everyone's singing and having a good time."

"How could she? Can't she see our faces? How can she think any eighth graders would like this?"

"Quiet. You know she's right inside the door," Patrick warned.

"Why if it isn't my little star pupil, yes he is! How are you, little Prince Patrick?"

"I'm fine, Miss Yost. How are you?" Patrick managed to say as she squeezed his cheeks.

"Oh, I am just perfectly fine and wonderful, yes, I am indeed."

"That's nice. I'm glad, Miss Yost."

Patrick's friends tried to muffle their giggles as the boys went to their desks. Patrick motioned for them to stop, but the sight of Miss Yost in her black dirndl skirt and rainbow apron always made them giggle. It didn't help that her white-blonde hair was braided into a bun atop her head.

"She looks like Mrs. Claus," Tim whispered.

Patrick shushed him. "There's no need to hurt her feelings. Be quiet."

The boys shrugged and stopped their giggles and jokes. However, almost all of the students grumbled when Miss Yost told them to stand for their favorite song. It was actually no one's favorite song except Miss Yost's. It remained her trademark, the song she sang more frequently than any other.

"Patrick, why don't you start us off while I play the piano," Miss Yost instructed.

"Okay," Patrick said and sang the first time of *The More We Get Together*. Miss Yost then joined in and motioned for the other students to do likewise. As Patrick had said, most of them either mouthed the words or barely sang them. Miss Yost and Patrick sang so loudly, however, that she never knew. Patrick was glad; otherwise, her feelings would be hurt.

"Now, come, children, you can do better than that, yes you can," Miss Yost said and stood from the piano. "You are not doing the hand movements, no you are not. Have you forgotten? I will lead you." Miss Yost placed a record on the player, and soon the instrumental of the song filled the room. "Let us all sing with joy and do our beautiful hand movements."

Patrick accompanied Miss Yost with glee, while everyone else barely sang or moved. Miss Yost never seemed to notice that and was in a permanent state of gratification. After all, above her desk hung a wooden plaque that read, *Valdavia's Favorite Music Teacher.*

After class, the students rushed from the room, except for Patrick who stayed behind to help Miss Yost straighten the desks and chairs. When they finished, she patted his head, squeezed his cheeks, and exclaimed, "Oh, you are such a joy to me, little Patrick! You fill my soul with pure happiness. Rarely has a student been as enthusiastic as you. I admit, I shall miss you after this term. I will lose my star pupil to the high school. Such is life," she said and sighed.

"Yeah, I guess it is. Well, see ya, Miss Yost."

§§§§§

The week before Prince Eric's graduation remained a swirl of activity. The Palace Press Office fielded hundreds of questions about the ceremony, Eric's Valedictorian speech, the suit he would wear, his class ring, his graduation party, and his summer plans. Eric had helped the staff to prepare answers they would provide to all interested callers. When he wondered why people were so interested in his suit and party, Gerard took him into his office for a talk.

"Eric, I know this kind of interest doesn't make much sense to you and Patrick, and that it makes you uncomfortable. But, to be blunt, you both are the sons of a king and therefore first and second in line to the throne. People are naturally interested in such stations of birth and titles. Take the Prince of Wales. Charles, too, endured press and public scrutiny. It happens to every heir. So, you, in particular, must accept that there is interest in everything you do, Eric. You must accept that with dignity and grace, never getting angry or temperamental when someone asks for an autograph or wants to take a picture or asks questions about your life. You do not need to reveal personal information, but you do need to respond. That is the mark of an in-touch and compassionate prince or king. Do you understand?"

"Yes, Father, I do. It comes with the job, and I just accept it. I suppose it could be much worse, right? People could dislike the king and his policies, and there could be the threat of an uprising or a revolt. I won't complain and whine about it, Father. If people are interested in me, that must mean that they approve of what I do. I'm grateful to have a caring father and mother and brother, and fellow citizens who do support me and my family. I will always remain grateful for all of that and all of God's blessings."

§§§§§

Eric arose early for a Saturday. He hadn't slept much but had lain awake thinking about this milestone in his life. He showered, dressed, and then sat at his desk. He took his annual diary off of its shelf and opened to the next blank page. He had a lot he wanted to write before the bustle of the day. He knew his mother would be extra excited and full of her nervous energy in a few hours. Eric took his pen from its holder and began writing about the next chapter of his life.

16 June 1972

Well, this is the day, the first major milestone in my life. In a few hours, I officially graduate from high school. I am 17, and my childhood ends today. In late September, I move to Cambridge, England to attend the University of Cambridge. I will study government and political science, subjects that will help me to learn more that will prove useful in my future job. Father began preparing me when I was quite young so that nothing would seem overwhelming or too intense later on. I'm glad he did, because knowing my birthright from early childhood has made it normal to me, not extraordinary. Oh, I know that few people inherit a throne and kingship from their fathers, but this is my normal.

I will do the same for my child, ensuring that he is as comfortable with the reality as I became early on. It is a lot to take in, that I will become the absolute monarch of Valdavia one day. Absolute monarch. I've studied absolute monarchies. Most such rulers aren't restricted by any rules or laws, and some are actually tyrants. None of the Kings de Valdavia have operated this way. First, none of my ancestors were tyrants. Second, all have abided by the laws each King established, beginning with Christophe. None have been lawless or godless.

I learned by watching Grandfather when I was young, and now by watching Father. Father and I also frequently talk about the job of king, and what it means to rule a nation. He tells me about how he makes decisions and drafts laws. I think carefully about everything Father tells me and teaches me so that I can absorb as much as possible and be prepared when I must take over. I know what kind of king I will be. I will consider the needs of Valdavians foremost, what is best for them at the time. I will craft policies and laws in alignment with that, ensuring their needs and rights are met in the most beneficial way to them and to the nation. One thing I have thought of for several years is establishing an Advisory Board, and I even have the roles planned in my notebook I use for notes and ideas for my future job.

There will be a Treasurer who will oversee public funds as well as my private funds and investment portfolio. Grandfather made investments, and so does Father; they both advised me to do the same, so I will. I will appoint a Military Advisor for knowledge and advice, an Education Advisor to provide information and advice about academic decisions; and I will maintain the Diplomatic Courier whom Father appointed, as well as the Amnassadeur Extraordinaire et Plénipotentiaire, the diplomat assigned to Washington D.C. I will also create an Arts and Culture Advisor. These people will be my personal team who advise, inform, and assist me. Even though I will be an absolute monarch, I do not want to rule in isolation. I need contact with experts in these and other fields so that I can make those best decisions for my fellow Valdavians. I can never know all about everything, and this Advisory Board can provide the outside ideas and influence I will need.

I may officially be an absolute monarch, but I will practice benevolent dictatorship: doing what is in the best interest of all citizens. My birthright essentially forces me into this job, but this job is not about me. It remains about Valdavia and its citizens. As king, my priority is my country and its people. As a man, my relationship with God and of course my family are my priorities. Any and all decisions I make when I am king will affect my family, for they, too, are citizens of Valdavia. I will always remember that. Anything not right or good enough for my family will never be right or good enough for all other Valdavians.

Most importantly, I will abide by God's law and word in guiding all of my decisions, laws, and policies. God destined me to be the next King de Valdavia, and my duty is to uphold His law and word and to do what is right according to Him. At the end of my life, God will judge me based on how I fulfilled my destiny and purpose as His child, who just happens to be a king. Any king who rules without God's guidance never lives up to his birthright and destiny.

I know that I was created to be the 19th King de Valdavia. God destined me for this life and this responsibility. He created me for this, and He expects me to rein with honor, compassion, and godliness. I vow to do so, no matter how short or long my life on earth. The quality of my life is far more important to God than the quantity of my years. Only God knows how many years I will live, so my duty is to do the right and best job I can do in the years He gives to me.

§§§§§

"Hey, Eric, do you have a couple of minutes before you have to leave?" Patrick asked from his brother's open bedroom door. Eric stood before his full-length mirror tying his tie, and Patrick smiled. Eric was such the proper gentleman; he had been as far back as Patrick remembered. Eric preferred suits and ties over more casual clothes, whereas Patrick had always been the exact opposite. Patrick became suddenly amazed at how well they had gotten along and trusted one another.

"Sure. What do you need?"

"Nothing. I just wanted to give you your graduation gift from me now instead of at the party later. Do you mind?"

"No, I don't mind. Some gifts are more personal or meaningful than the average party gifts. But you didn't have to get me anything."

"Sure, I did. You're the only brother I'll ever have, and this is your only high school graduation, and a big one at that. Valedictorian, you know. Making the speech and all. Mom's all teary-eyed about it," Patrick said.

"She always gets emotional over these sorts of things. Heck, she cried buckets when you took your first step." Eric giggled, remembering the scene. His baby brother holding a chair for support, his legs wobbly, letting go of the chair and taking one step before falling on his behind. Their mother covered her face and cried for what seemed like hours. Eric, like his father, now found his mother's sentimentality charming, for it showed she cared about the people and events around her.

Patrick giggled, too, and said, "Yeah. Anyway, here." He thrust a wrapped box at Eric, who asked if Patrick wanted him to open it then. "Sure, go ahead."

Eric carefully removed the paper and found a black, gold-engraved box that said *Passion Planet Stationery*. Eric had never heard of the company. "They're in France. A friend at school had their catalogue," Patrick informed his brother. Eric nodded and opened the box. Inside was a leather journal that had a ship's wheel clasp. Eric tried to open it, but he couldn't.

"There's a trick to it. Can I show you?" Eric handed the journal to Patrick, who showed him how to turn half of the ship's wheel a certain way to unlock the journal. "See, this is perfect for you to use at Cambridge, because no one can read your private thoughts. I know you have the diary Father gives you every year, but this can be more private. Those diaries are for the Palace archives and get read throughout the centuries. Sometimes, you might want to write things that aren't meant for others to read, that's all, so I thought this would do the job."

"Gee, thank you, Patrick. This will be perfect for more personal or private thoughts. I guess we all have those, don't we? Although most of the kings in the past wrote everything in those diaries, you know. I've read some of them. I understand why, but like you said, sometimes there are those private thoughts. Thanks. This is perfect," Eric said and hugged his brother.

Thomas came to tell Eric it was time for him to leave, so he placed the journal on his desk as he left his suite. Patrick stayed and looked around his brother's bedroom and sitting room until his father called for him, thinking all that he could never say to his brother.

"Well, this is it, Eric. You'll be leaving soon, and you will make new friends. You'll probably fall in love and get a girlfriend. Your life won't have room for a high school brother anymore. You're grown up now. I know you promised that nothing would change between us, that you'd still do things with me, but it will change. It has to. You'll have new experiences and friends without me. Your life will move in a new direction. I know you'll come back here because you're the next king, but things will change between us. I'll miss our talks. I always felt like you trusted me and could tell me anything. But you'll meet new best friends, people you trust and to whom you tell things. I won't ever be as important in your life. You don't have to keep your childhood promises to me. I release you from them. I'll keep my promise, though. I'll always support you and be strong for you. Always. But I'll miss you, Eric."

§§§§§

"We have now come to the point in our ceremony for the Valedictorian's speech. This year's Valedictorian maintained a 4.0 grade point average throughout his four years, as well as holding the offices of President of the Government Club and the History Club for three of his four years. In addition, this young man regularly performs official duties on behalf of his father. It is my supreme honor to welcome to the podium Eric DeBruce Martineau." Principal Saunders shook Eric's hand when the prince approached the podium.

"Guests, families, faculty, administrators, and most of all my fellow graduates of 1972, I am extremely honored to speak to you today. This ceremony closes one chapter in our lives, which can be exciting, bittersweet, and yes, frightening. We are excited because we have accomplished one set of goals for our lives and can begin working on a new set of goals. Furthermore, we look forward as the next chapter of our lives begins. New chapters are exciting. They are also bittersweet, because new chapters bring new challenges and experiences and changes. We make plans for that chapter, but so much is unknown and unpredictable as we venture forth. That can be scary.

"However, I look forward with joy and confidence and faith. I know that I am capable of achieving my goals, no matter how difficult that may become. We've all heard that nothing worthwhile comes easily. That remains often true. So, believe in yourselves.

Have the mindset that you can accomplish anything and that required to make your goals and dreams reality.

"That's where faith comes in. I have faith in God, that He knows what remains best for me and will guide me through all of the challenges of my life. I also have faith in myself. I know that I am capable and hard-working. I also have a clear sense of my life's purpose. Some of you do, as well. For those who don't, explore your dreams and what matters most to you. Ask yourselves what you want your mark on the world—your legacy—to be. What will you leave behind for future generations? The answer to that will define your life's purpose and mission, whatever that may be.

"Once you acquire your purpose and mission, determine the best ways to live that every day of your lives. Doing so is like climbing a tall ladder, one rung at a time. As you reach each rung, tell yourself what makes you unique and special. Also tell yourself what your future life will look like. Visualize that future life and bring it to existence in your mind. One other thing to do every day: think of or to write down all of the things and people in your lives for which you are grateful.

"Do that every day, with conviction, and over time that image will become reality. Why? How? Because you live it, create it as you visualize it. All of us can do this. Our attitudes and gratitude influence every other part of our lives. I read a study that concluded that happy people rarely, if ever, get angry or feel resentment, jealously, or revenge. Why would they? How could they? Happy people possess fulfilled, successful lives. And remember that success is not necessarily measured by wealth. Success often means doing what you love to do, what feeds your soul, what makes you feel good about yourself. That might be writing novels or designing skyscrapers or sailing boats. The point is, find what makes you feel whole and content, and you have discovered your life's purpose.

"So, my challenge to all of the 1972 graduates is to find your passion and to live it. Doing so will leave your mark on the world and establish your legacy."

Eric bowed and took his place beside Roger as everyone stood for the ovation. He looked down at his signet ring, a 15th birthday gift from his father, and prayed that all of his classmates and friends would find the inner peace that he had found. That peace had not come from having his job chosen from birth. It came from his understanding that job, his role, and the legacy left him by his ancestors. Eric had learned all he could at this stage of his life and had used that knowledge to forge his own position and identity as the next king. Whenever that happened, he knew he was ready.

§§§§§

"Eric, Patrick, the Sultan of Brunei is visiting the Palace the first week of August. That's before the school year begins and before you have to go to Cambridge," Gerard said and looked at Eric. "This is the first visit to Valdavia of a Sultan of Brunei, so this is an extremely important diplomatic trip"

"Yes, Father, I know. I've studied the visits by foreign dignitaries, and all of them resulted in our nations becoming allies. Valdavia has never been challenged with or threatened by a military attack or a war. That's almost unprecedented, isn't it?"

"Yes, Eric, it is. Valdavia has never threatened another nation, regardless of the situation or circumstance. Our predecessors always maintained and negotiated peace, which kept our military from actively entering any conflict. Diplomacy means using tact, sensitivity, and discretion in these interactions and discussions with heads of state. Few heads of state want their nations to enter into war, so many of these relationships have a mutual goal of preventing war and of maintaining peace. Because the desire to maintain peace is often mutual, these meetings become about fostering alliances," Gerard explained.

"I read about that, Father. Valdavia avoided entering both World Wars due to its strong alliances," Eric said.

"Yeah, but some of our soldiers chose to fight for our allies' armies. That showed support, too," Patrick added.

"That's correct, Patrick. You've been doing some studying, too, I see," Gerard said and smiled, pleased that his youngest son was also interested in the country's history and diplomacy.

"Yeah. The military fascinates me. I'm thinking about joining the Valdavian Army in a few years, maybe making it my career."

"I'm impressed, son. You're 14 now, so you have a while to make the decision by the time you graduate high school. If that's what you truly desire for your future, I will fully support you, Patrick."

"Gee, thanks, Father. I'm pretty sure now, but, sure, I'll think more on it," Patrick promised. The truth was, this conversation convinced Patrick that his convictions were the right thing. As Father and Eric continued discussing the Sultan's visit, Patrick thought, *"Eric's the one who told everyone to find their passions and to live them. He's the one who put me on this path. I know what my passion is, and talk of war only makes me surer about my decision. But if Father wants me to wait until I'm about 16, I'll play along. I can't join the Army until then anyway. But when I do, the world will have the biggest shock it's ever had."*

§§§§

A crowd of thousands filled the mall outside the Palace, awaiting the Sultan of Brunei's motorcade. On schedule, the cars pulled into the Palace courtyard, and the Sultan stepped from his limousine. King Gerard stood nearby, and warmly welcomed him when he approached. Press and spectators took photographs of this first meeting, and the two kings obliged by posing for a few photographs before they entered the foyer.

"Your Majesty, may I present my family, Queen Consort Matilda, Prince Eric, and Prince Patrick."

The Sultan shook hands and chatted with each before being introduced to the Palace's chief staff, including Gerard's assistant Thomas. The principal butler escorted the Sultan's manservant to the suite where His Majesty would stay for the week, and soon the Sultan's servants carried the Sultan's trunks and suitcases upstairs.

Meanwhile, King Gerard and the Sultan had tea in the sitting room, where they discussed their itinerary for the week. As Gerard had told his sons, the purpose of the visit was to form an alliance in the face of growing unrest in other nations. Neither ruler wished to find his country forced into a war, so common ground and alliance would help them to stand together should they be confronted with such a proposition.

The week's meetings with civic and military leaders proved promising, and they closed Friday's meetings by signing an alliance agreement. Both men served as absolute monarchs, which gave them the freedom to form the alliance without opposition from a governing body. Gerard knew the alliance would protect Valdavia and its citizens, and he genuinely felt it was in the country's best interest. Given the reaction to the news reports, so did the majority of Valdavians.

On Saturday morning, the Sultan treated the Valdavian Royal Family to gifts he had selected for each of them. For the youngest prince, he presented a golden horse adorned with a jeweled saddle. Patrick looked at it with wide eyes, never having seen anything like it. "Thank you, Your Majesty. I will treasure this always and remember your kindness when I look at it," Patrick said and stood to shake the king's hand.

Eric was gifted a priceless suite of diamond and sapphire jewels "for your future Queen Consort," the Sultan told him.

Eric felt amazed at the gift, and he blushed at the mention of his future wife. Still, he quickly stood, bowed, and thanked the Sultan for his thoughtfulness. "I know my wife will find these as exquisite as I do. Thank you."

Matilda received an even grander suite of jewels, which made her gasp and clutch her throat. The Valdavian Royal Family had always been more understated, she thought. This was very, well, extravagant. Still, it was a lovely set, and she graciously thanked the Sultan.

The Sultan reserved the most remarkable gift of all, however, for Gerard. Several of the Sultan's servants carried a huge wooden box into the sitting room. No one knew what to think, do, or say. The Sultan motioned Gerard toward the box, at which time, the servants opened it. The Royal Family stared in total astonishment.

"Wow! That's the coolest chair I've ever seen," Patrick exclaimed to the Sultan's delight.

"Yes, Patrick, this is quite a magnificent chair indeed. I have never seen another like it anywhere," Gerard said.

"I am pleased that you enjoy the chair. I had it custom made just for you, Your Majesty. A grand, well-loved king deserves such a chair."

"Thank you. That is extraordinarily kind of you, Your Majesty," Gerard said. "This truly is a masterpiece. I have no words for how I feel."

The Sultan beamed, bowed, and said, "No words are needed. The expression on your face is gift enough for me. I sincerely appreciate your family's hospitality and kindness to me and to my staff this week. I am sure our nations will remain strong allies."

With that, the Sultan and his staff left the Palace, drove to the airport, and boarded their private planes to return home. The visit proved quite successful, and Gerard was pleased.

However, he stared at the chair and said, "This is incredible. What am to do with this? Where would it go?"

"I'm sure I don't know, dear. It is rather large, isn't it?" Matilda asked.

"Large? It's monstrous. I suppose it will have to be stored in the dungeon, I mean the basement," Gerard said.

"No! I know the perfect place for it," Patrick said and ran to the chair.

"Where?" his father asked, almost afraid of his son's answer.

"My sitting room. This is awesome!"

"Your sitting room? What on earth for? How would you ever use such a large piece of furniture?" Matilda asked in horror.

"To sit in! What else? I can make a step so it's easier to get to. I like it!"

Eric couldn't help but laugh. "You would, Patrick. It's just your style. Let him have it, Father. What can it hurt?"

"Oh, very well. It will take most of the men here to get it upstairs to your room, but if you really want it, it's yours. Don't forget your golden horse, too," Gerard said and rolled his eyes as Patrick grabbed the horse and ran upstairs to make room for the awesome chair.

"I love him. He's a hoot," Eric said, still laughing.

"I love him, too, dear, but I find his taste in furniture abhorrent," Matilda said and went to her room with a headache.

"Yes, our Patrick is one of those rare souls who finds joy in the most unlikely of items," Gerard said and smiled at Eric. "He will certainly bring comic relief to your life when you assume the throne."

Eric laughed. "I hope so. I'll need and want Patrick's quirky sense of humor to alleviate my stress. Working with him will never be boring."

"That's an understatement if I ever heard one," Gerard mumbled and went to his office.

§§§§§

"Hey, do you need any help?"

"Sure. The main things I need to pack are suits and informal clothes, shoes, toiletries, everything like that. I'll buy my books and supplies there, so I don't need to take any notebooks and school supplies. I'm organizing everything first so it all will be easier to pack in the truck and suitcases," Eric replied.

"I never organize clothes before I pack. That seems like twice the work, but, hey, you roll like that, big bro."

Eric giggled. "I'm going to miss you, you know."

"You are? Really?"

"Sure. We've been together our entire lives. We've done everything together for the most part. This is the first time we'll be apart," Eric said as he folded a white dress shirt.

"Yeah, I know. I'll miss you, too. It's not gonna be the same without you here, not at all," Patrick said and picked up one of Eric's dress shoes.

"I won't be gone forever, you know. And I'll come home some weekends and on holidays. We'll have time to catch up and do things then. Roger will probably come home when I do, too, to spend time with his family. Neither of us wants to be away for long periods. To be honest, we've both talked about how we'll probably get homesick. That will make coming home for visits all the more special."

"I don't want you to feel bad while you're at university, but I am glad you want to come home and visit. Four years, huh? Maybe it won't feel so long with visits, holidays, and summers."

"Right, Patrick, it won't. Just look at my high school years. Four years, just like that," Eric said as he snapped his fingers. "You'll experience that soon. It all seems to speed by, even if some of it seems a bit too much at times. But there are clubs and organizations that help to fill the time, and I'm sure you'll find one or two you enjoy."

"Yeah, I'll check 'em out. I don't hate school, but I don't like the time it eats from life."

Eric looked at his brother. "You said that several years ago. Remember?" Patrick nodded. "You've never changed, Patrick. I like that. It gives me a sense of comfort and constancy knowing that you'll always be the same you no matter the time or season."

Patrick snickered. "You sound like a cheesy card. But I'm glad. I want you to know that you can count on me no matter what you need. I'll always be here for you, Eric. Always."

"I know, buddy. I know." The brothers hugged, and then Eric cleared his throat. "Hey, do me a favor and get my diary and the journal you gave me. They're both on my desk." A minute later

Patrick held them out to Eric. "Do you mind putting them in my carry-on? It's over there."

"Sure thing," Patrick said with a smile. *So, Eric is taking the journal and will use it.* The knowledge gave Patrick some comfort.

After they finished the packing, the young men sat in Eric's sitting room and reminisced about their childhoods. Eric shared with his brother his hopes and goals for his future, once more mentioning that he wanted Patrick to be his assistant. Eric noticed the look in Patrick's eyes, though.

"Hey, what's wrong? Is there something you want to tell me? I know you said something about joining the Army. Does that mean you don't want to be my assistant?"

Patrick shook his head. "No, nothing like that." After lots of persuading from Eric, Patrick told his brother. "I've said this before. You'll meet new friends and maybe even get a girlfriend. There won't be room in your life for a high school younger brother. You'll grow up and away from me. That's all. You're not obligated to keep that promise to me, you know."

"What? Are you serious? Sure, I'll make friends. That's normal. By the way, I'm not interested in girlfriends while I'm in school. I have priorities. There's a time for relationships and romance. And there will always be room for you in my life, Patrick. You're my brother, my only brother. We're together for life and beyond. Nothing and no one will ever break our bond. Is that clear?"

Patrick smiled and hugged his brother. "Sure thing, Eric."

Gerard had come to tell Eric it was time to leave, but he stood in the hall and listened to that conversation. He predicted how it would end, and his heart rejoiced when Patrick embraced Eric. Gerard swallowed his tears before he tapped on the open door.

"Come, boys, it's time to drive Eric to the airport. Manley will get your trunk. I'll take your suitcase, and you get the smaller bags," Gerard told Eric.

"All right, Father. Roger's parents are driving him to the airport, so he'll meet us there. Thank you for letting us use your plane."

"Why not use it? That's why I bought the thing, isn't it? Let's get your mother and go."

Soon, Gerard and Matilda hugged Eric, although Matilda also smothered him with kisses. She finally let go of him, and Patrick once more put his arms around him.

"Call me anytime if you need anything, and I'll come to Cambridge right away," Patrick said in his brother's ear.

At almost the same moment, Eric told Patrick, "Listen, call me anytime if you need me. I'll always be here for you."

The boys laughed, patted one another on the backs, and then Eric boarded the plane to write his new chapter.

§§§§§

By midafternoon, Eric, Roger, and Eric's bodyguard Stanley Porter arrived at the young men's apartment. With all trunks and bags inside, the boys began unpacking and organizing. Afterward, they walked through the surrounding neighborhoods, becoming familiar with the shops, department stores, and restaurants near the University.

After nearly two hours, Roger asked, "Are you hungry? I sure am."

"Now that you mention it, yes, I am. I haven't thought about food since breakfast. What do we want? We've seen Italian, Indian, Chinese, Mexican, American, and street cafes. What sounds good to you?"

"I'm game for anything. What about pizza?"

"Okay. Let's find that pizza parlor we spotted a little bit ago," Eric said.

Soon the three men sat at a table enjoying a pepperoni pizza and drinks. As they ate, Roger and Eric chatted about their classes and speculated about their coursework. "It's University, so it's naturally more challenging than high school. We're expected to put in more study and homework time. I'm so excited, though, I can't tell you, Roger. I just want to get started so I can learn as much as possible."

"Geez, man, I've never known anyone this excited about any school. But you've known your life's path since you were very young. You know what you'll do for the rest of your life. Most people don't. But I guess that's what your speech in June was all about, huh?"

Eric nodded as he chewed and swallowed a bite of pizza. "Yes. Sure, I've known my destiny most of my life, but that doesn't mean it had to be my passion. The whole point is that it is my passion, because I realized that God placed me in this position for a reason. I don't know that reason yet, but I know He has a reason for everything He does. With that in my mind and my heart, I reflected on my destiny and my heritage and what I wanted my role as king to be. I discovered my passion, Roger. Everyone can find their passion. That's what the speech was about," Eric explained.

"Sure, I understand that. I've thought some about that since graduation. I have a pretty good idea what's right for me. Some of the choice is out of my hands, but I've prayed about it," Roger told his friend. What he didn't tell Eric is what he had first mentioned after King Stefan's death in 1963. Roger would truly enjoy becoming Eric's valet. He knew that Eric had long ago tapped his brother Patrick to be his assistant, and he understood that choice. Eric and Patrick were close, and that was a natural selection. But Eric and Roger were practically lifelong best friends who had shared darn near everything. Roger knew and understood Eric better than anyone outside his immediate family. Roger loved his friend and wanted to support him.

"Well, whatever it is, I pray for it to come true for you, Roger. You deserve your dreams and desires."

"Thanks, man."

§§§§§

22 October 1972

Well, Eric is gone, at least for a while. I know it's not forever. Heck, he's the next king, so he has to come back sometime. He promised me he'll come home some weekends and on holidays, and of course during summers. He promised me, and he's always kept his promises to me. He's never lied to me. I believe him, and I trust him.

I believe him that he still wants me to be his assistant. He wouldn't say that if he didn't mean it. He wouldn't. Why would he saddle himself with someone he didn't want around? He wouldn't do that to the nation and to himself. Duty and responsibility are far too important to him to jeopardize his kingship by hiring an incompetent, unwanted buffoon as his assistant. He'd hire someone like Father's Thomas rather than me. So, I know he means it. He wants me there to help him and to support him.

I want to help and support Eric. I've always wanted to, as long as I remember. It's my duty anyway, to protect and serve my brother. To do the tasks that enable him to do his job as king to the best of his ability. That's what I was born to do, just as he was born to be king. I've known my birthright since Grandfather's death, and I will devote my life to being Eric's assistant.

Eric and I are the only children, the only supporters we have. We have to stick together, even when he gets married and has children. I'll be the best brother, assistant, brother-in-law, and uncle any man ever was. I love Eric. I will love his wife and children. I will do anything for them. Anything. My vow, as always, is to be strong for Eric and to do all he needs and wants me to do.

§§§§§

22 October 1972

Today, Roger and I moved into our apartment in Cambridge, England, where we will live for the next four years. The terms are different in England; there are three rather than two, each two months in length. Full Easter Term end 16 June 1973. Still, that break will, for the most part, coincide with Patrick's summer break from high school. The other nice news is that there are two term breaks during which I can go home for visits. The first is 3 December through 14 January. Christmas with my family is extremely important to me; it always has been and always will remain important to me.

Patrick took me by surprise in my room today by saying he didn't hold me to my promise to make him my assistant. Where did he get that idea anyway? What made him think I don't or wouldn't want him to be my assistant? Even Roger knows that I want Patrick to be my personal assistant. Patrick seemed to believe me when I assured him I do indeed want him in that position. Who better? Patrick is my first best friend, and he knows me better than anyone other than Roger. Actually, I've told Patrick things that I've never told anyone else. I hope this conversation never comes up again. I pray that my little brother knows how much I love him and that he can trust me with his life.

I am glad that Roger is here with me. It is comforting to have my second-best friend with me, someone else I completely trust. My friendship with Roger was instant, and it's only grown stronger with each passing year. He said years ago he'd like to be my valet. I'd like that. However, he mentioned today that he's been praying for his dream to come true, even though, as he put it, the decision is not entirely his. I have no idea what that means or what his passion is, but I do pray it comes to fruition for him. I'd like for him to feel satisfied, fulfilled, and happy in his life's work. It has to feed his passion and feed his soul. So, if this mystery desire takes him down a different path, I will of course wish him well. I know our friendship will endure regardless.

Life remains, in many ways, a mystery to each of us. I know what my destiny and passion are, but I do not know how my life will play out day by day, year by year. I do not know when or if I will marry or have children—or how many children. I don't perceive a large family in my future, though, even though I'm not opposed to that. I'll be content with whatever God provides for me. I haven't ever even thought of romance, even going on dates. I know dates are more social rather than romantic in high school, but I never had the desire to date just because it is the norm for most people. I liked my classmates, those I got to know, and I didn't object to socializing with them. I objected to the ritual of dating. Relationships are serious, and my personal belief is that there is only one person meant for each of us.

God pre-destined who I will love and marry. I have yet to meet her. I will know the moment I do meet her, of that I am sure. If I do happen to meet her while I am in Cambridge, then that is God's will and design. If not, then that, too, is His will. I will know in my heart when I meet her; God will let me know that she is the one destined, picked by Him, for me. Until then, I am content to continue my studies and to prepare as best I can for my future role.

§§§§

Eric kept his word and came home for several weekends and for each term break. The summer of 1973 proved enjoyable for the brothers. Eric had made friends at University, especially a third best friend, Daniel Sein, whom he brought home with him and Roger. He introduced Daniel to his parents as well as to Patrick.

"You know what I call Roger, Daniel, and me? The Three Musketeers," he told Patrick with a giggle. "You're the fourth musketeer."

"I am?"

"Sure thing. I'm going to ask Daniel to be my valet de chambre when we finish University. He wants to go into service, maybe be a gentleman's gentleman, so I figured I should ask him to be my valet. He's my good friend, and I trust him. What do you think?"

Patrick smiled, flattered that Eric asked his opinion. "I think it's fine. Grandfather always told me he had to have people he could trust working for him. Go for it."

Eric also shared what he was learning, as well as his plans for the Advisory Board, with Patrick.

"In fact, I'd like you to head the Advisory Board. You can remain in constant communication with the Board members regarding current situations and events, and then report back to me. What do you think?" Eric asked Patrick.

"I think an Advisory Board is a stupendous idea. No, really. Any leader or ruler needs input and guidance, and, well, an absolute monarch usually hasn't got any. As good as Grandfather was and Father is, they operate independently. They do their own research and make decisions. But a panel of experts in all these fields, that's unprecedented, Eric. You'll change the Valdavian monarchy for all time."

"I don't know about that, but it seems like the best way to receive input and information. So, would you be interested in heading the Board? You'd also still be my assistant. That's not too heavy a load is it?"

"Heck, no. I'd love to do both. Are you kidding me? It would make me feel like I was actually doing stuff that's worthwhile and means something. Plus, it sounds like it will help you, so, yeah, I'm in, man."

Eric laughed and said, "Thanks, Patrick. I was praying you'd say you would. And you'll be a strong asset to me."

§§§§§

"Happy Birthday!"

"Ah, come on. I'm too old for surprise parties," Patrick said with a slight blush tinting his cheeks.

"No one is ever too old for surprise parties, son. You know this family celebrates every birthday with full relish. Birthdays are celebrations of one's life, and a chance for family to let someone know how loved and valued he or she is. So, don't complain about birthday parties. Enjoy them!" Gerard exclaimed and smiled at his now 16-year-old son.

"Father's right, Patrick. Birthdays aren't about how old someone is, but about showing gratitude for people we love," Eric said.

"Yeah, okay. I never thought of them that way, I guess. Thanks, everyone."

Patrick did enjoy spending the afternoon with his family, especially since Eric had to return to Cambridge soon. The gift from his mother was predictable, a new sweater for the colder winter season. His father and his brother completely surprised him, however, with their gifts. Gerard gifted his son a Montblanc fountain pen, "for all the writing you do now," Gerard explained. Patrick breathed a sigh of relief realizing that his father referenced his high school career. Eric bought Patrick a collection of poetry. How had he known? Patrick wondered. Eric hadn't found his journals, had he? Patrick began to panic.

"I noticed you got some poetry books from the library, so when I saw this in a bookstore, I thought you might like it," Eric told his now-relieved brother.

"Sure thing. Thanks, Eric."

After a few hours of talk and laughter, the family members went their separate ways. Eric left to visit some friends, while Matilda supervised the dinner menu and Gerard returned to his office. There were no days off for a king. Patrick walked to his suite.

As he stood at the window, he thought about birthdays and what they meant. "How many more will I celebrate? I have no way of knowing that. Only God knows. But I feel something inside of me, this nagging feeling, that I won't live long enough to become Eric's assistant. I've kinda always felt like I had to rush through life. That I won't have enough time to do all I want. So, rather than worry about how long I've got, I'm going to make the most of the time I do have," he whispered.

Sighing, Patrick went to his desk, took a sheet of notebook paper from his school binder, and got his new fountain pen. Eric was right. Patrick liked poetry, and he decided to write his first poem, a traditional ballad, that day, his way of commemorating his sixteenth birthday.

My Purpose

Every day and every night, so many questions fill me;

They consume my time and my thoughts to my distraction,

As I seek the answers which I pray bring peace to my soul

And ease this tumult within which lead all to disruption.

Why am I here? Why was I born? My brain keeps asking

　　God.

What is my ultimate purpose? Why was I created?

What does my life mean to the rest of this vast universe?

Everything about me is a mystery, yet fated.

I feel such anguish as I ponder about my future,

Sensing that I shall never grow old and will stay alone—

Never truly a man, unwed, childless, with no legacy,

No mark, no inheritance, to leave behind of my own.

I live each day fearlessly, for I hide the fear and angst

The whole while I'm wondering if that is my destiny.

If I am meant to live fast and die young without children,

Then what is the reason, God's reason, for my brevity?

What will death feel like at the true moment it strikes me

      down?

What will happen after death requests me at my gloaming?

What influence will I make on those I must leave behind?

Will my shadow on this world grow dark or endure glowing?

Will I still matter to those whom I continue to love?

What purpose will I serve in my eternal life after death?

I wish I knew that, but I cannot know until I die.

'Til then, I must trust God and live life until my last breath.

When Patrick finished putting his thoughts and feelings on paper, he read the poem. His small, loopy cursive filled the page with words he never wanted anyone to read. Patrick positioned his hands to tear the poem to shreds, which he would immediately burn. Before he could, his hands froze, immobile at the top of the paper, as if held by an invisible force.

Patrick heard a voice tell him, "Do not destroy that poem."

Who was that? There was no one around. "God?" Patrick asked aloud, as if he would receive an answer.

"Yes, Patrick. Your writing is part of you that you must never destroy. Do you understand?"

"Well, yeah, but I don't understand why. No one's ever going to read any of this stuff, not if I can help it."

"There is a purpose to everything. You will understand everything when it is time for you to understand. Until then, trust me that I know what is best for you and that I know your purpose."

"Sure. If that's what you want. Okay, I'll hide this poem where no one can find it."

Patrick folded the paper into a small rectangle and placed it in the back of his bottom desk drawer, behind a piece of loose wood. No one would ever know to look there, he thought.

"So, God just told me my writing means something, but He didn't tell me what. He told me to trust Him. This is kinda trippy, but sure, why not? He's God, after all, and if He spoke to Moses and Abraham, why wouldn't He talk to little ol' me?" Patrick pondered, giggled, and ran down the hall.

§§§§§

Before long, Patrick was well established in his sophomore year at King Philippe High School. Three weeks before the end of the term, Principal Rodney Roceur announced an assembly in the auditorium. As the students and teachers walked there, most of them speculated on the reason for the assembly. No one seemed to know any information.

"Do you know what it's about, Prince Patrick?" a young lady asked him.

"Oh, hey, just call me Patrick. None of that prince business. And I don't know anything."

"Oh. I wasn't sure, Patrick, given that you're the most important student here and all."

"Huh? I'm not the most important anything. I just happen to be the son of the King, that's all. It's my father who's important, not me. And my brother, since he's the next king. I'm just Patrick, and I want to do things my way until I become Eric's assistant."

"You're going to be King Eric's assistant? Why, I think that's pretty important."

"Nah. I mean, I guess it is, the role that is. But I'm not. Say, I've never seen you before. Are you new?"

"No. I'm in the Honors Program. I rarely see people who aren't. Gee, that sounds snobby. I didn't mean it that way. It's just that we, the honors students, are like a cohort. We take all of our classes together. You wouldn't have seen me much at all, I suppose."

"Honors Program? I got a letter about that when the school year started. I ignored it. I guess I shouldn't have, huh? Tell me about it."

"Well, the assembly's ready to begin. Maybe we can talk later."

"Sure. What's your name?" Patrick asked.

"Maria Bouchard. I suppose the Palace numbers are for official use only. Here's my home telephone number. Call me later, and I'll tell you all about Honors."

"Cool. Thanks. And I have my own phone line in my room. Here's my personal number. You can call me, too."

"Wow. Thanks. I won't abuse the privilege, I promise."

"Don't worry about it. If I'm there and not doing something else, I'll talk. Call anytime. Oh, and if I'm not there, leave a message on my machine, and I'll call you back."

"You have your own answering machine. How neat. All right, if you're sure it's no problem."

"It's not," Patrick said as Principal Roceur began speaking.

"Students. Faculty. I received an incredibly important telephone call this morning about one of our students. Someone among you is soon to do something extremely noteworthy."

Everyone talked at once, trying to figure out who and what Mr. Roceur meant. It took him more than five minutes to silence everyone. "Please. If you talk over me like that, I will be unable to share this news. Thank you.

"I received a call from the personal private secretary to the General Assembly President of the United Nations."

At that, Patrick murmured "Oh no." Maria looked at him, confusion on her face. *Was Patrick sick?* she wondered.

"Our own Prince Patrick de Valdavia is to make a speech before the United Nations on Tuesday, June 4, at the UN Manhattan, New York City headquarters."

Before Mr. Roceur could continue, the students and faculty leapt to their feet in cheers. After fifteen minutes, many of them still cheered, while many others surrounded Patrick. Patrick's bodyguard had been alerted, so he stayed beside his charge throughout the assembly. Finally, the faculty and staff restored as much order as they could.

"I was not told the subject of the Prince's speech, but nonetheless, this is a first in the history of King Philippe High School. Never has a student of this school given a speech at the United Nations. The graduates who have include the Prince's grandfather in 1948 and 1956. The international spotlight shines on this young man, who will represent his father, King Gerard, and this school, named after his fifteenth great-grandfather. I, personally, am exceedingly proud of Prince Patrick, and I know all of you are as well."

As everyone cheered, clapped, whistled, and stomped, Maria leaned close to Patrick. "You told me you didn't have any idea what this was about."

"I didn't. I had no idea the secretary would call Mr. Roceur about this. Why would she?"

Patrick's bodyguard leaned near and explained. "Because your speech is important, Patrick. Besides, you did tell the General Assembly President that June 4 is a school day."

"Oh. I forgot. But, still, Father could have called the school. The UN didn't have to. Now everyone knows."

"Patrick, we would have found out that evening on the news," Maria reminded him.

"I forgot that, too. Oh, well, it's done. So, you still gonna call me tonight about that honors stuff?"

"Sure. I can't wait," Maria said and smiled at Patrick as everyone returned to their homerooms for dismissal.

§§§§§

"Hello?"

"Patrick? It's Maria. Are you free to talk?"

"Sure thing," Patrick said and tossed his long legs over an arm of his giant chair. "I'm glad you called. People don't often call me."

"Oh? Why not?"

"I don't know really. Someone told me it's because of who my father is. He's the King, I know, but he's still just my father. Heck, I got this private line in my room so that my calls won't bother him or anyone else. But everyone still seems to be afraid. They wouldn't be if they saw my room, though. Heck, it's not even in the same wing as my father's office and my parents' suite. I can't disturb them. I can't disturb anyone. I'm the only one living in this wing right now."

"I'm glad. I mean about my call not disturbing your father. I know he's busy. Of course, he is. He's our King. Is it just you and your parents there while your brother is at university?"

"Yeah, and all the people who work and live here," Patrick said with a laugh. "The employee's rooms are in part of the attic. My great-great-grandfather had it refurbished a long time ago. When I was very young, I wanted to live up there."

78

"I've seen the Palace from the outside, of course. It's lovely. I like the towers."

"Yeah, I do, too. You'll have to come over, so we can go up in them. There's this cool really old telescope up in one of the towers. You can see for miles with that thing. You'll like it."

"Oh, I'd like that, Patrick."

"Cool. What about now?"

"Now? Are you sure? I don't want to interrupt anything important or get in the way."

"Nah. If your parents say it's okay, I'll come over with Devon and pick you up."

"You come here? To my house? You here?"

"Come on, Maria, don't do that. I'm just me. I'm Patrick. Sure, I do things, I go places, I play basketball and soccer, I go to high school. I'm just another guy. Don't go all goofy on me. Please?"

"I'm sorry, Patrick, really. It's just. . . . . All right. Hold on and I'll ask my parents." A few minutes later, Maria returned to the phone. "They said it's all right. Thank you for asking me. I'll be ready when you get here." Maria gave Patrick her address, and soon Devon arrived at the Bouchard home.

"Oh my! He's in a Rolls Royce!" Mrs. Bouchard exclaimed.

"Mother, please. Patrick wants to be treated like every other 16-year-old boy. Please, none of this gushing and making a fuss," Maria pleaded as Patrick walked to their door.

Mr. Bouchard greeted Patrick at the door, welcomed him in for introductions, and talked to him briefly. Mrs. Bouchard managed to nod and curtsy.

"Devon and I will drive Maria home after dinner," Patrick told her parents.

Dinner? At the palace? Their daughter? Neither Mr. nor Mrs. Bouchard were prepared for that news, so Maria took charge. "That will be fine, won't it, Mom and Dad?"

"Of course," Mr. Bouchard barely managed to say.

Maria took Patrick's arm and led him from the house before things got more awkward and uncomfortable. To Patrick's honor, he acted as if nothing untoward had happened. Maria felt grateful, for she was embarrassed for him. She also looked at him as he talked and felt something else stir in her heart. Maria felt love for the first time in her life.

Patrick looked at her and smiled, enchanted by the innocence in her eyes. Maria was unlike any girl he had ever met, and he liked her—a lot.

§§§§§

When the two teens arrived at the Palace, Patrick gave Maria a tour of the main floor, including the dining room, waiting room, vestibule (most of them called it the foyer), and finally down a hall to the east wing chapel.

"Oh, this is so beautiful!" Maria said, her hands folded before her as if in prayer.

Patrick stared at her for a few moments. "Yeah, it is. I come here sometimes to think. It's always quiet here."

"I would so love a place like this to come to whenever I want, where I can talk to God. Quiet contemplation. That would be so, so heavenly," Maria said with a reverential smile.

"So, you like to be alone and think about life and destiny and things like that, too?" Patrick asked her.

"Oh, I like to be alone. I do often ponder life, my purpose, you know, why I'm even here, what I'm meant to do. I think about that a lot. Too much, my parents say. They think I should join clubs and be more social. But that's not me. I don't have many friends, because I am such an introvert. I'd never make a good princess or queen, like your mother. She doesn't seem at all introverted. She's good at talking to all kinds of people. I'm sorry. I'm rambling on and on."

"No. I want to know more about you and what makes you tick."

"All right. But tell me about you, too. What interests you, Patrick?"

"Oh, like I said, thinking about my life and my destiny. I've thought a lot about that since childhood. I have a pretty good grasp on what I'm meant to do, though. Eric tapped me to be his assistant when he's king. So, I'll be helping him, supporting him, kinda being his right-hand man, you know, the second-in-command. I can't wait for that.

"Gosh, I didn't mean that the way it might seem. I look forward to helping Eric is what I mean. I don't want our father to die. Gosh, no."

"I know what you meant, Patrick, really. It's got to be rough to be in the position your brother's in. I mean, his real job begins the minute. . . . . Well, it's just got to be awful to go through life knowing that. I don't know how people like Eric and Charles in England do that," Maria said and shivered.

"Yeah, I know. Hey, let's go up to the watch tower for a bit before dinner," Patrick suggested as a diversion to change the subject. He didn't want to think of his father's death at all.

Maria nodded, and Patrick led her up the marble staircase to the fifth floor. "What's on this floor?" she asked.

"Oh, the ballroom, the balcony, and the Throne Room. And the staircases to the towers. Come on. The watch tower is over here," he said and guided her toward an iron winding staircase. "You go first, and I'll be behind you in case you slip."

Maria didn't slip, and when she stood in the tower, she gasped at the view. "This is incredible. It's almost like you can see Heaven from here."

Patrick giggled. "Maybe, but even this telescope isn't that strong. Go on, look through it," he told her and pointed to it.

Maria and Patrick enjoyed seeing the sights surrounding them from a different perspective. Finally, he said, "Hey, let's go to my room so you can tell me about that honors stuff."

Several minutes later, they entered Patrick's suite. Maria looked around his sitting room, taking in the shag carpet, the antique furniture, the paintings on the walls, the books filling shelves—and the huge chair. "Wow! This room is a clash of eras, Patrick. And that giant chair! Where on earth did you ever find that?"

Patrick laughed. "I didn't find it. It was a gift to Father from the Sultan of Brunei a few years ago. Father was gonna have it stored away, so I took it. I think it's cool."

"It certainly is unique, I'll say that. Did the Sultan think King Gerard is a behemoth?"

"I have no idea. Father and Mother thought it was pretty ghastly and ostentatious. They never let the Sultan know that, gosh no. They were gracious and thankful for the gifts. He brought mother some beautiful jewelry. But Father was, well, overwhelmed by this chair. No one else wanted it, and I did, so here it is."

"Your family's lives are so amazing. Meeting all of these important people, traveling, just all kinds of grand things. And you'll be doing more and more of them, won't you?"

"Yeah, I guess."

"You're already doing great things, Patrick."

"Nah, not really."

"Sure, you are. Your UN speech is just as awesome as anything can be!"

"It's just a speech, and it happens to be at the UN. It's no big deal." He glanced at his watch. "What about those honors classes?"

"Well, they're more advanced classes for the students with the highest GPAs. Your brother was in the Honors Program. You got an invitation? Why didn't you do it?"

Patrick shuffled his foot, shrugged his shoulders, and said, "I don't know. I mean, I do, but I'm sure it will sound silly." Maria assured him it wouldn't, so he finally confessed. "I just didn't want to be labeled a brain like Eric."

"Why ever not?"

"Because then people always expect so much from me. I'm not as important as Eric, so I don't matter as much. And, well, oh, it doesn't matter." Patrick turned and walked to a window, staring out at the leaves blowing in the breeze.

Maria came up behind him and put a hand on his shoulder. "Sure, it does, Patrick. It matters to you, so it matters to me. I like you. You're very nice and easy to talk to. Making friends is a big deal to me, and I'd like to think we're friends. Don't friends share what's bothering them?"

After several minutes with just the clock ticking in the room, Patrick told Maria, "I just don't want to let people down. See, if they think I'm all smart and capable and stuff, they'll expect me to do anything well and easily, like Eric. He could write a 25-page research paper in one day, and it would be fantastic. He'll be a fabulous king. I'm just afraid of letting him down if his expectations of me are that high. So, I prefer to hang with the normal people in the regular classes. Then, if I excel, great. If not, no big tragedy."

"Oh, Patrick, no. You could never let anyone down. Your parents and your brother love you too much to be disappointed. That's what my parents told me last year when I got a B on a report card. I cried for hours after school, afraid to show it to them, and when I did, they were so happy and proud of me. So, what I thought was a failure—not getting straight As—was no big deal to the people who love me most," Maria shared.

Patrick stared out of the window for several minutes. "You really think no one would pounce on me, the future king's kid brother, if that happened to me? They sure would. Because of who my family is, I can never just be Patrick, no matter how much I want to be. I have to be this Prince Patrick person. I can't do this, Maria. I can't put myself out there like that and risk disappointing and embarrassing my family. I won't. Sure, I'd like to take those classes, but everyone will know."

"What if they didn't know?"

"How would I hide it, suddenly going from regular classes to honors? They'd notice."

"Yes, they'll know you're not in those classes anymore, but they don't have to know you're in Honors. Let me talk to the Sponsor and the Principal tomorrow and figure out what we can come up with. Okay?"

"This is the craziest thing I've ever heard, but okay."

§§§§§

"See, I told you everything would work out! I'm so happy that we'll be in the same classes," Maria said and grabbed Patrick in a hug.

The hug surprised—but pleased—Patrick. "Yeah, so am I. But, um, we're standing in the Principal's office in front of the staff."

"Sorry. I just got excited. Like I told you, I don't make friends easily, and I don't have many friends at all. So, meeting you at the assembly has been a real blessing, Patrick. You're the best friend I've ever had."

Best friend? We haven't known each other long, Patrick thought. He liked Maria, but still. "Yeah, I guess it was, Maria. Thanks to you, I'll start next year in the Honors Program, and I'll just let my friends think I'm in different classes. That won't be a lie, just a misunderstanding. I will be taking different classes. That's not a lie, is it?"

"No, it's not. Not telling something isn't lying. There is a difference. If they believe that you're in different classes than they are, that really is true. They don't have to know you're in Honors if you don't want them to. I knew everything would work out. I prayed about it. Why take chances?" Maria asked and smiled.

"Sure, why take chances? Next year will be fun. We'll be juniors together. We'll graduate together. Who knows what else we'll share in life, Maria. God might have His own plans for us."

"Yes. I'm sure He does. We know He has a plan for you, Patrick. I'm still waiting for Him to reveal my purpose to me. As soon as He does, I'll be sure to tell you. I'm so happy to have a friend I can talk with."

Maria and Patrick smiled at one another, not imagining what God truly planned for either of them. They could only pray that they would remain as happy as they were at that moment.

§§§§§

"What are all of these people doing out here?" Patrick asked as his father drove the car toward the gates.

"I'm sure they are here to send you off on your first major Royal duty. Your speech has been the biggest news story lately," Gerard answered.

"Wow, really? It was a bit much with the assembly at school, but to dismiss school for this? That's nuts. I know a lot of these people. This is just trippy."

"Well, whatever it is, it is also flattering that people think so highly of you, Patrick. Whether you recognize it or not, you are well liked and highly regarded. I hear only compliments and praise about you on my engagements and travels. I hear them about Eric, too. Both of you have the lens of the world's population on you, which I know can be quite trying. It can also be a benefit."

"A benefit? How?"

"Take your speech at the United Nations as one example. Because you are well known, people will pay attention to that speech; it will garner a lot of notice. You have the power to influence change in this world, Patrick. Causes which mean a great deal to you can receive global consideration through you and your actions. You need to think about that seriously, son."

Patrick stared out of the window as the car turned into the airport. "I hadn't thought of it quite that way, Father. I guess I do have a responsibility to take my role more seriously and to work for the things that matter most to me. That's what this speech is, something important to me. That's why I want to go to New York and talk to these powerful people about physical fitness and wellness and community."

Gerard smiled at his son and hugged Patrick before they exited the car. "That's my son. That's all you need to do, patronize causes you care about, promote them, and be their public voice. That's what you've already done with the Athletic Association of Valdavia. Now, come, let us get you settled on the plane, and you'll be on your way to changing the world."

§§§§§

Patrick, dashing in a navy-blue suit and red tie, his brunet hair characteristically tousled, stepped to the podium to a standing-room-only hall in the United Nations Headquarters. He carried only one index card on which he had written an outline of his speech. He knew his topic and what he wished to say to some of the world's most influential human beings. Standing in front of hundreds of people, Patrick felt oddly at ease for such a private person. He knew the reason: his topic was of utmost importance to him.

"Dear General Assembly President Benites, members, and guests, I am honored to speak to you today about a subject extremely important to me. Thank you for inviting me to promote this cause here today.

"Physical fitness means more than doing leg presses or lifting weights. Yes, such activities, when combined with a healthy lifestyle, do create strong muscles and stamina. More than that, though, physical fitness helps the whole person. I saw this first hand as far back as elementary school," the 16-year-pld Prince said, causing smiles among the audience. "I saw how gym class and recess helped my classmates who had issues such as attention disorders or behavior problems. After a game of soccer or basketball or running track, they had expended their pent-up energy in a positive manner. They weren't just sitting still in a classroom, holding it in and having it erupt in violence against their classmates. I saw several scuffles and bruises, but then, when we got introduced to phys ed, that all began to change.

"The children who had lashed out in frustration at not getting that energy out of them became calmer when they were sitting at desks. The outbursts became less frequent. There have been studies on this, in fact. Just two years ago, Doctors Algin and Porter of England released their research. They studied twenty-five fifth graders over the course of two years. They saw marked decrease in verbal and physical outbursts in the classroom, which they attributed to the school's physical education program. I have copies of their report with me should any of you desire to examine its findings.

"So, what I saw in my classmates is typical when physical fitness programs are established in schools. As I said, yes, these programs help people's bodies become fitter and stronger. They teach physical skills. But most importantly, they teach social skills; after all, teamwork is such a part of many of the games and tasks children do in phys ed. Cooperation is a huge lesson in athletics.

"So is motor skill development. Coordination is necessary to play any sport without accident. I can tell you what some of you probably know. The whole body works together when you are dribbling, dodging other players, and leaping for the hoop shot in basketball. You use your entire body to do something similar on the football field while going for the touchdown. Brian, eyes, ears, arms, abdomen, legs, back—the entire body is engaged in these sports.

"Children who have strong motor, social, and behavior control skills do much better academically, as well. They have more focus and stamina, and do not lose their attention during lessons. Sports trains the entire body."

"There are nations and parts of our world where children do not have these benefits. They do not have access to regular physical fitness. Their schools are underfunded and understaffed, lacking the essentials. Many children never get to make a run for the touchdown or to jump for the shot.

"In underdeveloped countries, where fewer children have a chance to attend school, we need to supplement physical education with other programs and venues. The more actively engaged people are, the more likely they are to lead healthy, productive, collaborative lives. The goal isn't to create a generation of athletes, but a generation of healthy, focused, successful people. Sports bring people of all nations together, like in the Olympics or the World Cup.

"I am living proof of sports' benefits. For once, I will boast a bit. I have played sports most of my life. Since first grade, I have been a straight-A student and on the Honor Roll every term. I took on my first patronage a short time ago, and I chose the Athletic Association of Valdavia, which promotes athletics in schools as well as professional sports. In addition to my Royal duties and eventually acting as my brother Eric's assistant when he becomes king, I want to pursue my favorite sport professionally. I want to be a speed boat racer.

"All children can have well-rounded, healthy, productive lives if they are exposed to the life lessons taught through athletics. This begins in school through physical fitness programs. Please join me in this campaign to bring global physical fitness to reality. Thank you."

§§§§

Patrick returned to school two days later to banners, balloons, and cheers. The sights and sounds stopped him in his tracks on the walkway. He turned to Devon and showed his bewilderment. "What is this for?"

"Your speech, of course. You didn't see Tuesday evening's paper or yesterday's? Your speech got everyone talking," Devon informed his charge.

"Oh. I guess that's good, huh? That was the whole purpose, after all. Get attention for global physical fitness. Like Father told me, this kind of attention comes with the territory. I better get on in there before the bell rings."

Dozens of high schoolers instantly surrounded Patrick, all of them talking at once. Autograph books, magazines, posters, newspapers, and pictures appeared in front of him, and classmates pleaded and begged for his autograph. He obligingly signed as many as he could before the first bell sounded, and then tried in vain to get to the entrance.

"Hey, come on everyone. We're all gonna be late for homeroom," Patrick moaned. He disliked tardiness; if he had a pet peeve, that was it. "Come on, please."

Devon took control, grabbed Patrick, and pushed their way through the throng of students. Devon and Patrick made it through the door, only to find themselves surrounded by more people.

"This is hopeless," Patrick said. "I'll never get to class on time."

Once more, Devon forced their way through the crowd and went into the office. He locked the door, preventing the imploring girls from getting to Patrick. "Is there any way to stop this mob scene?" Devon asked the secretary. "Patrick wouldn't have made it this far if I hadn't pushed and shoved our way in here. How can he attend his classes with this going on?"

"Oh, dear. We actually weren't aware the Prince had arrived yet. But short of calling the police or the Army, I'm not sure what we can do. Most of the student body has been in a tither for days, especially after watching the Prince's speech. That was the tipping point. There's no holding them back now."

"Then how can you expect Patrick to attend school during these last two weeks if this keeps up? I have to consider his safety foremost, and right now that's priority."

"We are well aware of the security concerns," Principal Roceur said as he bounded in from his office. "I have been in discussion with Prince Patrick's teachers this morning, and we have come up with a solution. Please come into my office."

Patrick's teachers greeted him, and then the principal continued. "Patrick is an excellent student, most excellent. Our solution is to have him complete his assignments in the safely of the Palace. Mr. Toine will come by every day to collect them. They can easily be left at the front gate, I presume?" Patrick and Devon both said they could. "Excellent, then that is what we will do. Every day, assignments will be left for Patrick to complete and the previous day's assignments collected. This folder contains the assignments from all of your classes for today. I trust this is satisfactory?"

"Well, if it has to be this way, but it kinda stinks that I can't be with my friends. It looks like my life is really changing, huh? I thought I'd have more time."

A short time later, at the Palace, Patrick and Devon explained why Patrick was home so early and that he would not return until September. His parents noticed his sadness and tried to reassure him.

"I know. I have to accept that my life is just different. It shouldn't be, but it is. I'm going to my room. I've got all my books, and someone will clean out my locker and bring everything here soon. This is just great," he said and shuffled up the stairs.

Gerard and Matilda knew there was little they could do. Patrick's life would always be different, that was true. He would rarely be able to do things the same way as others did them. Patrick would always be recognized, noticed, and sought. Now that he had entered the political arena with his UN speech, his life had drastically changed.

"I think I'll wait a while to tell him about those interview requests," Gerard said as he went to his office for a meeting.

In his room, Patrick did his history homework, and then opened his secret hiding place. He took his notebook and pen and sat against the wall as he wrote.

6 June 1974

Well, I never in a million years expected to be sent home from school today, and all because of that speech. I'm miffed, sure, 'cause I'm being treated differently, the one thing I never wanted. It's happened before, but now it's big leagues. I'm almost an adult, well, in a few years, and I always just wanted to live my life my way as much as I could. Looks like that isn't very much right now. I sure hope this nonsense dies down soon. I made that speech to get important things done, not to get attention for me. No one should want this kind of life. Poor Eric. What's he going through?

§§§§

"Hello?"

"Patrick, hi, it's Maria. Everyone was buzzing today about your having to leave because hordes of students mobbed you when you got to school. Gosh, that's just awful."

"Yeah. It really is."

"I'll see you tomorrow, won't I? We can find some time to talk."

"Um, not unless you come here."

"Are you sick? What's wrong?"

"I'm not coming back to school until September. Mr. Roceur and my teachers worked it out so that I can do all of my assignments from home. One of them will deliver and pick up my work. I don't want to talk about it. It's all I've thought about all day."

"Oh, well, all right. I'm so sorry this happened. You're the only person I've ever met in school with whom I feel comfortable talking to about everything inside me. I'm going to miss seeing you until September," Maria said, sounding like she was going to cry.

"Heck, you don't have to wait. You can come here anytime. Can you come over now? I'd like to talk to you, too."

"Let me ask my mother. Hold on, and I'll be right back." Two minutes later, Maria returned and said, "She's going to drive me. I'll be there soon."

Matilda watched Maria climb the stairs, and she smiled. *"What a relief that Patrick's good friends are visiting him. I know how upset he is, and he needs their company,"* she thought as she arranged some roses on a foyer table.

"Patrick?" Maria said at his open door. "Thank you for inviting me. I missed seeing you the past few days, at least in person. We all saw your speech. You were incredible, Patrick, just incredible! And your speech, why it really got a lot of the kids talking and thinking. No wonder you were invited to join the Honors Program; you're just the most brilliant thinker I've ever come across anywhere."

Patrick shuffled a foot in his characteristic self-conscious manner and his face turned pink. "Stop it, Maria, please. Please don't be like the others."

"I didn't mean to be. I'm sorry. You are full of these brilliant ideas, and you do make people think seriously. You have so much to offer the world, and I can't wait to watch what you do and how you'll change this world."

"Well, we all change the world in our own ways. I just get more attention because of who my family is, that's all. This isn't about me. It's about my family's titles," Patrick protested.

"Not with me, it isn't. I don't mean any disrespect, but I don't give two hoots what titles and positions your family members have. I don't care about your title. I care about you, Patrick. You. The sensitive, thoughtful, passionate young man I met in the hallway on the way to assembly that afternoon. You, not some prince. Got that?"

Patrick stood rigid, staring at Maria as if she had just karate kicked him. Finally, he managed to say, "Wow, no one has ever spoken to me like that before. You almost sounded angry at me."

"Well, I am! You're playing this victim, and it doesn't suit you. It's not you; it's not authentic. You were born a prince. That comes with duty, responsibility, and yes, public attention. Look at Prince Charles and his brothers and Prince Albert. And your brother, Prince Eric. They're all heirs to the throne. You're not the only prince, so get over yourself. Stop feeling sorry for yourself, and live that life you want to live so much. How do you expect to go out and do everything you told me you want to do if you're so afraid of people watching you, getting excited at seeing you, taking your picture, or asking for autographs? Like it or not, you were born a public figure, so get used to it already and stop whining about it."

"Holy smokes, Maria. Wow. You sure told me, didn't you?"

"And now you're mad at me, and you're going to throw me out. Don't bother, I'm going," Maria said and headed toward the hall.

"Wo, wait! I'm not mad at you," Patrick said as he ran and grabbed her arm. "I'm glad you said all that."

"You are?" she asked and looked at him with surprise on her face.

"Sure. I needed to hear that. I have been moping for a while. I mean, I do know all that stuff you said, in my head anyway. I know it's got to be worse for Eric. So, yeah, I need to just buck up and live my life my way and stop worrying about other people. I also need to be grateful for all I have. You know, my great-grandfather was taught here, in the Palace, by a tutor. He never went to school and met other children. I have it made in the shade compared to that, don't I?"

Maria smiled. "Yes, you sure do. And I'm glad you aren't mad at me. I understand that friends can tell each other anything, right?"

"Sure," Patrick said and smiled at her. "I'm really glad I met you, Maria. I like you a whole lot."

"You do? Oh, Patrick, I really like you, too, a whole lot."

§§§§

6 June 1974

Life is not as terrible as I'd been feeling it is. I have it a lot better than a lot of people, and I'm fortunate to have my family, this place to call home, food, clothes, my health, a body that works, and good friends.

Life is all about love. I love Mother, Father, and Eric, and I know they love me. I love God, and I sure know He loves me.

I did whine and complain about the public attention I was getting, and boy, was that ever wrong. Maria laid into me this afternoon! She told me the brutal truth. She told me straight up what's wrong with me, and by gosh did she ever shock me. No one has ever talked to me at all like that. She was angry at me! Angry!

And you know what I realized? Her anger told me a lot more. Sure, she got fed up with me, but she also cares about me—really cares. Someone has to care to get that wrought up over someone else. Why get so bent out of shape and, well, passionate about it all if you don't care, right? I mean, she told me before that I'm a close friend and she likes me, but today was different. She showed me that she cares, and I don't think she even knows she did that.

But it's time for me to be honest, too. I've liked her a lot for a while. She's not just nice. She's easy to talk with, and she listens to me, truly listens. She cares about what I think and say; she's interested. And she shares her thoughts with me. She trusts me enough to open up to me. I feel the same way. I finally have someone with whom I can share everything in me, all the stuff I keep down deep inside since I was a little kid.

Maria is my best friend. She's the one person above all that I can trust. That means so much to me, I can't say it in words. A lifetime of not being able to tell anyone any of my thoughts, feelings, and questions. I want to tell Maria everything. I want to pour out my soul to her. I want her to do the same with me. I want us to share everything, including life.

Maria is the one person for me. I know that. I feel that. I imagine us in ten years, married and with two children of our own. Sure, I'll still be Eric's assistant when he's king, but I'll have a beautiful life outside of that. Wow. I never thought I would feel that kind of love and care for someone. I know I'm only 16, but so many of my friends have been going steady for a couple of years. I felt left out, left behind. Not anymore, I don't. For the first time in my life, I'm in love! I love Maria. My life is perfect. Wow, thanks God. You're awesomely cool.

§§§§

"Maria, do you realize what today is?"

"Uh-huh. We met one year ago today right here in this hallway. Has it already been a whole year? It doesn't feel like that long."

Patrick giggled. "I know. You know, I'd never felt happy all the time until I met you. You changed me that day."

"What day?"

"When you gave me all heck for moping about my life like I'd been doing. You turned me around and changed the way I view things, the way I think about everything. It was like you flipped a switch inside of me, girl. No one ever had the nerve to talk straight to me, no one, except you. Know what I wrote in my journal that afternoon?"

"How could I?" Maria asked with a smile.

"Right. Well, I wrote that your anger at me must have meant that you cared about me in some way. I mean, friends do care about each other and all."

"Yes, they do. But I really care about you, Patrick."

"I'm glad, because I care about you, too."

"Well, um, I care about you not just because you're my friend. I care about you because—because I—because I love you, Patrick. There, I said it finally."

"Maria? Really?"

"Of course, really, or I wouldn't have said it. Oh, I hope this doesn't change things between us," Maria said, her lips trembling.

"Of course, it will. It has to."

"It does? Then we can't be friends anymore?"

"I think we'll be friends for all time, you kook." He smiled at her offended expression. "Don't you get it? Haven't you ever seen it?" She shook her head, confused. "I love you, Maria. I love you."

"Oh, Patrick, I prayed you would. I mean prayed to God about it. He knows how I feel, and I asked Him to further our relationship if it's what He wants for us. He answered my prayer."

"When did you make this prayer?"

"Three months ago."

Patrick laughed and told Maria, "I also wrote in my journal that day you got angry at me that I love you. That was nearly a year ago. So, I'm not so sure what's going on, but at least we're on the same page now, huh?"

"Yes, I suppose. You never let me know? Why?"

"I'm not exactly sure. I wanted to give you time. Both of us time. We were 16. I know we're still just 17, but one year brings a lot of maturity at this age. I wanted us to get to know each other and feel totally comfortable with each other. I mean, if this is for life, as I pray it is, then we will remain best friends for the rest of our lives."

"Oh, Patrick, that sounds wonderful."

As Devon watched from a discreet distance, the two teenagers walked arm-in-arm down the hall to Patrick's locker. There, they continued their talk until Maria saw her mother pull up in the parking lot.

"I'll call you later, Patrick," Maria shouted as she ran out the door.

Patrick smiled while he walked to Devon. "Life really is beautiful, isn't it?"

"I suppose it is," Devon agreed, knowing that first loves often came with heartache. That was the one thing from which he couldn't protect the Prince.

§§§§

"Hey, Father. Thomas stopped me when I got home from school and said you need to talk to me. What's wrong?"

"Nothing is wrong, Patrick, at least I hope not. I just want to talk with you, man to man. You will graduate high school soon, and you need to think about what you want to do. Plus, there are a few other subjects I'd like us to discuss. Come in and sit. I've told Thomas not to disturb us unless it is extremely important."

"Wow, this sounds serious, but okay," Patrick said and sat in the chair across from his father's desk.

"Oh, it's not as serious as you make it out to be. It's just that we haven't talked in a while, and a milestone like graduation makes a perfect time for such conversations. Patrick, I know Eric has asked you to be his assistant when he becomes king, but what do you want to do until then?"

"I told you and Eric a few years ago. I want to join the Army, and I want that to be my career."

"You will likely have to resign from your post when Eric becomes king, you realize. Being the assistant to the king is a demanding job. You might want to talk with Thomas about the job, perhaps even shadow him for a while to get a feel for what's required. Oh, I realize that Eric will develop his own style and methods as king, but Thomas can still be a valuable resource for you."

"Sure, I know I can't be a career soldier and Eric's assistant at the same time. But we have decades before, well, you know. There's no rush," Patrick said with a smile. "And, yeah, I'll hook up with Thomas."

Gerard smiled at his son's vernacular. "If you are serious about making the Army your career, you need to enlist soon so you can begin shortly after graduation."

"Yeah, I know. I did that already. I begin as a plebe on Monday, June 14."

"Well, I'm impressed, son. You have taken this seriously. If this is as important to you as you claim, you will do your best to become the strongest, most-disciplined soldier the Army has, and I have every confidence that you will. Have you told your mother yet?"

"No. I just did it yesterday. I'm not ready for her tears and protests. I was kinda hoping you'd tell her, but I have a feeling you're gonna tell me to be a man and do it myself."

Gerard smiled. "That's right." He cleared his throat. "What about Maria? The two of you have been close for two years now. How serious is this relationship, Patrick?"

"Well, we're best friends, and we love each other. We talk a lot, about all kinds of things. We trust each other." Patrick waited for his father to speak, but Gerard simply stared at him, making Patrick uncomfortable. "What else am I supposed to say? You know I'd never do anything wrong, right? Maria and I love each other. We talked about the future some, and when the time is right, we want to get married."

"I trust you, Patrick; I always have. I've never been concerned about your compromising your values or beliefs. I just needed to know from you just how serious this relationship has become. So, marriage has come up?" Patrick nodded. "Well, I am pleased that neither of you wants to rush into marriage. Being good friends will help maintain a firm foundation in the marriage. I'm sure you and Eric have noticed how Mother and I tease one another and that we have our private jokes and time alone. We entered our marriage as good friends, and this October 4 we celebrate our twenty-seventh wedding anniversary."

"Wow, yeah, I know. Maria and I have talked about that. Her parents have been married twenty-two years now. We both have examples of strong marriages, so we know what we want. That's why we're not in a hurry. God will tell us when it's our time. We both pray about it a lot."

Gerard nodded. "Fine, son, fine. Prayer is the best recourse when you have a major life decision to make. Ask for God's assistance and guidance. I have every faith in you."

§§§§§

"Come in," Patrick said in answer to the knock on his suite door.

"Patrick."

"Maria!" Patrick flung his pen onto his tablet and stood up. "This is a nice surprise. I thought you'd be busy getting ready for tomorrow. You know, picking out dresses, shoes, and all that stuff."

"No, I don't need any fancy clothes. Patrick, I need to tell you something."

"Okay, go ahead and shoot."

"Patrick, please, this is hard enough. It took every bit of my strength to come here. My mother's waiting in the car."

"Hey, what's wrong? Something happened. What?"

"Something happened all right. To me."

Patrick panicked. "You're sick? Tell me!"

Maria shook her head. "No, it's nothing like that. I've made the most important decision of my life." She held Patrick's hands in hers. "You know I love you. You do believe that, don't you?"

"Sure, I do. I love you, too. What is it, Maria?"

"I know we've talked about our future together. We talked about marriage."

"Yeah, I know. Tell me!"

"I love you, Patrick, and I will until my last breath. You must believe that. But, my beautiful Patrick, I love someone else far more."

Patrick went limp and fell back into his desk chair. He stared at the floor as his brain spun wildly. Had she just said that? Was he hallucinating? Was he having a nightmare?

Maria knelt before him and held his arms. "Patrick, I love you. You are the only man I will ever love. That's the truth, believe me."

"I can't, not after what you just said. You can't love two men, Maria. You made your choice, now just go."

"It's not what you think, Patrick. Please, I must explain, and then you'll understand better. There is no other man."

"I don't understand. You're not making sense."

"Oh, Patrick, my love, I have prayed about this for many years, since long before we met. I know I probably should have told you, and if you hate me for not telling you, I'll understand. I'll never

99

blame you. There isn't another man. I've been called to take the vows."

"Vows? You're getting married? You said there's no one else."

"I am getting married. To Jesus. Tomorrow after graduation, my parents are taking me to Santa Maria Magdalena Convent in France. I become Sister Maria Anna. Patrick, my life's calling is to serve Jesus."

Patrick slumped back against the chair and stared at her as his eyes filled with tears. After several minutes of quiet, he spoke. "So that's it, then. It's over between us. We will never have the future we talked about."

"Oh, Patrick, this hurts me, too. I love you."

"But you love Jesus more. That's cool, really. No one can compete with Jesus," he said with the tiniest of smiles. "You'll make a great nun, Maria. You've always been contemplative, as long as I've known you anyway. If God called you to be a nun, then you have to go. You must obey Him. I know that. But does it have to end completely? Can't we still be friends?"

A tear slid down Maria's cheek, and she shook her head. "Santa Maria Magdalena is a cloistered convent. Not even my parents will see me again."

"Wow. I think I've got it bad. Your mother must feel it the worst. Mothers are really connected to their children. This is a lot to take in, Maria. It's gonna take me a while to come to terms with this."

"I know. It's been rough on my parents, and it will be for a very long time. No contact between us ever. For all intents and purposes, I'll seem dead to them. We'll never know how each other is doing or anything going on. I also must take a vow of poverty, so I want to give this back to you. Keep it to remember me by," Maria said and took off the friendship ring he had given her. She placed the ring in his hand, folded his fingers over it, and kissed his hand. "I love you forever, my Prince."

Maria stood and ran down the stairs, out the door, and fell into her mother's arms in tears. Gerard watched the scene from the staircase landing, knowing his son had just suffered his first heartbreak. *"Dear God, please protect Patrick from pain and negative thoughts. He truly loves this girl, and for whatever reason, she has left him. Keep him strong and focused on his life's goals. Remain with him and remind him of the love he does have. Thank you."*

§§§§§

"Patrick, may I come in?"

Patrick stuffed his notebook and pen in a desk drawer and instantly said, "Sure, come on in. It's nice to have you here for a while. I miss not having you around."

"I know. I miss you, too." Eric sat in a chair near his brother. "Hey, I'm sorry I couldn't come for your graduation. They wouldn't let me leave even two days early. I wanted to be there, you know. I wanted to cheer you on and hear your speech. I knew you'd be this year's valedictorian. Way to go, little brother. Except you're not so little. You're taller than I am," Eric said and giggled.

Patrick smiled slightly but looked down at the desk. Gerard had told Eric what had happened the day before graduation. Eric knew how Patrick felt about Maria; the brothers had talked often, making several long-distance telephone calls. Eric had felt certain that, in a few years, Patrick and Maria would marry. Heck, Eric could still hear the excitement in Patrick's voice when he said, "I never imagined love would feel like this, all-consuming and all warm and comfortable. She's the best friend I've ever come close to having. I can see us now, living in the east wing all on our own, sharing everything. Maria's the swellest girl ever, Eric. You'll adore her."

Now, for some unknown reason, it had all disappeared. Eric cleared his throat. "Patrick, Father told me. I don't know what to say. Sorry seems insipid right now, but I am. I can't say I know what it feels like, because I've never been in love, but I know it hurts bad. Do you want to talk?"

Patrick shrugged his shoulders. "There's not a whole lot to tell. She left me for someone else, someone with whom I can never compete, someone much better than I am."

"Hey, stop that," Eric said, a hint of anger in his voice. "You don't have to put yourself down like that over some other guy."

Patrick giggled. "You wouldn't say that if you knew who."

"Who? The football star?"

"No. Better. Jesus."

"What? She became a nun?"

"Yep."

"Wow. And you had no idea she was even considering it?"

"Nope."

"That's brutal. Gosh. How do you fell? Really?"

Patrick shrugged again. "It stings, I'm not gonna lie. But what can I say? Being a nun is a noble thing. I can't be mad or angry with her for that. You know, I really feel for her parents, though. They've got it worse than anyone."

"How so?"

"She's a cloistered nun. No contact at all with the outside world. She'll never see anyone except the nuns in the convent. Her parents were allowed to watch her get her hair shorn and take her vows, and then they had to leave without even kissing her goodbye. Now that's rough."

"Gosh, it sure is. I can't imagine never seeing my daughter again until we're both in Heaven," Eric said and shivered.

"Yeah. Plus, she took a vow of poverty. She didn't take anything with her except her Bible. The clothes she wore were burned, her mom told me. Maria has no ties at all to the life and people she left behind."

"She has her memories. No one can take those. She loves you, and you love her. I know it doesn't mean much right now, but maybe someday you'll be with her again," Eric said. He was always so hopeful and optimistic, Patrick thought.

"You mean in Heaven after we die? Yeah, but it won't be the same there, and you know it. We were friends here. It was great, but it ended. So, I move on and do my thing starting Monday."

"I know. My baby brother will be a soldier. Why do you want to join the Army so much anyway? I think it's great, but you've had this idea for years."

"I have my reasons. It will help me to accomplish a major goal of mine. World peace."

"Huh? Being a soldier? How?"

"I'm also a prince. So, I'll have access to people in power, right? I can use my title and rank to promote peace instead of war. I've learned a lot about Valdavia myself, and I especially studied why we've never had a war in this nation or why we were never forced to enter a war. Negotiations. I can do what our ancestors did to talk others into adopting peace and avoiding war. This world is headed for destruction unless people find peace and avoid wars."

Eric sat silent for several moments, considering Patrick's comments. When he spoke, his words sounded thoughtful and measured. "Patrick, you are a special soul, almost too special for this world. You were born for a much greater purpose than to be my assistant. Most people would tell you that you're insane for thinking you can single-handedly bring about world peace. But I think this is your true purpose. There have been individuals who have changed the world on their own really. Martin Luther, Gandhi, Joan of Arc, and more than anyone, Jesus. You'll do the same, Patrick. You will single-handedly bring people together and change the course of this world. Can I tell you how proud I am to be your brother? You will do much more important work than I ever will, Patrick," Eric said and hugged his brother close.

CHAPTER 4

Eric sat up in bed, startled, stunned, and confused. "Is someone there?" he softly asked. "Where are you?" Receiving no answer, he turned on the bedside lamp and looked around his bedroom. He went into the bathroom and sitting room as well. The windows were all secure, and nothing seemed out of place.

"What happened? I saw her. She was there. I wasn't dreaming: I know I wasn't. I've never had any dream like this. She was there, in my room, near my bed. At the foot of my bed looking at me," Eric whispered. "Tell me who she is and why she was here. Please."

Eric put his hands to his temples in an attempt to erase the image from his mind. However, when he opened his eyes, he saw her again, this time standing in his bedroom door looking at him. He wasn't imaging her or hallucinating. She was real, and she was there. "Who are you?" he asked her.

She never said anything, but she smiled at him and extended her arm toward him. She moved closer, seeming to glide over the floor, and stopped just in front of him. She placed her right hand over his cheek. Her hand startled him, and his body involuntarily jumped. Her skin was softer than the finest velvet, and its warmth surged through his body. He could not stop staring at her no matter how he tried.

A lone tear fell from her left eye and slid down her cheek. The tear reflected the moonlight, allowing him to glimpse it. "What's wrong? Do you need my help? Can't you tell me somehow?"

Even though she was crying, she smiled at Eric and hugged him. Then she disappeared.

Eric didn't move for more than twenty minutes. When he did, he rushed through his suite looking for the girl. Where had she gone? Why had she come? She seemed to have some connection to him, but what could it be?

Frustrated and confused, he turned off the lamp and lay on the bed. He never went back to sleep, but he stared at the ceiling until his alarm sounded. After his workout and shower, he dressed in slacks and a shirt and joined his family for breakfast.

When his mother asked him his plans for the day, he told her that he, Daniel, and Roger wanted to drive to Compeile for a few hours. Soon, Roger and Daniel hopped into Eric's sports car and the three were on the country roads for a scenic drive.

"Man, I've got to look for a job soon, you know. Now that we're through with university, real life kicks into full gear," Roger said.

"I know. It's expected that I'll now take on full-time Royal duties. Remember I told you that Patrick wants to make the Army his career?" Roger nodded. "Well, he's got some grand ideas for sure. But he also gave me an idea while I was talking to him yesterday. I'm thinking about joining the Army for a few years to get some experience and knowledge of what it's like. After all, I'm going to be in charge of it one day."

"Hmm. Yeah, you will. So, you're going to enlist? For how long?"

"You are? When?" Daniel asked.

"I'm not sure exactly when. It can't be my career for obvious reasons, but I was thinking maybe two years or so, enough to give me the insight I need into how it's run and organized. Is that long enough you think?"

"Sure, but you can join the reserves, you know. Do Army work on weekends plus two weeks each year. That will give you time for your duties and give you insider info on the Army," Roger suggested.

Eric nodded. "I hadn't thought of that. Thanks, Roger, that's perfect. I'll get started on that Monday. That's the day Patrick begins his Army career."

"He's a cool kid, always was. I always thought he was too sensitive for something like the military, but I guess I was wrong."

Eric glanced at Roger and said, "You're not wrong. He's extremely sensitive. But that's part of the reason he wants to do this."

"Really? To toughen up, you mean?"

"No, not that. He's got some idealistic but great ideas for what he wants to achieve as a soldier. My younger brother is going to do some mighty powerful things, Roger. I think Patrick's life has another direction to take, and I think I'm going to have to recruit another assistant when the time comes."

"Wow. That important, huh?"

"Yeah. So, what kind of job do you want to look for?"

"I don't know. I majored in business, so I suppose I can find some sort of entry level office job to get in a company, and then work my way up. I'll start my job hunt Monday, too. Looks like all three of us will be busy Monday."

The young men laughed, and soon pulled into the small town. Eric parked on the main street, and they explored the shops for a while—until Eric was recognized and surrounded by screaming girls. Stanley, Eric's bodyguard who had followed in a separate car, quickly appeared at Eric's side and monitored the girls until all autographs were signed.

Daniel stood near Eric, ready if needed, although he wasn't sure what he would do if a girl grabbed or pounced on Eric. He had observed similar scenes in Cambridge, but he never got used to them; they always unnerved him.

"Whew, I don't know how movie stars put up with that all the time," Roger said. "How do you stand it? It sounds great having girls throwing themselves at you, but it's a nightmare. They can sure trap a guy, can't they? Thank goodness for Stanley. He's gotten you out of some pretty tight spots over the past four years."

"I don't know how you stand it, either," Daniel said and wiped his forehead. "This can be a bit scary."

"It's more uncomfortable than anything, really. I haven't done anything on my own to warrant this attention. Just because I was born a prince, people act like this. It doesn't make sense to me," Eric said.

Roger smiled, accustomed to Eric's typically modest reaction to his fame. "I don't think it's just because of your parents' titles. It's got more to do with you. You're the only one who never sees that. You might not have done a whole lot of Royal work yet, but you never had to, buddy."

"What does that mean?"

"You look like a rock star, Eric. Even in elementary school, girls stared at you, followed you around, and wanted to sit next to you in class. Don't tell me you never once noticed any of that," Roger answered.

"Well, I didn't. I was too busy to pay attention to all of that nonsense. Now, can we change the subject?"

Daniel smiled, realizing that his friend was quite a guy. Handsome, suave, smart, popular, and unaware of it all. Heck, if Daniel possessed those qualities, he'd flourish in social situations. Eric, conversely, remained almost all business.

"Okay. How about helping me find a briefcase so I'm ready for those job interviews and look professional from the beginning?"

After two hours, Roger found the perfect briefcase, which he stored in Eric's car trunk. The young men then decided to eat lunch at an Italian restaurant. The maître d' immediately recognized Eric and escorted the three men to the best table in the establishment.

As they awaited their food, Roger and Eric talked more about Roger's job search. Suddenly, a girl grabbed Eric's arm and startled him. "Oh, I just had to come over and ask if you'll sign my menu. Please, Prince Eric. I'm just your biggest fan. My name is Sydney."

"Hello, Sydney. All right, I suppose," Eric said and took the menu from her. He signed it, returned it to her, and was stunned when she bent and kissed his cheek.

After she walked away, Eric wiped the lipstick from his cheek and asked, "What was that for?"

"I told you. Your biggest fan. You don't have to do anything. The rest of us are invisible. I can't get one girl interested in me, and you have thousands throwing themselves at you. You can sit at a table and eat lunch, and you get mobbed. It's not fair," Roger complained good-naturedly.

"Then you take them. I know it comes with the territory, but it gets embarrassing."

"Embarrassing to be every girl's dream man? Eric, you need your head examined."

"You wouldn't like it either, and you know it."

"Maybe not, but I'll never even have the chance to find out." Roger recognized Eric's expression. "I know, change the subject. So, anything new with you since we got home?

"Yes, actually. Have you ever had a dream so real it didn't feel like a dream at all? So real you were actually awake and moving around and part of it?"

"Huh? What are you talking about exactly?" Daniel asked.

"Oh, nothing I guess, just a dream I had last night," Eric said, wanting to continue the conversation away from Stanley.

"Must have been a doozy," Roger said, picking up Eric's intentions. "Hey, I suppose I should get a new suit for my interviews, too. Want to help me find one before we head back home?"

"Sure."

The young men looked through three shops before they found a classic suit in Roger's size. Roger placed the suit in Eric's car, and they began the drive home, trailed as always by Stanley.

"Okay, what was that business about a dream that wasn't a dream?" Roger asked. Daniel wanted to know, too, and said so.

"I'm not sure, Roger, Daniel. I saw a beautiful girl in my room last night."

Roger looked horrified. "A girl got in your room? How?"

"I have no idea. She was there, then I didn't see her, and then she was there again. There was something supernatural about the whole thing."

"Supernatural? You mean, she's a ghost?" Roger asked.

"You saw a ghost?" Daniel asked in alarm.

"I don't think so. She looked as human as you do right now. She touched my cheek, cried, and hugged me. Then she disappeared. In an instant she was gone. I know I wasn't asleep. I heard something, saw a shadow, and turned on the lamp. I searched my suite and didn't see her. I was standing in my sitting room, and suddenly she was in my bedroom doorway. That's when she came to me and placed her hand on my cheek. Her hand, her skin, was so soft and warm, it sent warmth all through my body. And she cried. Okay, it was one tear that slid down her left cheek. I asked her if she needed my help, and I kid you not she smiled at me and she hugged me!"

"A ghost hugged you? You even have ghosts following you around? Beautiful ghosts?"

"Roger, please, be serious. I don't think she's a ghost. I feel something about her. I feel like I should know her. I know that

110

sounds crazy, but that's how I feel. She's someone important to me, but I don't know how. I've never seen her before."

Roger looked out of the window for a few minutes. "If she's not a ghost, she's a vision."

"A vision? Like someone I'm going to meet in the future?"

"Sure. God must have sent you a vision of her. Why, I don't know. Maybe he let you see the girl you'll marry."

"Wow, I'd like to see the girl I'm going to marry. That would be awesome," Daniel said. Eric smiled at him.

"My future wife? I didn't get that vibe from her at all. She never spoke, but she wanted me to know something."

"Then maybe she's an angel sent to give you a message," Roger suggested.

"An angel? She sure was as beautiful as what I always thought an angel looks like. But the thing is, she didn't actually say anything. She cried, and she hugged me."

"Well, the message is in what she did. You need to interpret it."

"You think so? All right. I'll think on it for a while when I get home, and I'll pray about it. Maybe God will tell me more."

"Maybe. Let me know what you find out. This is some mystery."

§§§§§

19 June 1976

Last night, I saw a girl in my suite, a girl I'd never seen before. This wasn't a dream. I was wide awake and even got out of bed to search my rooms. I was alert and awake. I told Roger about it today, and he suggested I analyze what the girl did, because the meaning lies in that. She never talked. So, I'm going to examine what she did do and try to figure this out. I need to know who she is and what she tried to let me know.

First off, Roger said she could be a vision of my future wife, but I just never got that from her at all. Her vibe wasn't romantic as much as it was concerned. About what? That's what I want to find out.

Roger also said she could be an angel sent to give me a message. That's more likely. She did try to communicate with me without words. And she does look like what I always thought an angel would look like. She has long blonde hair, with bangs. She's slight in build, and perhaps a foot and a half shorter than I am. She wore a long white gown or dress, light and floaty material, because it moved easily when she walked or moved. I didn't distinguish much of her face because of the shadows in the room. I only had my bedside lamp on, and when I got my best look at her, we were in the sitting room. I saw her clearly, just not the details of her face like eyes and lips, that sort of thing. She just has this airy, calm manner that I've always associated with angels.

Anyway, when she did clearly appear to me, she stood in the doorway between my bedroom and sitting room. I stared at her without moving, and I didn't say anything. She smiled and extended her arm toward me. She reached out to me. She has some need to connect with me, that I know. Then she came to me, not seeming to walk really, as there were no movements of her body. It was more like she glided across the floor. I suppose that could be an angelic trait, too.

The next part gets to me. She put her right hand on my left cheek. I have never felt skin so soft, softer than that imported velvet our robes were made from years ago. And her hand felt warm. The warmth filled my entire body, and it made me feel safe. I can't explain it any other way.

The next moment, a single tear fell from her left eye and slid down her cheek. I asked her what was wrong and if I could help her, but she never said anything. She gave me a small smile, and she hugged me. I've thought about this a lot over the past several hours. She tried to tell me something. She showed me concern, compassion. She cried for me. Something is going to happen, something that will hurt me. I'll need comforting. But what? To me? To someone I love? I have no idea right now. But that's the message I get from all of this. She's giving me a premonition of my needing concern and comfort. That's quite disturbing, if I'm honest.

The strangest part of all is that as she hugged me, she just disappeared. Gone. She didn't move. She was hugging me, and then she was not there. I have no idea what that was about. Did she let me know all she had to "say" to me?

Or did another force make her return from where she came? I have no way of knowing if she left on her own or if she was forced to leave.

Was she sent by God to give me a message? Did she come on her own? Will I ever see her again? Most of all, WHAT WILL HAPPEN, AND TO WHOM?

§§§§§

Eric tossed, moaned, and breathed heavily in his sleep. "Who are you? What do you want? Tell me!"

"Hey! Eric! Wake up, Eric!"

"No!" Eric screamed as he held the sheet over his mouth and sat bolt upright. "Who's there? What do you want?" He saw a shape, but in the darkness, not much else.

"Hey, it's just me, Patrick. You must have had a nightmare. Are you okay?" Patrick asked and flipped on the bedside lamp.

"Patrick. Oh, wow, you heard me all the way in your room? I was that loud?"

"No. I couldn't sleep, so I was just walking around trying to tire my body or get rid of this nervous energy. Tomorrow's my big day, you know. I become a plebe and start on my new path."

"Yes, I know. I'm happy for you, really. Like I said, you'll live your dream and you'll change this world for the better."

"I pray so. I won't do it alone, not really. God is with me in this, plus I'll need the cooperation of world and military leaders. I'm not so idealistic to think peace will overtake this old world in a mere few years even. This will be a lifetime's work. I'm not fooling myself. I'll get tons of opposition, but I'm never giving up, Eric. This is too important. God created this planet as humans' temporary home, and humans are destroying it. That has to stop. It has to. One more nuclear war will wipe Earth from the universe."

"I know. That was certainly a topic that came up in my classes at Cambridge. Our generation is scared for the future, Patrick. It's going to take strong people like you to undo the horrors that past generations unleashed. You're right, it's going to be tough and rough, and you'll be persecuted by many for your stance. But I know you. You won't back down or surrender. I feel proud of you, I hope you know that."

Patrick bowed his head; like Eric, he became uncomfortable with praise. "I know. I'm proud of you, too. You've got some rockin' ideas on how to run this country. I can't wait to watch you in action. But what about that nightmare? Anything you want to talk about?"

Eric shook his head. "No. I've already forgotten it," he lied. He'd never forget her.

§§§§§

Eric barely slept the rest of the night, his thoughts consumed with his mysterious visitor. He arose, showered, and dressed extremely early, wanting to write about the previous night's dream. He also wanted to take Roger's advice and get information on joining the Army reserves. He turned on his desk lamp, took out his diary, and wrote, still trying to figure out the purpose behind the girl's visit.

21 June 1976

She appeared in my dreams last night. Apparently, I talked to her while I sleptp, because Patrick heard me and woke me. This was a dream. It was the same girl, wearing the same dress. I still never saw her face clearly. Her mouth is faint, but I never see her eyes. That's weird. Why would her face be hidden?

In the dream, she stood next to the Saintes Lake. I'd recognize that lake anywhere. Patrick and I have gone there many times. She stood there, in the grassy bank, and stared at me the same way she stared at me when she was in this room. Even though I never saw her eyes, she faced me directly, and I felt her gaze bore through me. It must be what an ant feels under a magnifying glass. I felt warm. I also felt something I'm not sure I can describe. I don't know how. I felt close to her. It was as if I know her extremely well, except that I've only seen her twice now, and I've only seen some of her, not her face.

I just realized something. When I told Roger about her, I said she's beautiful. But I don't know what she looks like. How can I tell someone that she's beautiful, when I don't know what she looks like? Oh, I know God didn't make ugly people, but we all have our ideas of beauty, we do. I know what makes something or someone beautiful in the sense of pleasing my senses. But I said this with certainty and authority to Roger. Why?

Who is she, and why is she haunting me this way? Two nights, once here and once in a dream. I've seen her, and I've felt her. I know she's real, and I know she's trying to warn me about my future pain, and that I will be sad enough to need comforting. She comforted me two nights ago, as if telling me she's sorry. Sorry for what, though? What is going to happen?

God, if you are trying to tell me, please help me to understand this girl's message. Help me to know what will happen and to whom. Please.

§§§§

Before breakfast, Eric went to his father's office, hoping to talk with him. Gerard saw him, smiled, and beckoned him in. "You've been up for quite a while already. Is anything wrong?"

"No, Father. I just wanted to talk with you before we go down to breakfast."

"Oh? What about?" Gerard asked while he leafed through a file.

"Patrick got me thinking. He enters the Army today, and he plans to make it his career." Gerard nodded. "I'm going to be king one day, and I thought I should have firsthand knowledge and insight into the Valdavian Army. It would help me to make the most appropriate decisions regarding how the Army is run, organized, and functions."

Gerard plopped the file on his desk. "You want to enlist, too, is that it?"

"Not exactly. Not full-time like Patrick is doing. Roger actually suggested the Reserves, so that's what I'd like to do for the next six years."

"Army Reserves? Weekends and one two-week training each year?"

"Yes. One weekend each month, and two weeks in the summer. I spoke with a recruiter, and he said men do Reserves from three to six years. I figure since I will be the head of the nation, I should do the maximum, six years. My tenure would end in July 1982."

"I see. I never expected this, not from my heir. But, Eric, I am so proud of you, son. Your grandparents refused to let me even consider it. Father had to tell me the reason, so I wouldn't resent them. As you know, I was their only surviving child, and I was therefore the only heir. They could not risk my life, even though the risk was low, as we know. And even though you are my heir, and I have what the British call a spare, I will always worry about you. I know, though, that you are intelligent, prudent, level-headed, and obedient. There aren't any risks in your joining the Reserves. Neither is there a precedent for a future King de Valdavia to join the Army. You will be the first in the nation's history, Eric. I love you, and I am immensely proud of you."

§§§§§

After breakfast, Eric went to his brother's suite. "Patrick? Do you have a few minutes?"

"Sure. I have to report at 9:00 sharp. It's only 7:30. What's up?"

"I know you have to spend the first month of your enlistment at the Army base, and that you won't have furlough, so I just wanted to have one last talk before you do leave."

Patrick smiled. "Sure thing. I kinda wanted to talk with you, too. Father told Mother and me that you're enlisting in the Reserves today. The first heir to enlist in the Army! Wow, Eric, you're in the history books before you're even king. That's great!" Patrick grabbed his brother in a hug. "You're going to change this world in more ways than I ever will, big brother," he said softly.

"Well, neither of us knows exactly what the future holds, but I'd like to think that we'll each have an impact and make a difference in how people think and act," Eric said with a faraway look in his eyes.

"Yeah, I like that. The DeBruce Martineau brothers, a team for life. We are, right?" Patrick asked.

"Of course, we are! You're one of the most important people in the world, Patrick. Listen, I know you can be a bit reckless at times, but promise me that you will never do anything reckless ever again. Nothing. I'm not overly concerned about the Army. I know you'll be responsible and safe with other people around who could get hurt. But promise me that you won't ever risk your own life."

Patrick giggled rather nervously. "Wow, you sound worse than Father ever did."

"I'm serious, Patrick. Promise me you will always take care of and protect yourself. You have to."

"Hey, you really are worried. Okay, okay. I promise, Eric. I won't zip through the air like a speeding bullet or leap from tall buildings. You have my oath," Patrick said and held up three fingers.

Eric laughed despite himself. "You're something else. You better, because life would be extremely boring without you." Eric hugged Patrick, and said a silent prayer asking God to always protect Patrick.

"Um, hey, there is one thing I need to tell you, but I don't want you freaking out over it, especially after all that stuff you just said."

Eric's brow furrowed. "What?"

"Well, none of us knows anything about our lives, you know, and how we could die any time. So, I wrote out where I want to be buried, for when my time comes."

"You what?" Eric asked, shock evident on his face.

"Well, yeah, just in case. Just in case something happens. I'm not planning to jump off the Palace or run in front of a truck, but, well, we never know, so I thought I'd let you know what I want. Just in case. That's all."

Eric breathed deeply. "All right. Just in case. I'll never need it, though. I'm the oldest brother. You'll outlive me."

"Yeah, but, well, just in case, it's in my Bible at John 3:16. Okay?"

"All right. But I won't ever need it, I'm telling you that."

§§§§§

Patrick hugged his parents and brother, and then left with Devon. Matilda began crying as soon as the front door closed, and Gerard pulled her close. "It's only one month, dear. Most of that time will be spent in a classroom, you know that. This is to prepare the plebes for their weekend trainings, which they will do for the following three months. Patrick will return after the one month and live with us during those next three months. We've been through this. You said you understood."

"I do understand. But it's different when your baby leaves," Matilda said as she cried.

"Eric was away at university for four years, and you never cried."

"University is far different from the Army. Eric wasn't sent into gunfire," Matilda said and wept more vehemently. "And now I learn that my other baby is also enlisting in the Army today. I'm losing both of my sons."

"Mother, you aren't losing us at all. I'm only joining the reserves. That's not a major time commitment at all, you know that. And we will have Patrick with us quite a lot. Our Army is not active duty. It never has been. Don't cry, please, Mother." Eric attempted to soothe his mother, and she stopped crying and turned to smile at him. "That's much better," he said and smiled, too. "I have to go now and complete my enlistment, and I don't want you to be upset."

"Now? So soon after Patrick? Oh, what am I going to do, Gerard?"

"You're going to calm down. Eric will return this afternoon. Patrick will be back in one month. There is nothing to get this emotional about, dear."

"Maybe not to a sturdy man like you, but to a mother who adores her boys, it's akin to the end of the universe," Matilda said through her tears.

"Mother, I'm leaving now. I'll return well before dinner. I love you," Eric said, kissed his mother, and quickly left with Stanley.

Patrick was weighed, measured, examined, and issued his plebe uniform and camouflage outfit, plus boots and socks for both, hat, beret, coat, a duffel bag, and his dog tags. His street clothes were packed in his trunk, which stood at the foot of his bunk. His first two weeks would be spent in the plebe barracks at the Army school on the base.

Patrick breathed deeply, looked around the barracks, and smiled. His dreams had just begun to come true. "This is the start of my real life, Devon. This is what I've wanted for many years. I know Father told you to stay with me, but I want to be treated like every other plebe. You take the car and go home, and you can come back for me in one month."

Before Devon could respond, someone else spoke. "I'm afraid that's not possible, Plebe DeBruce Martineau." Patrick turned toward the speaker. "I am Sergeant Mullineaux, Your Royal Highness. You are the first member of the Royal Family to enlist in the Valdavian Army, and the officers have decided that your security is a top priority. Your personal bodyguard will remain in the barracks for the duration of your initiation period, and he will be present when you are on the base. Mr. Nance will have the bunk next to yours during this one month. I realize that this is a disappointment to you, but we are responsible for your safety."

Patrick knew far better than to question his superior officer, so he saluted and said, "Yes, Sir, I understand. I will do as you order. Thank you, Sir."

"Fine, Plebe DeBruce Martineau. Feel free to become familiar with the base until the other plebes arrive. Lunch is at twelve hundred hours sharp. Our first meeting is at thirteen thirty hours sharp. Punctuality is highly prized in the Army. Never arrive late."

"No, Sir, I won't."

Once Sergeant Mullineaux left, Patrick did as he suggested and explored the base. He learned where everything was located, and he committed the layout to his memory. He arrived early at the mess hall, where he got to know the other new plebes, and he was also the first one to arrive at the classroom. Plebe DeBruce Martineau made a favorable impression on his first day.

Likewise did Private DeBruce Martineau, who impressed the officers by willingly enlisting as a reserve soldier. No other heir to the Valdavian throne had enlisted in the military; Eric was the first, as officers continuously informed him. He graciously accepted their accolades, knowing that his enlistment made history. Although not a huge deal to him, he recognized that it was a cause for celebration for others.

Eric, too, was weighed, measured, and examined, given his uniform, camouflage outfit, boots, socks, duffel bag, hat, coat, and dog tags. He sat through a two-hour information session, took the oath, and told to report for his first weekend of duty on July 24, 1976. Eric shook hands with the offices, slung his duffel bag over his shoulder, and left for home more than two hours before dinner, just as he had promised his mother.

$$\S\S\S\S$$

Roger stood watching Eric do bench presses, smiling at how dedicated his friend always remained in everything he attempted. He noticed that the weights totaled 100 pounds and that Eric had worked up an extreme sweat. He could never be jealous of his friend, but being around Eric often seemed to cause Roger's self-esteem to plummet. Eric, in many ways, exemplified the perfect man: movie-star looks and physique, intelligence, charm, and charisma. How could Roger ever hope to compete with all of that? Next to Eric, Roger resembled the court jester. He stood quiet and patient until his friend stopped, sat up, wiped his face, and reached for his water.

"Oh, hi, Roger," Eric said, panting. "How long have you been here?"

"Not long. I don't mean to disturb you, but I wanted to share my news."

"Good news, by the looks of your smile. What?"

"I was offered the job I wanted, and I accepted. I start next Monday."

"Hey, that's great, man! Congratulations! I'd give you a hug, but I'm a mess. Tell you what, give me time to shower and dress, and I'll treat you to lunch. Do you have time?"

"Sure, but you don't have to treat me. I'm a working man soon," Roger said with a proud smile.

"Soon. And you'll probably receive your first paycheck two weeks after you start. And anyway, I want to treat you. We're best friends, and this is the start of our adult lives, right? You in an office, me in the Army Reserves."

"Yeah, I suppose it is. When is your first weekend?"

"Just over one week, on the twenty-fourth," Eric answered. "I'm looking forward to this, to seeing what being a soldier is really like. I know Valdavian soldiers are never on the front lines unless they volunteer to serve in an ally's Army during a war. Still, this will give me first-hand knowledge of what our soldiers do and how the Army is run. I should know all of that if I am to be in charge of this country."

"Well, I gotta tell you, you sure have people impressed and talking about what a strong king you'll be. Our former high school teachers and classmates, our Cambridge classmates, people around the neighborhood, all seem to be talking about how you're already changing the monarchy just by joining the Reserves. No other member of your family has done that, and now both you and Patrick are soldiers. You two sure know how to shake things up," Roger said and smiled.

"Well, I didn't do this to make history. That never occurred to me; you know that. I did this because I think the king should know as much as he can to run this country effectively. I'm not putting down my father, grandfather, or ancestors, but it's just how I feel about my role. The only soldier king Valdavia has had is the first king, and this country was created for Christophe because he was such a loyal and strong soldier to the King of France. He knew enough to establish the Valdavian Army. I need to know enough to keep it running effectively."

"You will, Eric. You will. People are saying you'll be the best king this country will ever know."

Eric brushed away the comment with a sweep of his hand. "How about I shower and change now? You know your way around this place. Do what you want until I'm done."

"Sure," Roger said and found his way to the fourth floor. He didn't want to disturb King Gerard or Thomas, but he couldn't forget Eric's suggestion that he learn from Thomas. He thought he might be able to ask Thomas a few questions about his job as the king's assistant.

"I do have twenty minutes before King Gerard's next meeting, Roger. This job entails keeping His Majesty's schedule running smoothly and constantly up to date. That is crucial. Every morning, I prepare a card with every appointment for the day, with details on subject, attendees, and location. I also attach all files His Majesty needs in order to prepare for his appointments: copies of correspondence or transcriptions of telephone conversations, prior meeting notes and agendas, and relevant current news articles. His Majesty's schedule must run like clockwork. Meetings held in his office may be booked close together, but meetings held elsewhere should never be arranged too close in time to other meetings, as traffic and other issues could cause delays.

"I also handle his mail, passing all personal correspondence directly to him without my opening any of it. I do open and annotate all other mail, underlining key names and words in the letters so that King Gerard can easily ascertain the main ideas by skimming them. I've developed a coding system, which His Majesty fully understands. He uses a dictation machine to record his replies, and at the end of each day, I remove the day's transcription tape and place a fresh transcription tape on the machine for the following day. I then type each reply on His Majesty's official letterhead and leave the letters on his desk for his signature the following morning.

"I handle most telephone calls for His Majesty, as well, and brief him on all calls twice each day. He returns those which he determines are most crucial and tells me how to reply to all other calls.

"His international visits require months of preparation, often in conjunction with officials of the host countries. I can give you those details when we talk again. I must go in for His Majesty's meeting now."

"Thank you so much, Thomas. This has helped. Eric said you could teach me, and you already have. I appreciate this." Roger shook Thomas's hand, and watched the older gentleman take a tablet, a pencil, and King Gerard's planner into the king's office.

"Gee, I'd love to do this for Eric, I really would. I know he pegged Patrick, but if Patrick becomes a career soldier, how can he be Eric's assistant? I guess I'll have to wait a few years and see how things play out with Patrick," Roger thought as he slowly walked to the third floor to find out if Eric was ready to leave for lunch.

§§§§§

Eric opened his eyes and tried to focus them in the darkness. Something had awakened him. Or someone. He had been asleep but had felt a hand touch his hand. A soft, warm hand. Her! Eric sat up. "Where are you?" he quietly asked. "What do you need to tell me? I want to help you if I can. You can trust me."

Suddenly, her hand appeared in a moonbeam and took hold of his hand. She tenderly squeezed his hand, as if to assure him she did trust him. Eric again asked her what she wanted, and this time, she gently tugged his arm, causing him to follow her to the bookshelf in his sitting room.

Eric dared not speak. He watched as she removed a history book and opened to a page, nodded, and placed the open book in his hands. Eric studied the two-page spread, which showed four pictures of boats. He was confused.

"Boats? What about boats? I don't get it. I've only been on a boat twice. What are you trying to tell me? Please, I don't understand." Eric looked at her in desperation. She clearly wanted to tell him something she felt was important, but without words, her message remained unclear. "Can't you just say what it is? Can't you talk to me?"

The girl shook her head. She pointed to the book, still open in Eric's hand, and once more shook her head and formed what looked like sign language with her fingers.

"I don't know sign language. I can't decipher your message. I'm not supposed to get on a boat? Is that it?"

The girl shook her head, pointed upward, and in the instant before she disappeared, Eric saw a tear glisten on her cheek. He stared at where she had stood, more baffled than ever. He scrutinized the book for what felt like days before he slid a piece of paper to mark the pages, returned the book to the shelf, and lay on his bed. Like before, he looked at the ceiling, attempting to uncover the mysterious girl's mysterious message.

Finally, his alarm sounded at 3:00, and he showered, dressed, and stared at the still-dark early morning sky for thirty minutes. He then went to his desk to write in his diary.

23 July 1976

She returned early this morning. She definitely tried to give me a message, but when I asked if she could just speak to me, she shook her head. I don't know why she can't. I need to research angels and learn more about them and their rules and restrictions.

She did take me to a book in my room and show me pictures of boats. I rarely go near boats, so this likely isn't about me. But I can't figure out the urgency she seems to indicate to me. She did try to communicate with me, only through some sign language, and I don't know sign language. When I told her that and asked her clarifying questions, she pointed up, toward Heaven, and disappeared, just like the last time.

She is warning me about some danger concerning boats. What? Who? That's what I don't know and need to know! How can I do anything to prevent whatever will happen that appears to sadden me if I don't know who's involved? My brain feels more scrambled than ever.

God, is she an angel sent to deliver this message to me? Can't she just speak to me? If not, how can she let me know what I'm supposed to do? Please, God, let me know. I must know.

§§§§

Eric and Roger decided to walk the Palace grounds, so they could talk in private. Stanley was always present in public, and although the young men understood why, there were some things that others never needed to hear.

Once they were several yards from the Palace, Roger told Eric about his job, the ups and downs and adjustments. "I'm grateful for this job, don't get me wrong. The experience alone is worth all of the office politics and gossip."

"But?" Eric asked.

"But, I need more. I'm not feeling this job, Eric. It doesn't make me wake up every morning excited to go to work. I'm not sure many jobs would, though, to tell you the truth. I feel stuck."

"Well, what do you want to do? What is your passion?"

Roger laughed. "Your graduation speech." Roger knew his passion, but he couldn't tell Eric that he wanted the job meant for Patrick. He wouldn't put his best friend in the position to choose between his brother and his friend. Therefore, he quickly asked God's forgiveness for the lie he was about to utter. "Something energetic, dynamic, challenging, constant. I want something that matters, that makes a difference. I'm looking at different offices to figure out if any meet my wish list."

"That's quite a tall order for an office job. Best of luck. There is one office I've seen that matches your list, though."

"Oh? Where?" Roger asked, never anticipating the answer that nearly knocked his feet out from under him.

"Thomas Kruger's, Father's assistant."

Roger stopped walking and stared at Eric. "You know?"

Eric smiled. "Sure. I can read you by now, you know. Besides, I have a confession. Thomas mentioned your talk with him." He noticed Roger's embarrassment. "He also told me that when he retires, he will recommend you to Father."

"He what? I mean, he did? But he doesn't know my qualifications."

"He knows you, and he knows you did well in your Business Management classes. If you can hold out a few more years, until Thomas retires, the job will probably be yours. You'll have the job of your dreams."

"Gee, Eric, that's more than I ever expected. I don't know what to say. Oh, hey, I didn't mean to ignore you. How is the Army Reserves?"

"Fine. They train us in using the various rifles, in tank driving, in physical fitness, and in problem solving."

"Problem solving? How?"

"Oh, they give us scenarios and divide us into teams. Each team has a specific goal or duty, and we must figure out how best to accomplish that with teamwork and safety. I find it interesting, and I learned a lot about leading a team. This is all going to pay off later in my life. Leadership skills are so crucial in my future job, and the Army teaches me that already. I'm so grateful for this training, Roger. Looks like we'll both get to do the jobs we want to do," Eric said and smiled.

"Yeah. Hey, if everything is going so well, why do you look tired? You've got dark circles under your eyes that I never saw before. What's wrong?"

"Nothing's wrong." Eric looked around, just to double check that no one else could hear him. "It's just that I've had dreams about that girl, and she's visited me again."

"Who is she? What does she want?"

Eric shook his head. "I don't know for sure." Eric told Roger about the dreams and the most recent visit involving the book.

"Boats? Who do you know who travels by boat? And she seemed urgent? This is more mysterious than ever. I'm at a loss." Roger walked in silence for a few minutes as he thought. "When she pointed up, was it like she was telling you she had to get back to Heaven soon?"

"Huh?"

"Well, if she is an angel, maybe she came to you without permission. Maybe she broke the angel rules, and she had to get back before anyone found out."

"Maybe. This is so confusing to me, Roger. But I've prayed to God for his guidance and to let me know what He needs me to know. So far, I haven't gotten a message. So, I'm going to just trust Him and focus on my duties," Eric proclaimed. "If there's something I'm supposed to do, God will tell me. Until then, it's life as usual for me."

CHAPTER 5

Patrick awoke early, showered, and dressed in blue jeans and t-shirt, as well as his red high-top sneakers. He walked slowly onto his balcony and stared straight ahead. He had been a plebe for one year, and he had matured in many ways in those twelve months. He had spoken to his sergeant about his plans to promote world peace. Although the sergeant had not openly discouraged the prince, he had never been enthusiastic or supportive of Patrick's idea. So, Patrick would wait patiently until he was a private, and then make appointments with world leaders. He would, it seemed, do this single-handedly, just as Eric had said one year earlier. Patrick shrugged his shoulders in resignation, but he could not shrug off the feeling that had nagged him for weeks.

He refused to let that feeling dampen his excitement, however. He was finally test-driving his new speed boat on the lake that day! He had waited over seven weeks for the boat to be built and delivered. Now it was here, and he would finally get to drive it on Lake Saintes! Patrick couldn't allow this feeling, this lingering fear, to dampen his enthusiasm and freedom. He had imagined the spray in his face and the wind on his hair so many times, and today he would feel them, actually feel them. He could almost taste the saltwater.

Patrick decided to purge that fear; he would extinguish it before it destroyed him. He went to his desk and wrote a poem in a notebook, a poem that gave voice to that fear.

Destiny

The sun shines so bright this morning,

Taunting me with its cheer

When I can't feel it deep inside.

So I'll put on my veneer

And continue to hide this fear.

I never let them see

The angst, the turmoil I keep

Hidden deep within me,

This persistent and gnawing pain

That I don't want to know,

Though it remains my constant friend.

Friend? No. It is my foe.

I can't bear this any longer.

When will this misery end?

I know the answer in my heart.

Today I'll meet my friend.

They say I have a destiny.

Today I hope mine sets me free.

It worked! Patrick read the poem and smiled. Writing it had released it from him. He signed the poem, wrote the date—*19 July 1977*—at the top, and decided to hide the poem, as he hid all of his writings. He found a large manila envelope, placed the notebook inside, and sealed the envelope. He then pulled his desk away from the wall and stapled the envelope to the back of the desk. He returned the desk to its usual position. No one would ever think to look there, he thought, and went downstairs to join his family for breakfast.

§§§§§

"Oh, Patrick, baby, why must you do something so dangerous as to drive a speed boat of all things? Can't you stay home and help me tend to the rose bushes?" Matilda asked in the early stages of a panic attack.

Patrick breathed deeply, well aware by now of his mother's overactive worry. "Mother, please relax. Boating is no more dangerous than driving a car on the highway. People do that every day, and most do not have accidents."

"Well, some do, and many are fatal. Oh, this is just the worst thing you could do," Matilda said and fanned her face with her lace handkerchief.

Eric put his hand on Patrick's arm as a signal not to speak. "Mother, if it makes you feel better, Roger and I are going with Patrick, and I have two doctors hired to be at the lake just as a precaution. I will take care of Patrick, I promise."

Matilda sniffed. "That's all very prudent and thoughtful of you, dear, but how can you protect your brother when he is on a speeding boat?"

"I can be at his side as soon as anything happens. I'm an excellent swimmer, you know that. Trust me, Mother, as you always have, and please trust Patrick. He promised me last year that he would not risk his life. This boat has been tested and has been certified by four mechanics as safe. I'll make sure nothing happens to Patrick, I promise you and Father."

"Make sure you do, Eric. Make sure you do. If anything happens to my baby, it will kill part of me," Matilda said and made her way to the stairs in tears. Her lady-in-waiting ran to assist her to her suite and to administer to her needs.

Gerard turned to his sons. "I realize that your mother is often dramatic, but this is one time I side with her. This whole idea is risky and careless. Forget that you are a prince and an heir, Patrick. You are our son, and we protected you from harm until now. We thought we taught you to be responsible. Now you are willing to risk your life, and for what? Not a noble cause or to protect others, but to tempt fate."

"Father, I feel I am responsible. I said I wanted to get into speed boat racing a few years ago, in that UN speech. You heard me, and you never said anything then. I'm a soldier. I've learned responsibility, and I've long shown you that. All things in life come with risks, and you know that. Walking down that marble staircase has risks of falling and breaking a neck. I need to do this for myself. Please don't hate what I love. Please."

Gerard stood quiet and thoughtful for several moments before he pulled his youngest son to him. "I love you, Patrick. You should know that by now. Yes, you have always demonstrated responsibility, your quirkiness notwithstanding. Please, promise me that you will exercise the utmost caution. You must. You must," Gerard repeated with unshed tears making his voice creak.

"I will, Father. I love you, too, and Mother. I didn't get a chance to say it to her, so please tell her for me."

Gerard nodded as Patrick picked up his duffel bag and headed to the garage. Eric turned to his father and held his hand. "I promise you, I will do all in my power to protect Patrick."

§§§§

Devon drove the young men, with Stanley also in the front seat, and they picked up Roger at his apartment before they went to Lake Saintes. When they pulled up, Patrick opened the door before the car had come to a complete stop, causing Eric and Stanley to also bolt from the car.

Eric grabbed his brother's arm. "What are you doing?! Here you just promised Mother and Father that you won't do anything dangerous, and you leap from a moving car!"

Patrick looked like he'd been punched. "Hey, calm down, Eric. The car was barely moving." He noticed Eric's and Stanley's disapproving looks. "Okay, okay. Look, I'm sorry. It's just that I'm so psyched to finally have my boat, man. You know what this means to me."

"I do. But how can you drive a boat or do anything else if you get yourself killed in a mindless move like that? I don't want to have to go home alone and tell Mother and Father that you're dead, Patrick. I don't. You promised me, you gave me your oath, that you wouldn't do anything, anything reckless. You've already broken that promise today."

"Hey, I am sorry. Really, Eric, I am. I don't want to hurt you. Look, I do promise, I'll be extra safe today. I've got a life vest, a helmet, and goggles in my duffel. I'll be as protected as I can be. And I won't do any fancy moves today. I know I'm nowhere near ready for that. It's my first time on the boat by myself. I promise you, Eric. Forgive me. Please."

Eric stared into his brother's steel blue eyes, his own turquoise eyes filled with love, concern, and fear. "I do. But, remember this. You have only one body and only one life. You must take care of both. You have to."

Patrick stared at his brother, too, realizing how serious Eric had become. All of the tenseness had brought that nagging feeling back, and Patrick felt uneasy. He hid that, though, determined to regain his exhilaration. He nodded and said, "I will. You have my word. Enough?"

"Sure. Have fun, but be careful. The doctors are here on standby, but we won't need them today, will we, Patrick?"

"Nah. I'll be fine," Patrick said and smiled his lopsided smile as he turned to get ready.

"Man, that was pretty tense," Roger said as he came to stand beside Eric. "Patrick's a good guy, and he's smart. He puts on a show, but he wouldn't do anything that would jeopardize his life. Right?"

"I pray so," Eric softly said.

§§§§§

Eric watched as his brother put on the protective gear, breathing a sigh of relief when the shipwright tightened Patrick's life vest and helmet. He knew Patrick had taken lessons with the shipwright, and he had captained the boat with the shipwright monitoring him. He also knew that the shipwright would not have permitted Patrick to captain solo had he not proven capable.

When Patrick put one foot on the boat, he turned, smiled, and waved at Eric. Eric returned the smile, and as Patrick started the engine, Eric took a deep breath and prayed for his brother's protection. He had to trust that the boat was safe and that he and Patrick would return home to tell their parents about Patrick's first ride with laughter and joy.

"He'll be fine, Eric. He knows what he's doing. He wouldn't have been given a permit otherwise," Roger said, attempting to reassure and relax Eric.

Eric nodded once, but he didn't say anything. He moved closer to the lake and watched Patrick increase the boat's speed gradually. He wasn't irresponsible, just as he had promised. He handled the boat with skill and care. Eric breathed calmly, smiled at Roger, and thought, *"Everything's going to be all right."*

Patrick turned, went up the other side of the lake, turned again several yards downstream, and came up the center of the lake. Eric studied his brother's face. Patrick concentrated on the lake, the boat, and made sure both stayed in sync and that there were no impending obstacles. When he did notice a tree limb in the water, he maneuvered the boat around it deftly. Eric smiled, pleased with Patrick's care and proficiency.

Another lap of the lake, and Patrick again passed Eric and Roger. Patrick constantly looked at the lake, keeping one step ahead of obstructions or animals so he could move around them. He didn't want to capsize on his first day and cause the boat to need repairs so soon. Patrick ignored the people on the shore; he couldn't afford distraction. If he wanted this as his chosen his professional sport, he had to stay focused, careful, alert, and steady.

What was that? I didn't see anything. I didn't. Something hit the boat! No! Patrick's brain screamed. *I've got to hold my breath. I'm going under.* Patrick's eyes shut tightly as the worst imaginable pain devoured his body. All he felt was pain, the most excruciating pain, throughout his body. *What happened? I don't feel anything. I've got to get to the surface.* Patrick tried to swim. *Huh? I can't move. Dear Lord, I can't move. I'm dying, aren't I, God? This is my destiny. You tried to tell me.* Patrick stared up, seeing the sunlight filter through the lake's water. He felt the water rush around him. He saw Eric's face above him. Then Eric began moving with him, and they reached the surface. Eric carried him to the shore and laid him in the grass.

Patrick stood on the shore, watching Eric kneel close to him while doctors ripped his shirt off and shocked his heart with a defibrillator. Eric screamed at Patrick, begging him to open his eyes, to get up and go home with him.

"I am standing, Eric. Come on, let's go."

"He can't hear you."

"Huh? Who are you?"

"I'm here to take you to your new home," a girl softly said.

"My new home?" Patrick slowly asked. "You mean I'm dead?"

"Your body is dead, but your soul is alive. That's your body," the girl pointed to the frantic scene before them. "You are now your soul form."

"I'm dead. This is it?"

She shook her head. "No, Patrick, your life if far from over. You have whole new experiences and adventures awaiting you," the girl said and smiled at him.

"But what about Eric? He's so upset. He made me promise to be careful and to come home with him today. What will happen to Eric?"

"I don't know exactly. I do know his life is far from over. He has many more things to accomplish here on earth before he can come with us."

"Oh. Mother and Father? They didn't want me to come out here today. They didn't want anything to happen to me. I broke my promises to all of them."

"No, you didn't. The boat accident wasn't your fault, Patrick. It wasn't. Please don't ever feel guilty."

"Yeah, but Eric. Look at him."

Patrick watched as the girl turned her head and stared at Eric, who stood and stared up at the sky. Her hands went to her throat when Eric let out a guttural scream. She looked deeply pained. Patrick then looked at his brother, who had tears streaming down his face and the worst pain in his eyes.

Then he saw Eric look at the girl and the girl look at Eric. Eric was still and quiet, staring at her face. She was still, staring at Eric's face. Patrick kept looking from one to the other. "You have the same eyes. She's yours, Eric. She's your daughter! My niece. Eric! She's your daughter!" Patrick shouted, but, of course, Eric never heard him. Eric never even looked at him. Only at her.

Patrick saw Eric's mouth open and his eyes flash. Patrick quickly looked at the girl. A tear fell down her left cheek. She was crying. *For who? Me? Eric? Why is she crying?*

Patrick saw Roger put his arm around Eric and gently shake him, but Eric still didn't move. Suddenly, though, movement caught Eric's attention.

"Don't take him!" Eric shouted. "Don't take my brother! Keep working! Keep working! You can't stop! You can't! He's my brother! I have to bring him home soon!"

Roger held Eric tightly. "Eric, there's nothing they can do."

"Prince Eric," Dr. Samuels said, "I am deeply sorry. Prince Patrick most likely died instantly. He probably never felt anything."

"How can you know that?" Eric asked, his fists tightly clenched.

"Sir, your brother's spine was broken in the accident. We will learn more in the autopsy, but we feel internal damage to several of Prince Patrick's organs. I truly am sorry for you and the King and Queen."

Patrick saw Eric tense. "You're sure?" The doctors confirmed the injuries. "Is an autopsy necessary? You saw what happened."

"No, Sir, it's not if you are satisfied with the cause of death."

"I'm not satisfied at all, but I, too, saw what happened. We all saw. Please don't do that to him."

"As you wish, Prince Eric. Shall we take the body now?"

Eric nodded and once more stared at the girl. He didn't watch the doctors take Patrick away. He couldn't.

"Who are you? It's you, isn't it? You're the same girl?"

"Eric? Who are you talking to?" Roger asked in concern.

"The beautiful girl. She's standing there," Eric pointed.

Roger didn't see anyone. The only people on the shore were Eric, Devon, Stanley, the shipwright, and him.

"She's the same girl who visited me and who was in my dreams, Roger. She had tried to warn me about Patrick. The boats. The sadness. This is her message. Why didn't you tell me?" Eric asked her as tears fell down his face again. "Why? I could have stopped him, saved him."

"No one could have stopped me, Eric. No one. You have to know that. Don't blame her." Patrick grew frustrated. "Why can't he hear me?"

"I wanted to tell him. I tried to tell him the only way I could. I was forbidden from warning him. I was forbidden from even going to earth, but I did. I had to do what I could. But then it became harder to sneak away, and I had to stop going. I tried," the girl said, tears in her eyes, as she still stared at Eric. "I never wanted this to happen. I didn't want you to die yet, and I didn't want him to hurt like this. I wanted to stop this, but they kept saying it couldn't be stopped. They said it had to happen. Why does something like this have to happen?"

"Hey, don't, it's okay. There's always a reason why things like this happen. We'll find out. Yeah, it's a bummer about Eric. I don't want him to blame himself. None of this is his fault. It was an accident. So, what next? Don't we have to go to Heaven?"

The girl nodded. "Yes, but not yet, though. Not yet. This is my only chance to get this close to him for a long time. Please."

"Sure. He can't see me, can he?"

"No. He's not supposed to see me, either. I didn't make that happen. I don't know why he can see me, but I'm glad. I had to hide my face all of those other times. He's forbidden from seeing me yet."

"Yeah. So, do you know when you'll see him again?"

"Do I know when I'll be born? No. Only God and Michael know that."

"Michael? Who's Michael?"

"The Archangel, of course."

"Of course. This is trippy." Patrick smiled as he watched her. "You love him very much, don't you?"

138

"More than anyone can ever know," she whispered. "More than life."

$$\S\S\S\S\S$$

"We have to leave now. I don't want to, but Michael is calling me back. Are you ready?" the girl asked Patrick.

"Hey, Eric, I know you can't hear me, but I hope you can feel this. I love you, Eric. I'm going to miss you. You'll join me someday, and we'll have a blast again."

For the first time, the girl smiled. Eric saw her smile, and his face changed. He wasn't crying anymore, although the hole in his heart and his soul felt enormous.

"Yes, he will enter Heaven for his eternal life. I know that. It will be a long time, though. I know that, too. But, yes, the two of you will have a blast." The girl looked at Patrick for the first time in several minutes.

"Are you an angel?"

"Yes. So are you now."

"Me? An angel? Really?" She nodded. "Now that's trippy."

"He won't hear me, either, but I have to say it. I love you, my magnificent Daddy. I love you. Hold tight to that until I come to you." She blew Eric a kiss, which he caught with his hand. "I love you."

The angel led Patrick to a staircase that only they could see, and they began climbing to Heaven. Eric watched, seeing only her. He saw her turn her head as she climbed, looking at him as she had since she had appeared. She looked at him with turquoise eyes that exploded with love. Eric felt his heart stop and his breath catch in his chest.

"I love you, too," he whispered, but loud enough that Roger heard him.

Roger never saw anyone, but he knew Eric did. Maybe it was the vision again. Who knew?

What Eric never saw was Patrick climbing the stairs alongside the girl. Patrick, too, turned his head to watch his brother as long as he could. Patrick couldn't stop smiling that lopsided smile that Eric often said made Patrick resemble Elvis. *My brother. My niece. Together before her birth. This isn't trippy. This is a miracle, and I'm the one who caused it to happen. I did. I brought you two together before you were meant to see each other. I did. I'm the reason you two met today. You're the reason for my death. Now, that's trippy.*

§§§§

Eric stepped to the boat wreck that the shipwright had removed from the lake. A gaping hole in the bottom told what had happened. The boat had hit a large, jagged rock under the water's surface, which had upset it, turning it upside down. Patrick had been thrown from the boat. He would have survived if. . . . . The boat had thrown Patrick against the large, jagged rock, breaking his spine and ripping his organs apart. A rock. A stupid rock had killed his brother!

Eric kicked the boat with all of his anger, his brute force cracking boards and veneer. Stanley moved to stop him, but Roger held him back. "Let him get it out. He has to do this."

After nearly fifteen minutes, Eric stopped, his shoulders sagging, drained of energy. He looked at the shipwright and in a firm tone said, "Destroy it."

The shipwright nodded, understanding Eric's anger and grief. The boat could be repaired, but it would always remain a reminder of this tragedy. Yes, Patrick's death seemed an accident, but for Eric, the King, and the Queen Consort, the boat would only taunt and haunt them. It should be destroyed. He would haul it to his warehouse and burn the wood and melt the metal.

Eric walked slowly to the car, got in, and sat unmoving and staring straight ahead. Roger, Devon, and Stanley got in and remained silent even after they arrived at the Palace. Eric went in through the back-patio door and asked a maid, "Where are my parents?"

"Their Majesties are having afternoon tea in the sitting room."

Eric nodded, and went slowly to the second floor, stopping outside the sitting room to steel himself for the one thing he never dared to think he would have to do. He took a deep breath and entered.

Gerard saw him and instantly knew. "No. No! Not our Patrick!"

Matilda collapsed from her chair to the floor, wailing, screaming, crying. Eric wanted to close his eyes and cover his ears, blocking his parents' pain from his consciousness. He couldn't. He had to tell them.

"Mother. Father. Patrick took every precaution. He drove safely. The boat hit a large rock below the surface and—and it—and it threw him against the rock. The doctors told me it was probably instant."

Gerard just stared ahead at nothing in particular, a veritable shell of himself. Matilda pounded the floor as she continued wailing and crying and screaming "Patrick!" over and over.

Roger sent Thomas and Lucie, Matilda's lady-in-waiting, to the sitting room, knowing Gerard and Matilda needed tending. Lucie rushed to Matilda, holding her as she cried and screamed. Thomas tried to soothe Gerard, who never moved; he was in shock.

Eric went to his father's fourth-floor office, closed the door, and wrote the most painful document of his life. He had to rewrite the announcement four times, because his tears kept falling and smearing the ink. Somehow, though, he found the strength to finish, knowing that his father was not capable of announcing his youngest son's death.

Royal Announcement

On behalf of my grief-stricken parents King Gerard and Queen Consort Matilda, I have the extremely sad task of informing you of my bother Prince Patrick's death this afternoon.

I witnessed by brother's death, when his speed boat capsized in Lake Saintes, and I rushed to him and brought him to shore. Two doctors were at the lake as a precaution, and they immediately tended to Patrick. Despite their best efforts, there was nothing they could do. They pronounced my brother dead at 1:33 this afternoon. The doctors assured me that Patrick most likely died instantly, and I pray that is the case.

Further announcement shall be made once Patrick's funeral arrangements are complete.

Prince Eric de Valdavia

CHAPTER 6

Eric stood on his balcony, staring at the sky, reliving the afternoon in his memory. Patrick had done nothing wrong; he had worn protective gear—not that it saved him—and had driven the boat at reasonable speeds. Patrick had kept his promise to be prudent, safe, and careful. What happened was not due to Patrick's actions. It was, in the end, an accident—a tragic accident—caused by Eric.

Eric would never see, talk with, or work alongside his brother as they had planned. Their partnership had ended without warning that afternoon. Patrick was gone. He would never bound up the stairs full of energy and joy. He would never drop into Eric's room just to check on him. He would never sing loudly to his records and 8-track tapes. He would never play another practical joke. He would never brighten Eric's life with sunshine and fun. It was all gone in a millisecond. Forever.

Eric slowly walked to his desk, opened his leather-bound Royal diary, and wrote, trying to make sense of and to accept the afternoon's events.

19 July 1977

I never thought I would write this. Patrick is dead. My little brother is dead. It happened so fast. But why? Why Patrick? Letting him go was the hardest thing I have ever done. I will never see him again, talk with him again, be the victim of his practical jokes again. Nothing. Just the past, just memories. This felt like such a bad nightmare. Until I had to return home, without him, and tell Father and Mother. Father just seemed to go lifeless, just sat in a chair, his back straight, staring ahead. Motionless. Mother crumpled into a heap on the floor, screaming, crying, wailing. Both of them ripped out what was left of my heart. They are devastated. And I am devastated.

Now I have to be the strong one, ignore my own pain, and plan my brother's funeral. Dear God, this is too much. How am I supposed to remain stoic and strong, when I am drained of everything? I don't know if my brain understands all of this. What was real today? All of it? None of it? Was today merely a dream? I don't know.

I almost feel as if I am not me, that I am not in my body, that I am an actor in a tragedy and the real me is watching this play. None of this makes sense to me.

Especially the girl. Who was she? Where did she come from? She seemed to come out of nowhere. No. She came out of the clouds, she stepped out of the clouds. Then she was standing there across from me, next to Patrick. She was crying. For Patrick? For me? For us both? I don't know. I've never seen her before. Was she real? She seemed real. She looked real. So beautiful. Like an angel. An angel with long ash blonde hair and bangs, pink lips, and my eyes. My eyes. How is that possible? No one in recent generations of my family had these turquoise eyes. Is she an ancestor? Did I inherit my eyes from her? Is she an ancestor who came for Patrick's soul? To escort him to Heaven? I don't know. But she won't leave my mind even in the pain. I've never seen her, but I feel like I know her. Like I love her. Insane.

There is just too much in my brain right now. I can't think. I feel empty. What am I supposed to do now? God, help me. Please.

Eric closed his diary, dreading his next task even more than he had dreaded writing the announcement.

§§§§§

Eric walked to the west wing, stopping outside of Patrick's suite. The main door was open, as usual when Patrick wasn't home. *Will this door remain open for the rest of time?* Eric wondered, as he looked into the sitting room and saw the so-called giant chair. Eric went to

144

the chair that had caused such laughter and, for the first time, sat on it. How often he had come by and seen Patrick on the chair, his long legs flung over one of the arms as he read homework or wrote.

The images made Eric smile, but it wasn't long before his tears finally came. He sat in the chair until the room was dark—until he had no more tears left inside of him. *"Oh, Patrick, why? Why you? Why?"* Eric would wait decades for the answer to this question that haunted him.

He rubbed his face, ruffled his hair—as Patrick had so often done—and turned on the light. He had to do this. His parents could not handle this, and he wouldn't let them delve into even darker despair.

He took a deep breath and picked up Patrick's Bible from the desk. He opened the book to John 3:16 and, sure enough, found an envelope, *Patrick's Burial Wishes* written on the front in Patrick's childish script. Eric held the envelope to his chest and felt the desire to cry again. The tears weren't there, though, and he pounded the desk instead, needing to release his emotions somehow.

Patrick, I'm older. I was supposed to die before you. This isn't how things should be. Don't make me do this. Wake me from this nightmare. Please.

Eric held the envelope close and tight for more than one hour. Finally, he slit the envelope and removed a sheet of notebook paper.

Eric,

You're the only person who knows about this document, so if you're reading this, it means I'm not here anymore. Everyone dies, so don't be sad. I had some fun along the way. ☺

When I die, I know where I want to be buried. Please don't let them place me in that church vault. Please. I know our ancestors are there; the entire Valdavian Royal Family is there. But I can't stand the thought of being cooped up in that dark, stale room for all time. I know it's just my dead body, but still, where I go, I'll know. It will bug me, you know that.

You also know how I've always adored being outdoors—the wind, the trees, the grass, the animals and birds, the wide-open freedom. So, here's what I want. I want to be buried in the churchyard, in a spot where the sun can shine on me at all times. Well, during the day anyway. I trust you to pick the right plot for me, Eric.

I also know that Father and Mother will raise a stink, but don't let them pressure you or commandeer my body. Please. I can't be in that vault. Show them this if you have to. But please do this one last thing for me, Eric. Please.

I'll miss being with you. But we know that we'll be together again someday, and then it will be for all time. That will be so cool!

I love you, Eric.

Your Brother,

Patrick

Eric stared at the letter, rereading it at least a dozen times. "Oh, Patrick, you know I'll do this for you. I'll do anything for you, you know that. I'm so very sorry I couldn't keep my promise and protect you today. I'm so sorry. How can you ever forgive me? How? How can I forgive myself for letting you die, Patrick?" Eric said aloud. He had no way of knowing that Patrick heard him, but he couldn't hear Patrick's answer.

§§§§

"No, Eric! None of this is your fault," Patrick said, and realized that his brother couldn't hear him. "I need to let him know it's not his fault. I need to tell him. How can I tell him, Grandfather?"

"You can't, Patrick. Unless God gives angels specific instructions to go to earth for explicit reasons, there can be no contact between us and the people on earth."

"But that's no fair! How can God want Eric to live with this guilt for who knows how long? I have to talk to him!"

"I understand, believe me, I do. I don't want Eric to suffer, either, but we must obey God's commands. Angilia knows this all too well."

"Oh, yeah, she told me when she came to bring me here. She visited Eric and. . . . . . I better not say anything else."

"It's all right if you do. We already know why she went. She tried to warn him about your boat accident. She thought she could convince him to keep you off of a boat and that would prevent your death. Her heart is compassionate, as were her intentions."

"Did she get in trouble for trying to save me?"

"Trouble? No, not as we think of trouble on earth. But Michael had a long talk with her. I can't say that she was pleased by what he told her, but she understood her purpose and restrictions better than she had. You see, everything in life is used for God's purpose, even events not caused by God. Satan has his forces at work on earth, as we know. But God can turn any tragedy to serve His purpose. Such was the case with your accident. God did not cause your accident, but He did foresee the accident. He used that, and Angilia, to further His purpose for your lives: yours, Eric's, and Angilia's," Stefan explained.

"She is my niece, right? Eric's daughter? She has his eyes."

Stefan nodded. "Yes." Patrick noticed that his grandfather looked troubled and asked why. "Eric saw her when she went to earth for you. He should never have seen her; that was strictly forbidden."

"But she told me she didn't cause him to see her. She knew he could by his expressions and reactions, but she didn't know why he could. She's not to blame for that, Grandfather."

"Hmm. I know she can't and doesn't lie. But how, then?"

"I can address that."

"Michael, it's good to see you. So, you know why Eric saw his unborn daughter that day?"

"Yes, I do. God allowed it. He knew how this would affect Eric, so he permitted Eric to see Angilia, even though he does not know she is his unborn daughter. God felt that seeing her would provide Eric some measure of comfort and hope and reassurance. At the least, he would recognize her as an angel, and that knowledge would reinforce his beliefs about Heaven and eternal life."

"Ah, very well," Stefan said with a smile.

"But they will not see one another until her physical birth, that is strict," Michael said. "No matter how long her crying and heartache persist, she must never see him again, nor he her. Is that clear to both of you?"

"Absolutely," Stefan answered in a firm tone.

"Angilia told me about you, Michael. It's nice to meet you," Patrick said and extended his hand. Michael shook his hand and nodded. "Yeah, sure, I understand. But, well, what about Eric? He's blaming himself for what happened to me. It's not fair to let him live with this guilt."

"I realize it seems this way, but as Stefan told you, God has a reason for everything. Eric's guilt will resolve itself in time, a time assigned by God. Your brother will heal."

"Well, okay. I just don't like seeing him hurting so."

"That is to be expected. God understands why you feel this way. But you must trust God, and that He knows and will do best for all people."

Patrick nodded, and Michael left. "Hey, if it's okay, I'm going to sit with Angilia for a while. She's also hurting."

"All right," Stefan replied, knowing the severe pain of his two grandsons and his great-granddaughter.

"Hey, Little One, come here," Patrick said and gently lifted her onto his lap. "Cry it out. I know you love him, and I know you want to be with him. Coming back must have been the hardest thing you've ever done."

"It is, Uncle Patrick," Angilia said as she cried against him. "I do love him, more than I ever imagined anyone could love. Daddy is my first and greatest love. How can I possibly stay away from him?

How? He's all I can see and think about. He's hurting so much, and I can do nothing to help him."

She cried in agony, and nothing Patrick said or did soothed her. All he could do was hold her while she cried without ceasing. *How long can she cry like this? God, how long will she suffer like this? I didn't think suffering existed in Heaven. Please do something to help her.*

"Angilia, I have come to play for you. I know how you enjoy music," the Archangel Gabriel said as he appeared beside Angilia and Patrick. He played a gorgeous melody on a harp, but Angilia didn't stop crying. Gabriel ran his hand down her long ash-blonde hair and kissed her cheek. He looked at Patrick, shook his head sadly, and returned to the Archangel Choir.

"Hey, um, Little One, there's something I have to do for a little while. Okay? I'll be back real soon. Is that okay?" Patrick asked her.

Angilia nodded but never stopped crying. Patrick tenderly placed her on the silk blanket on which she had been crying, and he quickly left while no one else was there. He knew he was taking a risk, but he had to for his niece's sake.

Patrick literally took a leap of faith and sped to earth, to his sitting room balcony. He quietly got some of his money from the desk drawer where he had kept it, and then he quickly left. He zoomed to a toy store far away where he wouldn't be as readily recognized and scoured the shelves until he found just what he wanted: a white, fluffy teddy bear with gossamer angel wings. He stood patiently in the checkout line—as patiently as he could, considering he had broken Heaven's rules—and finally paid. He refused a bag and ran from the store; one of the bear's wings ripped on his rush out. He would tend to that later.

Patrick found a secluded alley, and from there flew back to Heaven. He came upon an angel, whom he asked to mend the bear's wing. The angel smiled and quickly mended the rip with the finest silk thread. Patrick hugged the angel in gratitude and ran back to Angilia.

He sat cross-legged next to her, and he brushed the hair off of her cheek with his hand. "Hey, Little One. I have a surprise for you. He'll keep you company and help to make you feel better. Okay? Here," he softly said and put the bear in the bend of her elbow.

Angilia looked at the bear, who seemed to smile at her, and she took him in her hands. She rolled onto her back and smiled up at the bear. "Angel Bear, are you my new companion?"

"You like him?"

"Oh, yes, Uncle Patrick, I do," she said, sat up, and hugged him. "I can never forget Daddy, and I won't, but I know that I will be with him for a long time when I am born. And I trust God to help him, so he won't suffer too much. I have to trust God. I know He does what's best for us."

"Why the sudden change? It can't just be the bear."

"No. Great-Grandfather and Michael talked to me. They both told me that they, and God, too, understand how I feel, but that my sadness won't make my birth happen any sooner than God predestined it. God knows the exact moment of my birth, and it will happen then. Daddy and I will be together forever from that moment on. Michael promised me that. I have to do my duty as an angel until Michael comes for me and takes me to earth."

"So, you'll be okay?"

She nodded. "I'll always think of and see Daddy. I even sketched him. See?" She held up a parchment sheet. "He's with me forever. Here," she said and placed her hands over her heart.

§§§§

Eric stayed up all night, sitting in Patrick's large chair. He didn't want to sleep. He hadn't eaten since breakfast and had no desire to eat. He sat in the chair and replayed the afternoon in his memory time and again. If only he had ordered the lake searched prior to Patrick's trial run. If only he had made sure the lake was safe. If only he had been more aware. If only. . . . . The list of what he should have done angered him, sickened him. He was angry at himself for letting this happen.

Eric grabbed the chair arms as tightly as he could. "Why?!" he screamed.

Gerard heard his son's scream faintly from his west wing suite. Why? That question ran through his head constantly. Why had his son died? Why Patrick? *He was only nineteen. He had his whole life ahead of him. Why did you have to take him now, God? Why?* Tears slid from Gerard's eyes as he lay on his bed, not moving, not making a sound. He had too much grief to ever let it all out. Where would it go?

Matilda sobbed beside him, curled on her side, not sleeping either. *How can life ever feel normal again? How? My baby is dead. Patrick is dead, gone from me. I can never be the same again. My heart. He took my heart with him. My baby.* Her grieving brain kept saying the same things, asking the same questions. Life as she had known it ended when Eric entered the sitting room without Patrick.

Stanley and Devon heard Eric's pained question, too, from their post at the end of the hall. Devon bolted down the stairs and out the back-patio door. He couldn't handle Eric's grief, not with his own constantly taunting him. *My one duty, my only job, was to protect Patrick, and I failed. I didn't protect him. I didn't save him. He's dead, and it's my fault. How can I live with this? How can you ever forgive me?* Devon asked God.

The Palace servants barely slept, either. Many of them spent the night in tears, grieving the young man they had watched grow up since his birth, the young man they had come to love. Now his joyful, playful spirit was gone forever. The Palace would never seem the same ever again.

The guards at the gates wore black armbands, symbols of their grief. Throughout the night, people stood vigil, leaving flowers, cards, stuffed animals, lit candles, any tokens of remembrance that echoed Patrick's short life. The crying—constant and often intense—pushed the guards to their limits of self-control. How could they remain stoic when little Patrick was dead? His bouncy, perpetual motion, his love of life, his happy smile, his friendliness—all gone in the most unexpected manner. So quickly. They felt his loss, too, and yet they could never let it show publicly.

The citizens of Valdavia remained stunned. How on earth could Prince Patrick be dead? In such a freak accident? It wasn't fair; it just wasn't fair. He was so young, so full of life, so full of promise. He was meant to do great things. Now he was gone? Dead? It didn't seem real. It couldn't be real. Why Patrick? No one could answer that, because his death made no sense. How could it?

In desperation, thousands of people went to the Palace, congregating at the only place they could, to grieve collectively. Their sweet young prince was dead. No one wanted to believe it, but with the official word coming from his brother Eric, they had to believe. They would never again observe Patrick around the city, playing basketball in the park, eating at the local restaurants with friends and family, going for jogs, or simply sitting under a tree reading or writing. No one would ever see him again, and it all seemed so wrong.

§§§§§

Stanley drove Eric the short distance to the church due to the enormous crowds. He knew Eric's meeting with Reverend Simmons would be emotional enough on its own that he didn't need to deal with grieving throngs of people. Eric kept his gaze forward during the drive, never looking at people or the tributes to his brother.

They, of course, screamed at him as the car drove past, and some threw flowers at the car. Eric had to ignore everything in order to remain as strong as possible. His parents needed him to stay strong, so he had to remain strong for them. He had to do what they couldn't do. He had to plan Patrick's funeral with Reverend Simmons.

Reverend Simmons waited at the front door of the church for Eric, and immediately escorted the prince to his private office.

"Thank you for meeting with me, Reverend Simmons."

"Of course, Eric. I will do anything I can to help you and your parents. I can understand how difficult this is for you."

Eric nodded. "It is, but it has to be done. I will walk behind the gun carriage that takes Patrick to the church. Father and Mother shouldn't have to go through that. Both of them are ripped to shreds enough as it is. They will be driven to the church ahead of the gun carriage's departure.

"Reverend Simmons, Patrick's service will be here in the church. He liked traditional hymns like *How Great Thou Art* and *Peace in the Valley*. He liked I Corinthians; he read that book a lot, so he'll like verses from that book."

"I will select the scripture readings from that book. Who is giving the eulogy?"

"I am," Eric said, and swallowed hard to prevent crying. "Other than our parents, I know Patrick best, and, well, I have to. It's the least I owe him."

Reverend Simmons placed his hand over Eric's. "You and Patrick were always close." Eric nodded. "Eric, I am so very sorry for what happened and for your pain. Is there anything I can do for you?"

"Yes. Reverend Simmons, my brother had a specific request about where he wants to be. . .where he wants to be buried." Eric took Patrick's note from his suit jacket pocket. "He wants to be buried in the churchyard. He wrote his wishes and told me where to find them if. . .if something. . .if something happened to him. I know my parents aren't likely to approve, but as Patrick writes, he wants me to do this for him. He will be buried where he wants to be buried. It's the last thing I can do for my brother, and I am going to make sure he gets what he wants."

"Of course, Eric. Is there a specific plot you have in mind?"

"You can read what he wants," Eric said and passed the note to the reverend. "He wants a plot in the sunshine."

Reverend Simmons nodded and returned the note to Eric. "I know just the plot. Would you like to see it?"

Eric nodded, put the note in his pocket, and followed Reverend Simmons into the churchyard. "This is perfect," Eric said as the reverend stood next to a plot in full sunlight, with no trees nearby. "This is Patrick's."

"Very well. I'll have it prepared. When would you like the service?"

"Is tomorrow too soon?"

"Not at all. Thursday the 21st. Have you selected the casket, son?"

Eric shook his head, and tears filled his eyes. "I haven't had time. It just happened yesterday afternoon."

"Of course, Eric. I can take care of that for you. Do you have any preferences?"

"White. It should be white. Patrick has such a good soul. White. Classic."

"I will take care of the rest, Eric. If you need me, please call me, and I will come to you any time of the day or night."

"Thank you, Reverend Simmons. I appreciate your help."

Stanley drove Eric home, and he went straight to the Palace chapel, where he fell to his knees and cried until his eyes were swollen. *I found the perfect plot for you, Patrick, one you'll like. I promised you I would do this, and I am. But this is the hardest thing I will ever do, no matter how long I live. I never expected to do this. I am so sorry, Patrick, so sorry. Please forgive me for everything.*

§§§§

Eric explained the funeral arrangements to his parents that afternoon as they sat in the sitting room. Both looked beaten and war-torn, with swollen eyes, dark circles under their eyes, perpetual frowns, and overall lethargy. He hadn't seen himself in a mirror lately but was sure he looked no better.

"He really wanted to be in the churchyard, not with the family in the vault?" Gerard asked.

"Yes, Father. I have the note he wrote and had in his Bible, at John 3:16. Would you like to read it?"

Gerard nodded, so Eric took it from his pocket and gave it to his father. Gerard read it and surprised Eric by smiling. "Yes, he would feel this way, wouldn't he? Our Patrick loves open spaces and nature. He was always one for hikes and jogs. And I often saw him in the park either playing sports or sitting under a tree reading or writing. No wonder he got such good grades."

"This doesn't upset you?"

"Not at all. Patrick didn't like to be confined," Gerard said.

"Not even when he was a baby," Matilda said. "He kept trying to find a way out of his playpen, until one day I looked over and he was pulling himself up and over the top rail. Once he figured that out, there was no playpen for him. He started walking very early, too, and barely crawled. He never stopped moving once he began.

"I remember having the gardeners install temporary fencing in the back lawn to keep him from running off into the wooded areas of the property. I could hardly keep up with him. He ran my legs off, that child. Perpetual motion. He loved to explore, too, so everything had to be Patrick-proofed to protect him: drawers, sockets, bookshelves, pictures, vases, just everything. The maids and I forever went from room to room to make sure everything was safe from and for Patrick. He was a whirlwind."

Eric and Gerard laughed for the first time since the accident, and Matilda found the laughter infectious. The three of them laughed over Patrick anecdotes for more than two hours, the catharsis they desperately needed.

"I've been thinking of those times I found him with your father, Gerard, playing those wild make-believe games, like pirates or cowboys and Indians. They really did have such fun together." Matilda said.

"Hmm, yes, they did. Patrick tapped into a part of Father I hadn't seen since I was a young child and he played with me. I wonder what the two of them are doing together now?"

"Well, Patrick did tell me once that he planned to wear his jeans and t-shirts in Heaven and that he planned to have loads of fun," Eric said with a smile, remembering the conversation.

"Fun. I wonder what the angels in charge think of that," Gerard said in mock haughtiness.

§§§§

"Where have my paints gone?" Camillus asked the other angels. None of them seemed to know, but all helped him search for his paint box. No one could locate it.

"I'll go look in the Principalities," Angilia offered. She ran to the Choir where her great-grandfather lived and asked the Observers and Kings there if they had seen the paint box. They hadn't, but they helped her to look for it. "Thank you for your help. I'll try the Archangel Choir next."

Angilia ran there, and with the help of Gabriel and other angels, searched for the box to no avail. "Thank you all for your help. I'll return to the Angels Choir and look again. That was the last place Camillus had his paint box."

Angilia joined the ongoing search in her Choir, looking in every conceivable nook and cranny. She came to an empty room— or so she thought. Sitting on a ledge reading a book sat her Uncle Patrick. Why wasn't he searching?

She walked up to him and snatched the book from his hands. "Where is it?" she demanded.

"Huh? Where's what?" He looked surprised.

"You know exactly what. Every angel in the Angel Realm is looking for Camillus's paint box except for you, Uncle Patrick. Where did you hide it?"

"What makes you think I hid his old paint box?" he feigned offense.

"Because Great-grandfather told me about you and how you like practical jokes and games. Camillus wants to paint. Please, Uncle Patrick, give me the paint box. I won't tell anyone you hid it."

"You won't? Really? Okay, I'll get it. Patrick led her to the roof of the Angel Realm.

"What are we doing here?" she asked.

"To get the paint box. You want it, don't you?"

"Of course, but I don't see anything up here."

"That's because you don't know where to look," Patrick said with a smile. "I'm the master of secret hiding places. You should try to imagine all of the hiding places I came up with in my rooms at home. No one will ever find them," he giggled. He walked to a golden marble brick and pried it loose. "Here you go," he said and pulled out the paint box.

"Uncle Patrick! How on earth does that brain of yours work?"

Patrick laughed. "Wait 'til you get to know me even better. I'll amaze you."

"I can hardly wait. I have to give Camillus his paints now. We'll talk later," she said as she ran to return the paints.

Yeah, Heaven can be a lot of fun. There are tons of hiding places and lots of people. I can get away with a lot of gags here.

"You best rethink your plans, Patrick."

"Grandfather! What? I didn't say anything."

"I know, but you thought it. Higher order angels have the ability to read thoughts. So, beware the next time you decide to play one of your pranks up here. It might not be your playmate who hears your thoughts next time. Now, how about a game of pirates? There are plenty of capes and swords we can use."

"Really? Cool! Let's go!"

Soon, Gerard and Patrick were dressed as pirates and having a sword fight in one of the marble rooms of the Principalities Choir. Needless to say, the other Overseers gave them looks similar to that Matilda had given them many years earlier. Patrick laughed uproariously, thoroughly enjoying himself.

§§§§§

Early Thursday morning, a hearse arrived at the Palace, bearing Patrick's casket. Eric led the attendants to the chapel, where they sat up a bier and placed the casket atop. Two soldiers then entered to drape the casket with the Valdavian flag, but Eric asked them to wait.

"Please, can you allow me some time with my brother?"

They bowed, left, and closed the door, leaving Eric alone with Patrick's dead body. Eric bowed his head, took several deep breaths, and slowly opened the casket.

"Patrick, this is the last time I'll see you, your body anyway. I hope you hear me. I love you, Patrick. I always have, and I always will. My life will never be the same without you here, you know that I hope. We were supposed to rule Valdavia side by side. Yes, I'd have the title only because I was born first, but you would reign with me, help me, and make decisions, too. This was how I planned it, Patrick, I just hadn't told you because it was to be your surprise from me at the time. Even when I got married and my wife became my consort, you would have remained alongside me. This was to be our joint reign, Patrick. Now I will be alone, but I will do all in my power to also do the work you would have done. I will strive to maintain and to promote peace as you so wanted to do. I love you."

Eric bent and kissed his brother's forehead before he closed the casket and walked from the chapel. *I will always miss you, but I have many happy memories to keep me company throughout the years. I also know*

*that you will never be far away. I want you to continue to make me laugh, Patrick.
Please.*

§§§§

Patrick turned and walked away from his grandfather and his
niece. Angilia saw the pain on his face, and she moved to follow him.
Gerard grabbed her arm, though, and motioned for her to stop.

"Let him go, dear. He, too, feels guilt for Eric's pain and guilt.
He feels he caused his brother's deep pain. He needs to make peace
with this in his own way for now, just as you had to get over your pain
in leaving your father."

Angilia nodded and resumed watching her father. "I don't
want either of them to hurt. Their pain hurts me so dreadfully. I
never knew or felt pain until I went to earth to escort Uncle Patrick
and saw Daddy's pain. I felt something I've never felt before,
something deep inside me. It hasn't gone away. Seeing Daddy
changed me completely, Great-Grandfather."

"Hmm, yes, I was so afraid of this. I tried to convince Michael
that God should select another Spirit Guide for Patrick, but he told
me that God steadfastly insisted it be you. I was told that God had
His reasons. It was no longer my place to argue. God always knows
best.

"Angilia, I recognized your love for Eric when I told you
about him, and I knew what would happen when you stood before
him. I knew how difficult it would be for you to return here and to
leave him. I know full well what you felt at that moment. Eric's deep
pain and grief broke you heart, my child."

"Broke my heart? I don't understand."

Gerard put his arm around her, pulled her close, and recalled
his own earthly heartbreak to help him explain such an alien concept
to an angel. "When we love people with all of our beings, as you love
Eric, we feel the greatest joy and elation. But when they feel pain that
we cannot ease, we share their pain. We seem to take it into ourselves.
We feel as if someone has seized firm hold of our hearts and crushed

them to pieces. They break our hearts with their agony, not with their hands. That is what you felt."

Angilia watched her father and considered her grandfather's words. "Yes. It does feel that way. Will it ever end, Grandfather?"

"Yes, Angilia, it will. The day you are born, and you and Eric reunite, all of this will end forever, I promise you. Love will fill your beings for all time."

"Then I need to be born soon. Very soon," Angilia whispered and walked away. She found Patrick, sitting alone on a ledge, and stood beside him. "Do you mind if another broken heart joins you?"

"Come here, Little One. Grandfather told you about heartbreak. I was going to, but he said you weren't ready to hear about it yet. I know how much you want to be with him. I do. Heck, I saw your heart break that day. I saw it happen to you, and I knew. But there was nothing I could do, absolutely nothing I could do."

"You? What do you mean?"

"I couldn't stop his pain, either. I still can't. I'm forbidden. I know Michael said there's a purpose for all of this, and I know a big part of it is you and Eric seeing each other. I saw the love between the two of you. I brought the two of you together, and that really is cool and special. But there's more to this than we know yet. It just doesn't seem right that he has to suffer like this for however long it goes on," Patrick said.

"I know. He pain causes me pain. I don't completely understand how and why, but I do know I love him more than I will ever love anyone else. I feel such a need to be with him, Uncle Patrick. It isn't just that I had to leave him. I understand God's timeline for me and that I will be born when it is my time and not before. I know that. But there's this pull, this need, which feels so strong and almost urgent. I need to be with him, and I can't," Angilia said and began to weep.

Patrick held her close and felt his own tears fall. Michael stood in the shadows listening and watching, knowing how much they hurt, but unable to do what they each desired. "*Patrick, your brother's guilt will end at the appointed time. In the interim, Eric will learn to live with it. It won't dominate his life in this way much longer. He will have many important tasks to accomplish, and his life will keep him from dwelling in deep grief. Eric will cope and eventually heal.*

"Angilia, you intuit far more than you should. However, God has permitted this as part of His purpose for you and Eric. You and your father are deeply connected, and perhaps one day God will reveal the depth of that connection to you and to Eric. God has specific plans for Eric and for you, child, and your destines are meant to change Earth in the future. You will feel this connection with your father for all time, and nothing will alter or end this bond. Trust God and know that He has planned your life and Eric's life to fulfill His divine purpose.

"One thing I can do for you both now, Patrick and Angilia, is to erase your guilt. Yes, you will still react and respond to what happens with Eric on earth, but neither of you will ever again feel this guilt as long as you reside in Heaven. Now, resume your tasks as you did prior to this."

"Hey, wanna go on a treasure hunt?" Patrick asked his niece.

"I've never been on a treasure hunt. Sure!"

Michael smiled as Patrick took Angilia's hand and the two of them ran off in search of treasures. His duty in the Angels Choir done, Michael returned to the Archangel Choir.

§§§§§

A few hours later, Eric assisted his parents into a car for the short but dreaded drive to the church. He kissed his mother and his father and swallowed his tears as he watched them depart for their youngest son's funeral, a funeral they should never have had to attend. *I shouldn't have to attend my baby brother's funeral, either,* Eric thought as he made sure the gun carriage stood in place on the courtyard.

Eric escorted the military pallbearers into the chapel, where they respectfully carried Patrick's draped casket outside. Eric followed, and stood behind them as they waited for the salute. Three soldiers stood atop the Palace, and they fired a 21-gun salute for Prince Patrick, who had been amongst their ranks for just one year.

The gunfire and the sobs, moans, and groans of the people broke the otherwise deathly silence. Eric steeled his shoulders and stared at his brother's casket as the pallbearers placed it on the gun carriage. He blocked everything and everyone else from his senses. He had to in order to survive the day.

After the salute, the gun carriage began its slow and measured journey to Christ Church Valmondois. Once Eric cleared the gate, people fell into step behind him, crying and moaning still, creating the longest funeral cortege in Valdavian history. People who still lined the route tossed flowers at the gun carriage, and within minutes the carriage was covered in fragrant lilies, roses, and white carnations—Patrick's birth flower. Eric could not help but to notice the flowers, and he once more had to clench his fists and his jaw to stop his tears. *I can cry tonight, after I take care of Mother and Father.*

Finally, the gun carriage stopped at the church steps. Thousands more people filled the churchyard and the area across from the church. All of them loudly grieved it seemed. Even young children tossed flowers and cried. Devon, standing guard nearby, noticed several of Patrick's friends and former classmates in the crowd. He remembered the little boy who played basketball during recess or pinball games at the local arcade. He recalled Patrick's hopeful first—and only—love that indeed ended in heartache. He remembered bunking next to Patrick during his plebe training. Devon, too, would have to wait to let his tears flow.

Eric walked behind the pallbearers who carried Patrick up the stairs and up the aisle. He heard people sobbing as the casket passed, and he clenched his fists even harder. The walk up the aisle had never seemed as long. He stopped when the soldiers placed the casket on a flower-draped bier on the altar. When they stepped away, he bowed his head, said a silent prayer, and sat beside his mother in the Royal Family's pew.

Matilda took his hand and held it tightly, as if afraid to let go of Eric. She cried into her black handkerchief. Gerard sat tall and straight on her other side but stared at the casket without moving. The choir sang one of the hymns Eric had mentioned the previous day, *Peace in the Valley.*

Reverend Simmons then stood at the pulpit to deliver the service. "King Gerard and Queen Consort Matilda, the world grieves with you, sharing your pain and shock. Prince Patrick is loved and admired the world over. His life touched countless people. None of them, though, can ever share the pain you feel as Prince Patrick's parents. Prince Eric, your grief is unique and singular as Prince Patrick's only sibling. While no one can know your pain, we all feel the pain of this unfathomable tragedy.

"Prince Patrick blazed through this world and our lives for a brief nineteen years. We all knew him, whether personally or through his public role and reputation. We who were blessed to know him know that Prince Patrick was highly intelligent, kind, polite, active, fun-loving, seemingly always in motion, yet thoughtful and even rather philosophical and spiritual. In many ways, Prince Patrick was a contradiction in terms.

"Many of his former schoolmates have told me that he seemed studious but nonchalant about his academic performance. Well, from his former teachers, I have learned what his family always knew. You see, Patrick cultivated a persona of someone more concerned about a fun and fancy-free lifestyle that hid his true self. The real Patrick, according to his closest friends and his former music teacher Miss Yost, was quite helpful, thoughtful, attentive, serious, dedicated, and present in the moment. His report cards indicate a young boy and teenager of high intelligence and service. He often assisted his teachers before and after classes, tutored in the high school's English laboratory, and served as the Patron of the Athletic Association of Valdavia. He also performed Royal duties on behalf of his father.

"Prince Patrick seemed always to be thinking, not daydreaming as some people supposed. His brain was a whirlwind, never truly shutting down. It contained so many ideas and dreams for the future that Patrick often suffered from insomnia. I know, because he came to speak with me about this dilemma. He wondered if the way his brain operated was wrong or even sinful. Of course, it wasn't, I told him, and explained that God must have thought Patrick was capable of so many great things. That's why He filled Patrick's brain so full of these thoughts and goals.

"Prince Patrick brought joy and love wherever he went. We must hold onto that joy and love and continue to spread them as part of Prince Patrick's legacy."

Reverend Simmons took his seat, and the choir sang a beautiful hymn, *Crying in the Chapel*. Eric continued to stare at his brother's casket throughout the hymn, not wanting to accept this as reality. However, the hymn ended, and he knew the reality when he stepped to the pulpit to deliver Patrick's eulogy. He had no notes; he didn't need any. He intended to speak from his heart. He intended to speak the truth about his brother and what Patrick meant to him. No other speech would ever matter as much to Eric or hurt him as much.

"I was three years old when Patrick was born, and I was so excited when Father took me to the hospital on February 7, 1958. Mother sat on a hospital bed wearing a lavender nightgown and robe and holding a tiny thing wrapped in a blanket. Father sat me on the bed next to Mother, and I saw that the thing she held was actually a baby. I asked of this was our baby, and Mother told me yes, he was my baby brother Patrick Alain David. I reached over and touched his tiny hand, and he opened his eyes and smiled at me.

"Our bond formed at that moment. Patrick became one of the people who knew me best, one of the people whom I loved deeply, and my absolute best friend. Patrick seemed to know far more than other people, even when he was a baby. He had this way of looking at people when we talked to him, long before he could talk, that indicated he understood everything but was just waiting for his time to share all he did know. Patrick did like adventure, imaginative play, and motion. He and our grandfather often dressed up in old clothes found in the attic and played, or actually acted out, pirates or gunfights or explorers. They were the proverbial two peas in a pod, and I know things are no different now that they are together again in Heaven.

"Reverend Simmons is right. My brother was a contradiction in terms. He wanted to be seen as stoic, strong, athletic, and carefree. He did develop this sort of James Dean persona. The irony is that, just like James Dean, Patrick was extraordinarily sensitive and thoughtful. He would have made a perfect philosopher, because he

164

frequently pondered the purpose of life and the mysteries of the universe. He cared about this planet, about people, and peace, and most of all about life.

"When we were much younger, he told me at the end of a school year that he enjoyed learning and school, but that it took too much time away from his being able to do things. He had this drive to do as much as he could, to cram as much activity as possible into every hour. It seemed almost as if he sensed that his time on earth was limited.

"Patrick's dream, his life's goal, was to promote and to work for global peace. I told him last year, when he joined the Army, that he would change this world and its course. He would have. He plotted his roadmap, and he was on the verge of starting that journey. He told me his plans. When I become the next king, I will do so without my brother by my side as planned. I will, though, fulfill Patrick's goal in his stead. I will do what he cannot do on earth.

"Patrick's earthly life may be short, but crammed with amazing ideas, thoughts, and deeds that will influence me for the rest of my life. Patrick will never be forgotten, I know that. His nineteen years and his legacy will shine on Valdavia for all time."

Eric returned to his seat, and the choir sang *How Great Thou Art*, one of Patrick's favorite hymns. Most people stood during the hymn, except those too grief-stricken, including Matilda. She cried as Gerard held her to him, and Eric placed his hands on her shoulders.

At the hymn's conclusion, Father Simmons returned to the pulpit while soldiers opened the side doors that led to the churchyard cemetery. "Ladies and gentlemen, we will now convene to the churchyard for the interment."

Father Simmons led the procession, followed by the military pallbearers, the Royal Family, their close friends and staff, and then those who had been able to procure seats in the church.

The pallbearers carefully placed Patrick's casket on the lowering device. They saluted before they moved aside, giving Patrick respect as a comrade soldier. Gerard noticed and bowed his head in acknowledgement. They saluted their King and went to stand by the fence out of the way.

The churchyard filled to capacity, and the roads outside the fence also filled with mourners. Valmondois over-brimmed with people, later estimated at approximately one million in number. Some had come from other European countries, from Australia and New Zealand, from China, Japan, and Taiwan, from the United States and Canada, from Africa, Egypt, Israel, and Iran. Patrick's life, his personality, had touched more people than he ever realized.

"We gather as a nation, not of Valdavians, but of all people whose lives, minds, and ideas were affected by this exceptional young man. Prince Patrick would blush and cringe at the accolades given him today, and I am confident in saying that his humility remained one of his most endearing traits. His smile remained readily available to all, no matter what he was feeling at that moment. As we consecrate his body, we know that his godly soul lives eternally in Heaven. We will think of Prince Patrick quite often. Let us honor Patrick by smiling, not crying, when we do think of him or see him in our memories.

"From 1 Corinthians 15, verses fifty through fifty-seven: *Now this I say, brethren, that flesh and blood cannot inherit the kingdom of God; neither doth corruption inherit incorruption. Behold, I shew you a mystery; We shall not all sleep, but we shall all be changed, In a moment, in the twinkling of an eye, at the last trump: for the trumpet shall sound, and the dead shall be raised incorruptible, and we shall be changed. For this corruptible must put on incorruption, and this mortal must put on immortality. So when this corruptible shall have put on incorruption, and this mortal shall have put on immortality, then shall be brought to pass the saying that is written, Death is swallowed up in victory. O death, where is thy sting? O grave, where is thy victory? The sting of death is sin; and the strength of sin is the law. But thanks be to God, which giveth us the victory through our Lord Jesus Christ.*'"

The casket was lowered into the grave as the sound of crying filled the atmosphere. Eric put his arm around his mother, knowing she needed support and that his father desperately attempted to restrain his own tears in public. Gerard needed support, too, so Eric moved between his parents and put his arms around both of them, his strength keeping all three of them upright. Many people marveled at the 22-year-old's seemingly-superhuman strength and control on what had to be the worst day of his life.

The Royal Family stood, Gerard and Matilda in tears and Eric staring down at his brother's casket, as several thousand people filed by and dropped flowers into the grave. After more than four hours, most people had paid their respects, and Eric motioned for Stanley and Devon to escort the King and Queen home. That left Eric to deal with the remaining mourners.

"Excuse us, Prince Eric. I realize that you don't know us, but we knew Patrick. I'm Mrs. Bouchard, Elena, and this is my husband Ernest. Our daughter Maria dated Patrick before she entered the convent."

"Yes. It's nice to meet you, Mrs. Bouchard, Mr. Bouchard," Eric said and shook their hands.

"We loved Patrick. He and Maria had talked to us and to your father about their desire to marry. They were incredibly in love, probably never fell out of love. I know Patrick didn't, because he came to visit me at least once a month if he wasn't on military duty. He knew we could never see our daughter again, and he wanted to make sure how we were doing. He was so kind and caring," Mrs. Bouchard said and began crying. "I'm sorry, but he is such a beautiful soul, and I'm going to miss his visits."

"Thank you, Mrs. Bouchard. If you don't mind, I'd like to continue the visits," Eric offered.

"You are just as kind. If you can, I would truly enjoy that, even for a few moments here and there. I will never forget Patrick," Mrs. Bouchard said and kissed his cheek. Mr. Bouchard hugged him and gave him a floral arrangement to place on the grave.

Eric placed the flowers at the foot of the grave, only to feel a hand on his arm. He stood to face a gentleman with tears on his cheeks.

"Prince Eric, I love your family very much," Arthur Brennan said. "Prince Patrick was such a wonderful boy, full of energy and life, and so kind and compassionate. He once answered in crayon a card I sent him. Such a young thing then. That note he sent me means more to me than most everything else I own. I treasure it. I loved that boy so much, I want you to know. I hurt, but my pain is nothing like yours or your dear parents'. The entire world hurts. We lost a hero, you know."

"Thank you, Sir. That means a lot. Patrick is the best brother God could ever give me, and I'm so grateful for him," Eric said.

Mr. Brennan patted Eric's shoulder. "Here, add this to the flowers for our Patrick," he said, handed Eric a floral arrangement, and turned to salute Prince Patrick's grave. "Good night, sweet prince."

CHAPTER 7

"Devon, would you mind coming to my office?" Gerard asked four days after Patrick's funeral.

"No, Sir. I shall be there in two minutes." Devon had planned to meet with King Gerard that morning, but it seemed His Majesty would beat him to the point.

Devon knew it would take him exactly two minutes to walk from his attic room to the king's office, and he indeed arrived exactly two minutes after hanging up the telephone.

"Please, sit down, Devon," Gerard motioned. "I meant to talk with you sooner, but, well, other things interfered. I apologize for that. I owe you more than neglect, far more."

"No, Sir, I completely understand," Devon said and shuffled uncomfortably in the chair. He had dreaded the conversation himself. "You do not owe me anything."

"Oh, but I do. Patrick was quite fond of you. I hope you know that, Devon. I need to speak with you about your position here."

"Yes, Sir, I know. I planned to make an appointment to speak with you, as well. I have something important to tell you. This is difficult for me, because I became fond of Patrick a long time ago. He was quite a special little boy, as you know."

"Yes. I know you were engaged at the time of his birth as his personal bodyguard, and that since. . .since July 19 you have not had regular duties. How would it be if you were to become one of my guards? Tithers is retiring in a few weeks and will need to be replaced."

"Sir? After what happened? How could you ever trust me, let alone forgive me?" Devon asked.

"Trust you? Forgive you? I'm afraid I don't understand."

"I failed at my duty, Sir. My job was to protect Price Patrick, and I failed. I failed, Sir." Devon removed an envelope from his suit jacket. "This is my resignation. I am so very sorry, Your Majesty, sorrier than you know."

"Resignation? You blame yourself for the accident? Devon, that's ludicrous, and you have to realize that. Patrick's accident was no one's fault. I refuse to accept this," Gerard said and held up the envelope.

"I'm sorry, Sir, but I must resign. How can you ever trust me to protect you, Her Majesty, or Prince Eric? How?"

"Because you protected Patrick with your life every day."

"Not every day, I didn't. Not that day, I didn't. That was my duty, and I failed. Whether you accept my resignation or not, I must leave. I appreciate all you and your family have done for me. I care for and respect each of you. That is why I must leave."

"Patrick would not want you to leave, Devon," Gerard said.

"No, he wouldn't. Forgive me for interrupting. I didn't mean to overhear, but I came to talk with Father and couldn't help overhearing," Eric said. "Devon, Patrick thought you one of the coolest guys he ever saw, cooler than Clint Eastwood or Steve McQueen. Please stay. For Patrick."

"You really want me to after what I didn't do?"

"You couldn't have done anything, Devon. You had no way of knowing that jagged rock was under the lake's surface. You can't blame yourself, so don't. Please," Eric said. "None of what happened is your fault in any way." *Because it's my fault, all mine.*

"Devon," Gerard said, "take two weeks off. Visit your family or just get away for a while and come back refreshed and ready to resume your guard duties. All right?"

"That's kind, Sir, but I think it best if I keep busy. Would it be all right if I do take the afternoon off, though? There is someone I would like to visit."

"Of course, Devon. You know what time dinner is served," Gerard said. He stood, and Devon extended his hand. Instead, Gerard walked around the desk and hugged him. "If you do want more time off, you are free to do so at any time."

"Thank you, Sir, I appreciate it," Devon said and turned to leave.

"Thank you," Eric said and also hugged his brother's bodyguard. "If you ever need to talk, you know where to find me," Eric said softly. Devon nodded and rushed upstairs before he cried.

That afternoon, Devon stopped at a florist shop, bought a bouquet of flowers, and walked to the churchyard. Several people gathered at Patrick's grave, so he waited until they left before he approached. As he waited, he kept his head bowed, fighting the tears that formed in his eyes. He had watched Patrick grow from newborn baby to 19-year-old soldier. So much promise. So much potential. He truly did love this young man and did his best to protect him as if Patrick was his own son. None of this was fair. Finally, he saw the headstone for the first time and couldn't stop his tears:

Patrick Alain David DeBruce Martineau

6 January 1958

19 July 1977

*I will both lay me down in peace, and sleep: for thou, LORD, only makest me
dwell in safety.*

--Psalm 4:8

Devon kneeled to his knees in front of Patrick's grave, his
tears finally falling. *"I'm so sorry, Patrick, so very sorry. This should never
have happened, and it's all my fault. Please forgive me for failing you when you
most needed me. I'll miss you,"* he said and stood the flowers against the
tombstone.

§§§§§

"Devon, no! Hey, you didn't do anything wrong. None of us
knew that huge rock was there. Don't you do this, too!"

"Oh, Uncle Patrick, there's nothing we can do for Daddy or
for Devon. God will remove their guilt in time and heal them.
Besides, they can't hear us anyway," Angilia said with a tinge of
sadness.

"I know, but they have nothing to feel guilty about. Neither
do you."

"Me? I haven't said anything."

"No, but I can tell it. You tried to warn Eric, but you couldn't
stop this from happening. And that's okay, Little One, really. I'm
going to tell you something I never told anyone. For years before this
happened, I felt this nagging thought that I wouldn't live long. I knew
I'd never marry and have children or work for peace like I wanted or
work with Eric like we'd talked about. I somehow knew I'd die young.
That's one reason I felt I had to do as much as possible. I knew my
time was limited, so every minute mattered to me."

"Oh, Uncle Patrick, that makes me so sad. No child should
feel that," Angilia said as tears formed in her eyes.

"No. But it's okay. It's not that I wanted to die, leave my family and friends, and not do all I felt I was meant to do, but I was never afraid of death. Everyone dies. I knew Heaven is glorious and eternal. I'm fine! This is a blast, you know. I love you, I love Grandfather, I love Michael, and I love God. I'll always love Eric, Mother, and Father, and when they die, they will come to Heaven to live with me. It's all good, Little One, all good. And God will take care of those on earth, and all will be good with Eric and Devon, too, when God deems it the proper time. Everything's good."

§§§§

"Eric, is there anything I can do for you?" Daniel asked as he held Eric's suit jacket for him the next morning.

"No, Daniel, thank you. There's nothing anyone but God can do. I know people mean well, and they are kind and thoughtful, but this is something I have to do on my own. I have a few things to do this morning, so would you please check on Father while I'm gone?"

"Of course. I didn't know Patrick long, just a year, but I liked him. A lot. I never told him that, which bugs me. We never think to tell people things like that, do we? That's one thing I've made a vow to do, starting with you. I love you, Eric. You are one of my best friends and an incredible man."

"I love you, Daniel. You, Roger, and me are the Three Musketeers for life," Eric said and hugged his friend. "You're right, no one tells the people they care about what they mean to them, not nearly enough. We all need to do that more."

"Well, you and your family do it more than any other family I've known. Patrick knew how you and your parents loved him, still do. In the year I've been here, your family has changed the way I think about a lot of things that I took for granted. Thanks for that added benefit, man."

Eric smiled. "Well, it's learned behavior, you know. My grandparents were also quite demonstrative, which is where my father learned it. It just keeps getting passed down through the generations."

"Well, I look forward to the time your children are running through this Palace and filling it with laughter and love."

"Laughter. Laughter seems so wrong now. There's nothing joyful anymore, not here, not for me." Eric straightened his tie. "Well, I'm off. I'll be back this afternoon sometime."

§§§§§

Eric walked into the high school office, completely surprising everyone there. He stepped to the principal's secretary and asked if he could talk with Mr. Roceur.

"Certainly. I'll let him know you're here, Prince Eric," Miss Tillerson said and disappeared briefly. She returned with Principal Roceur, who greeted Eric with a handshake and condolences.

"Prince Eric, I am so extremely sorry about Prince Patrick. So very sorry. Is there anything I can do for you?"

"Thank you, Principal Roceur. I need to speak with you about something quite important if you have some time."

"Of course. Please come in," the older man said and guided Eric to a chair in his office. "I will do anything in my power for you, I hope you know that."

"Thank you, Sir. I just learned that you and the school board had asked Patrick to teach a four-week literature course that begins on Monday. I also heard that the course has been canceled."

"Yes, that's correct. Under the circumstances, we felt it best to cancel the course."

"I wish you would reconsider. Patrick never mentioned this to me or my parents, but he generally didn't boast about himself. Nonetheless, I know with certainty that he wouldn't want the course canceled just because he can't teach it."

"Well, that is wonderful news, Prince Eric, but with just five days until the course begins, I doubt we can find a qualified teacher in time," Principal Roceur said. "We created this course specifically for Prince Patrick because of his extraordinarily high achievements in Honors English."

"Sir, if you recall, I also studied Honors English here. I may not have quite the same high achievements as my brother, but I would like to teach this course for Patrick."

"You, Prince Eric? Oh, yes, well, let me call the School Board President to inform him. Do you mind waiting?" Eric said he didn't, so Principal Roceur quickly explained Eric's offer, which was met with both shock and enthusiasm. "Prince Eric, you have the job. I will get you the textbook and course materials." Within minutes, he returned with a large anthology and an envelope of papers and forms. "Your syllabus and attendance sheets are in this envelope, along with other pertinent information. Your pay cycle is every Friday."

"Please donate any salary to the Athletic Association of Valdavia in Patrick's name," Eric said.

"Of course, Prince Eric. "Of course. If there is ever anything else you need, do not hesitate to ask me or my staff. Your first class session begins Monday morning at 9:00 sharp and meets all five days for four weeks. We worked the schedule around Prince Patrick's Army duty. Is this schedule suitable for you, Prince Eric?"

"Yes, it is, Sir. I will spend the next few days preparing and be here before class begins. Thank you."

§§§§§

"Eric, I am very proud of you, son," Gerard said at Eric's suite door that afternoon while his son worked at his desk.

"For what? I haven't done anything unusual."

"Yes, you have. Roger told me about your visit to the high school this morning. First, Patrick never mentions being asked to teach this course, and now you do not tell us that you volunteered to teach it in your brother's place."

"It's not a big deal. I heard about the course and that it had been canceled, so I decided to persuade Principal Roceur to reconsider. He did, so I'm preparing. I found Patrick's notes and plans on his desk, so I'm using those. I'm doing his class the way he wanted it done. It's every Monday through Friday morning for the next four weeks, ending a couple of weeks before the school year begins. This won't cause any problems for you, will it?"

"Problems? For me? I should say not. And even if you had been scheduled for a public event, we could have easily rescheduled. Everyone would have understood. What you are doing takes far more strength than I know I have, Eric. You are a far stronger man than I am, and you will be a far stronger king."

§§§§§

Eric drove to the high school Monday morning, arriving at 8:40, and signed in at the office. "Your students are already in the classroom, Prince Eric. I went up to check a few minutes ago. They were all surprised when I called them last week to say that the class hadn't been canceled. Please don't hesitate to buzz the office should you need anything," Miss Tillerson said.

"Thank you, Miss Tillerson," Eric replied and headed for the staircase. His course used room 414, which he knew well from his Honors English courses. Followed by ever-present Stanley, Eric went to the classroom, opened the door, and walked in.

The gasps resounded when everyone saw their teacher, but Eric placed his books and papers on the desk as if he hadn't heard. He picked up a piece of chalk and wrote his name on the board, which garnered even more surprise. *How could no one recognize Prince Eric?* they all wondered.

"Good morning. I'll be teaching this literature course for the next four weeks. My name is Eric DeBruce Martineau. Why don't we begin by getting to know one another?" Eric asked, after which the students introduced themselves.

Stanley sat unobtrusively in a front corner, himself becoming interested as the class session progressed. He never expected that his charge would ever be a teacher, but he supposed royal princes had done far more surprising jobs over the centuries.

"Please take a few moments to read Whitman's poem titled 'There was a child went forth every day.' which is on page 257 in our text. Think about the main idea, the theme, of the poem, and we'll discuss this," Eric instructed. Ten minutes later, he began the discussion, listening attentively to each student's ideas.

"Most of you are correct that everything the child sees becomes part of him. He temporarily becomes what he sees. On a deeper level, Whitman's poem shows his mindfulness of the object he sees, of all shapes and structures, which is symbolic. Of what is this list symbolic?"

"Life," one boy answered.

"Himself," answered a young lady.

"How so?" Eric asked her to clarify.

"Well, everything he wrote is essentially about himself," she said.

"To an extent, every creation is about the creator," Eric said. "In this poem, the theme is becoming, which is a continual process. The more we witness and experience, the more we change and develop throughout life. Therefore, becoming is a lifelong phenomenon."

"I hadn't seen that before, but I do now. The young child becomes what he sees, but as he grows up, he changes. It's so clear now," the young lady said. Many other students added to the discussion, until Eric saw the clock.

"We are almost out of time. Your homework for tomorrow is to read the first act of Shakespeare's *Hamlet*, which begins on page 334. Come to class prepared to discuss the characters and their reactions to the events and people around them. Thank you for a lively class session," Eric said as students sat attentively still. "You may sign today's attendance sheet and leave."

One by one, the students walked by the teacher's desk, signed the attendance sheet, and looked at Eric in awe. Not only had no one expected Prince Eric to teach their class, they were amazed by his knowledge and insight.

"Prince Eric," a seven-year-old boy said, and Eric looked down at him. The boy hesitated, finding the right words. "Thank you for teaching the class. I had fun and learned a lot." The boy dared not mention Patrick. He didn't want to hurt Prince Eric.

"You're welcome. I enjoyed it, too, Samuel," Eric said with a smile. "What made you take this class?"

I can't tell him it's because of Prince Patrick. That will make him sad. "Oh, it just seemed cool, and they said anyone could enroll. So, my mother signed me up. It is cool. See ya," Samuel said and left.

Eric packed his briefcase, turned in the attendance sheet at the office, and went to his suite when he got home. He stood on his balcony and breathed deeply. *Patrick, I can never do this the justice it deserves. This is your course. You planned it. I'm just your substitute teacher. I'll tell you one thing, though. You're teaching me quite a lot, too, little brother.* Eric smiled up at Heaven and went downstairs to lunch.

"You're doing just fine, Eric, just fine," Patrick replied with a smile as he watched his brother from Heaven.

§§§§

After Tuesday's class, Eric drove to the Bouchard home. "You can take the car home, Stanley. I'll walk home. It will do me good."

"No, I can't do that, and you know it. I'll wait here in the car as long as needed."

"All right. But if you change your mind, don't worry about me," Eric said, knowing his loyal bodyguard would never leave him anywhere. Eric walked to the front door, rang the bell, and waited patiently for Mrs. Bouchard to answer.

"Oh, Prince Eric! What a pleasant surprise! Please, come in," she offered with a broad smile.

"Thank you. I hope I'm not interrupting anything."

"Not at all. I just put a load of laundry in the washer. Would you care for some lemonade on the veranda? I also have some sandwiches I made before I did the laundry. I don't know why, since I wasn't expecting any visitors, but, well, it turns out I got a most pleasant visitor after all. You go on out, and I'll bring the refreshments."

"No, please, allow me," Eric offered and picked up the tray. He followed her to the seating area, where they sat on the sofa and chatted for a while.

"Do you receive any news about Maria at all?"

"No. The convent doesn't have telephones, and they do not receive mail. They are truly cloistered. I have to trust that she is well, but I never know for certain. That's the hardest thing for me. I'm her mother, and she's my only child. Even if she weren't my only child, I'd wonder and worry. How could I not?"

"I don't think that's possible, Mrs. Bouchard. Our mother has always been overly protective about. . .about Patrick and me." Eric cleared his throat. "She calls it maternal instinct. My father calls her a lioness protecting her young," Eric said and smiled.

Mrs. Bouchard laughed. "Yes, that sounds about right. How is your Army training coming?"

"Fine. I do my two weeks after this summer course ends. They gave me a furlough because. . .because of everything that happened. So that allowed me to teach this course. I'm so glad I can, too, because it was Patrick's."

"Yes, I'd heard about that, and I even thought about enrolling, except, well, I didn't want to be that much of a constant reminder of Maria for him. He did visit me at least once a week, but every day for four weeks would have been too much for him. He never stopped missing her."

"Hmm. He never talked about her at home, at least not with me. I'm sure he did miss her. He loved her an awful lot, I know that. He did understand why she left, though, and he knew it wasn't about

179

him. He even told me he could never compete with Jesus," Eric said and giggled at the memory.

"Yes. My husband said something like that after we left Maria there. 'How can we deny Jesus our daughter? He gave her to us for the time we had her, and now He's called her to do His work.' Forgive me, I know Maria's not dead, but I like to think this applies to Patrick, too. Jesus has reclaimed both of them for His purposes."

Eric sat staring at a bird on a tree limb, considering her words. He smiled and looked at her. "Yes, Mrs. Bouchard, He has. I may never know the reason, but you must be right. Otherwise Patrick's death doesn't make sense. There must be a purpose. But that still doesn't exempt me."

"Exempt you? From what?"

"I'm sorry. I've taken enough of your time," Eric said and stood.

Mrs. Bouchard grabbed his arm and stood. "You blame yourself for Patrick's death. Eric, you can't. What happened was a tragic accident. It's just that Jesus uses such events to His purpose rather than letting them remain senseless, as you said. Jesus has a purpose for Patrick that we don't yet know, but He does. And you had nothing to do with causing or preventing the accident. You need to accept that. Please."

"I'll try, Mrs. Bouchard. I promise, I'll try," Eric said, kissed her cheek, and left with emotions swirling through his exhausted brain. *How can I accept it when it's not true? I'm the reason Patrick is dead.*

"Yes, Daddy, you and I are both the reason. Uncle Patrick's death brought us together long before we would have been otherwise. God has a reason for that. I don't know the reason, but it's enough to know He has one. We will learn the reason someday, and you will realize everything and heal   I pray that day is soon," Angilia said as Michael listened and watched. He knew far more than she, and he knew that Eric's guilt would remain inside him for quite some time. He also knew exactly when and how Eric's healing would occur.

§§§§§

Eric sat up in bed breathing heavily. *Was I dreaming? I don't know. It seemed so real, as real as being in my room does now. Why is she back? Why is she haunting me?*

Eric glanced at the clock on his bedside table. 1:42 in the morning. He knew he wouldn't sleep anymore that night, so he put on his robe and sat at his desk grading papers to return later that morning. *At least the course keeps me busy and gives me something to do*, he thought.

When he finished grading, it was 3:36. He decided to dress and work out in the basement exercise room. Roger heard him stirring from his next-door suite and knew that his friend still dealt with Patrick's death. He had no idea what, if anything, he could do to help Eric, except to always be there to support him. It was the least he could do, he pondered as drowsiness overtook him once more.

In the basement, Eric did bench presses and cardio for two hours. He found exercise not only kept his body fit, but that it had the added benefit of exorcising his guilt long enough for him to make it through the day. At this stage, getting through each day remained all he dared to hope for, because he didn't fathom his guilt suddenly disappearing.

How can it just disappear? I deserve to live with it since I can't live with my brother any longer. I'm the reason Patrick isn't here, and I should be far more severely punished. It was my job to take care of, to look after, my brother. I made a vow to myself and to God when he was born to protect him from all danger, and I failed. I failed my brother. I failed God. It should have been me who died that day, not Patrick.

Eric jumped back on the cardio machine and pushed himself harder than he ever had. After twenty minutes, he stopped, panting and beyond exhaustion. He wiped his face and looked up—to face her. The same girl who had been beside Patrick. He saw her face again, and he knew she was real, or at least her vision was real, not a dream.

"What do you want now?"

She still could not speak to him, so she held up her hand and said *I love you* in sign language. That sign Eric knew from films and television.

"You know me? How? I feel that I know you. But that doesn't make sense. I feel something else, too, that troubles me. I feel that I love you. How can I when I don't know who you are?"

The girl dared not touch him this time, so she placed her hands over her heart, her way of saying that they were bound together for all time. Suddenly, she heard her uncle calling her, warning her, and she signed *I love you* once more as she disappeared.

"Don't go! Tell me who you are. Please, my angel, tell me." *My angel? No. My Angel. She's mine. She is mine! She's mine. God, why have I seen her now? She's not my wife at all. She's my. . .she's my daughter. I've seen my daughter. When will I see her again? When will I hold her? When will she be born? When, God? When?"*

"Eric, you and she will meet again when it is time. When she is to be born, only I know. All you need know is that she is awaiting that moment, just as you are. She is your angel, and she is meant to restore your hope and inner peace regardless of all else you feel. You know that you must trust me and that my destiny for you unfolds according to the timeline I established for you and for her centuries ago. Live your life according to my word. That is all I require of you, my child."

Eric stood motionless for several minutes, not sure if he had hallucinated just then. He rubbed his head and focused his eyes. "God? Was that you?" Eric still stood unmoving, waiting for an answer or a sign. Then he felt a warmth surround his being, and he knew. God had spoken to him, confirming the girl's identity. His unborn daughter. He had seen—and felt—his unborn daughter.

I promise, God. I will follow your word and live the life you desire me to live. I can't promise that my feelings about Patrick will change, but I will do my best to trust you. That's all I can do, because I know there's a purpose to everything in Heaven and on earth. That's the best I can do right now. Thank you for allowing me to see her.

"Oh, Daddy, God did allow this visit. Michael sent me, but only for this short time. I am forbidden from ever coming again until the time of my birth. Until then, carry me in your heart, and I will carry you in my soul. I love you, Daddy," Angilia said while Patrick put his arm around her and smiled. Everything would be all right.

§§§§

"Good morning, everyone," Eric said as he entered the classroom on Friday, August 26. "As you know, this is our final class session. It has been a true honor to share ideas with each of you during these four weeks. Today will be a departure from our regular routine," he said and went into the hall. He and Stanley moved a table into the room, and the students, regardless of age, reacted with pleasant surprise.

Upon the cloth-draped table were doughnuts, pastries, juices, and cookies, as well as paper plates and cups. Once the men positioned the table, Eric encouraged everyone to fill their plates and cups. They all spent the three-hour session talking about the works they had studied, what they had learned, and also their goals for the future. Laughter reigned, including Eric's, which each person noticed. The students found his happiness the best conclusion to the course, as each of them told him as they regretfully left.

As Eric began packing his briefcase, he noticed young Samuel standing beside his desk and asked if anything were wrong.

"No, Prince Eric, nothing is wrong. I just want to give you this," Samuel said and placed a wrapped box in Eric's hand. "I want you to have this. I. . .I was going to give it to Prince Patrick, but you're his brother, so you should have it. Thank you for teaching me. I'll remember this all of my life," Samuel said, shook Eric's hand, and ran from the room before he cried.

Eric smiled and carefully placed the box in his briefcase. He and Stanley packed the leftover treats, and when Eric went to the office to turn in his final attendance sheet, he offered the food and drinks to the staff.

Principal Roceur heard the happy chatter and came to determine the cause. "Well, Prince Eric! Today is the end of your course. I've heard only outstanding reports from the students, I must say. I can never thank you enough for taking this on along with your other commitments and duties. We are truly honored to count you among our graduates and faculty."

Before he went home, Eric stopped at a florist shop, bought a colorful bouquet, and drove to the Bouchard home. Mr. Bouchard answered, which was unusual for a Friday morning. He welcomed Eric inside and asked him to sit in the living room.

"Elena has told me about your weekly visits, Prince Eric. They mean the world to her. She said you might stop by today, since this was your last class and you have your two-week Army training starting next week."

"Yes, Sir. I won't be able to visit during those two weeks, so I wanted to make sure to do so today. I hope Mrs. Bouchard is well."

"Well, actually. . . .," Mr. Bouchard began, only to be interrupted.

"Actually, I'm as well as can be expected, Eric. I have some news to tell you," Mrs. Bouchard said and sat beside Eric on the sofa.

Eric offered her the flowers, and she inhaled their perfume deeply. "I adore flowers. Thank you, Eric. My home in Heaven must have a large flower garden."

"Elena, please."

"It's all right, dear. I'm not the first woman diagnosed with breast cancer."

Eric sat stunned for a moment. "What can I do to help?"

"Nothing more than you already do, dear. Visit when you can. Pray for me if you will. Please, though, don't treat me any differently. Promise."

"I promise," Eric said, doing his best to control his tears.

"The doctors caught it early, and they are confident surgery and treatment will cure me. Right, Ernest?"

"Yes, dear, they are. And we are staying positive," Mr. Bouchard said with a smile.

"Oh, yes, we are, Eric. I've turned this over to God. Whatever happens is His plan for me. I know that. A positive attitude means more than any medicine, though," she said and smiled. "Now, how about some lemonade before your training takes you away from me for two weeks?"

Eric pushed his own emotions aside for the Bouchards, something he did often. He long placed others' pain and suffering above his own. In fact, he regaled the Bouchards with stories of his students and their often-hilarious interpretations of the literary works.

Mrs. Bouchard walked Eric to his car, where she hugged and kissed him in gratitude for his friendship and concern. Eric kissed her cheek and promised he would visit as soon as his training was complete.

At home, Eric sat at his desk and wrote in his diary.

26 August 1977

I know bad things happen to good people every minute of every day, but that doesn't mean I have to like it or understand why. Yes, I know God uses everything in His plans. That still doesn't account for or explain this kind of suffering. Cancer. Why do people get cancer? Or any potentially fatal disease or disorder? Why?

Mrs. Bouchard doesn't deserve her diagnosis. Neither does Mr. Bouchard. And Maria will never know that her mother is ill. Never. None of this seems right, but that is not my place to say what's fair or right. Only God can do that. I know my words are wrong, and I apologize to God.

I also realize that I do need to stop letting my guilt control my mind and my life. Starting now, I will bury it deep within me and not let it take firm hold on me again, no matter how long I live. God expects me to live a godly, obedient life, so I will do so. I will mimic Jesus and put my own suffering aside. Just as He thought of the thief on the cross beside Him, I will think of other people far more than I wallow in my own emotions and needs.

If I am to be King de Valdavia, I must do this. The people of this country, as well as my family, come before my own needs. That is my solemn vow to myself, to God, and to the people of Valdavia. This is one vow I will keep no matter what.

CHAPTER 8

Eric drove to the Athletic Association of Valdavia offices, accompanied as always by Stanley. The receptionist stared with wide eyes and open mouth as the prince approached her desk.

She finally managed to ask how she could help him, and Eric replied, "Is Mr. Jarvis available? I realize I don't have an appointment, but I would like to talk with him if possible."

"Yes, Your Royal Highness. I will let him know you are here." She telephoned the President's office, spoke quietly, and seconds after she hung up, John Jarvis rushed into the room to greet the prince.

"Prince Eric, what a pleasant surprise to see you," Mr. Jarvis said and shook Eric's outstretched hand.

"Thank you for seeing me without an appointment."

"Not at all. Please come into my office," Mr. Jarvis said and led Eric to his private office. As they walked through the large room filled with cubicles, the staff stood when they realized why their President had rushed to the reception area. They all stared, as amazed as the receptionist had been.

Stanley waited outside Mr. Jarvis's office, and he overheard quite the mild riot. "Isn't Prince Eric just dreamy?" "Oh my gosh! I never thought I'd ever see him this close up!" "I've had a crush on him since I was five years old." "I wonder if it would be inappropriate to ask for his autograph before he leaves." "I think I'm going to faint right here, right now." "He's the most beautiful man I've ever seen." "I'm in love." Even the male employees were impressed with Eric and his reputation, and were, if the truth revealed, equally star struck to be this close to their future king. Stanley was long used to hearing such comments; they became normal when Eric was a boy.

Inside the privacy of Mr. Jarvis's office, the men talked about Eric's purpose in visiting. "Mr. Jarvis, the AAV meant quite a lot to my brother Patrick. You know that. He felt so passionate about athletics, and so excited and overjoyed to become your patron."

Mr. Jarvis smiled at the memory of his first meeting with the then-15-year-old Prince Patrick. "Oh, I do know. He bounded into this office building with such energy and enthusiasm. He was the perfect patron for AAV. In fact, we are reluctant to select another patron in the foreseeable future."

"That's quite a statement in Patrick's honor. As his brother, I agree completely. In fact, I want to speak with you about the AAV's patronage. One of my missions in life is to continue Patrick's work. I have no intention of replacing him; I couldn't do that even if I wanted to. I agree there shouldn't be another patron. How would you feel if I unofficially took over Patrick's work on behalf of the AAV?"

"You? Take on Patrick's patronage?"

"I don't want to be the patron at all. That remains Patrick's role. I just want to do what he can't do. Of course, the decision is yours. If you prefer that I not. . . . ."

"Oh, no, of course I have no objections. It's just that I never expected you to offer your expertise to the AAV. We can never thank you enough, Prince Eric. How would the title of Honorary Patron sound?"

"That would be fine, Mr. Jarvis. Thank you. Please let me know whenever I can do anything to assist AAV. I'll do whatever I can, I promise."

"We will, most definitely. Now, would you like to meet the staff?"

"All right. I'd like that."

Mr. Jarvis and Eric left the office chatting, and Mr. Jarvis stunned his staff by announcing, "Everyone, please welcome our Honorary Patron, Prince Eric de Valdavia."

People gasped, then collectively stood to applaud Eric. They all knew, of course, about Patrick; most had met him and had liked and respected him. Now they would work with his brother, their future king. They all greeted and welcomed Eric, and a staff picture with the new Honorary Patron taken and released to the press that afternoon. Soon Valdavians began to grasp that Eric was stepping in for his brother, which made them love and respect Eric all the more.

"I love this young man very much, Charlotte," Arthur Brennan said to his wife that evening as he showed her the picture in the newspaper. "Prince Eric impressed me when he was ten years old, so poised and mature at his grandfather's funeral. We have watched him grow into a fine young man of twenty-two. Oh, what a good, compassionate man he is, and he will bring that to his reign when he becomes king. I dare say, dear, that King Eric will go down in history as the most benevolent king in Valdavian history."

Charlotte patted her husband's arm, smiled, and said, "Yes, I dare say he will. I do believe that the hand of God is on this prince, Arthur. Eric is meant to do many great things, mark my word."

The couple kissed, contented and peaceful knowing that their nation's future, and theirs, remained safe in Prince Eric's care.

§§§§

Eric went to his father's office at his request, where Gerard went through some invitations and other mail with Eric. Eric accepted invitations to two fundraisers on behalf of his father, one for the King Gerard IV Public Hospital, and another for the Valmondois Public Library.

"Eric, these requests for patrons arrived. Take a look through them and see if one or two interest you," Gerard said and passed his son a stack of letters.

After nearly fifteen minutes of reading and rereading the letters, Eric pulled five from the stack and gave them to his father. "I want to take these, Father."

"Five patronages? You already have two plus the AAV. Add the Army, and you'll be quite the busy young man."

"I know, but I don't mind. I like keeping busy." *It keeps my mind occupied so it doesn't slip into the guilt and derail me.* "I want these five, Father. I'm willing to take a couple more, too."

Gerard nodded. "Are you sure, son? Patronages seem easy, but they are time commitments. Think about this before you take on too much."

"I'm sure," Eric said and looked through the letters again. He added two more to his pile and had a total of ten patronages.

"Thomas will manage your schedule as well until you appoint your own assistant, Eric. I shall pass these on to him, so he can manage the events on your calendar. If you ever feel you have taken on too much, please don't ever feel you can't give up one or two patronages."

Eric shook his head. "I won't. I want to do this work. It helps people, and it helps me. It makes me feel productive and that I'm giving back to my country."

That evening Eric went to his suite exhausted but exhilarated after a 90-minute workout. Keeping busy, filling his time doing his duties and work, was the best antidote to the guilt that still tried to resurface from deep inside of him. As he showered, he went over the next day's schedule in his mind and felt relief. He had a busy day, which pleased him. He had scheduled one important visit into his agenda, as well, one that would do more to bolster his spirit than any other.

§§§§§

Eric began his work day at a meeting of the Valmondois Arts Council, one of his older patronages, followed by a meeting with the School Board, who had recently asked him to join; after his success teaching the accelerated literature course, they wanted his input on their plans and decisions. Eric shared his thoughts regarding the revised Honors curriculum, helping to guide the Board's decisions. He also offered to join the Board for the following academic term.

After that, he and Stanley had lunch at Eric's favorite French restaurant, and then went to a press conference at the AAV headquarters, announcing his Honorary Patronage. The publicity generated interest in the AAV's programs and scholarships. That, after all, remained the purpose of patronages: to garner interest, support, and charitable donations for the organizations. That's what Patrick had done with his tremendous enthusiasm for AAV; in the first year of Patrick's patronage, AAV's scholarships had received more than two million Valdems (the Valdavian dollar), and after his UN speech, the organization received nearly five million Valdems. Eric could only hope to do one eighth of his brother's good work.

The press conference ended inmid-afternoon, and Eric drove to the Bouchard home for a visit with Mrs. Bouchard. As usual, she answered the door with a smile and a kiss on the cheek. They took their regular lemonade and sandwiches to the veranda and caught up since their last visit.

"I notice that you're taking on more Royal duties, Eric. You're quite the busy man, but I suspect that's by design, isn't it?"

"Yes, Ma'am," Eric admitted. He did not have to hide his thoughts and feelings from Mrs. Bouchard, for she understood. She also could listen in sympathy and compassion without the emotional investment that his parents possessed. Had he brought up his guilt over Patrick's death with them, they would have felt hurt, confused, and possibly angry. He didn't risk those reactions with Mrs. Bouchard.

"Eric, I'm having surgery next week to remove the cancer. I'm having a mastectomy, and I've read a lot about this. A friend gave me this magazine with an interview Shirley Temple gave a couple of years ago after her breast cancer. She's the one who influenced me to have a biopsy to verify the diagnosis. I do have cancer, so the doctors will remove it. If I'm blessed like Shirley, I, too, will go into remission. That's what Ernest and I pray for, Eric. I'm not ready to die. It's not up to me, I know, but still. . . we can pray, right?"

"Yes, we can. I pray for you every morning and every night. I can't know how this feels, but I'm sure it's frightening. Please let me know if there's anything I or my family can do. If fate had been different, you'd be Patrick's mother-in-law, so you're practically family, Mrs. Bouchard. Family stands by one another no matter what happens. I'll always be here. I'll always be your friend."

Mrs. Bouchard began sobbing and dabbed her eyes with a tissue. "That's the sweetest thing anyone has ever said to me, Eric. I love Patrick, and I love you, too. You are the most amazing two young men I've ever met." She hugged Eric, and said, "The surgery is one week from today. Say an extra prayer for me that day, will you?"

"Of course, I will," Eric whispered and spoke a silent prayer right then.

§§§§§

After a fundraising luncheon at the AAV headquarters, Eric drove straight to the hospital and went to the third-floor oncology operating rooms. In a nearby waiting room, he found Ernest Bouchard sitting with his head bowed as if in prayer. Eric walked to him and put his hand gently on the man's shoulder.

"Eric. I didn't expect you to come here," Mr. Bouchard said when he looked up. "I'm glad you did, though. She's been in there over an hour and a half, and to be honest, I'm nervous."

"I know. I've been thinking about and praying for her all day. I wanted to be here before her surgery, but that wasn't possible. I don't have anything scheduled for this afternoon, so I plan to stay if that's all right."

"All right? Seeing you when she wakes up will mean the world to her, Eric. She loves you like the son we never had. Thank you for visiting her. It means a lot to both of us, you know. I've been sitting here with nothing to do but think. I've been wondering what Maria is doing. Praying for hours at a time? Does she pray for her mother and me? Does she wonder how we are? What is her life like? I'll never know. I'll never know if she's even still alive. Can anyone know what that's like? Does she know what she's caused us to go through?

"Oh, I suppose how we deal with this is part of our test on earth, right? If we blame Maria for committing to Jesus, we do wrong. If we blame Jesus, we sin. How are we supposed to feel? I'm sorry, I don't need to burden you with all of this. Forgive me."

"There's nothing to forgive. You can't talk to your wife, because she's hurting over this, too. She wonders if she did something wrong to turn Maria away from her. I told her she couldn't have. Patrick told me that Maria loves you both tremendously. She loves Patrick, too. She just loves Jesus so much that she felt called to become his bride. And that comes with sacrifices. Maria told Patrick she would miss you both and pray for you. You need to know that, Mr. Bouchard. I told Mrs. Bouchard already. Maria's decision is nothing against either of you or some punishment. It's a devotion and dedication to Jesus," Eric said as Mr. Bouchard listened intently.

"Thank you. That means more to me than you will ever know. That's as close as I'll get to hearing from Maria as I'll ever get, so thank you, Eric."

§§§§

Over one hour later, the surgeon came to speak with Mr. Bouchard. "Dr. Waycross, how is Elena?" Ernest asked as he stood to greet the surgeon.

"Elena came through the surgery just fine. She's in recovery, still coming out of the anesthesia. Once she's more alert, I'll take you back to visit her. Sit down, Ernest, so we can go over the surgery and all that comes after it," Dr. Waycross said and motioned for him to sit. He then noticed Eric.

"Prince Eric, I can't say I'm totally surprised to see you. Elena told me you have become a good friend and support to her in recent months. She thinks highly of you."

"As I do of her, Dr. Waycross," Eric said. "Mrs. Bouchard is doing well?"

"Yes, she is. Ernest, Eric, you both know the procedure she had done today. We removed her right breast and the lymph nodes under her right arm. We've removed all of the cancer. We did a full-body scan after the procedure to check for any other cancer cells, and none are in her body anywhere."

Ernest sighed and said, "Thank God. What now?"

"Of course, she will remain in the hospital for several days for healing, further tests to verify her cancer-free state, and physical therapy. If the tests in five days indicate no cancer, then we have some options. Elena can do a round of chemotherapy just as a precaution; some women have done so. But she may well elect to forego chemotherapy at this time. Either way, I want to see her for screening every three months for the next five years."

"Why so often, Dr. Waycross? Isn't radiation dangerous?" Ernest asked.

"We need to stay one step ahead of this. Cancer sometimes recurs, and if it does, the sooner we detect it, the sooner we can remove it before it does real harm."

"But she is cancer free? You're sure?"

"Yes, I'm sure, Ernest. But you are an intelligent man. You know that screening is the best way to discover any sign of a recurrence. If any cancer is found, we can remove it quickly and do a round of chemotherapy. But for now, your wife is as healthy as the proverbial horse. Come on, let's get you men back there so you can brighten her afternoon."

Eric followed Ernest and the doctor into the recovery room, and he smiled at Elena's first sight of her husband since before the surgery. *Thank you, God, for healing Mrs. Bouchard. She's a special lady, and I care about her very much. Please keep her well and cancer-free. Amen.*

Eric focused on his prayer and therefore felt startled to hear Elena's excited "Eric! You came!"

He went to her side, took her hand, and kissed her cheek. "Of course, I came. That's what friends do. It's so good to see your beautiful smile. Before you know it, we'll have lemonade on the veranda again. But not until you and Mr. Bouchard come to my home for lunch or dinner, or both. It's high time you meet my parents. After all, our families have a connection that can never be broken."

"Oh, Eric, that is the most beautiful thing I've ever heard. Yes, your Patrick and our Maria brought us together, and even though Jesus has both of them now and they can't be with us, we can keep their love alive. Can't we?" Elena asked.

With tears in his eyes, Eric managed to answer, "Yes, we can. For all time."p

§§§§§

Two weeks later, Eric answered the front door to welcome the Bouchards into the foyer. "Please come in, Mr. and Mrs. Bouchard. My parents look forward to meeting you. They're in the sitting room."

"Oh, my goodness, the Palace is just as magnificent as Maria described it. There must be centuries of history here," Elena said as the three of them walked up the staircase to the second-floor sitting room.

"Yes. My ancestors kept everything, it seems. The attic is filled with clothes, furniture, and sundry glassware accumulated by every family who lived here. Once in a while, someone goes up there and finds a treasure to bring down and use once more, maybe a flower vase or a table," Eric said with a smile as they neared the sitting room. Eric motioned the Bouchards in ahead of him.

"Father, Mother, it's my pleasure to introduce Ernest and Elena Bouchard." He turned to face his guests. "Mr. and Mrs. Bouchard, my parents, Gerard and Matilda DeBruce Martineau."

"I'm honored to meet you, Your Majesties," Elena said and curtsied. Mr. Bouchard voiced a similar sentiment and bowed.

"Please, call me Gerard. No stiff formalities, please. I can see why Maria is both lovely and charming, Elena. I may call you Elena, mayn't I?"

"Why, of course, Your—Gerard. And thank you. Maria came home raving about how kind and friendly and down-to-earth your family is. You might live in this grand Palace, but you are as nice and approachable as any man I've met."

"Well, thank you, Elena, but why shouldn't I be? I'm just a man, after all. I just happened to be born the son of a king and inherited this job. That's the only real difference between me and any other man," Gerard said with typical humility.

"That modesty was passed down to your sons, Gerard," Ernest said. "Both have been so kind and nice to Elena and me, finding time to visit us and talk with us despite their duties and schedules. We came to love Patrick, and we now love Eric, as well. What is that old saying? The apple doesn't fall from the tree? Well, your family proves that."

"Thank you, Ernest and Elena. We adored Maria. She is such a sweet, gentle girl. We—that is, Gerard and I—had every expectation that Patrick and Maria would marry in a few years. But she answered a higher calling, bless her. I am sure she is a jewel in God's crown," Matilda said. "She often referred to prayer or purpose or God in her talks. I could tell that her faith is important to her."

"Yes, we did, too, of course. I suppose her decision shouldn't have come as a surprise, but, well, it did. We never expected to never see our daughter again," Elena said, but quickly apologized for dampening the mood.

"Nonsense. Come, sit next to me, dear," Matilda said, and took charge of Elena. "It's perfectly understandable for a mother to miss her child, perfectly normal. I have an idea what you feel, Elena. Promise me that you will call me or, better yet, pop in for a chat when you need someone sympathetic with whom to speak."

"Oh, you are much too kind, but I couldn't just intrude on your life."

"I wouldn't have told you to visit if that would be an intrusion, now would I? Now, what do you say we get to know each other better over dinner?"

The five of them did, at a table brimming with food, friendship, and laughter. For the first time since Maria's vows and Patrick's death, the four parents and one brother joked, talked, and laughed so much their sides ached. Each of them found the camaraderie therapeutic.

The Bouchards left with promises of future visits with their new friends, the King and Queen Consort of Valdavia. How could they ever have dreamed that their daughter's friendship with a classmate would lead to this moment?

For the first time since his brother's death, Eric went to bed with a smile on his face. *Hey, Patrick, I don't know if you saw us tonight, but Maria's parents came for dinner. Mother and Father like them, and they all get along well. Dinner was the best, because, well, because for the first time in a long time we all laughed and enjoyed ourselves. Really enjoyed ourselves. And you know what? I don't feel guilty about it like I thought I would. I hope that doesn't upset you. I'll always miss you, Patrick, and I love you. But it does feel good to laugh and have some fun. I know you've got to be having fun where you are. Say hello to Grandfather for me, and tell him I love him. Goodnight.*

"Did you hear that, Little One?" Patrick asked with a smile.

Angilia nodded. "Daddy has a beautiful smile. I'd never seen him smile before. I want him to smile all of the time. I want him always this happy."

"Yeah, so do I. But life on earth isn't happy all the time, I can tell you that. But you know what? Bouncing back from sadness or anger or whatever makes the happiness all the more special. Yeah,

Eric is fine. He'll be just fine until he meets your mother and gets married."

"My mother. Oh, I wonder what she's like and what kind of relationship we will have," Angilia said dreamily.

"I dunno, but you'll find out, kiddo. I bet you and your mother will be best friends."

"Really? Oh, that would be just the most perfect life, Uncle Patrick."

Michael hung his head and flew away from his vantage point above them. Angilia's words hurt him, for he knew what the future held, a future he could never warn the girl about, a future she would have to live through on earth. All was part of God's plan and purpose for her life, although she could not know that then.

CHAPTER 9

Eric drove to Tamley's Department Store intending to purchase a new book that had recently been released and some sheets for his bed. He and Stanley took the elevator to the tenth floor, Furniture and Home Goods. Eric went to the bedding section and began searching for the Egyptian cotton sheets.

"Oh, my gosh, it's Prince Eric!" a teenager screamed and ran to him, grabbing his arm and taking him by surprise. "Prince Eric, it's you! I love you!"

"Hello," Eric said, trying to extract his arm from her grasp. "Have we met before?"

"Oh, I wish. No, but I sure know you. I have a scrapbook of all of your clippings, and your posters are on my bedroom wall. Oh, you're the dreamiest prince ever. You sure do have Prince Charles beaten by a long shot."

How was Eric supposed to respond to such a comment? "Prince Charles is a nice man."

"I'm sure he is, but, you know, you're just luscious. Can I have your autograph? Please?"

"Of course. I'll need my arm, though,"

"Oh, of course. Here you go," she said and let go of him. She searched her purse, pulled out her wallet, and opened it to reveal several pictures of Eric. She selected one and passed it to him. "This one. Please sign this one. It's one of my favorites of you. Your 21st birthday portrait. Your eyes are so, so luscious. And do they ever pop in person. Oh, my name's Teena, with a double e."

"It's nice to meet you, Teena," Eric said and dutifully signed her picture.

"Are you buying sheets for your bed? What does your bed look like? I always wondered."

"Sir, we must leave soon," Stanley said as he heard the sound of running footsteps. "Very soon."

"Yes, Stanley. It was a pleasure, Teena," Eric said and quickly followed his bodyguard to the elevator. They entered just as a group of girls caught up to them, screaming their disappointment.

"What was that all about?" Eric asked.

"It seems you are the new David Cassidy," Stanley replied.

"Me? Good grief. I can't even go shopping? This is ridiculous."

"Prince Eric, excuse me for overhearing," a woman in the elevator said, "but you are hugely admired and adored. It's clear to everyone how charming, polite, and unassuming you are. But to these young girls, you are an idol. It certainly doesn't hurt that you resemble a movie star, either. Don't be too hard on them. You are a fine young man for them to worship."

"Worship?"

"Well, maybe that was the wrong word, but we parents would much rather they follow you than some degenerate rock star. You are their future king, but you are an extremely attractive and personable young prince. What more could a girl ask for? If I were fifteen, I'd have your poster over my bed, and that's the truth."

"Thank you, Ma'am." was all Eric could manage to say as his face reddened in embarrassment.

§§§§§

As Daniel assisted Eric with his suit one morning a couple of weeks later, Roger came in the room. "Eric, there's a huge package for you in the foyer. I hope you don't mind that I signed for it."

"No, of course not. I didn't order anything, though. You're sure it's for me?"

"Quite sure. Your name is painted all over the wooden box."

"Wooden box? What in the world?" Eric pondered and went downstairs as quickly as he could. "Good night. This really is a large box. Who is it from?" he asked and searched the box. "Wales? I don't know anyone in Wales."

"Well, open it and find out what it is. It's probably a gift from a fan," Daniel said.

"I doubt it, but all right. I need to find some tools," Eric said, only to have one of the butlers appear with a hammer and a crow bar to open the box.

"I went in search of tools," Roger said. "Noah offered to open the box."

As soon as Noah pried the nails from the top, it sprang off and a girl stood up and shouted, "I made it!"

"Wo!" Daniel shouted. "That's some package, Eric!"

Noah sprinted to the alarm button, and within seconds guards appeared in the foyer and apprehended the startled girl. "I only wanted to meet Prince Eric," she protested. "I never meant any harm, really."

"Shipping yourself is how you meant to meet His Highness? You had to realize the security risk you took," said the guard who handcuffed her arms.

"Yeah, not to mention risk to yourself," Roger added.

"I just wanted to meet him, and I didn't know how else I could make sure I did. I'm sorry," she said and began crying.

Eric sighed and stepped forward, despite Stanley's warnings. "Let her go. She won't do anything, especially with this many people here." The guard removed the handcuffs but held the girl's arm as a precaution. "All you had to do was stand out there, and I'd have talked to you," Eric said and motioned toward the Courtyard. "I try to talk to people out there every day unless I'm on Army duty. You never had to do all of this just to see me. I'm not reclusive. I'm out about Valmondois all the time."

"I'm sorry, I am. I didn't know any of that. I've never been here before. I just wanted to make sure. At least I did get to see you. I'll go now, and I promise I won't bother you again, Prince Eric."

"Come here," Eric said, and the girl came closer to Eric, the guards moving with her. "This has got to be the most extreme measure anyone has gone to for me. What made this so important that you risked shipping yourself in a box?"

"I don't know, except you're the only man I've ever loved. I know you probably here that a lot, and it doesn't mean anything to you, but it's true."

"That's not true. It does mean something to me. What's your name?"

"Karen Klein."

"Karen, I'm flattered that you went to all of this trouble just to meet me. But please don't treat me differently just because my father is a king. I haven't done much yet to earn this kind of attention. I do thank you, though, for thinking of me this highly."

"You have, too, done awesome things, Prince Eric. You're a soldier when you don't have to be one. You do lots of charity work. I see all of the pictures and stories, and it's clear how much you care about people. I've seen you visiting sick people in hospitals. You love your family, and God, too. You're handsome, yes, and that's part

202

of it, sure. But you're just one of the best people in the whole world. I admire you so much. I just had to meet you and tell you that. And now I have. Thank you for giving me the chance to do that," Karen said and extended her hand.

Eric took her hand but also kissed her cheek. At Roger's suggestion, he also autographed a photo of himself for Karen, who left the Palace with her dream a reality.

§§§§

After a Wednesday School Board meeting, Eric and Stanley met Roger and Daniel at a new Greek restaurant for a late lunch. The maître d'hôtel escorted them to their table, leading through the center of the main dining area. The friends quietly chatted as they walked, when they were unexpectedly interrupted.

"Prince Eric!" a young woman screamed, started a veritable stampede of girls, young ladies, and teenagers who nearly knocked the maître d'hôtel to his feet. Stanley instantly placed himself between the throng of women and the prince.

"Wow! Here we go again!" Daniel exclaimed.

"This seems to happen every day," Roger said, barely heard over the demands for touches, kisses, and autographs.

"This doesn't make sense. I don't understand. I haven't done anything," Eric said in a bemused tone.

"Apparently, you don't have to do anything but show up somewhere," Daniel retorted.

"Let's get this over with and leave. I've lost my appetite. You two can stay if you want. I don't want to spoil your lunch," Eric said and started signing autographs and greeting his fans.

"We're okay. We can eat at home," Roger said.

Nearly one hour later, Eric drove them home to the Palace, where they made grilled cheese sandwiches in the kitchen. The young men sat on the back patio in the warm fall weather and talked as they ate.

"I'm sorry it's so hard for you to go out anymore. Man, those girls get one look at you and—wham!—they're all over you like bees on flowers. Buzz-a-buzz-buzz," Daniel said.

"I don't get it. I haven't changed. I don't think I have. I'm still me, the same old Eric. Why is this happening all of a sudden?"

"It's not all of a sudden, buddy," Roger said. "It happened all the time in Cambridge, too, you just didn't pay it much attention, I guess. Girls followed you everywhere you went, if you recall. We couldn't go anywhere or do anything unless they pounced upon you or took pictures of you."

Eric shrugged his shoulders. "I was new there, that's all, a novelty. But I was born here. I've lived here all of my life. Everyone has seen me out and about for nearly twenty-three years. Why are they acting like this now?"

"These might explain some of your superstardom, son," Gerard said as he came out onto the patio and placed some magazines, newspapers, and posters on the table.

"Wo! You are a teen idol!" Daniel said upon seeing the plethora of Eric memorabilia.

"These, too," Gerard said and added postcards, school folders, and even a metal lunch box on the table. "Your mother is amassing quite a collection of Prince Eric merchandise. Apparently, this feeds into the young ladies' interest in you, Eric."

"Mother?! My mother is buying all of this stuff? Whatever for?"

"You know I've kept scrapbooks on my sons since you were both born. I've bought and kept all of the magazines, newspapers, posters, and commemorative items and souvenirs I can find, as well. My precious sons bring me so much happiness," Matilda said and bent to kiss Eric's cheek.

"That's sweet, Mother," Eric said and smiled at her. "But do you know how weird and embarrassing it is to see myself on all of this, this stuff?"

"Embarrassing? Why in Heaven's name should you be embarrassed? Do you know that you are the thinking girl's heartthrob, dear?"

Eric nearly choked on his lemon water. "What?"

"Yes, dear. According to Albert Smithson of the *London Daily Express*, you are the intellectual teen idol, attracting well-bred, intelligent young ladies," Matilda explained.

Daniel and Roger snickered. When asked why by an offended Matilda, Daniel said, "They don't often seem well-bred when they notice your son in public, unless well-bred allows for chasing him, screaming in adulation, and grabbing for him."

"Well, that I don't know, but it's probably just because they become overcome when they do see Eric," Matilda said and put her hands on her son's shoulders.

"They're overcome, all right," Roger agreed. "Quite overcome."

"Please, can we discuss something else? This has gotten to the point of ridiculous," Eric said. "Never mind. You all talk about whatever or whoever you desire. I'm going to my desk to work on the school board proposal. Excuse me, please."

"Well, what has gotten into him?" Matilda asked after Eric went inside.

"Ma'am, if I may, I can explain," Roger answered. "This started when we were in elementary school, but it was nothing compared to this. He was followed by girls and asked for autographs. By the time we entered high school, it got to the point he barely had any privacy. I mean, forgive me, some girls followed Eric into the boy's restroom. It was worse at Cambridge, as Daniel can tell you, too. We couldn't go anywhere with Eric unless it was like a scene from David Cassidy's life. He was assaulted basically, just overwhelmed with girls. It's only gotten worse for him in the past two years. He can't even shop for a book unless he's pounced upon. Eric has no semblance of privacy, not even here."

"Oh, you mean the young lady who shipped herself here to meet Eric. I have articles about that in the scrapbook," Matilda said.

"Yeah, I wouldn't ever let Eric see those. That had to be the most uncomfortable moment yet for him," Daniel said.

"I agree, dear," Gerard said in answer to his wife's befuddled expression. "Enough is enough. Our son is a soldier and a future king. He is not a music or film star. This behavior is a bit extreme. I understand why he's an idol, but I also understand why he finds it so uncomfortable. Eric has always been a somewhat introverted as well as humble boy. If you must amass this collection, let us not flaunt it in his face any longer."

"Very well. I will contain my mementos to my office," Matilda said and began carefully gathering her treasures. "You do realize that those qualities you mentioned, dear, are among the reasons why Eric is such an idol and superstar," she added and took her items upstairs.

§§§§§

"We love you, Eric, oh yes we do. We love you, Eric, forever true," a crowd of a few hundred teenaged girls sang outside the Palace gates early on a Thursday morning. Eric tossed and tried to block the sounds, refusing to open his eyes and awaken completely. After more than an hour of the singing, which was just loud enough to drift through his slightly open window, he relented and got up to close the window.

As soon as his arms reached out for the window panes, someone screamed, "I see him! Eric is awake! He's in his room!" Immediately more girls joined the screaming and moved to prime locations for Prince Eric sightings.

"Eric, get in here," Roger said as he ran into Eric's bedroom. Roger leaned out, grabbed the panes, and locked the window. "They've been out there for at least three hours already. Why aren't their parents keeping them at home at this hour on a school day?"

"Why are they here?" Eric asked.

"You. It's your birthday, or had you forgotten? Your loyal public awaits the day's first appearance of its beloved."

"Stop it, Roger, please. Birthdays happen every day. They're not unusual."

"Most peoples' aren't, no, but yours are. They have cards, gifts, and flowers. I saw at least two girls with cakes. Just what you want for breakfast. Yummy."

"Cakes? This has gone too far, Roger. Cards, I understand, but this, no. What am I supposed to do? Go out there and once again act like this is normal?"

"Yep. This is your normal, Eric, get used to it," Roger said.

"I don't want to get used to it. Do people do this for the American President, I wonder?"

"For Jimmy Carter? I don't think so. But he doesn't look like. . . . ."

"Don't say it. Just don't. All right. I might as well get this over with, so the day can get back on track," Eric said. He quickly showered, dressed, and went downstairs, followed as always by an attentive Stanley, who had been alerted to the crowds by the gate guards.

As soon as Eric opened the door in the first blushes of daylight, the girls screamed with euphoric delight. "Eric!" "I love you, Eric!" "Happy birthday, Eric!" They then sang the happy birthday song in unison, which did affect Eric and elicit a smile.

"Thank you all, really, for thinking of me today. Your thoughtfulness truly warms my heart," Eric said in a loud, clear voice.

"We love you, Eric!" several girls replied. Others repeated the sentiment.

Eric went to the gate, asked the guards to open it, and greeted each girl, accepted cards, presents, stuffed animals, flowers, and yes, the cakes. He signed hundreds of autographs and said countless thank you replies. With the sun rising high in the sky, he smiled at the girls and said, "Thank you all so much. Now it's time for many of you to head home and get ready for school. My birthday is no excuse for missing school."

"Have a special day, Eric," one girl said before she left.

Many others once more wished him a happy birthday or told him that they loved him. Finally, all of them left, and a weary Eric carted armloads of presents, cards, balloons, and sundry other items into the foyer.

"What have we here? So, it's as I thought. My son's 23rd birthday generated all of that singing and screaming. You certainly received quite a load of offerings, son," Gerard said as he came to the foot of the stairs. He walked to Eric, put his arm around his son, and said with a fond smile, "People do admire you, son. I know the teenybopper brouhaha is a bit much, but never forget that this kind of admiration speaks highly of your character. You are honest, humble, compassionate, charitable, and loyal, and people recognize that in your everyday life. Being a public figure carries with it a responsibility to understand that so that you consistently represent your core values and morals. That is what these young girls respond to. That and your extremely good looks," Gerard said and winked at his son.

CHAPTER 10

Eric went to his brother's sitting room early, before most people awoke, and turned on the light for the first time in five months. "Merry Christmas, Patrick. It won't be the same without you here today, you know. You were always so full of enthusiasm and joy on Christmas Day. Even last year, you were like an overgrown child, constantly moving and wanting to do something fun. I know you're especially happy this year, because you're with Jesus—and Grandfather. I know this won't mean anything to you now, since you can't use it, but I bought this early in the summer when I saw it. It was supposed to be your Christmas gift from me. Anyway, I'll leave it here on the shelf next to your other books. Tell Grandfather I love him. Never forget I love you." *And that I'm sorry.*

Eric stood *The Possibility of Peace* by General Arrmond Tureille on the shelf and ran his hand along the spine before he left and closed the door.

"Hey, come on, Eric, enough of this moping and sadness over me. I'm fine! You know that, I know you do. I miss you guys, too. I love you and Mother and Father. You know that, too, and you have to know death doesn't end love. But, hey, thanks, man. That's one awesome book title! I can still read it, so your gift isn't in vain. I wish you could know that. Merry Christmas, Eric. Merry Christmas."

"Merry Christmas, Eric. I love you," Stefan said and put his arm around Patrick.

§§§§§

Eric next went down to the sitting room, the traditional location of the family Christmas tree. In the soft glow of the fireplace, he looked at the tree ornaments, remembering the past Christmases when many were first placed on a tree. He intentionally stopped at an ornament of a smiling snowman, and his memory came alive.

"Look, I got a new ormanent at school," Patrick said and held it up high for his family to see.

"What a happy snowman, darling," Matilda said.

"Here, let Daddy put it on the tree for you, son."

"I want to put it on the tree, Daddy. Can I?"

"Of course, you can, Patrick, anywhere you want."

"Okay," Patrick said and walked slowly around the tree until he found just the right spot. "Here. This is good." Patrick placed the ornament on a low branch—he was only in pre-school, after all—and smiled. "There. Now Santa Claus can see it when he comes down the chimaney."

Patrick's pure joy and large smile warmed his parents and brother, who surrounded the giggling boy in a hug.

"I wish I could hug you now, Patrick," Eric said and cried.

§§§§§

"Do you want me to go with you?"

"No. Thanks, though, Roger. I want to be alone."

"Sure. But let Stanley tag along, if for no other reason than to keep other visitors from bothering you. Okay?"

Eric nodded, patted his friend's arm, and walked to the churchyard with Stanley. They saw a group of girls at Patrick's grave, so they patiently stood unobtrusively under some trees until they left.

Eric then walked to his brother's grave and stared at the dates, his sadness and guilt rising in him yet again. They never went very far away, and anything could trigger them, often the most unexpected things.

Stanley stood at a distance to guard Eric from intrusions on his private visit. Eric felt free enough to softly speak aloud to his brother. "Patrick, it's been six months. One half year without you. This past six months has been so full of torture and loneliness. I miss you so, Patrick. Nothing is normal anymore, not really. It won't be until we are together again, whenever that will be. Maybe you know when. I just know that, more than anything, I'm so sorry for not doing more to stop it. I could have, I know I could have. But I didn't. I can't undo that, which hurts so much. I do want to tell you that I think of you nearly every moment. Everything seems to remind me of you: a joke, a basketball game, songs on the radio that you played on those eight-tracks all the time, the park, talk of peace, just everything. I've been visiting Maria's parents, too. I don't know if you know that. Mrs. Bouchard had a health scare last year, but her doctors say she's fine now. They miss you, too, Patrick, and they talk of you often. I'm sorry I haven't come here before today, but, well, you might know that I talk to you often without coming here. I don't like it here, seeing it carved in stone. It's so final. It hurts more. I know a gravestone doesn't mean anything except just that, a marker for your grave. I know you're in Heaven. So, if it's all right with you, Patrick, I'd rather talk with you at home rather than here. I love you."

"I know you can't hear me, Eric, but I love you, too. Hey, you don't have to come to the cemetery to talk to me. I hear you no matter where you are. Don't get hung up in the sadness of graves, please. Just remember me alive, because I am, Eric. I'm alive, and I'm here waiting for all of you to join me. I love you," Patrick told his brother.

"I love you so, Daddy. I wish I could take your pain away," Angilia said.

Eric raised his head from a prayer, and swore he saw the girl, the beautiful girl who had tried to warn him about Patrick, who had come one year earlier. Was she there? Was she just a figment of his grief-stricken mind? He closed his eyes tightly and opened them. She was gone. She wasn't real after all. She wasn't real.

§§§§

17 November 1979

Mother and Father gave me one of their surprise birthday parties today. 25. Like it's some magical age. I feel no different at all. Life goes on, as I suppose it does and has since the days of Adam and Eve and the murder of Abel, their son. God gifted Adam and Eve another son, Seth, and their lives went on. That's what humans are expected to do.

The pain never goes away. Never. I just learn to live with it. It's not the pain people might think it is, either. It's not the pain of grief. I know that Patrick's body died and that his soul lives eternally in Heaven. I know that, and that doesn't cause my unending pain. Sure, I love and miss him. We are brothers. We were close. I was his protector.

That's what hurts so very much. I failed to protect him when it mattered most. I failed to prevent the boat accident. I failed to save him. I failed Patrick, my younger brother, the one I should have protected and saved.

Celebrating my birthday doesn't seem fair when Patrick can never celebrate another birthday. His soul is forever 19. He will never fall in love, get married, and have children and grandchildren. That's not how it should have been. And it's my fault. Forgive me, God.

Eric closed his diary and placed his head in his hands. He felt drained of tears, unable to cry. He felt exhausted. He sat still and silent, until a voice intruded his brain.

Eric, there is nothing for me to forgive. Patrick's accident was not your fault. You could not have prevented it even had you tried. I cannot tell you why, but Patrick's death was part of my plan. Patrick's death opened the door for a new beginning, of which you are the central player. Trust that my plan is for the best, and that in time all shall be revealed to you. Trust that you will see your brother again when the time is right. Until then, you must accept that your life has a purpose. You must live that purpose, Eric, or Patrick's death will have been in vain. I have chosen you for a reason.

Eric sat, still unmoving for more than fifteen minutes as he subsumed all he had been told. *God, I trust you. I will do my best to put aside my guilt and to live my life the best I can. I vow to find joy in my family, friends, and in the people around me, in the little things, in life itself. I don't know why you would choose me, but I will do all I can to live as you want me to live, God. I am a man now, and I will live like a man of God.*

§§§§§

"Eric! What a surprise!" Elena exclaimed when she answered her front door on a sunny afternoon.

"I hope I'm not interrupting," Eric said.

"Of course not. I'm sorry I'm a mess. Spring cleaning," she said with a giggle.

"Do you need help with anything?"

"I wouldn't dream of asking you. No."

"Why not? I'm capable of doing housework," he teased her. "Tell me, and I'll do whatever I can. Maybe something is too high for you to reach or too heavy?" She paused. "Tell me what to do."

"Well, it's the armoire upstairs. It's solid oak and huge. I wanted to clean the floor under it, but I can wait for Ernest."

"Nonsense. Show me the way."

Within ten minutes, Eric moved the armoire, and Elena polished the floor while Eric stood on a stool and polished the top of the piece.

"What's this? You put Eric to work?"

"Ernest! You're home early!" Elena happily exclaimed and jumped up to hug and kiss her husband.

"The deal ended in success, so this is my reward. You're still cleaning? I thought I'd take you out."

"I'm nearly done. I just need to finish this corner, then the armoire can be put back." Elena quickly finished, after which Eric and Ernest began to move the armoire back into its corner.

Eric noticed Ernest stop, lean against the armoire, and clutch his left arm. "Ernest? Here, sit down," Eric said and helped him into a chair. "Mrs. Bouchard, keep him calm. I'm calling for an ambulance." Eric quickly dialed the number and told the dispatcher the address. For once, he used his title to elicit a quicker response. "Please hurry. This is Prince Eric, and my friend appears to be having a heart attack."

Eric then rushed to the window and shouted for Stanley to show the medical personnel to the master bedroom. Within five minutes of the call, they began treatment and lifted Ernest onto the gurney. Eric and Elena followed and went to the hospital with Ernest.

While Eric held and tried to comfort a terrified Elena, the doctors battled to restore Ernest's heartbeat. After thirty long minutes, Dr. Sanchez pronounced Ernest dead. At 3:51 on Friday, April 17, 1981, on what should have been an enjoyable afternoon with his wife, Ernest Bouchard died.

Knowing Mrs. Bouchard's medical history, Dr. Sanchez asked to speak with Eric first, telling him the tragic news. "I just don't know how she will react to this news, Your Highness. Her immune system has been weakened in the past by her cancer, and I don't want to just blurt it out coldly."

"I'll talk with her and break the news to her, but I prefer to do it here. She will want and need to see Ernest, and I want her to have the time and the privacy that she deserves. When she does leave, Ernest shouldbe treated with dignity and as if he were a member of my family. I will make the funeral arrangements and contact the morgue with instructions on where to take Ernest."

"Of course, Prince Eric. I have alerted Mrs. Bouchard's doctor, and he is on standby should she need medical attention," Dr. Sanchez said and left the unenviable task to Eric.

Eric prayed for strength and guidance before he returned to his friend. When Elena saw him, she ran to him and asked, "How is Ernest? When can I see him?"

The hope in her eyes cut him deeply. "Soon. We need to talk first." Eric tried to move her into a private waiting room, but she refused to move. He was forced to tell her in the hallway. "Elena, Dr. Sanchez and the team did everything. . . . ."

"No! Ernest!" she screamed and began crying hysterically. Eric could not calm her, and she struggled to breathe. Dr. Sanchez rushed to her before her own doctor arrived, and together the three men managed to get her into an examination room. "Ernest! I want—to—see—Ernest!" she screamed between agonized breaths.

Eric watched helplessly while they sedated her, so they could intubate her. She still tried to struggle, desperate to be with her husband. While the doctors worked to stabilize her, Elena turned her head and looked at Eric. Her eyes pleaded with him to help her.

Eric walked to her, placed his hands on her shoulders, and spoke softly. "Elena, let the doctors help you. You know Ernest would not want to see you like this. Do this for him, please. Do it for Maria."

Tears drenched her face. She managed to free her left arm, reached up and quickly pulled the breathing tube from her throat. She gasped for air, but managed to weakly say, "Let—me—go—to—him—please—let—me—go."

"Elena," Dr. Thomson said, "we need to stabilize you. If we must, we will fully sedate you in order to treat you. Nurse, quickly, prepare a syringe of propofol." Within two minutes, the nurse gave the doctor the anesthetic.

"There's no need," Eric softly said. "God gave her what she wanted."

§§§§

"Son, I commend you for taking on the task of arranging the double funeral for Ernest and Elena. How dreadful that must have been for you," Gerard said the afternoon of the funeral.

"It was, I won't lie. First, Ernest's heart attack without any warning, only to have Elena die from the shock of it all. She seemed to will herself to die, Father. Part of me understands, though. They have no family at all except for Maria, and there's no way to contact her. I've tried. But the cloistered nuns there give up their past lives completely and sever all ties to their families. No one would even attempt to get the message to her. That's the saddest of all, I think. She knows nothing of what happened since she took her vows. Nothing."

"No, but that was her choice, Eric. She understood what her life in the convent demanded of her. I'm not saying it's not a difficult adjustment for the young ladies, but they go into the life knowing what the life requires of them. She will likely pray for Patrick and her parents until her dying day, never knowing they are already in God's care." Gerard noticed Eric flinch, and he felt a pang knowing that his eldest son still dealt with his brother's death. "You say they have no family at all?"

Eric shook his head. "None, not even distant cousins that could be found. I had several people trying to find any relatives. Maria is the only one. That means it's us and their friends who will attend the funeral this afternoon."

"I wonder what will happen to their estate," Gerard pondered.

"I'm taking care of their belongings and home. I know that Elena had mentioned the cancer treatment center being someplace she'd like to support, so I'll also donate to that in their names. I'll place their belongings in storage in case any relatives come forward eventually, and I'll also have a real estate agent list the house. The proceeds of the sale will also go to the cancer treatment center."

"That's quite noble and generous of you, son. I'm proud of you," Gerard said and kissed Eric's cheek.

"It's the least I can do. They could have been Patrick's in-laws, and they were my friends. I'm just grateful that Elena wasn't alone when she died. I'm glad I was holding her hand. I know she and Ernest are well and happy, and that they have already caught up with Patrick in Heaven. That's the comfort I have."

"That's the comfort we all have when a loved one dies, Eric. Grief subsides with God's grace. Guilt should, too, my son. Turn it over to God. Do not continue to blame yourself for Patrick. He wouldn't like that, and you know that."

Eric looked at his father. "I know. I've talked to God about Patrick," Eric truthfully said. "I'm fine, Father, really. Guilt doesn't rule me any longer," he added, which was also true. *It doesn't rule me, because I've buried it deep inside of me. I can't serve the people of Valdavia and you and Mother if I allow the guilt to destroy me. You don't have to worry about me, Father.*

"That's good, Eric, that's good. I want you healthy and whole, son, not mired in guilt. You make me and your brother proud. I'll see you when it's time to leave," Gerard said and left his son's suite.

"You don't make me proud that way, Eric, not by repressing guilt you shouldn't even have. None of this was your fault, and you couldn't have stopped it. But if this enables you to live your life until you are healed, I'll lay off of you. Just let yourself be happy. Please. Fall in love, have a family, and be happy. That's what's meant for you. I know that for a fact," Patrick said to his brother—who couldn't hear him—as he smiled at his unborn niece.

CHAPTER 11

"*17* *November 1984*

Prince Eric Celebrates 30th As World's Most Eligible Prince

Valdavia's Prince Eric turns 30 years old today as the proclaimed world's most eligible—and most handsome—prince. Speculation is rife as to when this hot young man will find his Cinderella and crown her his princess."

"Your mother clipped this morning's newspaper article for her scrapbook," Roger informed his friend as he joined Eric and Daniel in Eric's suite.

Eric rolled his eyes and said, "The older I get, the more charming I think her scrapbooks are, but, boy, are they embarrassing. She's been known to whip those things out when we have visitors."

"Every child goes through that, Eric, just usually not with scrapbooks of newspaper clippings. Most of us suffer through photo albums," Daniel said and laughed.

"I know. She has plenty of those, too, believe me. I know it's part of her joy and love for us, so I just accept it the best I can. I'm too old to complain about it now, so I literally grin and bear it," Eric said and straightened his suit jacket lapels. "All right, I'm ready for the meeting. Let's go, Roger."

As Eric drove his car through the Palace gates, people outside the gates and on the mall screamed and cheered. He waved and smiled, reaching through his open window for some flowers and cards before he drove to the meeting.

On the drive home, he glanced at Roger. "I've been thinking, Roger. I've got a full calendar of duties now, and it's time I have an assistant of my own. Are you still interested, Roger?"

"You have to ask? Of course, I am, buddy. I'm with you for the long haul, you know that."

"Great. We'll tell Father and Thomas when we get home."

The young men walked up to Gerard's fourth-floor office to tell him and Thomas the news, only to be stopped by Thomas. "Sir," he said to Eric, "I've already talked with His Majesty, but I want to tell you, as well. I submitted my resignation, effective two weeks from now. I wanted to let you know, as His Majesty will hire my replacement soon, and I will train the new personal assistant to His Majesty."

"I'm sad to hear that, Thomas. I've known you most of my life. Do you have any special plans for your retirement?"

"I'd like to travel and visit some family who live elsewhere. Sir, His Majesty asked me to send you in when you arrived," Thomas informed Eric, who excused himself and went into his father's office.

"I'm sorry you're going, Thomas. I've learned a lot from you, by watching you and talking with you. I know King Gerard will miss your expertise," Roger said.

"I know you have, Roger. In fact, I recommended you to His Majesty as my replacement."

"You did? I-I don't know what to say. I don't deserve your kindness, and I'm not sure I'm worthy."

"I would never have told His Majesty you are did I not honestly believe so. The decision is His Majesty's, of course, but if my word means anything after nearly three decades, then you are guaranteed the job."

"Thank you, Thomas. Someday, I will do the same for someone interested in this type of position. You have been a wonderful teacher."

Just as Roger and Thomas shook hands, Gerard and Eric entered the hall. "I see the changing of the guard, so to speak, has just occurred," Gerard said and smiled. "As I told you earlier, Thomas, you will be greatly missed, but I think we have a solid replacement in Roger. In fact, Eric just told me that he offered Roger the position of his assistant. It appears my son and I will have our calendars and other matters handled by Roger. You begin on-job-training in the morning, Roger. Welcome aboard, officially."

"This is wonderful, Roger. I knew you were the right man for this job," Eric said and hugged his lifelong friend.

§§§§§

"Sir, here is your agenda for today," Roger said early one morning in the spring of 1985. "Sir, is anything wrong?" he asked when he noticed that Gerard put a hand on his right side and grimaced in pain. "Shall I call your doctor?"

Gerard closed his eyes until the pain subsided, and then looked at Roger. "No. It's just a twinge. Probably old age. I'll be fine," he said and took his typed agenda.

"Please let me know if you need anything, Sir," Roger said and slowly went across the hall to his office.

Two hours later, Eric appeared at his father's office for a meeting with him about the new water lines that would be installed throughout the country. Eric dropped his files and rushed to Gerard, who doubled over in pain beside his desk.

"Father! Roger! Call an ambulance!" Eric screamed. Roger quickly made the call, berating himself for not checking on the King more frequently throughout the morning. "Let me help you to the

221

sofa. Lean on me," Eric said and slowly moved his father to the sofa, where Gerard curled onto his left side.

Roger rushed to the main entrance to show the emergency responders to the fourth-floor office. They rushed up, knowing the King was ill, and took his vital signs. After examination, they speculated that, "His Majesty could have appendicitis or kidney stones, but only further tests can determine for certain. We must transport him to the hospital immediately."

"I'm coming," Eric said. "Roger, take care of Mother."

"No," Gerard said. "You are acting Monarch in my absence, Eric. Roger, issue the proclamation immediately."

"Sir, we must go now," one of the emergency medical technicians said. They placed him on a gurney, made him as comfortable as possible, and carefully carried him down the stairs. Palace guards shielded the public's view of King Gerard carried to and placed on the ambulance.

Eric and Roger quickly followed, and the sight of the worried Prince Eric triggered fear in the crowds that usually gathered at the gates. Eric walked to the ambulance and said, "I'm coming, Father."

"No, Eric. Your place is here until I am home again. Visit later if you must, but the people need you here."

"All right, Father, if that is your wish. I will visit later. In the meantime, you just do all the doctors ask of you so that you get well as soon as possible."

Gerard nodded, and the ambulance doors closed. At that moment, Matilda came down the stairs wailing for her husband. Eric and Roger quickly closed the doors, and Eric held his mother as he explained as much he as knew.

"We'll go and visit Father later this afternoon, Mother, but he needs tests so that the doctors can determine exactly what is wrong with him. We'll only be in the way there, so we need to stay calm and pray until we go and learn more. Come, Mother, let's have some tea," Eric said and led his mother to the small waiting room on the main level. Roger ordered the tea for Matilda, and a maid quickly tended to Her Majesty.

"Gerard has never been sick a day since I've known him, except the occasional cold. He's always been in excellent health. What is wrong with him, what? I can't lose him, Eric, I can't," Matilda said and fell into her son's arms crying uncontrollably.

"I know, Mother. But let's not panic until we learn more. This could be as simple as appendicitis, so we just need to wait. Cry it out, and then have your tea," Eric tried to soothe his mother.

Roger, meanwhile, rushed to his office and issued the proclamation that Prince Eric was temporarily acting King de Valdavia. Needless to say, the news sent the citizens of Valdavia into worry, panic, and speculation. Had King Gerard died? No, otherwise Eric would be the new King. What had happened to King Gerard? How serious was his condition? Why wouldn't the Palace provide more information? Within an hour of the proclamation, hundreds of people flooded the mall and gates, and dozens more telephoned the Palace for information.

"What can we tell them, Eric? We don't know anything yet," Roger lamented between calls.

"Issue a statement from me, Roger, as soon as I write it. Then I can get some work done for Father, so he won't be too burdened when he's released and home."

Statement on King Gerard de Valdavia

Late this morning, my father, King Gerard, was taken to hospital for tests and examinations after suffering from pain in his right side. At this time, there is no further information on his condition. My mother, Queen Consort Matilda, and I plan to visit him later this afternoon.

During his hospitalization, he has requested that I act as Monarch. I shall do so until he is well enough to resume his regular work schedule, and as much as feasible, I will consult with him regarding the running of Valdavia. I shall also fulfill his calendar of appointments and meetings during this time.

Rest assured that, as soon as we receive further updates regarding my father's condition, I shall inform you. Until then, my mother and I appreciate your prayers for his recovery.

Prince Eric de Valdavia

Roger released the statement, and also posted a copy on the Palace gates. With no information on Gerard's condition available, the staff and public became frantic. Matilda spent the afternoon in hers and Gerard's suite, tended by her lady-in-waiting, Lucie, wafting between tears and stoicism. The tears often won, much to Lucie's distress.

Finally, at 5:00, Eric appeared in his parents' sitting room, and managed to calm Matilda enough to let Lucie help her freshen for the visit to the hospital. Matilda reapplied her makeup, changed into one of Gerard's favorite dresses, and took her son's arm as they descended the stairs. Accompanied by a security guard, Eric drove his mother to the hospital—where news reporters gathered.

As Eric helped his mother from the car, dozens of cameras flashed, and dozens of questions shouted at the pair. Eric ignored them; his earlier statement should have proven sufficient. Shielded by the security guard and local police officers, the Prince and the Queen Consort entered the hospital and escorted to the King's room on the eighth floor.

"Oh, Eric, I'm so scared," Matilda confessed outside her husband's room. "I've tried not to be, but I am. I can't help it."

"I know, Mother. We're all worried. We should learn something soon. Let me know when you're ready to go in."

After drying her eyes, blowing her nose, and touching up her makeup, Matilda nodded, and Eric opened the door. Matilda gasped at the sight of her husband lying in a bed attached to various machines. Eric squeezed her shoulder in reassurance, and they quietly approached Gerard. He appeared asleep, so Eric made his mother comfortable in the chair next to him and went to find the doctor in charge of his father's treatment.

"Prince Eric, I am Dr. Neil Barnard, and I am the lead doctor over His Majesty's care. Please come with me so we can talk privately," the doctor said and took Eric to his private office.

Suddenly, Eric, too, felt fear rising in him, as much as he tried to dampen it. He swallowed and asked, "What is wrong with my father? Do you know yet?"

"Please sit, Sir," the doctor said, which only heightened Eric's fear. Eric did so, though, and listened intently while he placed his hands on his knees. "Our team performed several tests over the past hours, and we immediately ruled out appendicitis and kidney stones. We then did further blood and urine tests. His Majesty does have blood in his urine, and while that is also a symptom of kidney stones, we had ruled that out with imaging tests earlier. Therefore, we then conducted scans and images of his internal organs to determine the source of the bleeding.

"We scanned his liver, his kidneys, his pancreas, his bladder, his intestines, his lungs, and his heart. Prince Eric, our team found a tumor in His Majesty's right kidney. I will perform a biopsy soon, early this evening, to determine whether the tumor is benign or not."

Eric couldn't breathe. There was a chance his father had cancer. How? Gerard had never smoked or drunk alcohol, he ate fresh, unprocessed foods, and he remained active. How? Eric asked the doctor this question.

"It's true that His Majesty does not have most of the risk factors for developing kidney tumors, but our tests did uncover high blood pressure. There is no record of His Majesty having been treated for hypertension, so this is a new diagnosis. Hypertension is one risk factor. We have begun a regimen of hypertension treatment, so if this tumor is benign, then that treatment should help to prevent further tumors from developing."

"I pray so. Does my father know all of this?"

"Yes, Sir, he does. I spoke with him after the scans and tests. The biopsy is scheduled for 6:00 this evening. We are managing his pain until then. He is resting, but he did mention wanting to talk with you and Her Majesty. She is with him now?"

Eric nodded. "I'll spend some time with him before the biopsy, Dr. Barnard. Thank you," Eric said, shook the doctor's hand, and went to his father's room.

"Son, where have you been?" Gerard asked when Eric entered.

Eric went to his father's side, put a hand on his shoulder, and said, "Speaking with Dr. Barnard. He told me everything. You haven't told Mother, have you?"

"I most certainly have. I've always been forthright and honest with her. There's no need to change that now. It may be benign, but it could be cancerous. I'll face that when the doctor tells me the diagnosis."

"We will face it," Matilda said and grasped her husband's hand. "We will face it together, the three of us. We are a family, and we will share this experience whatever it is and whatever it brings into our lives. I can be as strong as Gerard. I won't go soft and weak when he needs me most. My marriage vows were for better or worse, sickness or health, and I will stick to those vows. No matter what, Gerard, I will be strong for you."

§§§§§

After 8:00 that evening, Dr. Barnard appeared in the private waiting room. Matilda clutched her hands together in a prayer-like formation, and Eric immediately stood.

"His Majesty is in recovery and will be awakened from anesthesia momentarily. He will remain there for half an hour at least to make sure there are no side effects from the anesthesia. The procedure itself went well. I removed the entire tumor, as well as some of the surrounding tissue. The pathologist rushed the test of the biopsy sample, and I received the results a few moments ago. Please sit, Prince Eric."

Eric sat, and Matilda held his hand tightly. They both knew before the doctor told them. Eric squeezed his mother's hand in reassurance and gave her a small smile.

"Your Majesty, Your Highness, the biopsy revealed that the tumor is cancerous. His Majesty and I did talk earlier today of this possibility, and he will begin chemotherapy and radiation therapy. He indicated that he would like to begin treatments as soon as possible, so we will begin as soon as he recovers from the procedure," Dr. Barnard said, aware of the import of the news not just for Matilda and Eric but for the nation, as well.

"When may we visit Gerard, Dr. Barnard?" Matilda asked.

"I'll take you to his recovery room. Do you have any questions?"

"No. You understand, of course, to do all in your power for Gerard. The rest is in God's hands," Matilda responded, keeping her vow to remain strong.

"Of course, Your Majesty. Please never hesitate to come to me with any questions or concerns. Prince Eric, this is my card, and my personal telephone number is on it. Please call me for any reason. His Majesty will receive the best care we can provide."

"Thank you," Eric said, and put an arm around his mother as they followed the doctor.

When they entered, Gerard was awake and having his vitals checked again. When the nurse finished, Matilda bent and kissed her husband. Gerard reached for her hand and squeezed it with a smile. Eric smiled at his parents, knowing their love endured strong and would bolster them through this trial.

"Dr. Barnard told you?"

"Yes, darling, he did. We will get through this together, as we have gotten through all of our other tragedies—together. I told Eric earlier that I meant every word of my wedding vows. I will stand beside you all through this, and I do all I can to help you to get well. In case I haven't said it lately, I want to say it right now. I love you, Gerard. You're the only man I've ever loved."

"You don't have to say it, dear. I know it. We were best friends before we married, and we're still best friends. This is just another valley in life. The mountains far outnumber the valleys. I'll do my part to beat this, and for the rest, well, I will trust the doctors and more than that, I will put it all in God's hand."

Gerard reached for Eric, and held his son's hand as he said, "Now, Eric, you will remain acting Monarch until I am released from the hospital. I shall then resume my duties, even through the treatments. But, son, I do need you to take on some of my regular duties, such as some public engagements and meetings. Dr. Barnard did tell me that the chemotherapy and the radiation often make people quite ill, so I most likely will be unable to travel during the treatments. I hate to burden you, but, I know I can depend on you."

"Of course, you can, Father. I will do anything I can to assist you during your treatments. I remember from Elena's cancer how sick she got from the chemo and radiation. Of course, you can't be expected to travel and take on too much. As long as you can advise me, I will do anything at all. You just concentrate on getting healthy."

"Thank you, son. The throne is in the best of hands. Let's just call this your on-the-job training, shall we?"

"I couldn't learn from a better man and King than you, Father."

§§§§

At Gerard's insistence, Eric released an update, informing the citizens of Valdavia of his kidney cancer and his treatment plan. Furthermore, Eric would operate in essence as co-monarch during the treatments and recovery, taking on the duties that Gerard would remain unable to perform.

People reacted in sadness, fear, and despair, gathering at Christ Church Valmondois to pray or outside the Palace gates to hold vigils. Eric spoke with the crowds every evening, comforting and reassuring them. "My father is deeply touched by your concern and greatly appreciates your prayers. He remains in good spirits, positive and hopeful. Thank you all so much," he told them one week after the update was released and posted on the Palace gates.

Once Gerard recovered from the biopsy surgery, he began a three-month series of chemotherapy and radiation treatments. Matilda accompanied him to each treatment, and she catered to him when he worked at home. He became weak, nauseous, unable to eat, and lethargic. Still, he spent several hours each day in his office, and he advised Eric regarding meetings and public engagements.

Though the schedule exhausted Eric when combined with his own Royal duties and his Army training, he relished the exhaustion, for it kept his brain too full to indulge in guilt or painful memories. Each night, Eric stared at the ceiling until sleep claimed him for a few hours, only to repeat the process the following day.

Daniel and Roger noticed their friend's overwork and his exhaustion, but neither felt it proper to say anything under the circumstances. After all, as Roger reminded Daniel, "His father has cancer. No one knows if he will survive this. Eric needs to do this so that his father won't worry about the country. He also needs to do this for himself. It's the first time since Patrick's death that he's slept for several hours each night."

Daniel nodded. "True. I just hope it doesn't make him sick, too."

"It won't. Eric's in excellent health. He's due for his annual physical soon, so his doctor will know if there's anything wrong, though. Eric's always eaten healthy, exercised daily, and overall been healthy. He's physically fine. I know this is tough on him and Matilda, though. It has to be. Just keep praying for them. That, and make sure Eric has all he needs."

By Christmas 1985, Gerard joined his wife and son on the fifth-floor balcony to greet the public. The cheers, banners, and shouts of love and appreciation warmed them all in the cool air. How wonderful to see their King Gerard once more, looking well considering all he'd endured. That was the best Christmas gift the people of Valdavia could have received.

In fact, at his post-Christmas examination and tests, Gerard his doctor declared him cancer-free. "Your Majesty, there is no trace of cancer in your body. You are free of the disease."

"When may I resume my full duties?"

"As your strength increases and returns to normal, you can resume more duties until you are back to full capacity. In the meantime, I advise against overdoing your public duties, as those can be more taxing and tiring. But in a month or two, you should be able to carry on as before."

"That's wonderful, Father. You do a much better job than I do, and besides, people want to see and meet with you, not me. I'll always be here when you need me, but I'm more than happy to step aside again and let the true King rule in every way."

§§§§

During 1986, Eric still effectively co-ruled, though unofficially, as Gerard remained rather tired and lethargic for several months. One day in the early summer, while Gerard met in his office with the President of Zimbabwe, Eric attended a Business Owner's Association meeting in his father's stead.

The people of Valdavia, particularly those in positions of authority and power, found Prince Eric knowledgeable, prepared, firm but open-minded, and always concerned about how any decisions would affect the citizens of Valdavia. That he always placed his fellow Valdavians first massively impressed all who dealt with Eric, and all who did knew he was more than capable and ready to take over when the time came—although no one felt anxious for King Gerard's death.

Far from it. Gerard had been popular and respected since his own induction into what Queen Elizabeth II of Great Britain referred to as the family business. And as he and Matilda expanded their family, people became enchanted with the young princes, Eric and Patrick, both of them handsome, charming, and quite beguiling as they matured into young men. Then, unexpectedly, the tragic accident that claimed Patrick's life at the age of only nineteen ripped a hole in the country that had yet to completely fill.

In fact, on the tenth anniversary of Prince Patrick's death, people gathered at the Church cemetery and outside the Palace gates for vigils. Flowers, candles, stuffed animals, cards, and notes, as well as posters of Patrick were piled at both places. Several young ladies who had been in their teens themselves at the time of the accident, wept as if a decade had not passed. Others played some of Patrick's favorite songs in tribute to the handsome, fun-loving prince.

"Must they do this right outside our home?" Matilda asked before breakfast that morning. "Isn't it enough that we live with this every day? Must we be reminded like this?" She began weeping and went back upstairs to her suite.

"I'll tend to her, Eric. You have breakfast," Gerard said, and followed his wife.

Eric sighed deeply as Daniel and Roger came downstairs for breakfast. Neither knew quite what to say; both knew the date and its significance. They knew what had upset Matilda. They also saw their friend's distress, and they feared the anniversary would reawaken his guilt.

"Go ahead and eat. I'm going out front to talk to the people there."

"Are you sure, Eric? It's pretty, well, sad out there," Daniel said.

"Of course, it is. These kinds of anniversaries always rekindle the grief. I want to, though," Eric insisted and opened the door.

The sight of Patrick's older brother brought a combination of tears and happiness. Eric, as usual, asked that the guards unlock the gates, and he went into the crowd to talk with and to console people who still missed his brother. "Patrick is quite special. I know that more than anyone. I miss him more than anyone, except our parents, especially our mother. I think about him every day. I know everyone adores Patrick and that you miss him, too. I won't tell you not to cry and not to be sad, because it's normal to miss people you care about. Just don't let the sadness linger too long. Patrick wouldn't want that, you know."

"We know, Prince Eric, but it's just so hard on days like this when the pain seems somehow stronger. I don't know why, but it does," one young woman said as tears fell down her cheeks.

"It's much harder for some of us, though. I cry most days," another young woman said. "I knew Patrick. I went to high school with him. He wasn't just beautiful on the outside. He was the nicest, kindest boy I ever met. And his laugh. I miss his laugh most, I think. I love his laugh. I'd give almost anything to hear it just one more time."

The woman burst into tears, which had everyone else in tears. Eric himself stiffened his shoulders in an effort to fight his tears. "I know. I would, too," he managed to say and reached to hug and comfort the woman. "Patrick would have been 29 on January 6, but he is eternally nineteen. We'll never see or know what would have been. We can only remember what was. Carry his memory in your hearts, but do him proud and find happiness in the memories. That's what I try to do. That's what Patrick wants. It's what God wants. Patrick isn't dead, we know that. He lives in Heaven now. Let that bring you solace. Will you all do that for Patrick? For me?"

"Yes, Prince Eric, I'll try," the woman he held said and dried her eyes. "For you and Patrick, I will try. Someday, we'll be with him again, I know that. And that will be most glorious!" she said and smiled through the tears in her eyes.

§§§§§

"Father," Eric said as he entered Gerard's office, "I don't mean to interrupt, but you are needed outside."

"Outside? Can't it wait until I finish my pre-meeting agenda with Roger?"

"I'm not sure. Everyone is already quite anxious."

"Anxious? About what?"

"Seeing you, of course. You do realize it's your birthday, don't you? Hundreds of people are on the mall outside the Palace pleading for you to make an appearance."

Gerard guffawed, and commented, "Birthdays are common occurrences. Mine isn't special."

"Might I remind you what you told me many times when I said the same thing? This shows that people love you and appreciate all you do as our King. You need to return their appreciation, not complain about it. Right?"

Gerard looked at Roger and said, "This son of mine certainly remembers everything I say to him. I can't complain about that, now, can I? All right, Eric, I shall meet with my friends, neighbors, and fellow Valdavians. Come with me, will you?"

"Sure, but I'm staying in the background. This is your day, Father, all yours."

Roger smiled as he watched father and son descend the stairs, and he said a silent prayer of gratitude for both Gerard and Eric, two equally amazing men whom he was privileged to know.

The screams of the elated horde wafted through the first floor, causing Matilda to slightly jump as she chatted with her lady-in-waiting. "What is going on?"

"I am afraid I do not know, Your Majesty. Perhaps Prince Eric left through the front door, or maybe it was His Majesty."

"Perhaps. I'm going to look," Matilda said, walked to the door, and peeked through a nearby curtain. "Of course! Today is Gerard's birthday, and people are gathered outside to greet him. How thrilling! Oh, Lucie, everyone loves him so. This is so beautiful to see. God kept Gerard here with us, and Valdavians are so grateful for that, aren't they?"

"Yes, Ma'am, we certainly are. We all love King Gerard immensely. He is so kind and caring, and it always shows. I am so grateful to know you both, Your Majesty."

"So am I, Your Majesty," Roger said as he joined them. "King Gerard truly is a godly ruler, one who cares about his people. I am so honored to work for him."

"I fell in love with him before I realized he was the Prince de Valdavia. When I learned he was the heir to the throne, yet was so thoughtful, kind, and compassionate, my love for him increased a thousand-fold. I vowed to support and help him all the days of my life. I never have and never could love another man," Matilda confessed, her eyes confirming every word.

"This is the one most loving and demonstrative family I have ever known of," Roger said. "Just being in your presence teaches me what true love and faith are."

"Yes, I feel the same way, Your Majesty," Lucie added. "Your family is a blessing to Valdavia and everyone who lives here."

"Roger, Lucie, that is so kind of you both to say. Who can we place our faith and trust in if not for God? God ordained each King de Valdavia, and God brought me and Gerard together so that we would create Eric and. . . .and Patrick. Everything in our lives is due to God, and we owe Him our love, gratitude, and obedience. We alone do not deserve these accolades, remember that."

"Eric says something similar often, especially when faced with the adulation of his fans. He attributes who he is to Gerard, you, and God. That's an amazingly strong belief system and attitude. Eric will become a most remarkable king many years from now. I have already seen evidence of that," Roger said.

"I have, too," Lucie said. "Valdavia is the most blessed country in the world."

§§§§

"Eric, I need to attend the zoning board meeting with your father later this morning. Do you need someone to accompany you to your meetings?"

"No, Roger, I'm fine. Father needs you, and I prefer that you accompany him as much as possible just in case. I will always worry about him. I just do after that cancer scare."

"I know. I still kick myself for not checking on him more often that day. Now I stay near him as much as I can," Roger admitted.

"Don't blame yourself. But thanks for looking after him. He's a notorious workaholic, and he doesn't always take care of himself. Sometimes, Thomas had to bring his meals to his office so he would eat. I want Father with us as long as possible, Roger. He's my father, not just my king, and I love him."

"I know. He knows, believe me. It's obvious in the way you talk to and treat him. He just radiates whenever you visit with him. He loves you, too."

Eric nodded. "I know. He shows it. He doesn't have to say it, but he does. I want my child to feel my love for her, just as I feel Father's. Well, I best head out. I'll be home mid-afternoon. 'Bye."

"'Bye," Roger said, thinking of Eric's comment. Child? Singular. Her? A daughter. *Is he still hung up on that girl from the visions and dreams?* Roger wondered. *"He must be. How long will this go on? It's been ten years already."*

§§§§

"Congratulations, Major General DeBruce Martineau," Gerard said as he pinned the two-star bar on his son's white uniform.

"Thank you, Sir," Eric said and saluted his father and Commander-in-Chief.

Gerard, as head of the country, and therefore the military, saluted his son, whose commitment to his country and his duty surpassed all expectations.

The soldiers and guests in attendance, including Matilda, Roger, and Daniel, stood in honor and respect for this young man who would lead Valdavia with faith, compassions, knowledge, experience, and dedication as yet unequalled.

Gerard said as much after the family and friends returned to the Palace after the ceremony. "Son, I have always been proud of you, you know that. However, my respect, admiration, and love for you have increased exponentially during the years of your voluntary military career. You began in 1976 planning to serve six years, and here you are in your twelfth year, and a Major General at that."

Gerard detected his son's expression, that typical embarrassed, uncomfortable countenance that told Gerard to stop talking.

"Eric, you have to realize what a historic moment this remains. Not only are you the first heir to the throne to serve in the Valdavian military, but you will be the first King de Valdavia who is a Major General in the Valdavian Army. You had to see and to hear the respect of your fellow soldiers and citizens today, Son. Never underestimate the importance of respect and love, Eric, especially since you will be their next King and Commander-in-Chief in the not-to-distant future."

"Father!"

"Gerard! Whatever do you mean? Have you not told me something?" Matilda asked in horror.

"What? Oh, Heaven's no, dear. I simply mean that I am nearing seventy years of age, and, well, my earthly life probably won't extend too far beyond that. That's all. Now, Son, back to our. . . . ."

"That's all?! Gerard, how could you treat your own death so cavalierly?" Matilda interrupted.

"I'm not. Not at all. It's just that I am well aware that most humans do not live to 100, dear, especially those who have dealt with cancer. I am quite realistic about that." As Matilda appeared on the verge of tears, Gerard quickly added, "I do not plan to go anywhere anytime soon, so don't get upset, please. Everyone dies, we all know that."

"Oh, I do know that, Gerard, but I do not want to discuss your death with you at our son's celebration."

"Father," Eric asked to change the subject, "did you ever know any Valdavian soldiers?"

"Oh, I've met several soldiers over the years, but I was never, shall we say, friends with a soldier. My mother didn't exactly forbid me from knowing soldiers, but she requested that I not spend time with them."

Eric nodded. "Grandmother didn't want you to become starstruck by them and their careers. She and Grandfather never wanted you to enlist in the Army, because you were their only surviving child."

"Yes. She feared the influence and the temptations would be too strong for me, and I would enlist against their wishes. I would never have done that, no matter how much I longed to enlist."

"I know, Father. I will never do anything else to displease you. I know I have, and I ask your forgiveness," Eric said, standing ramrod straight, his shoulders rigid, his fists clenched.

Roger, Daniel, and Lucie all stared at Eric in shock. Matilda's hands clutched her throat as tears choked her. Gerard appeared as if a prize-fighter had punched him in the gut.

"Forgive you? For what, pray tell? Eric?"

"In a few days it will be the eleventh anniversary of Patrick's death. I can never find true inner peace, when I know I am to blame. The main reason I've remained in the Army and worked so hard is to do what Patrick told me he longed to do as a soldier. This is what I can do for my brother, since I robbed him of the chance. These stars," Eric said and glanced at the symbol his father had pinned to his uniform, "are Patrick's."

Matilda turned pale, and Lucie rushed to her, helped her onto a chair, and held her. Roger and Daniel looked at each other in despair.

Devon's face betrayed his astonishment. How could Prince Eric blame himself? How? Devon took two steps toward Eric, but before he could say anything, Gerard spoke.

Gerard's shoulder's drooped, and for the first time in more than one decade, his eyes filled with tears. He looked into his son's brilliant blue eyes. "Is that what you believe, Eric? Is that what you truly believe?"

"Yes."

"How? Why? Your mother and I long ago accepted that the boat accident was just that—an accident, no one's fault. You know that."

"No. It was my duty to protect Patrick. I should have searched the lake. I should have discovered that jagged rock before Patrick entered the water. I promised God, myself, you, and Mother that I would protect Patrick all of my life, and I didn't. I let my brother die. I killed Patrick, because I didn't protect him."

"Eric, no. Son, you did nothing wrong. You did not cause, and you couldn't have prevented, the accident," Gerard said, tears at the corners of his eyes. "You have carried this inside of yourself for nearly eleven years. It is time to let it go, Eric. That is what Patrick wants and what I want."

"How can I let it go? I can never forgive myself. I can never expect anyone else to forgive me."

"There is nothing to forgive, Eric. Nothing. You are guiltless. What more can I say?" Gerard asked.

"Nothing. I'm sorry, Father. I don't deserve these stars," Eric said and reached to unpin them.

"Stop it, Eric! Just stop it! You did not cause Patrick's death!" Devon screamed and grabbed Eric's shoulders, taking everyone by complete amazement.

"Devon, I appreciate your concern. You protected Patrick diligently. He looked up to you. But this is my cross to bear."

"It shouldn't be. It can't be, because it's mine. I'm responsible for Patrick's death. I'm the one who failed in my duty, my one duty. From his birth, I was placed in charge of his protection. I failed. This isn't your fault. It's mine."

By this point, Matilda cried fervently, so much so that Lucie helped her upstairs to her suite. Daniel and Roger watched the scene in desperation, fearing for Eric. What could they do to help him? They quickly realized they wouldn't have to do anything.

"Devon. Eric. My office now," Gerard demanded. "Go."

The three men left their friends and solemnly walked up to the fourth floor in silence. Gerard opened his office door and ordered the younger men to "Sit." Although Eric was 34, he felt like a young boy chastised.

Gerard sat at his desk and looked at Devon and Eric. "You have both lived a lie for eleven years, pretending that you were healed. I expected more from both of you. How long do you expect to wallow in guilt and pity?"

Eric took a slow, deep breath. "As long as it takes, Father. I don't know how to end this without forgiveness. I can't forgive myself. How can I?"

"You can't forgive yourselves, because there is nothing to forgive. Neither of you is responsible for that rock that capsized the boat, just as no one was responsible for the Titanic's hitting that iceberg. Both were tragic accidents. I miss Patrick every moment. He is my son. But I made peace with his accident long ago, within the first year. So, too, did your mother, Eric."

Both Eric and Devon looked down, afraid of what their faces would reveal to Gerard. "Has either of you truly grieved?"

"Yes," they both answered. "Then the problem is here," Gerard said and placed a hand over his heart. "You need to accept that Patrick's death was an accident that neither of you caused." He saw them both move uncomfortably. "Eric. Devon. I forgive you both for not being able to prevent Patrick's death."

"You do?" Eric asked. "How can you?"

"Because you are my son, Eric, and I love you. And Devon, you are a valued member of the extended family, and I care about you."

"Sir?"

"Yes, Devon, I do. I hope you know that. You both know I speak the truth. Now it is up to you to find it in your hearts to forgive yourselves. Promise me you will try."

"Yes, Sir, I will," Devon said. "Your forgiveness gives me the strength and purpose to forgive myself."

"Good. Eric?"

"Father, I promise I will try. I will pray about it and seek God's help."

You already have my help, Eric. I told you years ago that you did not cause Patrick's accident, that it was not your fault. Perhaps now your heart is ready to accept that truth.

Eric sat still, staring, for several minutes as God's words took firm hold of his heart. *"I will try, God. I have to be honest. I will always blame myself, but now I can put the pain away and not let it interfere with my life. Thank you,"* Eric silently told God.

"Eric?" Gerard asked. "Are you all right, Son?"

Eric looked at his father, a smile illuminating his face and his eyes. "Yes, Father, I am. I am. Patrick's death won't rule my life anymore. Thank you."

§§§§

19 July 1988

Patrick, you know, I am sure, that I think of you every moment. Eleven years ago, our lives changed completely. My younger brother, the one I vowed to protect at all costs, you died. I failed you.

I carry that in me for the rest of my life, Patrick. No matter what Father or God tell me, I am to blame, because I didn't protect and save you. I promised God, Father, Mother, and myself that I would, and when it mattered most, I failed. I let you die.

I am so sorry, Patrick, more than you can ever know. But to appease Father and Mother, I will hide my pain and guilt from the world. No one shall ever see or know what my heart and soul feel.

This is my suffering, my cross, and I carry it as my rightful punishment. I do not deserve a happy life, one filled with a wife and a family of my own. I don't, because

240

I robbed you of that opportunity. I robbed the world of all of the good you would have accomplished.

Father says he forgives me, but I can never forgive myself. I won't blame you if you never forgive me, either, Patrick. I don't understand how you could. If this all means I am doomed to Hell when I die, so be it. I deserve to burn for eternity.

Until then, I will do my duty as heir and king, for I do care deeply about the people of this country and their well-being. I will never let them suffer because I am tormented. I buried my pain and anguish deep inside of my being. I hid my pain. But I will never forget the wrong I did and the pain I caused the world. I love you for all time, Patrick, and I miss you."

§§§§§

"Has Eric left for his meeting yet?" Roger asked Daniel after breakfast one morning.

"Yes. You know, it's good to see him back to his old self again. All of that gloom and doom over Patrick worried me."

"I know. They were extremely close, though, so Eric's guilt didn't surprise me. Still, he held onto it for quite a long time. Seems that talk King Gerard had with him and Devon did the trick."

"Yeah, and it's great to see him smiling again. It hurt me to watch him so miserable, even if he tried to hide it. I'm glad we got our friend back."

"And I am ecstatic to have my son back," Gerard said, joining the conversation as he came to get some files from Roger. "I understand his guilt, I do, but he clung to it as his symbolic sackcloth and ashes. I'm relieved he has finally found healing and peace."

§§§§§

"Eric, I just want to tell you how much I enjoy seeing you happy and relaxed," AAV President John Jarvis said after a board meeting of the AAV.

Eric had hoped no one would notice the difference in his behavior and attitude. However, some people were bound to, and he just had to accept that and keep trudging along. "Thank you, John.

It just took me a while to adjust to life, but I'm fine now, just fine. I'm just glad I can help AAV. Do we want to do some of the soccer team pictures at the Palace? I thought that would show our support of the team, sort of an official endorsement, if you will."

"Really? That would be awesome, Eric. Let me arrange everything."

"How about this Friday? My afternoon is free, so we would have plenty of time."

"Perfect. I'll contact the photographer and Coach Koonz. 1:00 Friday?"

"That's fine," Eric replied. "I'll see you then."

As he left the AAV offices, Eric thought, *At least my performance is convincing this time. They believe I'm healed of the guilt. Daniel, Roger, John, and several charity members have commented on how happy I am now, and Father and Mother seem more jovial and relaxed around me now. I just need to maintain this façade for the rest of my life.*

"No, Eric, you do not. Your guilt will truly end at the proper time. Oh, it will be many years, but it will end. And you will find genuine happiness before then. Your heart will not turn away from or deny you this, for all is part of God's plan for you. If this coping mechanism helps you until then, that is fine. You will learn to live with this until God's timeline comes to fruition. You will not permit the pain and the guilt to rule your life and to take you off of God's intended path for you. Allow the joy and love into your heart, Eric. Enjoy this life. That is how it should be," Michael said as he watched and read Eric's thoughts from Heaven.

"Michael! Oh, Michael, I have just seen the most beautiful sight ever!" Angilia gushed as she ran to Michael several minutes later. "Daddy! Daddy is happy, Michael, truly happy! I saw him smile for the first times since—since I went to Earth for Uncle Patrick. He watched two boys playing, and that made him smile. The boys must have reminded him of when he and Uncle Patrick played together. And the memory did not make him sad. Oh, Michael, this is a miracle!" Angilia gleefully said and hugged the strong, beautiful Archangel.

"Yes, it is, my dear."

$$\S\S\S\S\S$$

"Hi, Roger. I'm early. Is that a problem?" Eric asked in the doorway of his friend's office.

Roger smiled up at his friend. "Of course not. Come on in. I have a pile of charity requests to go over with you. I'll respond accordingly to each on your behalf. This is going to take a while. There are a lot of invitations. Nearly two dozen have arrived this week."

"Really? I wonder why? I haven't done anything unusual lately."

"Yes, you did. Your participation in the Heart Association fundraiser three weeks ago generated over three million francs for them. That got a lot of attention."

"Really? Well, this is one time I won't complain. The whole point is to raise awareness and funds for the charities. If I can help to do that, I am happy to do so. Let's get busy."

Roger explained each charity and fundraiser to Eric, who listened to all with serious consideration. He instantly chose an appearance on behalf of a British children's hospital.

"This one is in Santander, Spain, for the Maria Sabine Cancer Foundation's annual fundraiser banquet," Roger read.

"Maria Sabine? The actress, right?"

Roger nodded. "Yes. She was born in Santander in 1915." Roger cleared his throat. "She died from breast cancer in 1976."

"I will attend that one."

"Let me go over the details first, Eric."

"That's not necessary. I want to do anything I can to help them." Eric took a deep breath. "I want to do this for Elena."

"Of course, Eric."

After Roger went through each request, Eric selected thirty fundraisers to attend over the spring through the winter of 1989.

"You're going to be one extremely busy man, my friend," Roger said as he organized the piles of requests and prepared to enter them into Eric's calendar.

"I don't mind. I want to help people."

"I know, Eric. You always have helped others, even when we were children. You don't have to do all of this, but you do. That's what's so impressive."

"I do have to, Roger. One of God's expectations is that I take care of all people. As the next King, it's part of my duty to care for people. Besides, I want to do all I can to help as many people as possible. I will eventually inherit wealth. I don't want simply to hoard money away. I want to use it to help people and to do good. My life's goal is to help as many people as I can. I want to earn my birthright."

CHAPTER 12

"Son, why don't you and Roger leave for Spain today? This will allow you some time to acclimate yourselves before the banquet."

"Are you positive you don't need Roger to stay here?" Eric asked.

"Of course, I am. I don't have any meetings scheduled over the next four days, so I don't have any reason to leave home, except for tomorrow's church service, if I don't want to," Gerard responded. "I'll work from my office while you're gone."

"That's perfect. I still want Daniel to stay here should you need help with anything."

"All right, Son, I concede. But leave today and give yourself a few days to enjoy Santander before you rush back here to your routine. Enjoy a short vacation there, in fact. I order you to as your Commander-in-Chief and as your loving father," Gerard said with a smile.

"Are you sure?"

"It's Saturday. Enjoy an extended weekend. Return Tuesday or Wednesday. Be a tourist. See the sights. Meet people. Try new food. Relax."

Eric smiled and hugged his father. "I will. You know, I think I'm going to enjoy this trip."

§§§§

"Wow, Spain is breathtaking," Roger said as Gerard's private airplane landed at Santander Airport.

"It is. I've been a few times. It's always business, though, so I've seen little of the country," Eric replied.

"You will now. We both will. A long weekend in Spain; I won't complain about that," Roger said with a broad smile.

"I won't, either, actually," Eric softly said as the plane taxied to a stop. "I have a feeling that this holiday will change my life forever, Roger."

"Wow. Really? How?"

"Hmmm, in the most important way," Eric replied in a day-dreamy tone.

"Eric, we're ready to disembark," Stanley came to inform his charge. "I've been informed that there is a crowd gathered awaiting your arrival."

"We—or, rather, I—expected this. This fundraiser was well publicized," Roger commented.

"Like I said before, in this case, I won't complain. I just pray the Foundation raises lots of money. That's most important," Eric said.

"True," Roger said, and stood.

"Your luggage will be taken to the hotel. Your car is waiting to take you there when you're ready," Stanley explained to Eric.

"Let's go, then. I am looking forward to this stay," Eric said with a wistful expression.

Roger had no idea what exactly had altered his friend's attitude, but he was grateful. Eric seemed free of the gloom in which he's dwelt for so long.

The sudden burst of screams alerted Roger that Eric had been spotted. Girls and young women waved their arms, shouted, screamed, and jumped as he walked down the plane steps. He paused momentarily to smile and wave, eliciting more exaltation.

Stanley, as always, followed right behind Eric, scanning the area. His hand remained ready to grab his pistol at the first threat. However, no danger ensued, and the prince entered his limousine without any setbacks.

"Now I know what Colonel Tom Parker feels like most days. Limos, screaming girls, flashbulbs. He sees it all. My best friend is a veritable rock star," Roger said and smiled at the screaming throngs.

"Hardly, and I don't want to be a rock star. I wouldn't wish that life on my worst enemy."

"Why?" Roger asked.

"Because you lose your life completely. Others control your every move. Very little privacy. That does not appeal to me," Eric said with a slight shiver.

"Still. . . . . I suppose," Roger said and ended the conversation.

Soon, though, the young men arrived at the Grand Hotel, where more people awaited Eric's arrival. Eric obliged the autograph requests, smiled, and made small talk with those at the main entrance.

Once inside, the porter escorted the Royal party to the so-called Presidential Suite on the 25th floor, where Eric, Roger, and Stanley would reside over the next four days.

"Wow! If this is a perk of being a rock star, I'm in," Roger said and looked around the grand main room.

"It's not a perk, Roger. You should know that. I booked the suite, because it's the only one here large enough for the three of us," Eric said. "That's the only reason."

"You're paying for this? The Foundation isn't footing the bill?"

"Of course not. I'm not letting them pay for this suite, when we're here for their fundraising banquet. That would be counterproductive," Eric explained.

"Oh. I hadn't thought of that. Sorry. I still have a lot to learn," Roger sheepishly said. "Why didn't you ask me to book the suite?"

Eric shrugged his shoulders. "I'm still used to doing these things myself. I never bothered Thomas with my travel arrangements." He glanced at Roger. "I'll try to give the reigns to you, Roger, I promise. But you promise to let me know when you're busy with Father's business and schedule. He comes first."

"Sure thing."

A bellman delivered the luggage, and Roger quickly took charge of Eric's, primarily hanging his military uniform in preparation for the next day's steaming and brushing. He then placed all of Eric's clothes in the closet or bureau, placed Eric's toiletries in the master bath, and made sure the master suite contained all that Eric required.

"Roger, I could have done this," Eric said as he entered his suite.

"I know, but I wanted to. Do you need anything?"

"No. I have a brief meeting with a coordinator of the fundraiser tomorrow morning, but nothing until then. If you're up for it, I thought we could visit some of the sights, then find a restaurant at which to have dinner."

"Sounds good. Give me a few minutes, and I'll be ready," Roger said.

Eric informed Stanley of their plans, and he, too, took a few moments to freshen. Within ten minutes, the three men exited the hotel, and people instantly recognized Eric. For more than forty minutes, Eric signed autographs and posed with fans for photographs.

"Yes, you're a rock star, Eric. This long ago stopped being a teen idol thing. We're in our mid-30s now, and you have girls and women throwing themselves at you. This is your life," Roger said as Eric slipped on his dark sunglasses.

Roger noticed the attention directed at his friend, all of which Eric never realized. People stared at Eric, took pictures of him, followed him, and some even cried. That happened whenever Eric appeared out in public, and it had since Eric was a teenager.

"How can you never get all the fuss?" Roger silently wondered. *"You just aren't a normal man, Eric, and you never will be. You were born a public person. Before you were born, people were interested in you. This is your normal. I know you don't enjoy all of this attention, but it will always be part of your life. I know I tease you sometimes, but I do understand how uncomfortable this is for you. I'll try to help you deal with this. I promise to support you, so you can do what matters most to you."*

"How about authentic Spanish cuisine for dinner?" Eric asked. "We can do some sightseeing and return here in a few hours."

"Sure," Roger answered, and Stanley agreed.

Roger went inside the restaurant and made their reservations, and after four hours of visiting churches, museums, and walking ancient streets, they returned to the restaurant. Appropriately attired in suite and ties, the three men appeared stylish, sophisticated, and well-bred. However, once the host recognized Eric, he quickly escorted the three men to the best table.

"Thank you, but we don't need this table if another party may require it or has requested it," Eric said.

"No, Your Highness, no one has. We want you to have La Cienta's best, given that you are here to help a most noble cause," the host said.

"Thank you, Sir. That is kind," Eric replied.

Eric, Roger, and Stanley placed their food and beverage orders and chatted over the soup while the chef prepared their main courses. After the maître d' himself served their salads, Eric smiled and said, "I appreciate it here. We can enjoy our meal in peace. No one has noticed or interrupted us."

"They've noticed. They haven't interrupted yet, but they will. They always do," Roger said, speaking from years of experience.

One hour later, Eric smiled at Roger and Stanley. There were nearly finished with the main course when Roger's prediction proved true.

"Excuse me, Prince Eric," a female voice said.

Eric blotted his mouth, looked up, and asked, "Yes, Miss?"

"I was wondering if you would sign my menu?"

Eric had signed many menus over the years for people who approached him as he ate meals. He smiled graciously and said, "But of course. To whom should I address the message?"

"Anna."

A moment later, Eric returned the menu to an elated Anna, who read his best wishes inscription and gushed in gratitude. Anna returned to her parents' table, where she showed them her treasure.

Anna's act inspired others to approach Eric before he left the restaurant. Soon, a line of autograph seekers wound through the dining room. As usual, Roger and Stanley kept alert for the slightest sign of danger. With occasional assassinations in other countries, the Valdavian Royal Family's bodyguards remained vigilant and aware. Granted, most of the crowds that gathered around Eric all but worshipped him, but nonetheless, Stanley never relaxed for one second. Protecting the life of the next King remained his responsibility, and nothing or no one could ever make him forsake his duty.

For the first time during such a besiege, Eric smiled and exuded happiness. He explained why when the three men began their trek to the Grand Hotel. "Some of the people I met have purchased tickets to the fundraiser. Others gave me money and checks to pass on to the Foundation staff. How generous is that?"

"Very," Roger answered. "You do inspire people."

"Really?"

"In a manner of speaking, yes," Stanley added when Roger appeared somewhat uncomfortable.

"I'm not sure exactly, but like I've said, I want to help people.," Eric said.

Roger simply said, "You do, Eric," resigned to his friend's oblivion to his popularity.

§§§§

After the next morning's church service, Eric met with Rene Xavier, the representative from the Foundation, to discuss the agenda for that evening's fundraiser. "After the film and your speech, the dinner follows, and finally the audience with those who purchased V.I.P. tickets," Mr. Xavier said.

Eric nodded. "That's fine. I also have donations for the Foundation from other diners who were at the restaurant last evening," Eric said and pulled an envelope from his jacket's inner pocket.

"This is most unexpected, Your Highness. Thank you. Is there anything I can do to assist you this evening? Anything at all?"

"No, thank you. In fact, I want to ask if there is anything more I can do to aid the Foundation."

"Your Highness, you have done so much already just by publicizing the Foundation. Ever since your speech at the fundraiser was announced, we have received donations and interest. The fundraiser sold out in less than one week. Adding the V.I.P. meet-and-greet not only addressed public desire, but it brought 1,428,330 dólares to our coffers so that we can continue our work. That's the equivalent of 56,301.40 Francs. That is all due to you, Your Highness."

"That's the least I can do. I'm more than happy to do whatever I can. I mean that," Eric reiterated.

"We—I—appreciate that more than you know," Mr. Xavier said. "Everyone looks forward to your speech tonight, Prince Eric."

§§§§

Forty-five minutes prior to the fundraiser's start, Eric appeared in the suite's living room attired in his white dress Army uniform. He, Roger, and Stanley would go to the Hotel's ballroom before the fundraiser began.

"Do you have your speech notes?" Roger asked Eric ten minutes before they left.

"I don't have any notes. I have the speech in my mind, and I will speak from my heart. Elena Bouchard had weighed heavily on his heart in recent days and his memories filled with her cancer journey. She had defeated cancer, which thrilled him—but had succumbed to shock and heartbreak. The speech would challenge him, Eric knew that, but he felt strongly about the cause. No woman should go through that cancer journey.

§§§§

"Ladies and Gentlemen, thank you sincerely for attending the Maria Sabine Cancer Foundation's annual fundraising banquet. Ms. Sabine, as you know, was a goddess of film's golden era, enchanting audiences with not just her exquisite beauty but her heart-wrenchingly emotional and realistic portrayals of her characters.

"Ms. Sabine never married and had a family of her own, but she deeply cared about people. Her philanthropic work is well recorded and inspirational. When she learned of her own breast cancer and later that it had metastasized, Ms. Sabine worked with her lawyers to establish this Foundation so that research and education could flourish. Her desire, even though she knew cancer would end her life, was that doctors and scientists work together to seek treatments and ultimately a cure for this dreadful disease.

"Our mission remains dedicated to what Ms. Sabine considered her life's most important work: ridding the world of breast cancer. We will not stop until that is accomplished, no matter how long this battle takes. We will defeat breast cancer," declared Olivia Salvator, President of the Maria Sabine Cancer Foundation.

Eric swallowed his tears as Elena's smiling face flashed before him. If only. . . . . He would do all he could to help to win this war, he thought as he applauded with the other attendees.

"Now, we have a film which will show you the work brought about by the generous donations to this Foundation. You will see and hear from doctors, scientists, breast cancer warriors, and their families. This is a long, difficult fight for all involved, but with each new battle, there remains hope and optimism. Each battle is a chance to discover victory as our soldiers learn from their defeats. Those losses are heavy, and they do linger as guiding beacons. I know you will find this short film as emotional as I have," Mrs. Salvator shared as she took her seat next to Eric.

He found the film highly emotional, of course, as memories of Elena's cancer battle resurfaced as he watched and listened to the patients, families, and doctors. He also found the film galvanizing, prompting him to instantly increase his personal donation to the Foundation, a gift he planned to give privately after the event.

As the film ended, many people sobbed and had to dry their eyes. Eric cleared his throat, swallowed, and took several deep breaths. He had to deliver his speech soon, and he had to prepared. Yes, this was a somber moment, but he preferred to believe that it was filled with optimism and courage. He had witnessed both in Elena and Ernest. They endured as his motivation, his guiding force. He hoped to share that in his speech and provoke others toward more action if possible.

Mrs. Salvator approached the podium as the applause dwindled, this time to introduce Eric. "Thank you, everyone. This film touched my heart when I first viewed it, and I knew it would affect each of you similarly. Let us unite in this cause that Ms. Sabine cared for so deeply. She knew full well that none of this work would assist her, save her, but her prayer remained that it would assist and save others. Tonight, our cause is championed by one of the world's most benevolent public figures, the future King of Valdavia. You all know that Prince Eric is our featured speaker this evening, and his participation has garnered immense publicity and interest in the Foundation, as well as record-breaking donations in the months since his involvement was announced. Please join me in welcoming His Royal Highness Prince Eric de Valdavia."

Everyone stood in appreciation and applause as Eric strode to the podium, where he thanked Mrs. Salvator for her kind introduction. Eric slightly blushed as he motioned for everyone to sit. Taking a deep breath, he launched into his speech, one of the most emotional he would ever make.

"Ladies and gentlemen, Foundation staff, and Mrs. Salvator, I stand united with you in this fight. I know that some of you have been affected by breast cancer, and my prayer, like Maria Sabine's, remains that a cure for this devastating disease is soon discovered. No one should directly or indirectly suffer from this cruel disease. No one. I know what that battle is like, believe me, I do."

Eric looked at members of the audience as he spoke, making eye contact as he scanned the room. He stopped, staring at one face, a beautiful dark-haired, brown-eyes, ruby-lipped face. He felt his heart literally skip beats. He felt his pule pound in this neck. He felt slightly dizzy for a moment. He felt—what? He had never before felt such a reaction.

"On August 26, 1977 a dear friend of mine, the woman who should have been my brother Patrick's mother-in-law had fate taken a different path, told me that she had breast cancer. Elena Bouchard and her husband Ernest held strong faith in God, which guided every aspect of their lives. Their faith helped them through this frightening journey. Their strength and courage impressed me tremendously. Nothing seemed certain during this time, nothing except their faith."

Eric still stared at the beautiful brunette, his hands gripping the podium, as if he spoke only to her. He had never seen her before that evening, yet he felt like he knew her. How was that possible?

"Nothing would ever feel certain or guaranteed to them for the rest of their lives. I knew that. Elena and I talked frequently, and she shared her faith and her uncertainty with me. She also shared her love of life, of the small, commonly-overlooked things like a bird's song, a cloud, a butterfly, flowers, the smell of old books, and quiet understanding between friends."

The beautiful lady stared at Eric, too, her brown eyes locked onto his turquoise eyes. She gripped her clutch purse tightly, her own heart pounding fiercely against her sternum. Sure, she had seen the Prince's photographs dozens of times, and she found him handsome. But this was vastly different. Seeing him in person was unlike any feeling she had ever experienced. No other man had ever caused such feelings in her.

"Elena had read about actress Shirley Temple's breast cancer treatment and its success, so she followed suit. Like Shirley, Elena, supported by Ernest, took charge of her treatment. Like Shirley, Elena insisted on what is called a simple mastectomy, in which only the breast tissue is removed, not the chest muscled and lymph nodes. She understood the surgery, and she trusted her surgeon to remove all of the cancer. He did. Of course, she followed that with chemotherapy, and after six months, Elena was declared cancer-free."

Eric remained transfixed on that one woman, and during these moments, no one else existed. She alone mattered to him now. At 34 years old, he felt something he had never felt for any woman. He felt love.

"However, she and the oncologist never knew if or when the cancer would recur, or where in her body, so Elena endured full-body scans every three months as a preventative measure. The benefits far outweighed and negatives, as it assured the earliest possible detection and treatment should her cancer recur. We all remained grateful that Elena consistently received clean bills of health. God answered our prayers."

How could he feel love for a woman he had just seen for the first time? Love at first sight? A fairy-tale, a Hollywood movie, a fantasy. No. It was as real as he.

"However, the Bouchards did receive bills, massive bills, for the scans, on top of their share of the surgery bill. Their health insurance didn't cover the costs one hundred percent. I am grateful to be in a position to have financially assisted my friends, but I know that many people struggle with the resulting medical bills."

She continued to stare at Eric as his brain traversed two paths: delivering the speech and attempting to make sense of his feelings and emotions. She, too, struggled to comprehend her emotions at that moment. She had never believed in love at first sight. She found it childish. But it wasn't. It wasn't, she thought, as her heart pounded, nearly deafening her.

"The Maria Sabine Cancer Foundation provides hope, yes, and funding for research, but they also provide financial assistance to those who, like Elena and Ernest, face this brutal physical, psychological, and financial battle. The toll all of this takes on a patient and a family soars astronomically. I know that. I saw that. No one can endure this alone, and with this Foundation, no one has to."

I must talk with her. She cannot escape me, like Cinderella did the Prince at the ball. I cannot lose her now that I have found her, my one true love. I cannot.

"I want every woman to receive the diagnosis which Elena received—that she is cancer-free. I want every woman to be as inspired by Elena as I am, and to be her own advocate, to fight for what is best and right for her."

We will be together soon. I am almost done. We are so close to our happily-ever-after. Soon, Eric thought.

"I want to help the Foundation to make every breast cancer patient's battle less frightening, more hopeful, more supportive, and more compassionate. Together, we can all make that the reality for all breast cancer patients and their loved ones."

The audience erupted in thunderous standing ovation, but Eric never lost sight of her. The applause dragged on far too long, Eric lamented while he smiled, nodded, and thanked everyone. He only wanted to sit with her and talk with her.

Thankfully, Mrs. Salvator appeared at the podium, and she soon encouraged the audience to sit. "Thank you for such an emotional and inspirational speech, Prince Eric. Ladies and gentlemen, we shall now serve dinner, after which will follow the meet-and-greet with His Royal Highness for those of you who purchased that option. Please enjoy."

Mrs. Salvator and Eric returned to their table, and Eric immediately leaned close to Roger, who never even got to congratulate his friend on his speech.

"Roger, I need you to bring someone to our table now. She is the beautiful brunette with large brown eyes, wearing a red gown. She's at the fourth table back from the podium. I want her here. Go."

"Okay," Roger said, stunned. He quickly made his way to this mystery woman's table, surprising her when he tapped her shoulder. "Excuse me, Miss, but I am Prince Eric's assistant. He requested your company at his table, if you will please come with me."

Her eyes sparkled. "Of course, I will."

Eric beamed when he saw Roger and the beautiful woman winding their way to his table. He stood when they approached. He extended his hand and gently took hers. "Thank you for joining me. I am Eric."

"Yes, I know. I am Marisol."

§§§§

Roger discreetly placed another chair at the table and sat between Marisol and Stanley. He looked at his friend, whose eyes seemed lit from within, glowing with wonder and—love. In the more than thirty years he had known Eric, he had never seen that look in his friend before. Eric had often said that God would bring his true love to him. Had He? Time would reveal the answer.

Eric and Marisol talked to one another throughout dinner, ignoring everyone else. Not long after they sat, Marisol lifted her left hand to her throat, and Eric could not help but notice a ring on her third finger. Given how she had looked at him and talked with him,

Eric never thought she was engaged or married, though. She perceived where his gaze landed, and she held her hand out toward him.

"I have worn this ring since I was thirteen years old. Most people presume it to be an engagement or a wedding ring, but no, it is not. Read what is says, Eric," Marisol said, her voice nearly drowned in the noise of the crowded ballroom. She noticed his hesitation. "Go on, I want you to. I do not reveal this to most men I meet, for I truthfully do not mind if they think I am taken. Go on."

"I never thought you are taken, Marisol," he said with a smile as he lifted her hand to read the inscription. LOVE WAITS the band declared. A purity ring. Eric's heart swelled. "Marisol. My faith is the most important part of my life, too," Eric softly said and lifted her hand for a gentle kiss.

"Yes, I can tell that and feel that. Besides, magazines often speculate about your love life, or rather the lack of one. They often write that you have no time for romance. Pero eso no es verdad, ¿correcto? You are waiting for your one and only."

"Yes. And you, too, right?"

Marisol nodded. "Sí. Mi madre told me when she gave me this ring that God will bring me and the man meant for me together and that I will know instantly that he is the one." Marisol leaned closer to Eric." "Ella tenía razón."

"So was my father," Eric whispered in her ear.

Roger watched their interaction as he ate, aware that his friend and the beautiful woman felt the beginnings of love. He smiled, elated for his best friend, and prayed silently for Eric's continued happiness. *"Please, God, do not let him suffer another loss and heartbreak. He's been through enough, and he needs love and happiness."*

At that moment, both Eric and Marisol laughed, a joyous sound to Roger and to Stanley, who, as a man, had long hoped that Eric would find romance. He was all work, and that wasn't healthy.

"Tell me about what is truly most important to you, Eric. Oh, like most people, I read articles about your work, but I want to know your heart," Marisol said and placed her right hand over his heart. "Tell me if I know you. You are caring and kind, and you live a godly life. God is most important to you, followed by your family. You love tu padre y tu madre mucho. You do all for them and for the country you will rule as Rey. You want your people to have peace, prosperity, and justice." She looked into his eyes. "You seek absolución for Patrick's death."

Eric's breath caught in his chest, and he couldn't breathe. How could she know this? He fought the tears that formed in his eyes, but she noticed them and took a silk handkerchief from her clutch. Marisol tenderly patted his eyes and leaned over to kiss his cheek.

"Eric, no. You ask for something that God cannot give you, do you not realize?" She saw the anguish in his eyes. "He cannot give absolución, because there is no sin, no crime for God to pardon. How are you to blame for an accident, Eric? How? You have carried this guilt far too long, and you must let it go."

"I know, Marisol, I do, but I can't just let it go. I've tried. I have. I need to get to a place where I can release it. I need something more than God's forgiveness. I have His, I know that. I need—I need Patrick's," Eric said as tears once more filled his eyes.

Marisol again dabbed his eyes with her delicate handkerchief, and at the same time cooed her sympathy to him. "Mi pobre hombre, do not torture yourself so. Patrick has nothing to forgive, either, nothing. If he could, he would tell you this, Eric, you must realize that. You will be in Santander tomorrow?" Eric said he would, but asked why. "Tomorrow, I will take you to my church. We will talk to the Father there, and he can help you, I know he can. We will go, ¿sí?"

Eric looked into Marisol's soul, and felt trust and love. "Yes, we will go. But I need to get myself together tonight. You are already helping me unleash feelings I have kept buried deep inside of me for so long. But this is neither the place nor the time. Perhaps we can talk more after the fundraiser?"

"Sí. There is so much more I want to hear from you and to tell you about me, Eric," Marisol said in her enchanting Spanish accent.

For the remainder of the dinner, the couple discussed their favorite music, movies, foods, and books. They pleasantly discovered that they shared many similarities, which caused many smiles and giggles. Eric's brain swirled with so many emotions. How could someone he had just met know him so well, read his heart and soul so accurately? Surely, she was Heaven sent; she had to be the one for whom he had waited his entire life. Nothing else made sense.

Before he knew it, the dinner ended, and Mrs. Salvator returned to the podium to announce that the audience with His Royal Highness would shortly begin. "Those who have V.I.P. tickets will go to the sitting room off of this ballroom, where Prince Eric will meet with you for two hours. Photographs and autographs will be allowed. Prince Eric will be escorted in once all ticket holders have entered."

Those without V.I.P. tickets exited the ballroom, while all who had purchased the extra tickets lined up for entry into the sitting room. When Marisol told Eric that she would await him in the Hotel lobby, Eric shook his head.

"No. You wait here with Roger. After this, we will go to our suite," Eric said and indicated himself, Marisol, Roger, and Stanley. "I'll order coffee, and we can talk privately. Please?"

"Sí, Eric, I will wait for you. What is another two hours after thirty-eight years?"

Eric froze momentarily as Marisol's comment registered in his brain. She felt as he did! He smiled at her when Mrs. Salvator indicated it was time for the V.I.P. event. "Soon, Marisol. Soon."

Roger saw the reluctance in his friend, even though the fundraiser was quite important to Eric. Marisol watched Eric until the sitting room door closed behind him. While she waited, she asked Roger how he and Eric had met, and Roger shared their history with her. Then he revealed some of his insights into his friend with her.

"Eric has always been rather serious, with no time for frivolity. It's as if wasting time is the worst crime in his mind," Roger said.

"Sí. I understand that, too, Roger. I have never enjoyed spending time in mindless pursuits. I never had many friends in school, or rather outside of school. I loathed spending my time shopping or going to movies or just walking the neighborhood with no purpose. I did not fit in with most of my classmates. School was a path to the life I was meant to live."

"Wow. Eric used to say the same thing essentially, from when we were in elementary school. School remained a stepping stone to knowledge, thoughts, and ideas that would assist him with the job for which he was born," Roger said.

Marisol nodded. "How much responsibility he must have felt his entire life. What a huge obligation to be born with your job already known and to spend most of your life preparing for that job. I do not envy that, but I do know that Eric will make one astounding King. He has such strong faith, compassion, and drive to help people. A leader should possess those qualities and traits."

"Yes. King Gerard, Eric's father, is such a King, too. Eric has learned much from his father."

"King Gerard is well now? I read about his cancer," Marisol said, her hands unconsciously going to her heart. "How dreadful that the job for which Eric was born will become his when his own father dies. What a wretched feeling that must be for him. I cannot even imagine," Marisol said and shivered.

"Yes, it is," Roger said. "Gerard is Eric's King, but most importantly, his father, and Eric loves him tremendously. The Royal Family's faith got them through His Majesty's cancer treatments, but I'd be lying if I said the process wasn't scary for them all. But, yes, Gerard is free from cancer, thank God."

"Sí, gracias a Dios for His protection of King Gerard. I must admit that I have followed Eric's career for years, via the magazines, newspapers, and television news. He is unlike anyone else on this planet in this time. He is destined for many great things, Eric is. I

261

see this in him. He will change this world, not just Valdavia, I know that. He is touched by God," Marisol said, firm conviction in her voice.

Roger smiled at her. "You seem to know my lifelong friend as well as I do, Marisol. I have a feeling you two will hit it off fabulously."

Marisol laughed, a charming sound that warmed Roger's heart. He knew that Marisol was smitten with Eric and certain that Eric felt love for this pretty woman. An undeniable connection had formed between Eric and Marisol that evening, and Roger predicted a Royal Wedding in the not-too-distant future.

§§§§§

After the V.I.P. guests left the ballroom, Mrs. Salvator thanked Eric for helping the Foundation. "We have already generated far more donations during this fundraiser than the past four fundraisers combined, and this is entirely due to your participation, Prince Eric."

"Whatever the reason, I am elated. Please call on me anytime, and I will do whatever I can to help. Mrs. Salvator, I want to do more than just make a speech. In memory of my friend Elena, this is for the Foundation," Eric said, pulled a check from his uniform pocket, and slipped it in Mrs. Salvator's hand.

Mrs. Salvator gasped and said, "This is beyond generous, Your Royal Highness. Thank you, and may God continue to bless you." She shook his proffered hand, and only looked at the check after he walked away. "Dios Mio! Cinco mil dolares!" She looked back at Eric and uttered a prayer for his safekeeping and happiness.

Eric smiled as he neared Marisol and reached for her hand. "Shall we go to the suite now for our talk?"

"Sí. I have enjoyed my talk with Roger, but I do look forward to our conversation, Eric," Marisol said with a sparkle in her eyes.

"So do I," Eric replied.

As soon as they entered the suite, Roger and Stanley excused themselves, saying they felt tired. Both realized that Eric and Marisol desired to talk in private. Eric called room service for coffee, and while they waited, led Marisol onto the balcony to enjoy the gentle warmth of night.

"I've never been to Santander before. I never realized the beauties it held," Eric said and looked into Marisol's eyes.

"Nor did I," she whispered just as the doorbell rang.

"Our coffee. Excuse me," Eric said and rushed to the door. He wheeled the coffee cart to the patio, served the coffee, and sipped it as he thought how his life had suddenly and irrevocably changed. God had brought him love, as irrational as love at first sight seemed. Eric now knew how real and true that love feels.

"What are you thinking, Eric?" Marisol softly asked.

"How fairy tales do come true. How God keeps His promises. How happy I am for the first time in a dozen years." He stood and walked to the railing. As he clutched it with his hands, he bared his soul for the first time outside the pages of his diary. "In ten days, it will be the twelfth anniversary of—of—of Patrick's death. Twelve years. He would have celebrated his 31st birthday this past January 6. He was robbed of his life. Nineteen. He was only nineteen, so young and full of life and plans and ideas for the future. My younger brother died right in front of me, and I could do nothing to stop it. Nothing. I let him die. I let Patrick die. I will live with that forever."

Marisol went to him and put her hands on his shoulders. "Where is he now?" She felt Eric tense. "Where?"

"Heaven."

"Is he suffering still?"

"Of course not."

"He is healed, ¿sí?" Eric nodded. "He was healed by God as soon as his body died, ¿sí?" Eric nodded. "Your brother is alive and well and living in Heaven, with Dios y tu abuelos, ¿sí?" Eric nodded.

"Then let yourself live healed and whole, Eric. Exist with this guilt if you must, but do not let it stop you from actually living the life God intends for you. Patrick would not want that, would he?"

"No, he wouldn't. God brought you into my life, Marisol. You are my happiness, I know that." He turned toward her. "God must have a reason for everything, even if I don't understand. You are part of His purpose for me. Am I wrong or crazy? It doesn't feel wrong or crazy, does it?"

"No, it does not. It feels right. We both felt it instantly, sí, during your speech? I never once believed in this little-girl notion of love at first sight, but I swear on all that is holy that it is true and real, I feel it. So do you. Neither of us can deny its truth."

"No, we can't, Marisol. Yes, I felt it the first moment I saw you, as unbelievable as that sounds. If what I feel is not love, may God strike me right this minute," Eric said, his voice filled with emotions.

Several seconds later, Marisol smiled at him and said, "God did nothing to you just then. He obviously approves of our merger." Eric laughed. "Why do you laugh at me?"

"I am sorry, my dear. I'm not laughing at you, but at your word choice. Merger. It sounds like a business deal," he giggled.

"Oh? I should use a different word? Which one?

"In French, the word is mariage."

"Oh? In Spanish the word is matrimonio."

"So it is," Eric said and smiled.

"You will stay happy now? You will keep this smile?"

"With you in my life, Marisol, yes, I will. How could I not?"

Marisol traced one of the medals on Eric's uniform. "Bueno. Live in happiness and light, Eric, not unhappiness. Do not punish yourself any longer. That is wrong. God does not want us to live without joy. You know that. Carry Patrick in your heart. Remember him and honor him. Be forever grateful that he was your brother for on earth for nineteen years. But do not let his death cast you into a life of unhappiness. Now that you have opened yourself to happiness, embrace it. Welcome it. Cherish it. Please."

"I will. I promise. God brought your light and beauty and kindness into my life. You have brightened my life. How can my soul ever return to sorrow and deny its happiness ever again?"

The couple talked for another three hours, at which time Eric escorted Marisol to her car and watched her drive away—after promising to meet her later that day for the promised visit to her church.

Eric returned to his suite, sat at the desk in his room, and wrote in his diary.

10 July 1989

I am in love. I know love. I always had faith that she and I would find one another when the time is right. I never worried or really wondered. I left it up to God. He brought us together.

I saw her as I gave the speech. I knew at that instant. Love at first sight. Plain, simple, wondrous, and miraculous. She is the love of my life, my one and only. She is my future wife, the mother of our children.

I had to force myself to look at other people during the speech. My eyes quickly returned to her. She stared at me. We both know. We are meant to be together. We are.

It is not just that she is beautiful. Oh, she is very beautiful. It is far deeper than that. After the speech, I asked Roger to bring her to my table. We talked the rest of the night. She is everything to me.

Leaving her early this morning was the most difficult thing. We will see each other today and tomorrow, before I must return to Valmondois. I have been to Spain several times, and never saw her before. Our time is now.

I feel—what? Elated? Ecstatic? Buoyant? All of that and so much more. I have only heard men talk of love in this way in Shakespearean plays. Not in real life. I feel like poor Romeo. He was a child. I am 34. That has no bearing.

I am in love! I love Marisol. Marisol loves me. God has begun writing my love story.

Eric could not stop smiling. His happiness contained no boundaries. Inspired by this new feeling, he wrote a poem on the following page, one that expressed his emotions and elation. Unlike Patrick, Eric never wrote poetry to articulate his thoughts, ideas, and feelings. He preferred the prose of his diary entries, even though he enjoyed reading and thinking about the poetry of others. However, this night would remain the most magical of his life, that he knew.

Love at First Sight

All of my life I have dared never dream

That love at first sight could happen to me,

But the truth is greater than any dream.

With one look I know we are meant to be;

At first glance I knew we will be a team,

A pair in love throughout eternity.

You alone allowed me to believe

The truth of happily-ever-after,

That love is real and will never leave.

I sent up my prayer and have the answer.

In my heart and soul you forever weave

The story that writes my greatest chapter,

The rest of my life lived in blissfulness.

We share love, we share joy, and we share life;

Now I truly understand happiness.

I am yours, you are mine, to be my wife

For a lifetime of only peacefulness,

Not just this life, but in the afterlife.

You made my heart believe in fairy tales.

§§§§

Marisol drove to her childhood home, where she still lived with her parents. Once there, she tiptoed into her parents' bedroom and gently shook her mother. "What is wrong, mi hija?"

"Shh. Do not wake Papá. Come with me, please."

Juanita groggily sat up, slid her feet into her slippers, and put on her robe. She followed her daughter into the living room, where Marisol grabbed her mother's arms and sat her on the sofa. "What is this about? Is something wrong?"

"No. Everything is perfect, Mamá, absolutely perfect and beautiful!" Marisol exclaimed and twirled, her gown floating around her legs. Oh, Mamá, I have finally done it! I have done it!" Marisol smiled, clasped her hands in front of her, and said, "I am getting married!"

Juanita leapt to her feet, stunned, but before she could ask any questions, her daughter launched into the detailed story of this magical night. As she finished, Marisol said, "Oh, Mamá, he is the man meant for me, and I am the woman meant for him. We both know that. We both felt love at first sight. Oh, I know I poo-pooed that most of my life, but I felt it as soon as I saw him in the flesh. I felt it! There is nothing like this feeling! You always told me that I would know when I am in love, and I do, Mamá, I do!

"This is my one true love. We were brought together by God. We both waited until our mid-thirties for this moment, and now we have found each other. We talked most of the night, and we have so much in common. I know him so well, even his lifelong best friend said so. He is such a godly man, and he is so kind and caring. You will love him, too, Mamá, and so will Papá. I know that. So, too, will Eduardo. Oh, Mamá, I never dreamed I could feel so happy!

"He was at the banquet, the one I feared would be boring. But it was far from boring. He was there! Life can never be boring with him!" Marisol sat beside her mother and took hold of her hands. "Mamá, I am in love! For the first time in my life, I feel love! Now I know what you meant when you said my heart will tell me when I have found love, when I have met the man I am meant to marry. I have found him, and we will marry!"

Marisol stood and said, "I do not know when, but I do know we will marry. Oh, and Mamá, he is a Prince, and his name is Eric." Marisol blew her mother a kiss, opened the front, door, and left.

Juanita, her brain spinning crazily in the wake of her daughter's dramatic monologue, looked at the clock. 3:45. She might as well make the morning coffee so she could prepare Alejandro for Marisol's bombshell.

§§§§§

Not long after, Roger arose, attired in pajamas and robe, and made his way to the suite kitchen for a glass of orange juice. He noticed Eric on the balcony, watching the stars still glimmering in the sky. He carried his juice to the balcony, where he greeted his friend.

"You're up awfully early. Aren't you tired?" Roger looked at Eric for the first time, noticed he still wore the military uniform, and he quickly amended his questions. "You never went to bed? You've been awake all night?"

"Good morning, Roger," Eric said and giggled. "Yes, I've been awake all night. Marisol left around 3:00. We talked for hours. I feel wonderful, Roger."

"You and she talked quite a lot last night. I think it's safe to say you two hit it off, huh?"

"We did more than that, Roger. She's my soulmate, my one and only. Listen, I'm going to shower and change now. I'm spending the day with Marisol. You don't mind, do you? I know we planned to sightsee."

"Mind? Heck, no, man. I saw you two during dinner. I knew. Stanley did, too. Don't worry about me. I'll take in some sights and relax. Enjoy your time with Marisol while we're here."

"Thanks, Roger."

A few hours later, Roger informed Eric that Marisol telephoned. Eric beamed when he heard her voice. "How are you, Marisol? Have you gotten any sleep?"

"Sleep? No. But I'm running on felicidad," she said with a giggle. "About today. After our talk last night, do you still need to talk with Father Tervas?"

"Not particularly. I was able to open up about Patrick for the first time, and that really did help. You are my guardian angel, I swear. From the first moment, you changed me completely."

"God is responsible, my love. God is in charge of this."

"I know. He brought us together."

"Yes. I thought today we can visit my family, and you can meet mi Mamá y mi Papá y mi hermano. ¿Sí?"

"Yes. I will like that a lot."

"Good. I will pick you up at the Hotel at diez. Is that a good time?"

"It's perfect. I'll be ready. There is just one thing, Marisol. We'll have company. Stanley. He goes everywhere I go."

"Ah, but of course, tú guardia. I am glad he does. In this world, you need him. But what about Roger? He will be alone, will he not?"

"He said he'll see some sights, but yes, he'll be alone. We had planned to sightsee together, but that was before last night," Eric said.

"Then he will come, too. He is part of your life, sí. He is your longest friend, and he works with you. We cannot ignore him. Tell him to be ready, too."

"I love you more for that, Marisol. Thank you for having such a kind spirit. We'll be waiting."

"Roger. Stanley. Marisol is coming here at ten to pick us up. She's taking me to meet her family, and you two are also invited."

"I figured Stanley would go, of course, but you didn't have to weasel an invitation for me," Roger said. "I'm fine with going to some museums on my own."

"I didn't weasel you an invitation. Marisol mentioned you first. She invited you. She knows we're best friends, and she doesn't want you to be alone most of the day."

"Wow. She is something special. Most women wouldn't want their man's friends hanging around. She's a keeper."

"Yes, she is, Roger. She most definitely is a gem."

§§§§§

"Mis padres live not far from here," Marisol told the three men when they left the center of Santander. "I still live with them, one of the old customs which my family observe. It used to be that a daughter lives with her parents until she is married, and then she and her husband live together. Not many families still follow these customs, and these are considered old-fashioned to many people now. All of my friends constantly tell me to get an apartment or to move in with a man. I tell them I cannot live with a man to whom I am not married. That is a sin. They laugh at me, but I do not care."

"Good for you, Marisol. I got some teasing when I was at Cambridge for not getting my own home. I still live with my parents, too, which is, I know, unusual for a man. I am so proud of you for staying true to yourself and your values, enormously proud," Eric said.

"It is different for you, ¿sí? You are the next king, and you help your father, King Gerard, ¿no es cierto? I suppose you could get a home of your own, but it would never be as secure as the Palace, and besides that, you work at the Palace, too. It makes sense for you to live there, Eric. You must be such a blessing to tus padres," Marisol said and smiled at Eric.

"I'd like to think so. The most important factor about where we live is the love that fills the home. Without love, it's just a house, a shelter, but with love, it's a home, a nurturing haven from the ills of this world. My family has always had a home, regardless of its age and size. The people who dwell within its walls are the most important part, and I've been surrounded by the most loving people all of my life," Eric said with certainty.

"Sí. My life has been the same, with Mamá, Papá, and Eduardo. So much love to fill our hearts and our lives. Oh, Eric, I know they will love you so, and that you will love them, too. I told Mamá about last night's magic early this morning, after I left the Hotel. I told her everything in one fell swoop, and then I left for a drive. I could not sleep, and I could not stay confined to such a small space, so I left for the wide-open city."

"I didn't sleep after you left, either. I didn't even shower and change until around 3:45. I feel like I've been floating on a cloud since the fundraiser," Eric admitted, though not to Roger's and Stanley's surprise. They had seen it all throughout the banquet, especially Stanley, who had kept his eyes on Eric's viewpoint during the speech. He had seen the brunette who had caught the Prince's attention, and he had noticed that he held her captive, as well. Both Stanley and Roger knew that the proverbial fireworks show had heralded the couple's love during the dinner.

"Sí, yo también, mi Eric." Marisol smiled, and said, "We are almost there. Soon you meet mi Papá y mi Mamá. I can barely wait until they meet you," she gushed as a teenaged girl does.

Eric smiled at her and felt his heart swell with love. His first sight of their charming cottage enchanted him. He seemed to have stepped into an animated fairy tale, the perfect setting for this most quixotic of experiences he would ever know.

Marisol leapt from her car, ran to Eric, grabbed his hand, and ran into the house yelling, "Mamá! Papá! Conoce a mi amor!" An attractive brunette woman entered the living room, wiping her hands on her apron. "Mamá, this is him, the marvelous man I told you about last ni. . . a few hours ago. This is Eric, mi amor."

"It is you who has won corazón de mi hija. Who else? She said your name is Eric and you are a Prince. You are here for the fundraiser, I see that for months in the papers. And this one almost did not go. She said these dinners are always boring. 'They have the money I sent, so why must I go?' she continued to ask me. I tell her, 'Then do not go.' But soon before it begins, she comes out in this red gown, tells me she might as well go, because one never knows. 'Tonight may be quite different, Mamá.' And she returns at the most irrazonable time, makes me sit here, and tells me she is enamorado. And then she leaves me sitting here as if un huracán hit me. What do you think of that, I ask you?" Juanita said, charming her guests.

"I say that this is the most enchanting tale I have ever heard. I say that I, too, am enamorado, Mamá," Eric said as he held Juanita's hand and smiled at her.

"And who is directing this play? Walt Disney?" a man asked from the doorway.

"Eduardo! Usted vino!" Marisol exclaimed and ran to hug the tall, dark man.

"How could I not? Mi hermana calls and tells me she has a very important and special person for me to meet. She does not tell me anything else. Incredibly mysterious. And then I arrive, and I hear nuestra Mamá tell this fairy tale, and I find you standing here with the future King de Valdavia. How is this possible? The fundraiser was but a few hours ago."

"Eduardo, mi hermano lógico, have you never heard of love at first sight?"

"But of course! For many years, you condenar this idea, say it is not true. Now you say it happened to you. What am I to believe?"

"Believe tu hermana," another man said from the kitchen door. "Look at her. Listen to her. Can you not see it is true? Está en sus ojos."

"Papá!" Marisol said and ran to hug her father. "You were listening. I knew you would understand, I knew it. You believe, too, ¿sí?"

"Sí. Tu madre y yo sabemos. It happened to us many moons ago, mi hija." Alejandro removed himself from his daughter's embrace and walked to Eric. "I see it in you, young man. Amas a nuestra hija, ¿verdad?"

"Sí, lo hago mucho, Señor," Eric replied in flawless Spanish.

"She loves you. You love her. I see that. It is all I need," Alejandro said.

"Mamá, ¿y usted?" Marisol asked.

"Sí, it is enough for me, mi hija y Eric," Juanita said and kissed them both on their cheeks.

"Eduardo?" Marisol asked. "Quiero tu bendición, también."

"You have my blessing, mi hermana." He kissed his older sister's cheek, and then he turned to Eric and hugged him. "As do you, Eric. Bienvenido a nuestra familia. Welcome to our family," he translated.

"Come, we have tea and cake to celebrate," Juanita said. "Alejandro, you help. We will prepare the tray."

"Let me help, Mamá. I want to," Eric said and linked his arm with hers.

"You are a blessing for tu Mamá y tu Papá. And now you are a blessing to nuestra hija y para nosotros. You love Marisol. Marisol loves you. Alejandro y yo te amo. Eres ahora nuestro hijo, Eric. We now have two sons, Alejandro and you," Juanita said and kissed his cheek.

§§§§

After a lengthy lunch overflowing with delicious food, conversation, and laughter, everyone went off in pairs. Juanita and Marisol cleaned and then washed dishes so that they could talk heart-to-heart. Eduardo asked Eric to take a stroll with him, so they could get to know one another. Stanley discreetly followed them. That left Alejandro and Roger to chat for a while.

"Mamá, you like Eric, ¿sí?"

"Sí, mi hija, I do. Eric, he is a very kind and caring man. I have read about him, sí, but now I see him with my own eyes and with my heart. I can tell that his heart and his soul are godly and good. I can tell that his love for you is real and sincere."

"Oh, Mamá, I am so alegre, because I, too see that. I see his love for me, Mamá, I do. Not lust or physical attraction, no. Love. Eric is unlike any man I have ever met. I recognized that instantly. I knew that. I felt that. When Eric walked to the podium, and I saw him, when I looked into his soul, I knew. I knew that Eric is my one and only love, the man God sent to me. I prayed for him for many years, Mamá, and I waited patiently for him, and now he is with me, in my life and in my heart."

Juanita touched her daughter's left ring finger. "When you were thirteen years of age, I told you that you should wait for Dios to bring you and your soulmate together. I gave you this ring as a symbol of your promise to trust Dios and to avoid temptation. I knew in my heart that Dios would provide the man for whom you dreamed and prayed, because He had brought tu Papá y yo together as one. I told you that your heart will tell you when you have met him, did I not?" Marisol nodded. "And how could I know that? I knew, because the same thing, it happened to me. The first time I saw Alejandro, my heart told me that he is my one true love. And we are now married for forty-one years this past April 20. I have never one time thought of another man."

"Oh, Mamá, I know. I pray that Eric y yo remain as incredibly happy together for as long as tu y Papá."

"Longer, mi hija, longer. I pray tu y Eric celebrate twice as many years as esposo y esposa."

Marisol pulled her mother into a hug as both women shed tears of joy.

§§§§§

"Eric, I have seen you in newspapers, magazines, and on television. I have read what kind of person you are, but now I meet you, and I learn you are more than people say. I see the way you look at Marisol. I do not see in you what I see when other men look at her, nothing more than lust and desire. I see love. It is in your eyes, the way you smile at her, the way you watch her, the way you attend to her. For the first time, I see a man look at mi hermana with love and respect," Eduardo said as he and Eric slowly walked through the neighborhood. Stanley followed, but provided the young men as much privacy as possible.

"Gracias, Eduardo," Eric said. "I appreciate that, truly I do. I never even dated all through school and university, nor after. I never had any desire to date merely because it's what most people do, and I certainly never desired a romantic relationship outside of marriage. Most of my life, I have trusted that God would bring me and the woman He chose for me together when it is His time, not mine. He has, last night. I'm sure it sounds highly romantic and perhaps immature and, as you said, straight out of a Disney fairy tale, but it's true. I knew that Marisol is my one and only love as soon as I saw her. I knew in my heart and soul and mind; all of me knew instantly. How can I say it any other way?"

"You do not need to, Eric, "Eduard said with a smile. "I see it in you, and I hear it, too. It fills every part of you. I never put any truth in the childhood ideal of love at first sight, never. I will be honest with you, man to man. I have had a few relationships. Have I ever been in love? No, I have not. I have not met someone who does this to me. Besides, I am too busy with my career anyway to make time for love, as much as that seems wrong. But, it is my truth. If we are to become brothers, Eric, that relationship must be built on truth and honesty, ¿sí?"

"Absolutely, Eduardo. I have my beliefs and values, but I also know that your sister and I are in the minority. Not many people wait until marriage. That is a personal decision, and it is not my place to condemn or judge prople for the choices they make. Marisol and you have a beautiful bond, I can tell. She was your protective big sister when you were both children, looking out for you. Right?"

Eduardo giggled. "Sí. Marisol stood up for me many times, and she fought bullies who threatened me. She is fierce, that one.

She will become a lioness with your children, I tell you, Eric. She will not let anyone or anything hurt them in any way."

Eric smiled. "Our child. I can see her now," Eric said in a day-dreamy tone.

"Her? You see a daughter of yours and Marisol's? She will be a pretty brunette, ¿sí?"

Eric looked at Eduardo and smiled, but he didn't respond. *No, Eduardo. She is blonde and beautiful. Angelic.* Eric put his arm around Eduardo's shoulders and said, "I can hardly wait for her to be born and to meet her uncle."

§§§§§

"Eric, I wish we could stay together forever," Marisol said the next morning as they stood on a lush hill overlooking the heart of Santander. "I do not want to be apart from you."

"Nor I from you. But we will visit each other as often as possible. I want you to meet my parents. They will love you, I know that. You will love Mother and Father, too."

"I know I will. You are their son, and they made you. They are wonderful people. I already love then for making you for me," Marisol said and put her arms around Eric.

Eric laughed joyously and held her close to him. Te amo, mi amor. I love you. It's just that those words can never express what I feel for you, no matter the language in which they are spoken. No word can."

"I do not need words. All I need is to look at you, and I see your love for me. I see it in how you look at me, as if you see me for te first time with each look. I see it in how you treat me, tenderly and respectfully, as if you place me up high in your thoughts. I feel it when you hold my hand or like now, when you hold me to you and I feel tu corazón beating. We do not need words."

"Just like three nights ago when we were the only two people in that crowded ballroom. You will forever be the only woman to me and for me, Marisol, the only woman," Eric said, his voice dripping with emotion.

"I feel that I am Lucy Muir and you are Daniel Gregg. We are meant to be together for all time, mi Eric. Not even time and space will ever separate us or weaken our love," Marisol said.

Eric sighed. "No. Never. Ours is a strong love, an eternal love, a love blessed by God. Our love remains indestructible."

Marisol snuggled closer to him in their final moments before Eric left Spain. "I like that. I love our love." She smiled up at him. "I will visit Valmondois, mi amor, and see my future home. I live for our reunion, Eric."

"As do I," Eric softly said. "Let me know when you will come to Valmondois, and I will come for you in Father's plane."

Marisol smiled and traced his shirt collar with her finger. "Or perhaps I will surprise you, no?"

§§§§

12 July 1989

I arrived home from Spain a short time ago, and I miss Marisol dreadfully. I don't know how to continue as normal with these feelings swirling through me: love and need. Yes, I love her, and I need her with me. Now that I have found her, now that God has brought her to me, I cannot exist without her.

However, my next task is to tell Father and Mother about Marisol and our deep love. I know they will understand and believe me, just as Marisol's family do. What a wonderful union this will be, merging our two families for all time. How I look forward to my future! Thank you, God.

§§§§

"Hey, Eric, you have no idea how this makes me feel! It's been far too long, bro, and it's about time you opened your heart to love and happiness. I look at you and see my brother the way I remember him, smiling, happy, content with life.

"I know this is a forever thing for you, and I also know that God has a huge part in this. He placed you two together. Roll with it, you know, follow where it leads. She's not gonna break your heart, and she's gonna bring you a lifetime of happiness and love. Way to go, Eric!" Patrick enthused as he looked down from Heaven at his brother.

"Daddy!" Angilia nearly shouted as she joined her uncle. "He's so happy! Oh, this is what I have prayed for so long."

"Yeah. That's what love does to a man," Patrick said and smiled at her.

"Love? Daddy is in love? With—with my mother?"

"Yeah, sure."

"Then I'll be born soon? I'll be with him soon? When can I see my mother?"

"When you are born, Angilia," Michael said from behind her. "You will be born when it is your time, as well, just as we discussed before. There are some things you are not meant to see or to know before your earthly life begins. You know that. I understand your feelings, but God's guidelines must be obeyed."

Patrick saw her overwhelming sadness. "I understand. I promise to remain patient, no matter what I feel. God knows what is best for me," Angilia said, hiding her pain from Michael—or so she thought. "Excuse me, Michael and Uncle Patrick. I am going to assist Gabriel," she said and ran off quickly. She didn't want to cry in front of Michael.

"This is gonna be rough on Angilia, you know. She loves Eric so much, almost too much, and she's prayed for his happiness since she brought me here. There's no risk of her seeing her mother?" Michael assured him there wasn't. "So, her mother is essentially invisible to her. I guess Eric will be, too, when he's with Marisol, which will be quite often. Wow. Everyone else sees this, just not Angilia. That's tough."

278

"It seems so, I know. But it must be. Never discuss Marisol around Angilia, not for any reason."

"Sure thing. I've seen Marisol. I've heard her and Eric talk. This is his forever happiness. They'll be together for decades. I've waited for this myself, you know. This is the grooviest thing that's happened since I moved here," Patrick said, flashed a peace sign, and ran off.

How long Eric and Marisol remain together has long been known, son. Their love will endure no matter what else befalls them, though, rest assured of that. Their love will buoy them through all of the storms and trials that assail them. Eventually, they will live eternally joyful, with their daughter, in Heaven. That is guaranteed, Patrick. You will be with them then, as well, Michael thought. *Eric and Marisol will face pain, but their love will prevail.*

§§§§

Eric's parents returned from meetings; they hadn't been home when he and Roger got back. Roger, already back in his office, greeted Gerard with telephone messages. Gerard asked Roger to inform Eric he wanted to speak with him, so Roger called Eric's sitting room, where he worked at his desk.

Within minutes, Eric tapped on his father's office door, and Gerard happily said, "Come in, Son!"

Eric stood, his hands on the chair back, and smiled. Gerard glanced up at his son and dropped the papers he'd been holding onto the desk.

"Eric, I take it your trip to Spain was quite productive. Something remarkable happened there."

"It was pretty amazing, yes," Eric said, still beaming. "I've never experienced a more incredible trip."

"Yes, I see. What is her name?"

"Marisol," Eric instantly replied. "Father, I knew the moment I saw her that she is the one true love of my life. It's not her beauty or the location. It's her. I just knew the first moment I saw her. I can't explain it any other way. I stared at her. She stared at me.

279

During my speech, we stared at each other. It's as if we were the only two people in that ballroom, it was. We both knew instantly. We talked until around 3:00 that morning, and that day, she took me, Roger, and Stanley to her parents' home, where we spent the entire day. I met her parents and her brother, and they are so wonderful, Father. I felt so at ease with them from the minute I entered their home. Marisol and I spent nearly every moment together until I left Spain. Nothing has ever felt as real and as natural as being with her, Father. I know love at first sight sounds ludicrous to many people, but I can testify how real it is. Nothing is more real than our love."

Gerard looked into Eric's eyes, and he, too, saw what Juanita, Alejandro, and Eduardo had seen. "I can recognize that clearly, Son. I wondered when love would find you. It has. Love does have a way of changing everything in a man's life. We view everything through different eyes, through a different perspective. No longer is every decision selfish, about just us. Now everything contains and concerns her, too. That is not such a bad thing, I can tell you that," he said and smiled.

Gerard continued. "Love is a partnership, Eric. Every decision is a joint affair. Social circles and social lives change. Behaviors change. When you love another, you consider her preferences, her desires, her beliefs. You no longer live a solitary existence. All of that disappears. So, too, do loneliness and sadness. When you share life with someone, you also have a confidante, a best friend with whom you can share your thoughts, emotions, ideas, and to whom you can unburden your troubles. That is what your mother and I have shared for over forty years now. Such a union is a miracle of sorts."

"I know," Eric said and walked to the office window. "I shared my deepest pain with Marisol that first night, after the fundraiser, on the Grand Hotel balcony. She talked to me with compassion and sympathy, but she also talked straight and told me what I needed to hear."

Gerard looked at his son, whose back and shoulders no longer slumped even slightly. "By the looks and sound of you, Marisol herself performed some sort of miracle. She set you free from bondage after a dozen years."

Eric turned and faced his father. "The pain and guilt will live in me for the rest of my life, but they do not control me any longer, Father. Marisol finally helped me to acknowledge what I knew but had denied. I thought that my guilt was some sort of penance I had to pay. I told her that I sought, that I needed, absolution—from Patrick. I have God's forgiveness, I know that, but I needed Patrick's. Marisol helped me to admit that Patrick is fine where he is, whole and healed, and that he has nothing to forgive. Somehow, it took those few minutes with Marisol to purge my soul."

Gerard nodded and stood facing his son. "I told you the same thing, yes, but the messenger is the difference. I've known and loved you since your birth, and you think I'm partial. Marisol had just met you, and she loves you in a far different manner. What she said, she told you from her heart in order to heal the heart of the man whom she loves. A woman's love works wonders, Eric. Treasure it, cherish it, treat it as the golden fortune from God that it is. A man is gifted this rare gift only once in his lifetime, my son."

§§§§§

One week later, Eric typically arose quite early, exercised, showered, dressed in a suit, and then sat at his desk. He bowed his head in silent prayer, and when finished, took some stationery from a desk drawer.

19 July 1989

Dear Patrick:

How I love you! You are my brother, and I will forever love you. You are so very special, and by now you would have accomplished so much. You would have completely blown my mind, as you used to say. You would be among the leading officers in the Valdavian Army. You would have met with various world leaders in your quest for world peace, and you would have given them many ideas and tactics that would have changed their minds and their policies. You would have changed this world, all for the better, Patrick. I know that. Your drive and your passion remained firm and contagious. You would have won over so many world leaders on the strength of those alone. Let's not discount your charm and charisma, either. You could melt the heart of the mythical Ice King.

I miss you more than you will ever know. Oh, Patrick, you were supposed to co-reign with me. We were a team. Now I must face this life and this duty without my strongest supporter and ally, without my closest friend.

You should have been here for all of life's milestones, yours and mine. I was to be your best man when you married the love of your life, and you were to be mine. Now I will marry Marisol without you beside me. I will not have a best man, Patrick. No one can replace you.

I so wanted to rush to your room last week and tell you all about my true love: everything—every detail, every emotion—everything. We would have celebrated to your kooky music, with our favorite drink, lemonade. You would have shared my joy. And you would have been here when Marisol visits, and the two of you would have bonded instantly as the two most important people in the world to me. You would have loved her as the sister you never had, and she would have loved you as a second brother.

Gosh, Patrick, you would have been with me when I first saw my newborn daughter, my blonde-haired, blue-eyed Angel. Oh, Patrick, she would have had the best uncle in the world. You two would have shared secrets and played games. You would have nourished her creativity and her imagination. You would have read poetry to her. You would have helped her with her homework. You would have sung her to sleep with your versions of lullabies. You would have helped her to become a zebra in a field of horses, just as you are.

But none of that can ever happen. Twelve years ago, our lives changed. I am so incredibly sorry, Patrick. I know you well enough to know that you do not blame me. No matter what had happened, you would never blame me, even if I deserved blame. Your loyalty and love are too strong for that. That does not exempt me from blaming myself for robbing you of all of this and more. I would give up my own life if it would reverse what happened twelve years ago. You are so important for this world, my brother, and I would thankfully and willingly change places with you in an instant.

I suppose that is wishful thinking, huh? God doesn't rewrite history. That means I am stuck here, on earth, without my brother, my partner, my best friend. I pray we reunite someday, when this life of mine ends. I will do all in my power to make sure that happens.

Until then, Patrick, carry my love in your soul. I do love you.

Eric

Eric folded the sheets and placed them in an envelope, which he closed and then placed his wax seal over the flap. He wrote *Patrick* on the front, and then carried it to his brother's suite. He placed it inside *The Possibility of Peace*, the book he had bought as Patrick's 1977 Christmas gift. He slid the book back onto the shelf, patted it, and closed Patrick's door behind him when he left.

Patrick looked around, saw several angels, so went to an upper room in the spheres, where he made sure he was alone. He quickly went to earth, to the Palace, and lighted on his balcony, where he quietly went into his sitting room. He slid the book off of the self, slipped the envelope out, and returned the book.

He then went to his desk and got a piece of paper and a pen. He poised the pen, only to hear Angilia calling for him, telling him, "Great-Grandfather is looking for you, Uncle Patrick! You better get back here fast!" Patrick had intended to write his brother a note, but he realized the error in that. He grabbed a puzzle box from his desk and stuffed it in his hoodie pocket. He replaced the paper and pen and zoomed back to the Angels Choir.

"Where were you? You left the Spheres, didn't you?" Angilia asked.

"Yeah, but just for a moment. No one missed me."

"They almost did. You are fortunate that another angel needed Great-Grandfather's council before he discovered that you had left. What is so important that you had to risk rebuke?"

Patrick dared not tell his niece the truth, for she might try to go to earth again and see Eric. "I had to get something, that's all."

"I hope it's worth it if Grandfather or Michael find out."

"I brought you something. I bet you no other angel has one of these," he said with a smile and pulled the box from his pocket.

"What is it?" Angilia asked as he held it out toward her. "It is pretty."

"Yeah. It's from Japan. It's a puzzle box. To open it, you have to solve a puzzle. I thought you'd have some fun with it, Little One. Go for it."

"You are not going to help me, are you?"

"Of course not," Patrick said with a laugh. "The fun and challenge lies in figuring it out. Go on, give it a try, and I'll go find out what Grandfather wants."

Patrick did, but after that, he went somewhere private where he could read Eric's letter. He did, and even if his brother couldn't hear him, he answered the letter by talking to Eric. "Hey, has it really been a dozen years? There's no time here, you know, so I had no idea. I love you, too, Eric, you know that. I always will. I hope you know that, too. You should. Yeah, we were the best of friends. I'd have done anything for you, buddy, anything.

"I miss being around you. I so wish I could be there for all that's going on with you. General DeBruce Martineau. I would have cheered you the loudest that day. I would have helped you when Father was sick. You are so strong. You always were. But even strong men need help and need to let go of baggage they carry. Don't ever think you caused my accident, Eric. No one did. It just happened. I do know that I was meant to die that day. For a few years before the accident, I felt that I wouldn't live a long life. I sensed I would die young. I accepted it. That's just how my life was planned. Maybe someday I can tell you all this, and it will help.

"I wish I was there with you to celebrate yours and Marisol's love. I've seen it, which you can't know, and I see how true and deep it is. I wish you knew that I am friends with my niece, your unborn daughter. You've seen her, and you know she's your daughter. She loves you so, so much, Eric, and she will for all eternity. You and she will be the ones who change the world, I know that from eavesdropping on Grandfather and Michael.

"I wish most of all I could tell you the purpose for my death. I brought you and Angilia together before her birth. I'm not sure why, but that's part of God's plan. See, she snuck off against orders all those times before my death, and some after, but the day she came for me was God's doing. He let you see her. And when you did, the puzzle pieces finally came together, and you figured out the truth. Your angel visitor is your future daughter. Just hold out a few more years, Eric, and she will be with you. I look forward to watching that. You'll have a most wonderful life, Eric, even with the pain and heartbreak that come into your life.

"I'll always be with you, even if you can't see me or hear me. Okay? Be happy and be the mind-blowing man and king I know you'll be. Love you, bro."

CHAPTER 13

“As Eric worked on a school board proposal at his desk, he received a telephone call from the front gate security. “Yes? Is anything the matter?”

“No, Sir, not exactly. You have a visitor at the gates. She said to tell you it’s your surprise.”

Eric stood and excitedly said, “I’m coming down,” and ran down the stairs without replacing the receiver on the phone. As soon as he opened the front door, he asked the guards to unlock the gate, and he sprinted. “Marisol! This is the most beautiful surprise!” he said and held her at arm’s length as if seeing her for the first time.

She laughed joyfully, a sound which filled Eric’s entire being with ecstasy. “I had to. It has been far too long, mi amor, far too long. Our daily telephone conversations have been lovely, but to tell you the truth, they make me long to see you all the more,” Marisol said as she smiled up at him.

“Where are your things, your luggage?”

“I brought only this,” she said and lifted a round train case. I did not take the time to pack a lot of things, because, well, because seeing you is too urgent. I will buy new outfits in my soon-to-be ciudad natal, my new hometown, ¿sí?”

Eric laughed. "You will have everything your heart desires."

"Mi corazón solo te desea, mi Eric. Only you."

Eric leaned closer and whispered, "And mine desires only you, my love." He took her hand, smiled, and said, "Come. Meet Father and Mother! They'll be as surprised as I am."

"Lucie, do you know where Mother is?" Eric asked as his mother's lady-in-waiting walked toward the back-patio door.

"Yes, Eric. Queen Matilda is in her car waiting for me. She has a visit to Hamley's Department Store to officially open the new rooftop restaurant. I must go, I am sorry. She is waiting for me. Please excuse me."

"Of course, Lucie. Thank you." He turned to Marisol. "That is frequently a risk around here. Both Mother and Father have busy schedules, I'm afraid. I think Father has appointments this afternoon. Let's check his office. It's on the fourth floor. Are you up for all of these stairs?"

"Sí," Marisol said with a giggle. "I need the exercise. Marisol glanced around as much as she could as they climbed the stairs. "Your Palace is magnifico, Eric, incredible."

Eric laughed. "It's not my Palace. I just live and work here."

"It will be yours, ¿no? You will become the country's next Rey, and you will be the mayordomo of this Palace, the custodian, is that the right word?"

"I suppose it is, actually. This Palace was given to Christophe in 1331, and each King de Valdavia has lived here since then. Each King protects and cares for the Palace and its history for future generations, so I guess we are custodians. Well, we've made it. Father's office is just ahead."

Roger nearly bumped into Eric as he walked toward the stairs. "If you're looking for your father, he's not in there. He's getting ready for a meeting of the banking consortium. Anything important?"

Roger noticed Marisol and smiled. "I see it is. Gee, I'm sorry, Eric and Marisol, but there's nothing I can do at this point."

"It is all right, Roger," Marisol said. "I came without telling even Eric. It was a surprise. I will meet Eric's parents later. Go, Rey Gerard is waiting for you."

Eric smiled at Marisol. "Thanks for being so understanding about this. Let me get you settled in your rooms, and you can freshen up. After that, what do you say I give you a tour around this place? This will be your permanent home one day, after all."

"Sí, mi hogar. Mi hogar permanente," Marisol reverentially said. "I would live in a one-room shack with you, Eric, and be the happiest woman in this world. Wherever you live, my happiness lives."

"Hmmm," Eric sighed. "I like that, mi amor, and I feel the same. This past month without you has been so torturous for me. It will be the same when you return to Spain."

"I have a second surprise for my Eric," Marisol said and smiled at him. "I am not returning. I talked to mi Mamá y mi Papá y Eduardo. I tell them that I want to live in Valmondois, to know the city where I will live with you, Eric. I will rent an apartment close to the Palace and be with you every day. I will never leave you again!"

"Marisol? You're staying?" She nodded. "This is the happiest news you can tell me right now. But you are not renting an apartment."

"But I must. I cannot live here, even with all of these rooms. I cannot. You understand that, ¿sí?"

The despair in her eyes stabbed Eric's heart. "I do understand, but you still do not need an apartment. Let's get your things to your suite, and then I must show you something."

Marisol remained mystified as Eric took her hand and led her out onto the expansive back lawn. Separated from the Palace and shrouded by trees and shrubs sat his surprise for her. "This is a mostly unused guest house. You will live here, in your own house on the

Palace grounds, my love, and we will be near one another. Come, let me show you around the house," Eric said and took keys from his pocket.

"This huge mansion for just me? This is far too much, Eric, really."

"Then use only the man floor, darling. Use what you need. This is perfect. You will be near, plus you will have the security of the Palace grounds. This is ideal. See," Eric said when he opened the door. "It's fully furnished, and it has every convenience. You can have your clothes and things sent from Santander to here. Say yes, Marisol."

"Sí. I will live here until we are casado. If your parents approve, I will. We will ask them, ¿sí?"

"They'll approve, Marisol, but, yes, we'll ask them this afternoon," Eric said and kissed her forehead.

§§§§§

Matilda returned from her event half an hour before Gerard's meeting ended, much to Eric's excitement. He longed for his parents to meet his future wife. He turned to Marisol as they sat in the music room and asked, "Are you ready to meet Mother, darling?"

"Not now, please. I would like to meet them together, at the same time, if that is all right, please. I know that sounds silly, but that is what I kept seeing in my head when I imagine this first meeting."

Eric leaned forward and took hold of her hands. "It is far from silly, Marisol. Father's meeting is over soon, so we won't have long to wait. I want to have tea waiting in the sitting room for them when I ask them to come here. It's just across the hall," Eric motioned. "We can meet and talk there. While you were changing earlier, I asked the cook, Pierre, to prepare the tea and some light sandwiches. I hope that is all right."

"It is perfect, mi amor. You are so pensativo, thoughtful, as you say. Your parents return home after these meetings and events, and you have alimento, refreshments, ready for them."

290

"For you, too, after your flight."

"It was a short flight, you know that," Marisol said with a giggle. "But I love you more for your concern and care for me. You will mimar me, sí."

"Mimar is one word for which I don't know the translation, I'm afraid. Teach it to me."

"Let me think. Oh, perhaps spoil, pamper," Marisol said in her thick Spanish accent.

Eric beamed. "I most certainly will do that, my darling, happily so."

They heard Roger and Gerard on the stairs, and Eric put his finger over his mouth, so their surprise wasn't ruined. A moment later, he left Marisol and went to the kitchen to let the staff know to have the tea and sandwiches please brought to the sitting room in five minutes. He then went to his parents' suite, where both of them were, to let them know, "Mother, Father, I'd like your company in the sitting room in a few minutes. I'd like to talk with you both. Tea and sandwiches will be there by the time you arrive."

"Talk to us? Is it important, dear?" Matilda asked as she straightened her dress.

"Yes, Mother, it's quite important. I have the best surprise in the entire world to share with you both. Don't dawdle," he said before he rushed down to the music room to retrieve Marisol.

"Dawdle? Wherever did Eric learn that word?" Matilda asked, sounding utterly perplexed.

"From you, dear. You must have said that word thousands of times when Eric and Patrick were children," Gerard replied and reached for her hand. "Come, let's go to the sitting room for this surprise."

"Eric isn't the sort to spring surprises on us, though. I wonder what on earth it can be."

"We will find out as soon as we get there. You'll never get there if you move at this snail's pace. Hep to it."

"Gerard! Really," Matilda reprimanded, much as she used to chastise Stefan and Patrick.

With Gerard leading his wife at a steady pace, they soon arrived at the open sitting room door—and stopped when Matilda froze to the spot and gasped audibly.

Eric stood. "Mother, Father, I'd like you to meet Marisol," he said and reached for her. She stood beside him and smiled at his parents.

"Your Majesties, I am so happy to meet you," Marisol said and curtsied.

Matilda quickly recovered from her initial shock and went to Marisol. "I am delighted to me you, my dear young lady. So, you are the one true love of my son's life. Welcome," Matilda said, held Marisol's arms, and kissed her on both cheeks.

"Thank you. I did not tell Eric I come today. I hope that is all right. I wanted to surprise him," Marisol said and smiled at Eric.

"Of course, that is all right. I trust Eric has shown you around and gotten you settled in a suite."

"Yes, Your Majesty, he has. Your home is just beautiful, maravilloso."

"Thank you, Marisol. Someday, you will make this yours and Eric's home, where your family will live. Gerard and I shall be the doting grandparents to your sweet children," Matilda said.

"Perhaps the doting grandfather can welcome his future daughter-in-law before the grandchildren are born, dear," Gerard said, moving in for the greeting.

Matilda sniffed, feigning disdain, while Eric and Marisol laughed. "Oh, you have already brightened things up, Marisol, with your laughter and your joy. I'm Gerard, Eric's father. Welcome to our home. Stay as long as you like, my dear." Gerard kissed her cheek, and the four took seats, Eric and Marisol on a love seat and his parents in matching chairs nearby.

Marisol poured and served the tea, much to Eric's delight, and he smiled as he watched her. As they sipped, Eric opened the conversation. "Father and Mother, Marisol and I actually want to talk to you about Marisol staying here." Eric and Marisol charmingly explained her desire to move to Valmondois, but why she felt she couldn't live in the Palace before they married. "I instantly thought of the guest house. Marisol doesn't need the entire house, just the main floor. That solves her problem of finding a place to live, and it affords the security she needs as my soon-to-be fiancée. So, I wanted to ask if. . . . ."

"Of course, Marisol may move into the guest house," Matilda interrupted. "It is the ideal home for her until you marry. Perfect. You can have your things sent here, and the staff can assist you in setting all in order. Gerard, this is perfect."

"Yes, it is. Besides, your family can visit you here any time they desire, dear girl." Gerard sipped his tea. "Of course, you know you are welcome in here any time. You'll eat your meals with us, or at least I hope you will do so. We will enjoy your company. Have you thought of when you want to marry?"

"We talked about late next year, mid-December 1990," Eric said.

"A Christmas season wedding. How lovely," Matilda said.

"Fine," Gerard said. "Moving here now will allow you to acclimate yourself to Valdavia and to get to know the people. When your engagement is announced, you may do a few public engagements with Eric to become familiar with your new role as a Princess de Valdavia. Yes, we will enjoy having you with us, Marisol, very much so."

§§§§§

That evening, Eric escorted Marisol to the house, which maids had cleaned and aired, and helped her settle in. She stood in the main hallway and looked in amazement around her. "Eric, this is far too beautiful for me to use. There are valuable antiques and expensive furniture. This is too much for me."

"No, it is not, Marisol. Nothing I can give you is too much for you. Besides, a house is meant to be lived in, and the furniture is made to be used. This is your home until our wedding day. Make yourself comfortable in your temporary home," Eric said and put his hands on her shoulders.

"All right. I do like that I am so close to you now. I will see you almost first thing every morning."

"Next Christmas, you will awake in my arms, darling," Eric softly said.

"I wait for that. Our first Christmas as esposo y esposa. I will become your wife, and I will make you happy, I promise you that."

"You already make me happy, Marisol, exceptionally happy. I honestly never thought I would feel true happiness again. All it took was that first sight of you. God granted me so many wondrous gifts at that moment, gifts of which I am not worthy, but for which I am eternally grateful," Eric said and pulled her closer to him.

"You are worthy, my gallant, godly prince."

After a few blissful minutes, Eric said, "Oh, let's call Mamá and Papá and tell them where you're living now. They can pack and send your clothes and other items on Father's plane."

"All right. They will have a surprise, too," she said as she dialed their telephone number. She held the handset so that Eric could hear as well. Together, the couple told Juanita and Alejandro the news, and as expected, they responded in elated shock.

"I am so exaltado that mi hija is safe with tú y tus padres," Juanita said. "So is Alejandro. This has eased our hearts, Eric. We will have Marisol's clothes and her things ready for the plane. Los amamos a los dos."

"Eric y yo los amamos a ambos, Mamá y Papá," Marisol said, loud enough for both of her parents to hear.

"Te amo, Mamá y Papá," Eric said. After Marisol hung up, he said, "My life is perfect. I love you, Marisol."

§§§§

Manley placed copies of the morning newspaper, as usual, in the dining room, Gerard's office, the foyer, and the kitchen. The kitchen staff, therefore, first read the headline story, which sent them into near shock at how so much could be learned in such a short period of time, especially with no word from Eric. The fact that fans suddenly resorted to spying on the Royal Family raised concern, particularly amongst security.

The Valmondois News

22 August 1989

Prince Eric Finds Love

Monday afternoon, visitors at the Royal Palace gates witnessed the arrival of a dark-haired beauty. A security officer telephoned inside the Palace, and seconds later, a smiling Prince Eric rushed to the gates to welcome the lovely lady. Witnesses report that the pair appeared quite affectionate and happy.

While we do not yet know much about this mystery love interest, witnesses near the couple did report hearing Prince Eric refer to her as Marisol. Further eyewitness accounts report that Marisol was not seen leaving the Palace grounds. In fact, one ingenious Royal fan climbed a tree in front of the Palace, gaining a view of the Palace grounds.

This anonymous source reveals that Prince Eric took Marisol to the guest house on the estate that afternoon. Later that evening, he once again accompanied her to the guest house, this time carrying the train case that she was seen with when she arrived that morning. The Prince left the guesthouse, but our source reports that Marisol remained throughout the night. The logical presumption amongst Royal watchers is that Marisol has taken up residence in the guesthouse.

Could this indicate that Prince Eric has finally found his love? All early indications point to an imminent engagement—and Royal Wedding.

Gerard typically went to his office before breakfast, where he, too, read the article. He expected public interest in his family, so the report raised little concern for him. However, Devon tapped on his office door shortly thereafter and requested to speak with him.

"Sir, have you read the headline story?" When Gerard said he had, Devon continued. "Sir, in my nearly thirty-two years in service, never has someone gone to such extremes to spy on your family. What should my colleagues and I do to better protect Prince Eric and Miss Martínez?"

"True, as far as we know, no one has climbed a tree to ascertain our actions. Eric greeted Marisol at the gates, in front of everyone, so people are bound to be curious. After all, they have speculated about his lack of a girlfriend since he was in high school— or, in some cases, whether he was hiding her away somewhere. At this point, I don't think there's any need for alarm. Just keep a vigilant look for anything out of the ordinary, Devon. And thank you for caring so much."

Daniel alerted Eric to the headline as well, and surprisingly, Eric seemed unconcerned. "I'm far too elated to get upset over this, Daniel. I did rush out there and talk to her while dozens of people stood nearby. I realize now that I should have brought Marisol inside first, but her visit was such a beautiful surprise that I just didn't think of privacy. She's protected here, and that's all that matters."

"I suppose. But everyone knows, and you two won't have much privacy in public at all."

"True, but as soon as I would have gone anywhere with her, this public brouhaha would have started. It happened to Prince Charles every time he looked at a woman. It comes with the birthright. Eventually, we have to announce our engagement, and our wedding will be public. That's just how it must happen. Do I enjoy it? No. However, I'm far too happy to let that irritate me. Come on. Let's go down to breakfast."

Eric heard the back-patio door unlock, and he rushed to open the door. "Marisol! Happy Tuesday! How was your night?"

"¡Feliz Martes! I slept wonderfully, and my dreams, they filled with our future together," Marisol said as Eric took her arm and escorted her into the dining room.

"Lucie, take this up to my office, and please do not fold it. I must clip that and add it to my scrapbook today," Matilda told her lady-in-waiting. She then smiled up at Eric and Marisol. "I now have my first item about the new Royal couple to add to my collection." She held up the front page of the newspaper for them to see, and then handed to carefully to Lucie.

"Already? Ah, well, people were bound to figure it out, ¿no?" Marisol asked.

"Yes, they were, the first time we went anywhere together. People are naturally interested in our family, and even though it makes me highly uncomfortable, I just live with it." Eric turned toward Marisol and held her hand. "This is all new to you, darling. I'll do my best to help you through this adjustment period. You shall never go out by yourself, not because there are threats, but because this becomes overwhelming much of the time. I will make sure you are shielded as much as possible."

Tears filled Marisol's eyes. "Gracias. Yo amor, Eric."

§§§§§

As autumn progressed, Marisol gleefully explored Valmondois, met her neighbors, and garnered the affection of Valdavians who felt elation at Prince Eric's love and joy. As more than one person said to her in passing, they loved her because Prince Eric loved her, and she brought him such happiness. Furthermore, they recognized that Marisol possessed abundant faith and kindness.

She often cooked some of her mother's recipes for Eric and his parents, sometimes inviting them to her house for dinner. The invitations thrilled Eric, for he relished watching her do things for him and his parents, things she unmistakably enjoyed performing.

One evening, Matilda whispered to her son, "Marisol is a most lovely girl in every way. She will be a marvelous wife and mother."

"I know," he replied in that day-dreamy tone.

"She has exquisite taste, as well. The times I have taken her to boutiques, she never fails to select clothes that reflect modesty, style, and class. We have talked over lunches, and Marisol possesses strong Christian faith and values. But you know that."

"Yes, I do, Mother. I knew that July 9 at the fundraiser. Marisol is a beautiful gift to me from God. He sent her to me."

"Yes. I know you will never lose sight of that blessing," Matilda said and patted his hand as Marisol brought the main course to the table.

Eric knew that, no matter what occurred during his life, he would remain grateful for Marisol. In fact, that gratitude began every prayer he uttered.

§§§§§

"Come help us, Marisol. You are part of our family now," Matilda said just as Eric entered the sitting room carrying a tote filled with Christmas tree ornaments.

He kissed his mother's cheek and then Marisol's, carefully placed the tote on the floor, and said, "Yes, you are. Get on over here and help decorate our tree."

Marisol smiled and helped the DeBruce Martineau family place heirloom ornaments on their tall tree. In one year, she would decorate the tree as Eric's wife. Her smile lit the room at the notion, and Eric smiled at her as if he read her thoughts. Gerard noticed, and he, too, caught the happiness bug and smiled at his wife.

Suddenly, Eric's smile disappeared when he unwrapped a snowman ornament. Marisol instinctively knew it was Patrick's, and she put her hand on Eric's arm. Matilda saw, and her spine tightened at the fear of Eric's reaction.

"I vividly remember when he proudly showed us his new ormanent, as he called it," Eric said with a smile. "He wanted to place it on the tree all by himself, somewhere Santa would see it when he came down the chimney. Patrick placed it here, and this is where it's hung on every Christmas tree since then," Eric said and knelt in front of a low branch. "Merry Christmas, Patrick," he softly murmured and carefully placed the snowman on the branch.

Marisol kneeled beside him and put her arms around him. "What a beautiful snowman. In a few years, our child can place him on the Christmas tree for Patrick."

Eric smiled at Marisol, tears of love filling his eyes. Gerard put his arm around Matilda, who wiped tears from the corners of her eyes. She whispered to her husband, "Our Eric is healed. God brought Marisol to him, knowing she is the one to heal his deep pain and open his heart to happiness. This is the most miraculous Christmas ever, Gerard. Our family is healed."

§§§§

Eric picked up the handset from his sitting room telephone and dialed the guesthouse number. When Marisol answered, he said, "Happy Valentine's Day, mi amor. Do you have plans for this evening?"

Marisol laughed and answered, "You know I do not, Eric."

"You do now. I am taking you to the most romantic restaurant in Valmondois for a special dinner. You go to your favorite boutique and buy yourself a new gown for tonight. Lucie will accompany you, and security, too, of course." He heard her start to speak. "I've already cleared it with Mother, darling. She doesn't have any appointments this morning, so Lucie is free to go with you and assist."

"I do not need a new gown, though, not with all of the clothes I have," Marisol protested.

"Maybe not, but I want to treat you to a new gown for our first Valentine's Day. I want you to have a new gown for tonight, one you like."

"All right, mi amor. I will go. You want me to surprise you with the gown, ¿sí?"

"Sí. Now be a good girl and go shopping. I thought most men had to stop their girlfriends and wives from shopping. I have to force you."

Marisol giggled, but said, "I do not love you because of your money, Eric. I do not need you to buy things for me. I love you."

Eric breathed deeply. "I know that, darling. I love you more for that. However, I want to buy things for you. Now go," he ordered her with a laugh.

During lunch, Marisol refused to reveal anything about her shopping, even when Matilda asked about her gown. All she said was that Eric wanted it to be a surprise.

When Eric rang the guesthouse doorbell, he felt quite unprepared for the sight that greeted him. His breath caught in his chest when he looked upon Marisol, resembling the Disney princess Eduardo had said she sounded like back in July. Marisol's long dark hair cascaded onto her shoulder and back in natural waves, a diamond barrette gifted by Matilda holding back the right side. She wore a red satin strapless sweetheart gown, with full skirt and cummerbund. Over the bodice, she wore a coordinating embroidered red lace bolero.

"Are you all right, Eric?"

"Oh, yes, darling. You are always beautiful, but the sight of you just now took my breath."

"You approve of the gown?" she asked and daintily pirouetted.

"Absolutely. The important thing is that you bought the gown you most like."

"I did. Lucie will tell you this. I liked this one as soon as I saw it. The boutique had just this one, and when I try it on, it is a perfect fit. It is meant to be mine, ¿sí?"

"Yes. You must wear it often. Red suits you with your dark hair, brown eyes, and olive complexion. You are radiant. Come, let us go. Stanley is already in the car. Of course, he must come, but he will allow us privacy."

"I am glad he comes. I do not want you to be bothered so much when you are not working. You need your time, too, Eric."

"I know, but when one is born to famous parents, then this is part of the life," Eric explained.

"I know. No one ever harms you, do they?"

"No, darling. I will warn you, though, sometimes there are quite a few people, and it can seem overwhelming. I want you to get used to this, Marisol, because it will increase when we do announce our engagement."

"I understand, querido. I am used to my privacy, and this will be desafiante, challenging I think you say. But with you beside me, I will never fear or worry," Marisol said.

"I'll make sure of that," he said as he helped her into the back seat.

Ten minutes later, Stanley pulled up at a five-star French restaurant, La Vie Belle, where Eric walked around the car and held Marisol's had as she stepped out. Patrons both leaving and entering the restaurant noticed the dashing Prince and his lovely lady in red. People stopped and watched them enter, followed as always by Stanley, who handed the car key to the valet.

The maître d'hôtel immediately escorted the Royal couple to their table, where Eric held Marisol's chair for her. Stanley sat at the nearest table, alert and attentive. Eric and Marisol typically garnered reams of attention on their outings and dates, and even though the Prince's admirers posed no threat, his one duty remained to stay aware of every person near Eric. Stanley essentially watched the Royal watchers throughout dinner.

Meanwhile, Eric and Marisol ordered dinner—grilled salmon steaks and vegetables--and sparking water to drink. Neither ever drank alcohol, which by now was well documented in the newspapers. The waiters received several orders for the same meal, much to the chef's delight. Prince Eric brought him great fortune and reviews.

While they ate, the couple talked about sundry topics, as they had that first night at the fundraiser, and finally dinner plates cleared, and dessert menus presented to them. They both ordered Ispahan and coffee, and as they waited, Eric removed a black velvet jewel box from his inner jacket pocket.

"Happy Valentine's Day, Marisol, mi amor," Eric said and placed the box in front of her.

"Eric, ¿qué has hecho?" Marisol asked, her eyes large and her mouth prettily agape.

"I have bought you your first Valentine's gift from me. Open it," he said and smiled.

"Eric! This is far too extravagante para mí!" she exclaimed and pushed the box back toward him.

Eric stood, walked behind her, and replied, "Nothing I could ever give you is too extravagant for you." He lifted the diamond and ruby necklace from the box and fastened it around her neck, lifted her hair, and tenderly kissed her cheek. "Para ti, mi amor, con mi amor."

"Your love is all I want, Eric, but I will tell you that these tokens of your love, they do touch my heart. I thank you," Marisol said and kissed his cheek.

Diners who witnessed the scene found it charming and romantic, but many noted that the couple had never been seen kissing on the lips, at least not publicly. Still, the couple's love and devotion remained undeniable, and when they finally left the restaurant, lifelong residents of Valmondois celebrated Prince Eric's first real Valentine's Day.

§§§§§

When Eric and Marisol returned to the Palace, many fans awaited the glamorous couple. One approached the car with a huge bouquet of long-stemmed red roses for Marisol. "Gracias," she said with a smile, further charming her admirer. Eric radiated at the love Valdavians displayed for his future wife.

Once inside the garage, Eric took hold of Marisol's arm and said, "Let us go inside for a while." He guided her down an east wing corridor to the chapel.

In front of the altar, Eric held her hands. "Marisol, we met seven months ago. These seven months have only strengthened my love for you." Still holding her left hand, Eric kneeled on one knee, pulled a ring from his jacket pocket, and asked the most momentous question of his life. "Will you do me the honor of marrying me?"

Tears filled Marisol's eyes, spilled from their corners, and nearly blinded her. Through her tears, she nodded and said, "Sí. Oh, my Eric, yes, I will so happily marry you, mi amor. I love you so, Eric."

Eric slid the ring onto the third finger of her left hand, kissed her hand, and shed a few tears of joy. He stood, smiled at her, and said, "I never thought I could or would be happy again, but God placed you in my life. My happiness returned the instant I saw you. You remain the light, joy, and love in me, Marisol."

Marisol placed her hand on Eric's cheek and softly said, "And you are mine, all of time, Eric, all of time. I have never loved any other man, only you, and forever will I love only you."

"I thank God for you each day. Marisol, do you mind if I pray now?"

"Por supuesto que no, mi amor."

Eric held her hands, they bowed their heads, and Eric spoke to God. "Dear God, you told me that you have a plan for my life, and I believe and trust you. You brought Marisol and me together. Our love is part of your plan. Our union and our future child are part of your plan. You destined us for one another, and you aligned circumstances so that we met at the appointed time. I remain eternally grateful for the blessing of our love and for the rapture it brings to me. Thank you, God. Amen."

"Amen," Marisol whispered.

"Come. How about a moonlit stroll through the garden?" Eric asked.

"On, sí, mi amor. It feels I am already in Heaven standing here with you. Oh, Eric, I am muy dichoso," Marisol said and leaned into Eric when he put his arm around her.

The couple slowly walked out of the east wing corridor just as Gerard and Matilda came into the foyer. "Gerard, it's happened!"

"What has happened?"

"Just look at Eric and Marisol!"

"Yes, dear. They're home from their dinner date. I must say, her red gown is appropriate for Valentine's Day."

"Yes, Gerard, Valentine's Day. Of course, it happened tonight. It's the perfect date."

"For what?" Gerard asked just as Eric noticed his parents.

"Mother! Father! You are the first to know," Eric said with a smile while he and Marisol walked closer to his parents. "Mother, Father, this is the most blessed moment of my life. I asked Marisol to become my eternal wife, and she said yes," Eric said and smiled at Marisol.

"This! This is what happened! I could see it; I could feel it. Oh, Eric, my baby, what a fine young man you've become! How I've prayed for your happiness," Matilda gushed as she grabbed her son in an exuberant hug and practically smothered him with kisses.

She then turned to Marisol, grabbed her, and said, "You are the love of my son's life. I know in my heart that you two will be happy for many decades."

"Thank you, Mother," Marisol responded, her joyful smile reflecting her inner happiness.

"Now it is my turn," Gerard said and hugged his first-born son. "Congratulations, Eric. I am elated for you. And you, young lady," he said and hugged Marisol, "are the perfect daughter-in-law. You and Eric are a match made in Heaven."

"Sí. Estamos," Marisol agreed and smiled up at Eric.

§§§§§

"Hey, Eric, you sure kept this a secret," Roger said later that night. "I mean, I knew you and Marisol would marry, just not when. Congratulations," he said for perhaps the thirteenth time.

"No one knew, not even the jeweler who made the ring. I merely told him it was a gift, so that its design remained top secret. I wasn't lying."

"No. Do you two have a wedding date?"

"Yes. We've known that for a while, actually. We want mid-December."

"So, you'll announce the engagement soon?" Roger asked.

"May 21. That's Marisol's birthday. No one else needs to know until then if I don't want them to know. I don't want people, especially reporters and photographers, stalking Marisol's every movement. No one needs to know everything she does."

"Yeah, but what about that ring on her finger? People will notice that thing. It's not exactly tiny."

"We'll work out something. I want her to be able to plan her wedding without an invasion of privacy," Eric stated as he and Roger climbed the stairs.

"I'll do everything I can to help with that. This is the best news ever, buddy. I'm so delighted that you're happy and in love," Roger said and hugged his friend.

"I am. Thanks for everything, Roger. Good night."

In his suite, Eric sat at his desk and wrote that day's diary entry, the entry he at times thought he would never write. For so long, Eric never felt he deserved happiness. Marisol—and God—changed all of that.

14 February 1990

 This evening was magical! My first real Valentine's Day—and with my love, Marisol. Our dreamy dinner at La Belle Vie, and then into the Palace chapel. I proposed! She accepted! I slid the ring on her finger, alongside the purity ring Mamá gave her when she was 13. She told me, when I walked her home, that she will wear both rings together until our wedding. I admire that! Marisol really is the perfect woman.

 I am happy—fully, truly happy—for the first time in many years. Marisol healed me, or rather God used her to heal me. For that, and for her, I remain eternally grateful, as clichéd as that statement has become. I am grateful to God. He told me years ago that He has a plan for me, and He does. Thank you, God, for loving me as you do. Thank you for Marisol.

CHAPTER 14

"Eric, can you talk now?" Marisol asked at his sitting room door.

He turned from his computer and instantly said, "Of course, dear." He stood, put his hand on her elbow, and guided her to the sofa. "What's wrong? You seem worried."

"I am. ¡Mi tonto hermano! He has gone to Iraq to report on the Invasion of Kuwait! Mamá and Papá asked him not to go, but he went. It is muy peligroso, so very dangerous, there, and I am so afraid for him, Eric. He has gone, and there is not one thing I can do."

Eric listened in disbelief, for he and his father closely watched and read about the invasion, and Gerard received regular briefings. Eric fully understood the risks to members of the press, as two French television news anchors were victims of well-publicized assassinations in retaliation for reporting the atrocities of the Hussein regime.

Eric pulled his fiancée to him, and Marisol cried against his shoulder. "I don't know what to say, darling. I understand your fear, I do. I hurt for you, but I feel so helpless. I'm not sure if there is anything even Father can do to have Eduardo removed from Iraq. I will talk with him. But first, we'll pray for his safety."

While Eric held Marisol, he closed his eyes and prayed. "Dear God, I come to with a request for your protection of Eduardo, who has placed himself in the face of danger in his quest to reveal the truth about the invasion. Please bring him home safely to Mamá, Papá, and Marisol. This we ask you in love and faith. Thank you, God. Amen."

Eric kissed her forehead and said, "Let me speak with Father. I'll be back soon, darling."

Half an hour later, Eric returned to his sitting room, where Marisol stood on the balcony. He walked to her, put his hands on her shoulders, and said, "Father called the French Embassy in Iraq, and he spoke with the Consulate General of France. Mr. Arautier will try to locate Eduardo and have him flown to France. He'll contact Father as soon as he learns anything."

"Then there is a chance? Oh, Eric, I never thought anything could be done. I will pray every moment until mi hermano is out of the Middle East. Oh, Eric, mi amor, gracias. And bless Father."

§§§§

Ten days later, on August 15, Mr. Arautier telephoned Gerard with information. After the conversation, Gerard immediately called Eric into his office. "Close the door, son. Mr. Arautier just called. There is no trace of Eduardo Martínez in Iraq. The publisher of *Verdad* confirmed that Eduardo was sent and arrived, and the hotel staff verifies that he checked in. His possessions are still in the hotel room. However, he is nowhere to be found."

"He could be investigating the events or chasing down interviews," Eric said, attempting to rationalize Eduardo's apparent disappearance.

"Perhaps. That is why he was sent. Mr. Arautier and his team will continue the search and keep me updated."

An excruciating two weeks later, Gerard faced the task of calling his son and Marisol into his office for grim news. Eric held Marisol's hand, feeling her tremble.

"Mr. Arautier telephoned. A representative of the Hussein regime told him that Eduardo and nine other journalists were taken hostage."

"No!" Marisol screamed.

Eric put his arm around her and held her tightly. *How could this have happened?* he thought.

"Mr. Arautier and his team are trying to locate Eduardo and the others. I have telephone calls placed to Prime Minister Rabin, President Sadat, President Bush, and President Mitterand. We will work together to help find them and release them." Gerard came around the desk and knelt in front of Marisol, held her hand, and promised, "I will do all in my power to locate your brother."

"Gracias, Father," Marisol said, tears straining her voice, and hugged him.

Two months later, however, no further news of Eduardo had surfaced. As Marisol and Eric sat in the chapel, she told him, "Eric, I love you, and I long to become your wife. But I cannot be married until Eduardo is safe. I just cannot. Please, can we wait until Eduardo is safe?"

"Of course, darling. Many powerful people are working to find Eduardo and the others. We cannot give up hope, darling, as frightening as this remains. If it will help, I will go to Iraq and search for Eduardo."

"No!" Marisol shouted in response, fear in her voice. "You cannot! Mi querido Dios, I will not let anything happen to you, Eric, no. You cannot leave me."

"I won't," he said and held her close. "I will never leave you."

Eric informed his parents and Marisol's parents that he and Marisol would postpone their marriage until Eduardo's release. All of them understood and supported Eric and Marisol, and Gerard issued a statement informing the public, who supported their future King and Queen Consort with love and prayers.

§§§§

Christmas 1990 proved rather somber, with the cloud of Eduardo's unknown status over the Palace. Gerard sent Roger to Santander, and he returned to the Palace two days before Christmas with a surprise for Marisol and Eric. By chance, Eric skipped down the stairs seconds after Roger and the special Christmas gifts entered the foyer.

"Mamá! Papá!" Eric exclaimed and ran to them. "How wonderful to see you!" He hugged them both, and he felt their tenseness and stress. His heart ached for them.

"It is good to see you, mi hijo. Yo amor," Juanita said and kissed his cheek.

"Yo amor, Eric. We are happy to be with nuestra Marisol and you at Christmas," Alejandro said.

Eric noticed Alejandro's eyes filled with tears, and he knew that Alejandro yearned for his son. "I will take you both to Marisol," Eric said and walked with them up the stairs to the second-floor sitting room.

Marisol heard someone enter, and she turned from the window where she stood. She immediately ran to her parents and hugged them both simultaneously. Roger had alerted Gerard and Matilda, who witnessed the reunion from the doorway along with Eric.

Matilda and Gerard met them, welcomed them, and expressed their sympathy and concern. Matilda motioned everyone to the sofas and chairs, where they could relax and talk.

"You try to find nuestra Eduardo," Juanita said to Gerard. "Nuestra hija tells us that you have many world leaders trying to find Eduardo. Muchas gracias," she said and kissed his cheeks.

"Sí, muchas gracias," Alejandro added.

"I sincerely with I could do much more," Gerard said. "Please let me tell you one thing that I pray gives you some hope. The intelligence officers and experts with whom I have spoken assure me that the hostages must be alive. The Hussein regime always broadcasts executions and murders they commit. None of their executions since the invasion involve any of the ten journalists."

Juanita turned pale at the word executions, and Gerard took her hand. "Gracias. I do not feel that mi hijo Eduardo has left this earth. I feel he is alive. I keep saying this to Alejandro. My heart feels this." She told Gerard.

He patted her hand, and Matilda came to kneel before her. "A mother's heart feels what her children think and feel. It is a lot like ESP. We know, don't we, Juanita?"

"Sí sabemos," Juanita agreed and hugged her ally.

"We must believe that Eduardo is alive," Gerard said in that well-known authoritative tone that leaders and Valdavians heard many times. "I receive updates and news daily, and none of the ten hostages has been reported as dead. They must be held for political bargaining, and the moment any word of this comes to me, I will work to free your son."

Juanita sobbed tears of gratitude, and Alejandro held her shoulders. "We remain agradecido for your kindness," Alejandro said and smiled at Gerard even though tears threatened to overtake him. Gerard patted his hand, understanding a father's love and concern for his son as Patrick's image filled his mind.

§§§§

Alejandro and Juanita remained in Valmondois for two months, staying with Marisol in the guesthouse, although they dined with the DeBruce Martineau family most evenings.

On Valentine's Day, however, Eric received a call from Marisol inviting him to dinner that night. "Mamá is cooking comida deliciosa for us, mi amor. This is her gift to us."

"I look forward to it," Eric softly replied.

That evening, Daniel helped Eric to get ready by brushing and steaming his black tuxedo and polishing his shoes. Eric strode to what he called the Martínez house carrying two bouquets.

311

Alejandro answered the door, attired in a suit, and welcomed his second son, as he and Juanita considered Eric. "The women finish in the kitchen. We go into the sitting room, ¿no?"

Eric smiled and said, "I'll enjoy a visit with you, Papá." However, the two men had little time to chat, as Juanita appeared and announced that dinner was served.

Eric stood, kissed her cheek, said, "For you, Mamá," and handed her a bouquet of yellow long-stemmed roses.

"Gracias, mi hijo. The roses are muy hermosa." Juanita quickly placed the roses in a vase and rejoined the men in the dining room.

Eric assisted Juanita and Alejandro, and had just walked to his seat when Marisol entered carrying the main dish. Eric instantly smiled at the sight of her, and he glowed at her graceful movements. He held her chair, kissed her cheek, and then placed two dozen long-stemmed red roses on the table before her.

"Oh, mi amor Eric. Our second Saint Valentine's Day together. ¡Qué hermosa!" Marisol said and kissed his cheek. She nuzzled her cheek against his and added, "Your beard is so soft, mi Eric. Everything about you is just perfecto."

Eric shook his head, but she kissed him before he could once again deny her praises of him. "You are the second-greatest person in my life after God," Eric said as he sat. "Speaking of God, shall we say grace?"

"May I?" Juanita asked, and Eric nodded. They bowed their heads, and Juanita prayed, "Querido Dios, gracias for your blessings. You have brought our two families together, and that is a great gift. Thank you for Gerard, who does all for nuestra hijo Eduardo. Please watch over Gerard and Eduardo. And please bless Eric and Marisol as they wait to become esposo y esposa. Te amamos, Dios. Amen."

"Amen," everyone said, and then enjoyed the delectable homecooked meal of traditional Spanish dishes. After Juanita served dessert, Eric placed a box in front of Marisol.

"Again? Eric, you gave me a beautiful gift one year ago. This is too much."

"Nothing is too much for you. Yo amor usted," Eric said and kissed her.

"We are prometido one year. I have been happier than ever this past year. Gracias, Eric," Marisol said and held his hand.

§§§§§

Despite the lack of news regarding Eduardo, and the concern for him, life had to continue. Gerard, of course, carried out his duties and schedule as usual, but he (and Roger on his behalf) made frequent telephone calls and wrote dozens of letters and e-mails in attempts to locate or to find information about Eduardo.

Matilda likewise fulfilled her appointments and public duties. Her graciousness and charm never faltered, even though everyone knew of her anxiety for Marisol's brother. Many peopled considered their Queen Consort as Valdavia's Mother, always caring and compassionate.

Eric, as always, performed a full-time load of duties and meetings, appointments, and charity support. He also worked at home to assist his father: researching, writing reports, and answering many of the letters that arrived for Gerard. Eric's poise, strength, knowledge, and commitment continued to impress people, as they had for more than two decades.

After a walkabout following the official opening of Gathered Leaves Bookstore, Eric and Stanley walked toward their car. A bedraggled teenaged boy ran to Eric and grabbed his arm. "Prince Eric, please. I need to talk to you. Now."

Stanley placed himself between Eric and the boy, but Eric calmly said, "It's all right, Stanley. This seems urgent," Eric said to the boy. "How about we go to that café," Eric pointed across the street, "and have lunch while you tell me?"

The boy nodded, and the men walked to the café, sat at two tables (Stanley nearby), and ordered. The boy glanced down, hiding his tears. "What's your name?" Eric asked him, placing a hand on the boy's arm.

"Jacques."

"I'm here whenever you're ready to tell me, Jacques."

"I just don't know what to do. My mom left, my dad is mean, and kids in school make fun of me 'cause I look like this," Jacques said, still looking at the table.

"I'm sorry, Jacques. I'm going to help you, but I need a bit more information. Okay?"

Jacques nodded, so Eric asked his first question. "You said your dad is mean. How? What does he do?"

"He throws things. And he hits."

Eric's stomach lurched, but he maintained his calm. "Is that why your mom left?" Jacques nodded. "He hits you, too?" Jacques once more nodded. "Are you still at your father's house?"

"A little, mostly when he's passed out. He gets drunk a lot. He comes home late and just passes out wherever he's at. So, I hide in the shrubs beside the house and go in after he's out cold. I get a couple hours sleep, sometimes shower if it's not full of junk he throws in there, but there's no food in the house since mom left. I grab leftovers in the school cafeteria. Some of the kids saw mw, so they tease me for that, too. I told some teachers, but they told me to be nice to the other kids and to talk to our pastor about my paents. That's all. No help. I'm just sick of the whole thing. I want out."

"I'll help you get out, Jacques. I will. I know people who can help, too. But first, you need to eat. We need to get you new clothes. Then I'll take you back to my place to shower and take a nap. We'll get through this."

"Your place? The Palace? You'll take me inside?"

"Of course. You'll be safe there. I promise."

"But your folks. I mean, King Gerard and Queen Matilda. They won't like me traipsing through there," Jacques said.

"They won't mind. Don't worry."

Jacques looked at Eric, nodded, and scarfed down his sandwich. Eric ordered dessert for them so that Jacques would ingest as many calories and carbohydrates as possible. *When had he last eaten?* Eric wondered.

Stanley had long ago trained himself to not overhear Eric's conversations, although he watched the boy vigilantly. He refused taking any chances with Eric's safety.

After the meal, Eric asked Stanley to drive them to Hamley's Department Store. "Why are we stopping here?" Jacques asked.

"You need to pick out some new clothes. Come on," Eric said.

Eric always gained attention, but the sight of him shopping with a dirty, scruffy teen drew speculation as well. Regardless of the circumstances, every witness agreed that Eric helped the teen. People watched Eric purchase several slacks and shirts, undershirts, undershorts, socks, pajamas, and two pairs of shoes for the boy, all of which the teen selected. Alerted press photographers snapped dozens of photographs, which later appeared in the local newspapers and magazines.

At the Palace, Eric led Jacques to an unoccupied third-floor suite, and he showed Jacques where everything was located. Once Eric demonstrated how to operate the shower for Jacques, Eric reentered the bedroom to retrieve Jacque's worn clothes. Both Stanley and Eric heard the loud thud when Eric picked up the jeans.

Eric looked at Stanley and, in a veritable whisper, said, "I was never in danger. Jacques had other plans for this." Eric picked up a revolver, emptied the bullets, and placed them all in a bag with the clothes. "Stay with him. I'm going to call a couple of people who can help him. He bought some pajamas if he wants to take a nap."

Eric rushed to his sitting room, closed his suite door, and called Pernell Stouffer, the lead counselor at Life Matters: Depression and Addiction Treatment and Suicide Prevention Center. Eric explained Jacques's situation, including the gun and its implications. "Can you please come to the Palace as soon as possible?"

Pernell promised he would, so Eric next telephoned Sawn Shivier, the President of the Family Crisis Coalition of Valdavia. Eric repeated all Jacques had gone through and that Eric had found a gun in his pocket. Shawn, too, headed for the Palace.

Eric breathed deeply and said a prayer. "Dear God, please help Jacques find safety and peace. Please watch over him and protect him. Please heal his father. Please, God. Amen."

Eric calmly returned to Jacques's suite, where he found the boy asleep. Eric motioned Stanley to the adjoining sitting room, and he quietly updated Stanley on the impending assistance. "Pernell and Shawn will get Jacques to safety and counseling. They'll take care of him. I'm just afraid he'll think I somehow betrayed him by calling in other people."

"Even if he does at first, he won't for long. He actually got teary-eyed when he put on the new pajamas. He seems grateful. I don't know his situation, but you think he's suicidal?" Stanley asked.

"That, or the gun was for protection from his father," Eric said.

"Wow. Okay. He sure came to the right person, I guess. You got him the help he needs."

While Jacques slept, watched over by Stanley, Eric met with Pernell and Shawn, providing every detail that Jacques had shared. Both men agreed that the boy required immediate intervention.

Shawn explained that he would locate a foster home for Jacques, where he would receive compassion, kindness, and stability. "I have a list of families willing to foster, and you know we thoroughly check each person. I will begin calling them now if there's a phone I can use."

"Of course," Eric said and led Shawn to an empty suite.

"I'll talk with Jacques today," Pernell said, "and we'll have daily sessions to start. You're right. He's either contemplating suicide or he's planning to use the gun on his father. I'll work with him to determine which and then to help him find his self-love and self-worth. It'll take time, but a stable foster home and environment will help a lot. Your kindness has already cracked the shell from all you've said. That's all he needs, kindness and love. Is it all right if I talk with him here? He already feels safe here, so I'd rather not force him to leave until we get him to a foster family."

"Of course. I didn't do anything extraordinary. Anyone else would have done the same thing," Eric characteristically said, deflecting praise.

"I don't think so. His teachers didn't do anything, even when he told them what was going on. Neither did neighbors who likely heard or saw what happened. The people who saw him on the street today didn't offer to buy him food and clothes. You did. A lot of people don't get involved. It's just a sad fact of the late 20th century."

"Jacques ran to me. He grabbed me. Otherwise, I probably wouldn't have noticed him."

"Maybe, maybe not. The point is, people have seen him every day, and no one stepped in to help. You could have walked away and done nothing," Pernell said.

Eric's expression and tone indicated his disgust at the idea. "No, I couldn't. How could I just ignore someone in need? That's impossible."

"You possess compassion and concern, Eric. Yes, I know, so do other people, but the difference is, you're not afraid to live them. Not everyone does. Everyone sees these qualities at work in you. You innately live them. You're one of those people who put others' needs first."

"Lots of people do," Eric said, typically deflecting attention from himself. "Let me check on Jacques. If he's awake, you can meet him."

Eric entered Jacques's bedroom at the moment he slipped a t-shirt over his head. Eric smiled and asked, "Did you get enough sleep? How do you feel?"

"Yeah. I'm okay. It feels good to be clean again." Jacques tied his sneakers, stood, and extended his right hand toward Eric. "Thank you. I didn't know who else to go to."

Eric grasped Jacques's hand and said, "You're welcome. It's my honor. Remember I said I know people who can help you?" Jacques nodded. "Well, they're here. I'd like you to meet one of them as soon as you're ready."

"Do I have to tell them everything? I don't know if I can."

"You told me. You trust me. You can trust Pernell and Shawn. I did already fill them in on what you told me, but I'm sure they'll both have questions for you. When you're ready," Eric said.

Jacques breathed deeply a few times, stretched his arms behind him, and said, "Okay. Let's go."

Eric led Jacques to the suite down the hall where Pernell waited, and introduced them to each other.

"Hi, Jacques. Eric works on behalf of my organization, so he called me to come help you. I'd like to, so why don't we begin?"

"Okay, I guess. How are you going to help me? What do you do?"

"I help people with emotional issues, you know, like fears, depression, loneliness, things like that. Eric tells me you've been through a lot. Those things cause a lot of stress. I can help you learn to deal with all of the feelings and emotions."

"You're a therapist?" Jacques asked.

"Yes."

"I don't know," Jacques said and shuffled his feet nervously.

"I understand," Pernell said. "But Eric wouldn't have called me if he didn't think I can help you. Right?"

"I-I guess. I've seen therapists on TV. You're gonna ask me all kinds of questions about my innermost thoughts and dreams and psychoanalyze me. I don't know about that. I mean, blaming my dad for everything and stuff like that."

"No, nothing like that. I promise. We'll deal with the immediate issues that you told Eric about. Okay?"

"Okay, but only if he will stay here," Jacques said and turned toward Eric. "Will you?"

"If you want me to, yes," Eric said.

"Good. Sit where you want, Jacques," Pernell said.

Jacques grabbed the desk chair and sat backwards, his arms resting on the back of the chair. Eric and Pernell sat on the sofa.

Pernell asked some questions to confirm all that Eric had shared, and then asked, "Where were you the night your mom left?"

"In my closet. Since I was a child, I hid there when the yelling and fighting started. They were yelling. Nothing unusual. Then I heard actual fighting, you know, punching and hitting, and I heard my mom scream. My dad threw something that broke, and then he left. I heard his car leave. Mom got up as soon as he left. She must have been pretending to be knocked out. She ran to their room, and I heard her opening drawers and stuff. Then I heard the front door open and close again, heard her car leave, and then it was quiet."

"She hasn't been back since?"

"No. Nothing. She never came for me. She left me with him. You know, he came back a few hours later. It was dark, just the moonlight through my window. I jumped back in my closet when he came in screaming mom's name. He started looking for her, so I went into the little crawlspace in my closet and stayed there until he left early in the morning. I actually fell asleep, I was so tired. When he came home and passed out, I left. Went to school in the same clothes, probably smelled, too. Kids made fun of me. I hate school."

"Your father is violent and abusive. He hit your mother, and she left because of it," Pernell said. "How does that make you feel?"

"Mad. I'm mad at her for leaving me there. If she came back now, I wouldn't see her." Jacques balled his hands into fists, which both Eric and Pernell noticed.

"How do you feel about your father?" Pernell asked.

"I know he's got a problem. He drinks too much. But he's never been nice. Not to mom and me anyway. I'm not sure why he has a family. I don't really know him. I don't want to."

"You don't hate him?"

"How can you hate someone you don't know?"

"Jacques, you told Eric you want to get out of everything. Coming to Eric was the first step. But, did you have a backup plan?" Pernell said.

"Like what? Running away? No." Jacques looked directly at Eric. "You know. You found it. Yeah, I thought about putting that gun in my mouth and pulling the trigger. Then I saw a newspaper in the library. That's where I hang out. It said something about you helping a family whose house burned down. So, I figured, what have I got to lose? If you helped me, great. If not, I had the gun."

"Jacques, thank you for trusting me," Eric said, his voice choked by tears. "You can come to me anytime, you know that."

"Sure. Now what?"

"You didn't really want to kill yourself, or you would have. Your survival instinct is strong. You asked for help. That's the one thing so many people don't do. You want to live, don't you, Jacques?" Pernell said.

"Yeah, sure. I'm only 15. I want to be a scientist, but I messed up everything in school."

"Don't worry about that. Shawn and I will help you get into a different school where you can catch up and get back on track. You'll be okay. We'll make sure of that."

"Speaking of Shawn, let me check if he's ready," Eric said and returned shortly with Shawn, who met Jacques.

"Jacques, part of what I do is find foster homes for children and teens who need stable, safe homes. I spoke with a couple who is on our waiting list, and they are excited to meet you. They'll be here soon. Do you know what a foster family is?"

"Yeah. They're kinda like surrogate parents. They'd take care of me, and I'd live with them."

"That's right. Some foster parents become adoptive parents. Mr. and Mrs. Cormier can't have children of their own, and they want to adopt. They are on the adoption waiting list, but they also applied to become foster parents. I told them about you, what Eric shared, and they really want to meet you and help you. They want you to live with them."

"But both of my parents are alive. How can I be adopted?" Jacques asked.

"Your mother abandoned you. Your father is an abusive alcoholic. King Gerard actually heads the Supreme Court de Valdavia, and he will approve your adoption, whether by the Cormiers or another couple," Shawn said.

"Really? You're not just saying that?"

"Of course not."

"Then I will get out of this," Jacques said and cried. "Thank you." He rushed to Eric and hugged him.

"Everything is all right now. We're all going to make sure it remains that way," Eric said as he held the teen.

§§§§§

Shawn escorted the Cormiers to the second-floor sitting room, where Eric, Jacques, and Pernell waited. As soon as Mrs. Cormier entered, she ran to the teen and sat beside him.

"You're Jacques! Oh, I'm so happy! I'm Beth Cormier, and this is my husband Louis," she said and glanced at her husband.

A tall dark-eyed man shook Jacques's hand and said "Hello, Jacques. You're going to live with us. We live about fifteen miles from the Palace. Our house is modest, I suppose, but it's roomy, and we have four acres. Lots of space. If you like it there, and if you like us, we can go shopping for a bike for you. Would you like that?"

Jacques shrugged his shoulders, and Louis sat to his other side. "You don't have to buy me things. I've never had a whole lot, so I'm used to not having things."

"No, possessions are not the most important parts of life, but there's nothing wrong with having things. Why shouldn't you have a bike? Heck, I had one when I was sixteen," Louis said.

Jacques again shrugged. "I don't know. I suppose it's okay. But don't buy me stuff just to win me over."

"We wouldn't do that," Beth said. "We want you to love us because, well, you just do. Okay?"

"Okay."

"We know it will take time. You don't know us. We don't know you. But we will. I hope you like chocolate chip cookies, because I took some out of the oven just before we left," Beth said with a smile.

"I do, but I've never had homemade cookies."

"You'll have lots of cookies. Beth likes to bake," Louis said.

"When is your birthday?" Beth asked.

"November 12. Why?" Jacques asked.

"We need to know so we can plan the party and buy your gifts. And so I can bake your cake," Beth replied.

"A birthday party? I'll be sixteen, too old."

"Who cares? Birthday parties are for everyone."

"So? Do you want to go home?" Louis asked.

"Sure. Why not?" Jacques said and stood. Everyone else stood, too. Jacques walked to Eric. "Thank you for everything." He extended his right hand, but Eric put his arms around Jacques and hugged him.

"Keep in touch," Eric said.

"Okay."

Three weeks later, Eric flipped through his mail, and Jacques's name stood out in the upper left corner of an envelope. He slit the envelope and removed a card. Pictures fell out, pictures of Jacques with a new bicycle, with Louis and Beth, and with a dog. The teen smiled broadly and genuinely in each.

Eric smiled, too, read the card, and bowed his head. "Dear God, that you for saving Jacques and bringing him to a loving family and secure home. I know we all face struggles in life, but let Jacques always remember that he has people who love him who can help him. Amen."

§§§§§

The next morning, Matilda picked up a copy of the morning newspaper in the foyer. The headline stunned her.

The Valmondois News

24 October 1990

Prince Eric Rescues Teen from Abusive Home

She rapidly read the story, which included the press pictures of Eric and Jacques clothes shopping several weeks earlier. "Gerard!" she yelled as she quickly walked up to his office. "Gerard!" She arrived breathless and panting. "Have you seen this?" She held up the newspaper.

"Yes, dear, I just read it. Quite impressive, I must say. Our son has confirmed that he will be a compassionate, wise, and efficacious King. I shall have no qualms when I die."

"Gerard, really. But, how could we not know about this? He brought the boy here weeks ago, and those men, Pernell and Shawn, were here, too. No one saw anything? How is that possible?" Matilda said.

"I'm sure staff members saw, but I doubt they knew anything at the time. I think this proves how discreet and loyal our staff are, don't you?"

"Of course. But still, to find out by reading it in the newspaper almost one month later. How could Eric do that to us?"

Roger had come to Gerard's door at that moment to relay a message, but turned to leave when he realized Matilda and her husband talked. Gerard stopped him. "Roger, what do you know of this?"

"Of what, Sir?" Roger asked and walked forward to read the headline. "Wo! When did he do this? No, I didn't know anything about this. Eric never said anything."

"Typical, just typical," Gerard said. "There's no sense interrogating him about it. He's never been one to boast or to like praise, so let's not say anything. Paste the article in your scrapbook, dear, and cherish our son as our most valuable gift from God."

"Yes, but. . . . . You're right. He doesn't like all of this fuss, as he calls it. I shan't mention it," Matilda said.

"Eric!" Marisol ran up the stairs calling for her fiancé. Roger quickly went to divert her to Gerard's office, where she appeared concerned. "Eric? Is something wrong with Eric?"

"No, dear," Matilda said. "We had just seen the newspaper. You have, too, right?"

"Sí. Isn't it wonderful? Eric, he is the most magnificent man, so kind and loving."

"Yes," Gerard said, fighting a smile at Marisol's lovestruck expression. "He is, but we just promised not to mention this to him. You've seen how much he dislikes attention like this. Eric's compassion is first nature, not contrived for public approval. He does things like this because they're in his heart. He doesn't feel that what he does is so extraordinary as to warrant weekly, sometimes daily, newspaper articles. He feels that such acts are done from sincere concern and kindness, not for reward or attention. He's told me many times when we've discussed this that the only reward that matters will be the one God gives him on his judgment day. Let us allow him to live his life without any additional ballyhoo."

CHAPTER 15

On Christmas Eve, Gerard spent a few hours in his office. Eric arrived with a huge smile, and said, "Father, carollers are outside the gates. Why don't we all go out and listen to them? Father?"

"Oh, Eric, it's you. I just can't get my eyes to focus. This headache."

Eric went to his father and helped him stand. "Come on. I'm taking you to your doctor. We're not taking any chances." Eric buzzed for Roger, who rushed to help support Gerard as they walked down the stairs. "Tell Mother and Marisol where we went," Eric told Roger after they helped Gerard into the passenger seat of a car.

Gerard's doctor, Dr. Davis, ordered an MRI of the King's brain and requested the reading receive top priority. Eric sat with his father in a private examination room, where Gerard kept his gaze on the door. Neither man talked, but both silently prayed.

Ninety minutes later, Dr. Barnard, Gerard's oncologist, knocked on the door and entered. Eric's heart pounded. He knew the results before Dr. Bernard spoke.

"Gerard. Eric. There's no easy way to say this."

"The cancer has returned," Gerard said matter-of-factly. Eric gripped his father's hand.

"I'm afraid so. This is the hardest thing I've ever had to tell a patient."

"How long?"

"Gerard, the cancer has metastasized in your brain," Dr. Barnard said.

"I expected you to say that. There's nothing that can be dome. I know that. I can buy a little time with chemotherapy. I know that, too. How long? Give me the estimate."

"It's difficult to predict, because every patient is different. With chemotherapy, which slows the tumor's growth, up to two years."

Gerard nodded. "Fine. That's plenty of time to make sure everything is in order. I'm not spending my last Christmas in a hospital. Bring me my clothes, Eric, and let's go home."

"You'll want to begin chemotherapy next week, Gerard. My nurse will call Eric with the appointment information. Call me day or night if you need anything," Dr. Barnard said. "Merry Christmas."

"Merry Christmas. Don't be so glum. This isn't the end of the world," Gerard said and smiled. "We are all born, and we all die."

Dr. Barnard smiled and left.

§§§§§

Lucie entered the foyer with a tea tray just as the patio door opened and Gerard and Eric stepped in. "Oh, Sir, everyone is so worried. Matilda and Marisol are in the sitting room. This is the fourth pot of tea. I'm just taking it up."

"Fine, Lucie. Go on ahead. I'll be there soon." Gerard turned to face Eric. "Let me tell your mother. This doesn't have to dampen Christmas." Gerard smiled. "Next year, you'll recite the nativity story for the first time, Son."

"Dr. Barnard said up to two years," Eric said.

"Even so, I'm well aware that I will not be the acting King come December 1992. It's not that I want to die, but I am realistic. The cancer will destroy parts of my brain, and I'll be unable to do certain things. I'll be bedridden in my last months. Son, I've known about this for a couple of weeks. It's terminal. Chemotherapy will buy me a little time, that's all, but in the end, it really doesn't matter. I'll die from this when God decides my time is up."

Eric nodded. "I'll do anything, everything, to help you. Everything."

"I know. God sure did give me the two best sons," Gerard said and walked up the stairs, Eric alongside him.

When Gerard and Eric entered the sitting room, Matilda steeled herself. She refused to let her fear and sorrow show in front of her husband. Instead, she gently placed her cup and saucer on the tray and asked, "Would you both like tea?"

"Yes, dear, I would." Gerard said and sat beside her.

"Yes, please," Eric replied and sat in a chair near his father.

Marisol studied Eric—his eyes in particular—and noticed the hint of tenseness on his temples, where the tiny veins pulsed. He caught her watching him, and he smiled at her as if in reassurance. Somehow, she felt more concerned, for she knew he frequently buried his feelings. The cup rattled against the saucer she held, so she placed the saucer and cup on the table and tightly clasped her hands on her lap.

"Roger told you where we went?" Gerard asked his wife.

"Yes, dear, he did." She sipped her tea and then asked, "What did the doctor say?"

Gerard, too, sipped the tea before answering. Somehow it tasted better that afternoon. "I've been having headaches. Eric

329

walked in during one, so he took me to the doctor's. I already knew what Dr. Barnard would tell me after the MRI." He sipped his tea. "The cancer returned in my brain. I'll have some chemotherapy to slow the tumor and give me a few more months."

Marisol's knuckles turned white and strained as she desperately fought her initial reaction to scream and cry. Eric observed, moved closer to her, and put his arm around her. She looked up at him. He stayed so strong. *His father way dying!* She held his hand tightly, and he kissed her cheek.

"When do you begin treatments?" Matilda asked.

"Next week. The office will call with the date and time. It's Christmas Eve. We've missed the carollers, so let's go in the music room and sing carols. Marisol, do you play the piano?'

"No. I have no musical talent at all," she said and giggled.

"We don't need the piano. Let's sing a cappella here, near the tree and the fire. In fact, let's get more people up here to join in," Gerard said and went to the call button. He told Manley to send as many staff members as possible to the sitting room. He called Roger and Daniel, as well, and soon the room filled with people.

They sang traditional carols and hymns, ending with Gerard's favorite, *Away in a Manger.* Soon thereafter, everyone prepared for the midnight church service.

After Reverend Simmons's message, Gerard stood at the pulpit and recited the nativity story in Luke chapter 2, as he had done since Christmas 1963—27 years. As he spoke, Gerard saw what no one else could see: five-year-old Patrick swinging his legs as he sat on the pew, between his mother and his brother, smiling at his father. *Oh, my Patrick, how I've missed you. I will be with you soon, son. Soon.*

"Oh, Father, I want to be with you again, but why do you have to suffer so? You never did anything wrong. You never hurt anyone. Why is this happening to you? Why? I'm so sorry you have to go through this. I'm so sorry. I love you, Father. I'll be waiting for you," Patrick said, sadness in his voice as he watched his father from Heaven.

§§§§

"Eric, would you call Marisol and ask her to come to the sitting room? I want to talk with you both. Your mother ordered tea and sandwiches for us," Gerard said in the door of Eric's suite.

"Of course. Nothing is wrong?"

"No. I have a wish to ask of you both, though," Gerard said.

"All right. I'll call her now. We'll do whatever we can." Gerard thanked his son and left. Eric dialed Marisol's number and relayed his father's request.

Eric went down to the sitting room, and Marisol arrived shortly thereafter. Matilda served the tea. Gerard smiled at each of them.

"I know, Marisol, that you do not want to marry without Eduardo present, and, believe me, I do understand that. My condition, however, leads to my question." Gerard looked at his son. "Eric, I want to see your wedding. I will not stop working with the other leaders and investigators to locate Eduardo. However, I am quite realistic.

"This cancer may claim my life sooner than Dr. Barnard estimated. I could die before Eduardo is found. Eric and Marisol, would you consider marrying in the next few months?"

Marisol leapt from her chair, kneeled before Gerard, and said, "Of course, Father. I gladly do this for you."

Gerard placed his hand on her head, and, tears filling his eyes, thanked her.

Eric said, "You know we will, Father. We'll choose a date for this summer." Eric looked at Marisol and said, "Darling, come with me. I want to show you something."

Marisol went with Eric to his sitting room. "When I was sixteen, I wrote a letter to God. I sealed it in an envelope and placed it in my Bible." Eric picked up his Bible, turned to the letter, and removed it. He slit the flap and said, "I want you to read this."

"No. This is private. I cannot."

"Please," Eric said and held the letter toward her.

Marisol took the letter and read it—four times.

26 June 1971

>*Dear God,*
>
>*I know my life's destiny remains in your hands. You planned my life long before I was born. You chose my parents and brought them together.*
>
>*God, I trust you to do the same for me. Bring me and the woman you designated for me together. Align the universe. Let my heart, my mind, and my soul all know instantly and simultaneously the moment I see her.*
>
>*I place my trust and my life in your discretion and wisdom. I know she and I will meet at the time you have already appointed.*
>
>*I love you, God, and I will love her.*
>
>*Thank you,*
>
>*Eric*

Before she could say anything, Marisol cried. When she managed to force herself to stop, she softly said, "Sí. We marry June 26. That date is ordained through this letter you wrote to Dios. That is our wedding date. Oh, Eric, yo amor usted."

"I love you, mi amor. Shall we tell Father and Mother?"

"Sí."

Eric and Marisol returned to the sitting room holding hands. "Father, Marisol and we will marry on June 26."

Gerard smiled and went to hug his son and future daughter-in-law. "Thank you. I need to go write the announcement so that the world may celebrate with you."

Within the hour, the Palace Press Secretary, Carol, released Gerard's statement, and Roger also fastened a copy to the Palace gate.

31 January 1991

With the greatest pleasure, Queen Consort Matilda and I announce the wedding date of our beloved son Prince Eric to Miss Marisol Martínez, daughter of Alejandro and Juanita Martínez.

Prince Eric and Miss Martínez will wed on 26 June 1991 at Christ Church Valmondois.

Gerard R

§§§§§

"Eric! We want Eric! Eric!"

'Why don't you two give them what they want? You've finally announced your wedding date, and they want to congratulate you. Go on," Gerard said to Eric and Marisol after lunch that day.

"Eric! Eric! Eric!" people continuously screamed.

"All right. I don't mind talking to people. Marisol? I suppose this is your first official duty," Eric said with a smile.

"I-I suppose. I have to get used to it, no?"

"Yes," Gerard answered and winked at her. "You are the next Queen Consort de Valdavia, dear girl. You'll talk to more people than you can count and shake even more hands. This is your so-called baptism by fire."

Eric took Marisol's hand, opened the front door, and immediately the screams on the mall became deafening. As usual, Eric asked that the guards open the gates, so he and his fiancée could meet everyone. People surrounded the couple as soon as they left the Courtyard, leaving Marisol overwhelmed. Still, she managed to shake hands, accept congratulations, and chat with people.

Eric began walking through the crowd, holding Marisol's hand as he did, and soon they had armfuls of cards, flowers, stuffed animals, and other gifts. Roger and Daniel went to assist, carrying presents into the foyer.

Gerard watched from a window. "Valdavia has it's best leader right there. My son is already in the history books, but his story is far from over. Eric has done so many noble deeds for Valdavians, and he will do many more. History will proclaim him our most effective and strongest King. I know that. I've already seen the evidence. I will leave this world in peace."

§§§§§

That afternoon, after Alejandro normally returned home after work, Marisol telephoned her parents to share the news. Eric picked up an extension, and they both talked with Juanita and Alejandro.

"Mamá! Papá! Eric and I have something very important to tell you. You will return to Valmondois in June."

"You are inviting us for a summer visit?" Alejandro asked.

"You never need an invitation, Papá and Mamá. You are always welcome," Eric said. "You know that. You may come now and stay forever if you want."

"Oh, we know that, Eric, we do. But I cannot leave this home. What if Eduardo returns here and we are gone? No, I must wait for mi hijo," Juanita said.

"Mamá, I understand. If you want to come, we will leave word that you are in Valmondois. Eduardo will come here to you and Marisol," Eric said.

"Sí, Mamá, Eduardo will come here to us. Please come. I will need your help," Marisol said.

"¿Qué está mal?" Juanita asked, fear in her voice.

"Nothing is wrong, Mamá and Papá, not with Marisol. Please don't be scared," Eric quickly said.

"Eric and I will marry on June 26," Marisol said.

"Mi hija! Eric! We are happy for you, but you wanted Eduardo there," Juanita said.

"We do, Mamá, but you know my father's cancer returned. This morning he told us that his one desire is to see my wedding. We can't refuse him. I hope you don't mind," Eric said.

"No, Eric, we do not," Alejandro said. "You must do this for tu Papá. It is right to do this. Our Eduardo will understand."

"Sí. And when Eduardo is home, you have what they call a vow renewal, ¿sí?" Juanita said.

"Yes, Mamá, we will. We love you all," Eric said.

"Mamá, you help me with the dress and flowers. My hair and makeup. ¿Sí?"

"Sí. I dream of this since you are born. You make me tan feliz," Juanita said and sobbed. "Los amo a ambos."

"I will love to come, but my job. I cannot take that much time," Alejandro said.

"Quit your job. We need you. We'll take care of you," Eric said. "You don't have to move here, but you don't need to work if you don't want to. You are my second mother and father. I'll transfer money to your bank account today," Eric said.

"Eric, no. That is not right," Alejandro said.

"Of course, it is. We are family, Papá and Mamá. I want to take care of you. Besides, we will have a child, and we will want you here when Marisol is pregnant and for her birth," Eric said, unaware of his pronoun. No one else noticed in the excitement of the conversation.

"Your parents will not mind?" Alejandro asked.

"No, of course not. I want to do this. I have my own money, inherited from my grandfather and grandmother, and I can never use all of it on myself. Nor do I want to. I'm transferring the money today. Give me your account information and resign from your job. My father's plane will come for you when you are ready to come here. Just call us and let us know. Marisol can come and fly here with you. You'll like that, won't you?"

335

"Sí. Gracias, mi hijo," Juanita said.

Alejandro provided his bank name and account number, and Eric called his bank for the equivalent of a $10,000 cash transfer. His parents-in-law would never worry about financial issues again.

§§§§§

After a chemotherapy session in early March, Dr. Barnard ordered another MRI of Gerard's brain to check the tumor's growth. Once more, the radiologist and Dr. Barnard rushed the analysis.

"Gerard, Eric. The tumor hasn't grown since Christmas. That's good. This is your third cycle of chemotherapy. How are your side effects?"

"Oh, not bad. I usually feel tired the week of the treatments, but nothing too serious."

"Good. We'll continue these four-week cycles as long as they're successful. As long as the tumor responds to the chemotherapy, we'll keep with it. I'll check every month for growth or changes to the tumor. When it starts growing, that means the chemotherapy is no longer working. When that will be, I have no way of knowing," Dr. Barnard explained.

"Only God knows, Neil. I'll see this son of mine married, and that's my greatest desire."

"You have three cycles before then, so let us continue praying that the tumor doesn't grow, "Dr. Barnard said.

Eric accompanied his father to the one-week chemotherapy sessions the first week of every month. He stayed beside Gerard during the treatments, sometimes holding his hand, sometimes sharing the wedding plans.

"Well, Gerard, your June MRI shows no changes," Dr. Barnard said on Friday, June 7.

Gerard smiled and let out a sigh. "I thank you, but most of all, I thank God. Neil, the next time we see you, Eric will be a married man."

Dr. Barnard smiled and hugged his King, his patient, and his friend. "I'm not going to tell you to enjoy the day, because you will. Just have fun with your family and friends and make memories."

"I plan to. I'll carry those memories to Heaven with me."

§§§§

"Mike is going to Santander and back with you. So is Daniel. They'll take care of and protect you, Mamá, and Papá. I know they don't want to move until Eduardo is located, and I do understand. But I'm happy Papá retired. He can spend more time with Mamá and make furniture again. I'm also glad they're staying here until after our wedding. When do you think you'll return?" Eric said at the airport two days later.

"Probably tomorrow, darling. Mamá and Papá have nearly finished packing. I just want to bring some more of my things, jewelry from family, books, childhood toys. I have a muñeca, a doll, my abuelo gave me. I want our daughter to have it," Marisol said with a smile.

"Our daughter. I can hardly wait for her," Eric said and smiled wistfully. "I'll miss you, but the sooner you go, the sooner you can come back to me." Eric kissed her, while members of the public watched from a distance and took pictures, as did press photographers.

Mike, one of King Gerard's body guards, promised to protect Marisol and her parents, and Daniel vowed to help them in any way. Eric watched until the airplane vanished from his view, and then he and Stanley drove home.

As promised, two days later, Marisol, Alejandro, and Juanita arrived at the airport. Eric welcomed them, drove them to the Palace, and spent the afternoon talking with them. To their delight, Matilda and Gerard joined them on the back patio with lemonade and sandwiches. Eric and Marisol held hands and smiled as their parents chatted. The families easily connected, forming an eternal bond.

Despite everything, the pain and suffering, life is perfect. Thank you, God, Eric thought.

337

§§§§§

As before, Alejandro and Juanita moved into the guesthouse with their daughter for the summer. Eric assisted his father as much as he could while maintaining his commitments and agenda. Matilda, as well, kept to her public duties as the Queen Consort. Alejandro ate lunch with Gerard when no other family members were home. The two men became fast friends, and they often took long walks through the vast Palace property after lunch.

Marisol and Juanita spent much time at the workshop of Bernice Bellencamp, the couturier whom Marisol had selected to design her wedding gown. In the early stages, mother advised daughter, they examined fabrics and trims, and finally Marisol made the final selections. With the design a true collaboration, work progressed, and regular fittings made.

Marisol never hid her whereabouts when she left the Palace, accompanied by Mike, which meant people knew the identity of her dress designer. Regardless, speculation about the gown's color and style grew steadily throughout May and June. Neither she nor Eric concerned themselves with such trivial pursuits. Far more important matters preoccupied the couple: Gerard's cancer and Eduardo's hostage situation.

Nevertheless, both Eric and Marisol anticipated beginning their shared lives—and the birth of their first child, the daughter Eric had seen in 1977.

Tourists and royal watchers began arriving in Valmondois two weeks prior to the date in order to obtain hotel rooms and to stake claim to premium spots outside the church and along the route. Thousands stood outside the Palace gates every day, which prompted regular evening visits from the engaged couple—to the thrill of Eric's fans. Thus, was the buildup to the second Wedding of the Century.

§§§§§

Reverend Simmons began the traditional ceremony that would bind Eric and Marisol for eternity. "Dearly beloved, we are gathered here in the sight of God and in the face of this congregation, to join together this man and this woman in Holy Matrimony; which is an honorable estate instituted by God himself, signifying unto us the mystical union that is betwixt Christ and his Church; which holy estate Christ adorned and beautified with his presence, and first miracle he wrought, in Cana of Galilee, and is commended in Holy Writ to be honorable among all men; and therefore is not by any to be enterprised, nor taken in hand, unadvisedly, lightly, or wantonly; but reverently, discreetly, soberly, and in the fear of God, duly considering the causes for which Matrimony was ordained.

"First, It was ordained for the increase of mankind according to the will of God, and that children might be brought up in the fear and nurture of the Lord, and to the praise of his Holy name.

"Secondly, It was ordained in order that the natural instincts and affections, implanted by God, should be hallowed and directed aright; that those who are called of God to this holy estate, should continue therein in pureness of living.

"Thirdly, It was ordained for the mutual society, help and comfort, that the one ought to have of the other, both in prosperity and in adversity.

"Into which holy estate these two persons present come now to be joined.

"Therefore if any man can shew any just cause, why they may not lawfully be joined together, let him now speak, or else hereafter for ever hold his peace." Reverend Hutchins paused for 30 seconds, allowing the traditional time for anyone to address this matter if needed. No one spoke.

Reverend Simmons looked directly at Eric and Marisol. "I require and charge you both, as ye will answer at the dreadful day of judgment when the secrets of all hearts shall be disclosed, that if either of you know any impediment, why ye may not be lawfully joined together in Matrimony, ye do now confess it. For be ye well assured, that so many as are coupled together otherwise than God's word doth allow are not joined together by God; neither is their Matrimony lawful."

Eric felt his heart overflow with love for the moment for which he had trusted God. Reverend Simmons spoke the vows.

"Eric Richard Constantin, wilt thou have this woman to thy wedded wife, to live together after God's ordinance in the holy estate of Matrimony? Wilt thou love her, comfort her, honor, and keep her, in sickness and in health; and, forsaking all other, keep thee only unto her, so long as ye both shall live?"

"I will," Eric said, his voice loud and clear, yet strained by tears.

Reverend Simmons looked at Marisol. "Marisol Maria, wilt thou have this man to thy wedded husband, to live together according to God's law in the holy estate of Matrimony? Wilt thou love him, comfort him, honor and keep him, in sickness and in health; and forsaking all other, keep thee only unto him, so long as ye both shall live?"

"I will."

"Who giveth this Woman to be married to this Man?" Reverend Simmons asked as he looked at Alejandro, who stood at Marisol's left.

"I, her father, do," Alejandro said with tears in his eyes.

"Eric Richard Constantin, say after I do," Reverend Simmons ordered, as he recited the vows line by line for Eric to repeat.

"I, Eric Richard Constantin, take thee, Marisol Maria, to my wedded wife, to have and to hold from this day forward, for better for worse, for richer for poorer, in sickness and in health, to love and to cherish, till death us do part, according to God's holy ordinance; and thereto I plight thee my troth."

Marisol likewise repeated her vows after Reverend Simmons.

"I, Marisol Maria, take thee, Eric Richard Constantin, to my wedded husband, to have and to hold from this day forward, for better for worse, for richer for poorer, in sickness and in health, to love and to cherish, till death us do part, according to God's holy ordinance; and thereto I plight thee my troth."

Eric and Marisol placed the gold wedding bands upon the book which Reverend Simmons held. The congregation bowed their heads as Reverend Simmons said a prayer for the blessing of Marisol's ring.

"Bless, O Lord, this ring, and grant that he who gives it and she who shall wear it may remain faithful to each other, and abide in thy peace and favor, and live together in love until their lives' end. Through Jesus Christ our Lord. Amen." Reverend Simmons placed the ring in Eric's left hand.

Eric smiled at Marisol as he slid the ring onto the fourth finger of her left hand and said, "With this ring I thee wed; with my body I thee honor; and all my worldly goods with thee I share: In the name of the Father, and of the Son, and of the Holy Ghost. Amen."

Reverend Simmons offered his prayer for the blessing of Eric's wedding ring. "Bless, O Lord, this ring, and grant that she who gives it and he who shall wear it may remain faithful to each other, and abide in thy peace and favor, and live together in love until their lives' end. Through Jesus Christ our Lord. Amen." Reverend Simmons placed Eric's gold band in Marisol's left hand.

Marisol slipped the ring onto the fourth finger of Eric's left hand as she fought tears of joy. "With this ring I thee wed; with my body I thee honor; and all my worldly goods with thee I share: In the name of the Father, and of the Son, and of the Holy Ghost. Amen."

At that moment, Eric and Marisol knelt onto kneelers that had been made specifically for their wedding. Alejandro discreetly stepped to his seat in the Royal pew, between Matilda and Juanita.

"Let us pray," Reverend Simmons said. The congregation all stood and bowed their heads. "O eternal God, Creator and Preserver of all mankind, giver of all spiritual grace, the author of everlasting life; Send thy blessing upon these thy servants, this man and this woman, whom we bless in thy name; that living faithfully together, they may surely perform and keep the vow and covenant betwixt them made, whereof these rings given and received are a token and pledge; and may ever remain in perfect love and peace together, and live according to thy laws; through Jesus Christ our Lord. Amen."

"Those whom God hath joined together let no man put asunder." Eric and Marisol bowed their heads, both overcome with emotions.

"Forasmuch as Eric Richard Constantin and Marisol Maria have consented together in holy wedlock, and have witnessed the same before God and this company, and thereto have given and pledged their troth to each other, and have declared the same by giving and receiving of rings, and by joining of hands; I pronounce that they be man and wife together, In the name of the Father, and of the Son, and of the Holy Ghost. Amen."

At that precise moment, the crowds outside erupted in thunderous cheers. Eric and Marisol beamed at one another, elated to finally wed, and ecstatic that thousands of people wished them happiness.

The blessing continued. "God the Father, God the Son, God the Holy Ghost, bless, preserve, and keep you; the Lord mercifully with his favor look upon you; and so fill you with all spiritual benediction and grace, that ye may so live together in this life, that in the world to come ye may have life everlasting. Amen."

Eric assisted Marisol, and while the choir sang a selection of hymns chosen by the groom and bride, they took seats to the right of the altar.

Afterward, the Father Jose Garcia, who had led the services at the Martínez family church in Santander, Spain, approached the altar to read the Lesson, I Corinthians Chapter 13.

Reverend Simmons returned for the Address, which no one had heard or read prior to the ceremony. "Today, the world witnesses a real-life Cinderella story, in which the handsome and kind prince meets, falls in love with, and marries his one true love. Yes, the world loves fairy tales, and Eric's and Marisol's story has all of the trademarks of a classic fairy-tale, to be sure. Rest assured, though, this is no fairy tale.

"Fairy-tales famously end with the wedding and the words that the couple lived happily ever after. Yes, we all pray that Eric and Marisol live many decades together filled with laughter and happiness.

Yet, these are two very human people, and each of us face trials and tribulations as we journey through this earthly life.

"The real prayer is that Eric and Marisol support one another through these trials and tribulations, these valleys, that they surely will face as the years march forward. Love does not mean never having to say one is sorry. Love truly means remaining present and caring when your life partner faces a struggle or a hardship. As our next King de Valdavia, Eric will undoubtedly encounter many such moments and will turn to God and to Marisol to provide comfort and healing and reassurance.

"Likewise, when Marisol finds herself in life's valley, she will call upon God and her husband Eric for solace and comfort. That is love. That is what these vows are truly about: in good times, in bad times, in sickness as well as health. Not only when everything is rosy and seemingly perfect, but more importantly, when things seem hopeless does the partnership's strength itself get tested.

"This couple has already faced hardships, and yet their love has only strengthened. Anyone among you who has seen them recognizes this. God sees this. God will see Eric and Marisol through every storm that batters them, that threatens to overtake them. Their faith is strong and steadfast, and that is by far the most important ingredient in a successful marriage."

"God tells us that love is the greatest gift. Eric and Marisol give that gift to one another, to their families, and to all of us. Love reigns in their lives, and when Eric reigns with his beloved Marisol alongside him, love will guide him."

Reverend Simmons stood to the left of the altar. The choir sang The Lord's Prayer, Psalm 23. Afterward, Reverend Simmons continued the blessing of the Royal couple. "Almighty God, gracious Father, heap upon you both his grace and his sanctity, that you may honor and please him in body, in heart, and in soul throughout your earthly lives, so that you may live together in holy love not just in this life on earth but in your eternal life in Heaven."

The congregation rose to sing the National Anthem of Valdavia, and Eric looked at his wife, tears once more in his eyes, as they, too, filled in Marisol's.

When the National Anthem concluded, everyone remained standing while Eric and Marisol held hands and followed Reverend Simmons to the Register Room. Gerard, Matilda, Alejandro, and Juanita followed.

For the first time, Eric kissed his wife on the mouth, a gesture both sacred and romantic. Yes, their love remained strong and true, the ceremony merely providing a public forum for what Eric and Marisol felt in the hearts.

In addition to signing the church register, bride and groom and parents shared private hugs and kisses before retuning to the ceremony. When they did, the collective happiness remained evident for all in the church to witness.

Reverend Simmons offered his final blessings to Eric and Marisol with a recitation of an Orlando Gibbons prayer. "God the Holy Trinity make you strong in faith and love, defend you on every side, and guide you in truth and peace; and the blessing of God Almighty, the Father, the Son, and the Holy Spirit, be among you and remain with you always. Amen."

Reverend Simmons made one last statement before the newlyweds led the processional. "Honored guests, I am pleased to present to you His Royal Highness Prince Eric de Valdavia and Her Royal Highness Marisol, Princess de Valdavia."

§§§§§

"Ladies and gentlemen, I am honored to present Mr. and Mrs. DeBruce Martineau, Eric and Marisol," Roger announced at the ballroom door just before the couple entered.

The guests greeted them with a standing ovation, which made both Eric and Marisol blush. When Marisol leaned her head against Eric, the diamonds in the tiara he had gifted her the evening before caught the lights and gleamed. The central heart motif represented their never-ending love, a symbol no one missed.

As guests watched from tables that lined the massive ballroom walls, Eric took Marisol's hand and led her to the center of the dancefloor. She had told him to pick the song for their first dance, to pleasantly surprise her. When the disc jockey pushed the button and the song began, she smiled up at her husband, overcome by the emotions of the moment.

Eric and Marisol slow-danced to The Association's 1967 hit song, "Never My Love," charming guests and touching their hearts. Gerard smiled happily as he watched his son and daughter-in-law, and thanked God for allowing him to to witness his eldest son's marriage to his true love. *Despite everything, you have blessed me greatly, God. Thank you.*

§§§§

After the reception, Eric carried Marisol across the threshold of their suite, and she laughed joyously. He carried her into their bedroom, gently stood her, and kissed her lips. "I love you, Marisol," he softly said. "I love you. You fill my heart, my soul, my being. I love you."

"Yo amor usted, Eric," Marisol said and placed a hand on his cheek, caressing his skin. "I am so feliz, so very happy. I have no words."

"Neither do I, but we don't need words, mi amor."

Marisol's clothes and belongings had been moved to Eric's suite during the wedding, and she noticed a white lacy nightgown on the bed. "I bought that for you, only you," she whispered in his ear. "For you, and only you, I removed the ring Mamá gave me years ago." Indeed, she slipped off the purity ring permanently that morning as she prepared for her wedding.

"And I have waited for you, darling, only you," Eric said and kissed her. "Do you need help removing the tiara or gown?"

"Sí, gracias. Mamá did the buttons down the back of the gown, but I cannot reach them. Will you undo them?"

"Of course. First, the tiara," Eric said, gently removed it from her thick black hair and handed it to her. Then he slowly undid the three-dozen tiny pearl button down the back of her ivory brocade gown. When he finished, he kissed her shoulder and said, "No bride has ever been more beautiful than you."

Marisol turned and once more kissed him before she went into the dressing room to remove her wedding gown and carefully hang it. She put on a robe, brushed her hair, and then went into the bathroom to wash her face and brush her teeth.

While she did that, Eric removed and hung up his white military uniform and changed into his pajamas in the wardrobe—which he now gleefully shared with his wife. His wife! He and Marisol had married, and they became eternal partners. Eric knew that. *God, you know my heart. Marisol is the only woman meant for me, the only woman I will ever love, the only woman who will own my heart. She is my wife for life, God, and I pray our lives remain joyous and loving despite any hardships we face. Your strength and your love will assure that. Thank you for loving me enough to bring me Marisol and her love.*

Soon, Marisol emerged, attired in the white lace nightgown, angelic and perfect. Eric had turned back the sheets, and for the first time, they shared a bed. Eric leaned over her, kissed her, their love and passion increasing until their bodies merged and became one, forever one.

§§§§§

"Hey, Eric! I wish you could hear me tell you how happy I am for you. I am. You deserve this more than anyone, and your life is perfect now. Father's cancer is the only dark cloud over the family, and I'm truly sorry about that. But today was so beautiful, bro, and I so wish I could have been there to stand beside you, to support you. She seems wonderful, and I can see she loves you as much as you love her. Here's to eighty years of wedded bliss, Eric!" Patrick said as he watched Eric and Marisol kiss in their bedroom after the reception.

"Daddy and Mommy are married?"

"Little Bit! You shouldn't be here!"

"Why? I can't see them. I can't see him when he's with her. I suppose I'll never see him again until I'm born," Angilia said and frowned. The tears in her eyes dampened Patrick's happiness.

"I'm sure they won't be together every moment. Heck, Eric has many public duties, you know, so you'll see him when he's working and stuff like that."

"I will? Really?"

"Sure. You're just not supposed to see your mother until your birth, that's all," Patrick reminded her.

"Uncle Patrick, do you know when I'll be born?"

Patrick put his arm around her. "No. Only God and Michael know. They won't tell anyone else. But Eric and your mom are married now, and I do know they want a child soon. It's really all up to God, Little Bit."

Angilia nodded. "I know. I'll take the moments when I can see Daddy and be grateful for those. I love him so much, Uncle Patrick, and all I want is to be with him."

Patrick hugged his niece to him. "I know. He wants to see you again, too. I shouldn't have told you that, but what the heck? You're miserable, and I hate seeing you like this. I'll tell you one thing. I'll sure be watching when you are born, and you and Eric are reunited!"

§§§§§

"The garland looks beautiful. I'm so happy we've been able to preserve it as long as we have," Matilda said.

"It is old, ¿sí?" Marisol asked.

"Yes, dear," Matilda answered. "This belonged to Gerard's grandfather, also Gerard."

"Yes. I was named after Grandfather. He was such a jolly man, and Christmas was his favorite time of year. He enjoyed making people happy, especially children, so he was Valdavia's Santa Claus. When he went on any appointments and duties during December, he always went with a car trunk filled with wrapped toys. You know how people show up at all appearances, so Grandfather was prepared. He gave the presents to the children in the crowds wherever he went. I'd like to think I learned a few things from him. I see a lot of him in Eric.

"Grandfather was born in 1835, and he became King in 1895. The garland was a gift from Queen Victoria upon his coronation. Prince Albert had bought the original of this garland for his and Victoria's first tree, and she had it replicated for Grandfather."

"Oh, my goodness! This is inappreciable. I think your word is priceless. Such history!" Marisol said.

"Yes. Every family's past is filled with history. I want to learn more of your family's history," Eric said to Marisol and smiled.

"Now it's time to place the ornaments," Matilda said. "Place them where you want, but all I ask is that they are balanced. Gerard, you don't overdo it, promise me."

"Yes, dear."

Gerard had grown weaker. Three weeks earlier at his MRI, he and Eric learned that the tumor had grown one centimeter. Dr. Barnard planned to continue chemotherapy for the time being, so Gerard's next treatment would be January 2, 1992. Dr. Barnard also warned him to slow his schedule of public events and meetings, much to Gerard's displeasure. After all, that meant the end was nearer.

"I know, Mother. Balance makes for a lovely tree," Eric said and giggled. "This is my thirty-seventh Christmas."

"Ah, youth," Gerard said and winked. "Treasure yours, you two."

"We will, Father. We love you," Marisol said.

"And I love you both."

The four of them chatted and laughed as they unpacked the ornaments and placed them on the tree. Eric reached for one swathed in yellowing wrapping paper and carefully removed the paper, placing it safely in the ornament's compartment. He held the ornament, and even though he smiled, tears filled his eyes as he knelt to a low branch which pointed to the fireplace.

Marisol kneeled beside Eric and put an arm around him. "Patrick's snowman."

"Yes. This is our fourteenth Christmas without him. He should be hanging this on the tree."

"Oh, Eric. I know your pain at his loss. When it happened, I cried for days. It broke my heart, someone so young and so beautiful in spirit. You hurt me, too. I watched you, in newspapers and on the television, and I knew how deeply you hurt. But I also knew that you hid your pain, and that caused me great pain for you. I prayed to Dios to help you to find healing and peace. Long before we met, you touch my heart."

Eric smiled at his wife and said, "He did, mi amor. You. He sent me you, and you helped me more than you will ever know. God is my Savior, but you, too, are my savior. You must never leave me for any reason, Marisol. Never."

"I could never leave you, mi amor Eric. You are part of my heart."

§§§§

After Gerard's January 2, 1992 MRI and chemotherapy treatment, Dr. Barnard reported no changes in the tumor. "So, we stay the course, do we? Business as usual?" Gerard asked.

"We continue the chemotherapy treatments the first of each month, yes. However, as I warned you before, you need to slow down your workload, Gerard. Your body has been and is going through a lot. Chemotherapy alone is enough of a burden on one's body, let alone working as much as you do. I see the news. Five or more meetings and public appearances each day is far too much. You must cut back. I know what you're going to say, so don't even bother. I'm your doctor, and I know what's best for you."

"I do, too, Father. I'm taking half of your appointments. No debate," Eric said, recognizing his father's expression. "I'm not going to let you exhaust yourself with all of this work. You can advise and brief me on any meetings and other appointments. You're the King, but more importantly, you're my father."

"Eric is right. You need to lessen your workload. Do I need to remind you that this will not get better but only worse? Isn't the point of the chemotherapy to give you more time with your family, Gerard?"

"Yes, Neil, it is. Work can't take priority, can it? Eric will be my Solomon, then. When this cancer gets worse, I will declare him acting monarch. My family is the most important part of my life. I admit that I can no longer carry a full schedule and still enjoy the people who matter most to me. According to your initial estimation, Neil, I'm in my final year of life. This young man will be King in a few months anyway, so why not let him get some more on-the-job training?"

Eric smiled, hiding his sadness as he often did. "I need it, too."

"You do not. Regardless, you'll get it. I'm just sorry it's going to take you away from Marisol."

"Don't worry about that. We make the most of every minute. Besides, we both want to do all we can for you."

"Just what a young couple needs, taking care of an invalid," Gerard scoffed.

"Father, don't say that. We want to help because we love you. I love you. You have to know that."

"I do, son. I'm sorry. I never wanted to be dependent on anyone, especially my son. I never wanted to be a burden."

"You are not a burden, Father. Never. Don't you realize that love means giving all of yourself to those whom you love?" Eric said and held his father's hand between both of his.

§§§§§

"Father, the zoning committee meeting is tomorrow morning, and the military briefing is tomorrow over lunch. The Business Association meets tomorrow afternoon, and after that is the opening of the new hospital unit. I've read the agendas and your notes. I've added some of my ideas in pencil. Would you inform me of anything else I should know?" Eric said in Gerard's office two months later.

"All right," Gerard said and took the files from Eric. He reviewed the zoning committee and Business Association notes. "These are prudent additions," he said and returned all the files. "You know far more about the military than I do, so I have no need to review your notes, Eric. You've opened stores, dedicated buildings, and broken ground for new developments, so opening a hospital unit is not a major task for you. You're doing me proud, son, very proud."

Gerard breathed deeply and closed his eyes for a moment. Eric of course noticed. As if sensing his son's concern, Gerard opened his eyes and weakly smiled. He buzzed Roger and said, "I'm going to take a nap. Please wake me in one hour, Roger."

"Of course. Shall I help you upstairs?" Roger asked.

"No. I'll sleep here. Eric, show Roger the Murphy bed, please.

Eric went to a paneled section of the wall and pushed a hidden button. A bed automatically lowered, and Eric made sure it felt comfortable. He then helped his father to the bed, removed Gerard's jacket and passed it to Roger, and helped Gerard to sit atop the bed. "Here, let me remove your tie and shoes," Eric said, and then, like a father himself, tucked his ailing father under the blankets. Eric kissed his father's forehead and said, "I love you."

In the hallway, Eric whispered to Roger. "Don't close his door. Can you work from his desk, so you can answer his phone and watch him?"

"Sure. I'll bring a few things over and be as quiet as possible. I'll mute his phone and watch for the lights for incoming calls."

"Thank you. I hate being away from him, but it's the only way to keep him from working. Please call me if anything at all happens. Anything."

"I will. I'll take the best care of him. Plus, I've got Dr. Barnard's number if he gets sick," Roger said. "Just give me a second to grab a couple of things." Roger rushed back with Gerard's agenda and a notepad. "I won't leave until you're back, I promise."

"Thank you," Eric said, and grasped his best friend's hand before he reluctantly left.

On his way to the garage with Stanley, Eric heard his mother call to him. "I know you have some meetings, but how is your father?"

"Resting. He's napping on the Murphy bed in his office. Roger is working at Father's desk to keep watch over him. Why don't you get some rest, too? This is exhausting you, Mother."

Matilda sighed and said, "Yes, I think I will. Now is a good time, while Gerard is sleeping. You be careful, dear."

Matilda walked to the fourth floor, tiptoed to Roger and whispered, "I thought I'd nap on the sofa there while Gerard rests."

Roger nodded and smiled when she bent to gently kiss her husband's cheek before curling up on the sofa. Their love charmed him like a real-life fairy-tale. *People can live happily together, even when they do face tragedy and heartbreak. The loss of Patrick, Gerard's cancer—yet, these two never once lost their bond or forsook their vows. Heck, their love just seems stronger since I met them more than thirty years ago. That's so rare. I pray this for Eric and Marisol, I really do. Eric deserves happiness, more than anyone I know. I want to raise the toast to them on their fiftieth anniversary,* Roger thought as he watched the King and Queen Consort.

§§§§§

Three weeks later, in April 1992, Eric met with his father, as usual, in Gerard's office. Eric treasured the meetings, as they allowed him more time with his father.

"Eric, you know I trust you in all of your thoughts and ideas. You don't have to ask me to approve your notes before every meeting," Gerard said early one morning after breakfast.

"Are you sure? Or is there another reason? Are these talks too tiring for you?"

"Talks with you tiring? Nonsense. Our conversations are bright spots in my day. It's just that you really don't need my approval. You are more than capable to take the reigns solo," Gerard said and sipped his tea.

"You are the King, Father. I feel it's my duty to pass my ideas and intentions before you," Eric said.

"If that's how you feel, then by all means continue. I enjoy our talks. There's no other reason than that I really don't think you need me to approve your meeting notes."

"I'm flattered, but you are the King, and I am acting on your behalf. You should know my intentions," Eric said.

Gerard smiled. "Very well. I don't have anything pressing for the time being. When is your first meeting?"

"Nine. Do you need something?"

"Your company," Gerard said. "It's been a while since I walked through the gardens, and I thought you'd like to join me."

"Of course, I would." Eric stood and slowly helped his father from his desk chair. Gerard stumbled in the hallway, causing Eric to hold his father's arms and guide him back to his office. As Eric neared the sofa, Gerard lost his balance again, and Eric fought his panic. Eric held onto his father and lowered the Murphy bed, lifting Gerard atop it and covering him.

He rushed to Gerard's phone and called Dr. Barnard, who arrived within minutes. After an examination, Dr. Barnard told Eric, "His breathing is labored, but I tend to think that is his frustration at the imbalance. His heart sounds good. I do want an MRI, so I can see if there are any changes. Normally, I would call an ambulance, but we will take him in your car to preserve his privacy as much as possible."

Eric nodded, remaining outwardly calm, yet his face tight and tense. "He shouldn't walk. I'll carry him." Eric called for Roger. "Both of you walk one step behind me and be ready to grab Father if I stumble."

Eric took one stair at a time, very slowly, until Devon and Mike saw them and ran up to assist. "Let me carry His Majesty," Mike said. Mike's strength remained legendary among the Palace guards, and Eric trusted him. He carefully placed his father in Mike's arms, and soon, they placed Gerard in one of the dark-windowed Rolls Royce cars. Eric sat beside his father, letting Gerard lean on him, and Dr. Barnard sat on the King's other side. Mike drove, and Devon sat in the passenger seat.

Within the hour, Dr. Barnard told Eric and Gerard the MRI results. "Gerard. Eric. The tumor has grown early two centimeters and is affecting the motor skills area of your brain in the frontal lobe, an area called the precentral gyrus. This caused you to lose balance this morning. Gerard, when did you first notice this?"

"This morning when it happened. I might as well tell you that I also noticed that my handwriting is shaky. My hands shake, almost as if I have Parkinson's," Gerard said.

Dr. Barnard shook his head and looked at the floor for a few seconds. "Gerard, we'll do the May chemotherapy to see if and how the tumor changes."

"And?" Gerard asked.

"Depending on the results, we either suspend the chemotherapy or we continue the treatments. We'll know in two weeks."

"The end is nearer. I know that. What I don't know is exactly when. I don't know the date or the time of day or the location. Only God knows all of that. I just need to be ready at every moment," Gerard said.

§§§§§

Eric spent as much time as he could with Gerard, as did Matilda, who canceled many of her appointments for that spring. Marisol, too, sat with Gerard often, especially when Eric was away fulfilling his father's obligations. All of them noticed the further deterioration of his equilibrium and had also heard his slurred speech.

Matilda went to the watch tower atop the Palace frequently, where she could cry away from Gerard. She prayed constantly for God to cure her husband, and she did so once more. *Please God, remove this cancer from Gerard's brain. He never did anything to warrant the cancer in the first place. You know that. He's always lived according to your commandments and laws, and he loves people as you instruct us to. He is loving, kind, and hard working. He has never willingly or deliberately hurt anyone. You know him, God. He is a good man, one of the best. He does not deserve this. Please do not let him go through this, God, please. I know you can heal him, and I ask you to please do so. Please, God. Please. I love him. I love you. Amen.*

On the first Monday in May, Eric drove his father to the hospital for the MRI and for the chemotherapy session. While Eric sat beside his weakened father and held his had as he leaned back in the chair during treatment, Dr. Barnard entered.

"Eric, I have the MRI results." Dr. Barnard cleared his throat.

"Just say it, Neil," Gerard said, not opening his eyes. "The tumor has grown. This is my last treatment."

"Yes, Gerard. I am so very sorry."

"You have nothing for which to be sorry," Gerard said, some of his words slurred. "We knew this would happen. There's no need for me to cry about it. This is my truth. Now I wait to die."

Eric's grip on his father's hand tightened, and he swallowed his tears. Gerard waited until the nurse removed the IV, and then he patted Eric's hand.

"Death is part of life. We all know that. It's not death that saddens me, for I'm reasonably sure where I'll spend eternity. The saddest part is leaving you and your mother and that sweet wife of yours. I will miss you all terribly until God reunites us."

"I'll miss you more than you will ever know, Father," Eric said, tears filing his eyes.

"Are those tears for me?"

Eric nodded. "You don't deserve to suffer like this, Father. Not you."

"Then who does?"

"No one deserves cancer. Elena didn't. Maria Sabine didn't. No one does. It's just that so many benevolent and godly people suffer so. Why does Satan attack you like this? Why? His hatred for God's children sickens me."

"It's his only resort. He never tempted me away from God, so this is how he punishes me. This is my battle wound as a soldier of God, Eric. All soldiers will bear their own wounds. They may kill our bodies, but they will never kill our souls, which belong only to God Almighty. Remember, all of life's trials you face are Satan's attacks. Never get angry at Satan. Pity him. His being is filled with envy and hatred, because we have what he lost: a seat in Heaven with God. Remember that and fight the good fight."

"I will, I promise," Eric said and held his father's frail hand between his strong hands.

§§§§

"Mi pobre amor, you work too hard, too much," Marisol said as she massaged Eric's shoulders one night a few weeks later. "I know why, and I love you more for doing all of this for Father, but you are agotado, exhausted."

"Not exhausted, darling. I've never needed much sleep. Don't worry about me."

"I do not mean sleep. I mean in your soul. You hold everything inside. You remain strong for everyone, but what about you? Who is strong for you? How do you let it out? You do not, and that is not right. This started with Patrick?"

Eric shook his head. "Grandfather. Mother told Patrick and me to not cry or get upset in front of Father and cause him more distress. I vowed then to remain strong for Father, Mother, and Patrick, to bury it all. I've kept that promise."

Marisol moved in front of Eric and looked into his eyes. "Eric, no, you must not do this. You are amazing, and I love you, but you must think of yourself, too."

Eric offered Marisol a tired smile and put his hand on her cheek. "I don't want to become one of those self-absorbed men who forget everyone else and think only of their own needs and desires. That isn't what God wants from me."

"Dios does not want you to suffer by burying all of your feelings deep inside of you, mi amor. Please do not do that. Share them with me, su esposa. ¿Sí?"

"For better or for worse," Eric said and closed his eyes for a moment. "All right, I will. I will share with you all I feel and think about Father's cancer. You won't mind?"

"Mind? Why would I? We are life partners, Eric. We tell each other everything. Come," Marisol said and pulled him down to rest against her.

He held her hand atop his stomach, and took a deep, relaxing breath. "Father showed me what a godly man is just by living his life and treating everyone with love and compassion. He never seemed to get angry, not like some people who scream and curse and attack at the least little thing. Father has met millions of people, and each one would tell you that he was respectful and kind.

"Even when he was displeased or disappointed, he never lashed out in anger. He taught me by example to do the same, to follow Jesus's command to love all people. More than Reverend Simmons's sermons, Father's daily life has been my greatest teacher.

"He never deliberately, intentionally hurt anyone. Even when someone attacked him, he responded with kindness. He's such an incredible man. Yes, he is my King, but foremost, he is my father, and I love him. I love him.

"He never did anything to deserve cancer. He ate well, he exercised, and he lived a clean, healthy lifestyle. There hasn't been any alcohol or liquor in this place for at least one hundred years. Father never smoked or took drugs other than vitamins. He's kind and caring. What wrong did he do? He told me Satan attacked him because of his godly lifestyle.

"I understand that, but that doesn't change the fact that my father is dying. I know we all die, and I believe that the death of our bodies is not the end. I believe, as you do, that our souls live eternally, either in Heaven or in Hell depending on whether we accept Jesus as God's Son and our Savior. I firmly believe that.

"But it's Father's pain and suffering that hurt me, Marisol. And there's nothing I can do. I would take his pain, take the cancer, if I could, but I can't," Eric said and, for the first time since Gerard's brain cancer diagnosis, cried.

Marisol knew not to counter his comments, but she held him tight while he finally expended his own pain. For more than three hours, she held her husband close to her and gently rocked him while he cried.

§§§§§

Royal Proclamation

15 June 1992

As you know, my cancer returned—in my brain—and is terminal. The tumor is growing and affecting my motor skills and my speech. I love all of you, and I love Valdavia, and the last thing I want is to fail you or to do you a disservice. You deserve far better.

Therefore, I hereby declare my son, Prince Eric, as acting King de Valdavia. As much as my condition permits, I will continue to advise Eric, but soon I shall be unable to do so. You know that Eric will serve you well and that he will do everything for your benefit.

God has blessed me with a loving and devoted wife, your Queen Consort Matilda, and two remarkable sons, Eric and Patrick. My blessings far exceed the heartbreaks, and I owe all to God.

This is the last message you will receive from me, my dear friends, neighbors, and fellow Valdavians. Know that I feel honored to have worked for and with you these twenty-nine years. Thank you for adding to my life's richness.

God's blessings to each of you.

Gerard R

§§§§§

"Welcome to the midday news on this June 26, 1992. I'm Franklin Sydney, and it is my extreme honor to bring you this live interview with Prince Eric de Valdavia and Marisol, Princess de Valdavia on their first wedding anniversary."

"Welcome, Franklin," Eric said and smiled at one of the few reporters whom he trusted and considered a friend. "Marisol and I both welcome you on this special day."

"Congratulations, Your Royal Highnesses. Your wedding one year ago has been proclaimed the most romantic and love-filled Royal Wedding the world has seen in decades. Have either of you read the multitude of articles and books written about your wedding?"

Eric slightly grimaced but offered a small smile. "I haven't, no. I wasn't even aware that more than a few existed, to be honest. Have you, darling?" Eric asked his wife.

"No. People show them to me when I am out, but I have not read any of them."

"Do you mean that people ask you to autograph them, Your Royal Highnesses?"

"Only once or twice," Marisol said and smiled at her husband, knowing he had signed far more than she had.

"Yes," Eric merely replied.

"What is your one favorite memory of your wedding?"

"Oh, the entire day, really, but if you ask about the ceremony, for me it is when Eric slid the wedding band on my finger. That moment meant that we are man and wife forever," Marisol said, tears gleaming in her brown eyes. Eric gently squeezed her hand as he sat beside her on the sofa in his father's office.

"The entire day is my life's dream come true, so choosing just one moment is very difficult for me. If I must select one, though, it's the moment when Reverend Simmons asked, 'Who gives this woman to be married?' When Papá, Mr. Martínez, said he did, his voice cracking with his emotions, that touched me deeply. My father is very important to me, and I love him dearly. I know Marisol feels similarly about her father. Marisol and I share our strong Christian faith and our love of our families. Now our families are eternally bound through our marriage. The DeBruce Martineau and the Martínez families are now one family. Love is all about touching people and creating bonds, so, yes, that moment stands out for me for many reasons," Eric said.

"That is beautiful, mi amor, just beautiful. You have not told me that before," Marisol said and dabbed tears from her eyes.

"That is emotive and heartfelt, Your Royal Highness," Franklin said. "What has been the most surprising part of marriage for each of you during this first year?"

"Nothing," both Eric and Marisol answered simultaneously, and then laughed.

"Nothing?"

"No. Both of us have parents who have been married over forty-four years. We grew up with parents who are best friends, share private jokes, romance, and tremendous respect and love for one another. My parents, as well as Marisol's, share everything, and I mean everything, good and bad, happy and sad. Our parents provided each of us perfect examples of the partnership, trust, and honesty that grow a marriage and keep it strong and fresh," Eric said. He looked at Marisol. "Don't you agree?"

"Sí. I can never say it better than my husband, so I will not try. No, no surprises, because we, too, share everything and we deeply trust each other," Marisol said as she looked at Eric.

"Your Royal Highnesses, what advice do you offer to couples who are contemplating marriage?"

"Trust your heart," Eric immediately answered. "I long ago prayed to God to send me the one woman he intended for me and to let my heart know her instantly. That's exactly what happened to me at the fundraiser on June 9, 1989. I saw Marisol as I gave the speech, and I knew in my heart that she is my one and only. I never felt anything remotely similar about any other woman. I trusted God to bring her to me when I was meant to meet her, and He did. My heart knew," Eric said, finally explaining to the public why he had never dated and played the field.

"A wedding is about your love, not about outdoing someone else. Weddings are about you and your fiancé, not about what other people want. Yes, Eric is the next King de Valdavia, and his wedding would bring much interest, but our wedding was really quite—what is the word? Understated?" she asked Eric, and he nodded. "We planned our wedding together. We did not want something huge and dramatic. We wanted to respect the ceremony and our love, so we did not want to overshadow what is most important: our vows. I hope that does not offend anyone," Marisol said. Eric again squeezed her hand in reassurance.

"Of course not, Your Royal Highness. If you had read many of the book and articles, you would have known that many people felt that sentiment in your wedding. Yes, it was the marriage of the Valdavian heir, but it did not, as you say, overshadow the traditional Christian ceremony. People were touched by that emphasis," Franklin said.

"Gracias. Thank you," Marisol said.

"Your Royal Highnesses, one question frequently asked is when you will have your first child."

"When God has already determined we will," Eric said. "Again, Marisol and I trust and have faith that God long ago decided he—our child's birth date." Eric breathed deeply. He had stopped himself just in time before saying *her birth date*. Neither Marisol nor Franklin seemed to notice.

"Finally, what is your wish for your future?"

"Wish? I don't make wishes," Eric said. "My prayer for Marisol and me is that God grants us many decades filled with the love, happiness, and respect that filled our first year," Eric said and beamed at his wife.

"Sí, for me, too," Marisol said, looking at only her husband.

§§§§§

"Eric! Help!"

Eric bolted from his bed at this mother's scream and ran to his parents' bedroom. His father lay face down on the floor, unable to get up. "Father?!"

"He tried to get out of bed, and before I could get to him, he fell," Matilda said, crying. "Why didn't you wake me, Gerard?"

"I just wanted to go to the bathroom," Gerard weakly said, tears in his eyes.

"Here, let me help you," Eric said. He carefully lifted his father and made sure he wasn't hurt. "Come on, let's get you taken care of and then back to bed."

Eric assisted Gerard to the bathroom, feeling for his father's mortification. He understood that the lack of privacy and the inability to perform even the simplest tasks greatly upset and humiliated his father, so he maintained as much privacy as he could.

"You should not have to do this for your father," Gerard said, his words slow and garbled.

"I don't mind, Father. I know this is difficult for you, and I understand, but I want to help you in any way I can. You took care of me when I was too young to care for myself, and I owe you a huge debt. I do this because I love you."

Gerard nodded as he turned from the urinal. "I know," he softly said. "I know."

Eric lifted his thinner and weaker father onto the bed and covered him. He kissed his father's forehead and said, "Just call for me if you need anything at all. All right?"

Gerard nodded, and Matilda dried her face and lay next to her husband, as she had done for more nearly forty-three years. Eric captured that image in his brain, and he smiled as he turned out the light and went to his desk.

He opened his diary, picked up a pen, and wrote his feelings.

13 August 1992

Father fell trying to get out of bed a short time ago. Such a simple thing as going to the bathroom on his own is now impossible for him. I knew this was coming. I was also prepared for his reaction to its reality.

He has been independent and self-sufficient for so long, and having to depend on someone else for the most basic and personal of needs is not just humiliating, but a clear sign that his life is near its end. My heart aches for this strong, brave man. He does not deserve this!

Still, even while suffering these indignities, Father faces them with faith and strength. He doesn't want to be a burden, to cause us further turmoil—but he can never do that. I will do all in my power for him in his last days with us. How could I not? This isn't about me, but about Father and his needs.

God will heal Father as soon as his body dies, and his soul reaches Heaven. I know that. I will miss him, but I pray I am judged worthy enough to reunite with him and Patrick someday.

§§§§

"Eric, hey, you doubt that you'll be here? Really? If anyone will be here, it's you, bro. Don't worry about Father. Like you said, he'll be healed and fine—just like I am. I wish you could hear me and see me, Eric, but maybe somehow you can feel me around you.

"And, hey, you sure have a cool wife. She managed to do what no one else could. She got you to let out your feelings. You need to do that more, you really do. Yeah, you write in that diary, but you've got her now. Share it with her. Please. Don't bottle up all this stuff with Father like you've done with me. The angels pray for you, Eric."

Patrick heard crying, an unusual sound in the Angel Realm. He instantly knew, and he followed the sound. "Hey, Little One. You've been watching, too?" She nodded. "What you didn't see is how your mom has helped him. She got him to talk about it all, to get it out. That really helps, believe me. With her, Eric will get through this. Plus, he's got God."

"Mommy loves him. She helps him, because she loves him. Daddy helps Grandfather because he loves his father. I love Daddy, and I want to help him. I can't, though. I am helpless, Uncle Patrick. I can't do anything for Daddy."

"Sure, you can. Pray for him and talk to him."

"He can't hear me," Angilia said, still sobbing.

"He can't hear me, either, but I talk to him every day. Somehow, he feels us, I believe that, Little One."

"You do?"

"Sure. Besides, I have a feeling your birth can't be too far away."

"I pray so, Uncle Patrick. I just do not feel complete since that day I came for you and had to leave Daddy standing there. I can never explain it, but I have not felt whole since then."

"Well, you two are connected, you know. You're father and daughter. That's a very special bond."

"I just want him to hold me, Uncle Patrick. And I want to grow up taking care of him. That is all I long to do," Angilia said.

§§§§§

The next morning, Dr. Barnard arrived to examine Gerard, who stared at the ceiling throughout. Dr. Barnard assessed the bedroom, and as he looked around, Gerard said his first garbled words to his doctor.

"I am staying here until I die. That is nonnegotiable. I don't have much longer, and I want to die in my home with my family."

"Of course, Gerard. I was just thinking the logistics through."

"What logistics? This is my bed, and I am staying here. No hospital bed. No big machines. No more MRIs. The tumor is growing. I know that. I feel it. Nothing you or any doctor can do will change that. My time here is short, I know. I'm leaving on my terms, Neil."

"All right, Gerard. I would like to have an IV set up with a morphine drip and saline solution. I'd also like to have a nurse stay here around the clock to monitor you and to address any needs. Is that all right?"

"Fine. The nurse is not sleeping in here, though. There's a room next door," Gerard said. "I want to be alone with Matilda as much as I can be."

"I understand. I'll place the order now, and everything will be set up soon. Then we'll be out of your way," Dr. Barnard said.

Within the hour, the nurse arrived in her uniform with the IV and medicines. Eric stood in his father's doorway watching, knowing the truth before Dr. Barnard told him. The doctor briefed the nurse before he turned and beckoned Eric into the hall.

"Father's time is imminent, isn't it?"

"Yes, Eric. I prayed some miracle would intervene. I never wanted this to happen. I will come every day to check on Gerard, and I will be here in a flash if you need me. Just call at any time. We will keep him comfortable and control his pain. I'll increase his morphine as much as possible as needed," Dr. Barnard said.

"Thank you," Eric said and squeezed the doctor's hand. "We all appreciate it. I want to sit with him for a while before I must leave. He doesn't want me canceling any appointments to stay with him," Eric said with a sad smile. "I grab every minute I can. Excuse me."

Eric pulled a chair beside his father's bed and held his hand. Gerard seemed asleep, so Eric sat quietly, his head bowed.

"Why are you here, son? You have meetings today."

"Father, I thought you were asleep. I'm prepared for the meetings. I don't have to leave yet. There are a few minutes to sit with you. Am I disturbing you?"

"No. Just don't be late."

"I won't be," Eric said as his father did fall asleep.

Roger quietly came in several minutes later and whispered to Eric. "It's time for you to leave. Stanley is waiting. I'll sit with Gerard for a while."

"Thank you, Roger," Eric said and reluctantly left. Although no one could tell, his thoughts constantly returned to his father, and pangs of guilt stabbed him for not being with him. Still, he knew that canceled meetings would only distress Gerard, and Eric never wanted to do that. Even amid tragedy and sorrow, life continued.

§§§§§

"Mother, you need to eat. You've sat here for more than fifteen hours without sleep or food. What would Father say?" Eric said one evening in early September.

Matilda lifted a handkerchief to her eyes with one hand, while her other hand held Gerard's hand. "I can't. I don't want to leave him for one minute."

"Then I'll bring your dinner here. You can eat while you talk to him. That way, if he opens his eyes, he won't be concerned about you. Okay?"

"All right, for Gerard. I lie beside him with a hand over his heart just to feel his heartbeat. I want him to feel me here," Matilda said, wiping her eyes.

"He knows, Mother. He knows you're here with him." He patted her shoulder, kissed her temple, and said, "I'll get your dinner now."

Ten minutes later, Eric returned with a tray, which he placed on a table near his mother. "You eat. I'll sit here, too, and keep you and Father company," Eric said and moved a chair close to the other side of his father's bed.

"I'm here, Father. The meeting with Vice President Quayle ended amicably, and we signed the trade initiative between the United

States and Valdavia. The negotiations proved smooth and agreeable. I hope you'll be proud of the results," Eric told his father.

"Good, son," Gerard weakly said, his eyes barely open. "Very well done. You had a long day of it?"

"Actually, we agreed on most points, so our negotiations finished ahead of schedule. I was able to introduce the Vice President to some of our business owners and entrepreneurs who will become involved in the trade of goods."

"Most excellent, son, and prudent. I am proud of you."

Inwardly, Eric's heart lurched, for his father's voice sounded weak and his words quite indistinct. His father's pain and weakness deeply affected him, even though he never let it show except to Marisol in the privacy of their bedroom. Eric reached across the bed and held his father's hand.

"Thank you, Father. Filling in for you is quite the challenge, you know."

Gerard very slightly smiled. "Nonsense. Now, go to that wife of yours. She needs you. Go," he repeated when Eric didn't move.

Eric looked at his mother, and Matilda nodded. "All right, Father. I'll give you and Mother some privacy." Eric bent to kiss his father's forehead and went to his bedroom.

Eric pulled off his tie and jacket and tossed them carelessly on an upholstered chair. He stood silent, his hands on his hips for a moment, and then hit the chair several times as hard as he could. He fell to his knees and cried into the chair, muffling the sounds.

Marisol ran to him and wrapped her arms around him, holding him tight from behind. She never said anything, just let him cry and release his pain. She held him for a few hours until he stopped crying—and then, in utter exhaustion, fell asleep.

Marisol carefully unwrapped her arms from him, got pillows and blanket off the bed and gently lay Eric on his side, removed his shoes and socks, unbuttoned his shirt collar, and covered him. She lay beside him, wrapped her arms around him, and then silently cried into her pillow.

§§§§§

"Eric, I'm afraid Gerard will remain mostly unresponsive from this point. As the tumor grows and interrupts more functions, he can no longer perform those functions." Dr. Barnard recognized Eric's expression, for he had seen similar responses. He placed his hand on the younger man's arm. "Your father is at the beginning of the death process. He could transition any time in the next three days or so. The nurse will monitor him more frequently. His morphine has been increased to ensure that he feels no pain. I will come several times each day, but call me at any time for any reason, please."

Eric nodded. "Thank you, Dr. Barnard. We all knew this was inevitable, but the reality of it is just. . . . . Thank you."

"This transition is never easy, Eric, even for the strongest of faith. Someone we love is preparing to leave us, and that is painful, emotional, and yes, stressful. Call me if you just need to talk."

"Thank you," Eric said. After the doctor left, Eric went into his parents' bedroom and told his father, "I love you, Father," and kissed him.

He hugged and kissed his mother and held her for several moments. Neither of them spoke for a while until Matilda softly said, "Your father loves you so very much, Eric, more than I think you ever knew."

"I know, Mother. He never had to say it. I felt it." Matilda squeezed his hand and, through the tears, smiled at him.

When Eric left, he walked to his father's fourth-floor office and, for the first time, closed and locked the door. He looked around, realizing how little the room had changed from when his grandfather had worked from this office. Soon, he would be the King and this would be his office.

Eric sat in the brown leather chair both his grandfather and father had used. He placed his hands on the arms, where decades of handprints had created a patina. *Grandfather. Father. You are both part of me. You taught me. You prepared me for this. I am facing what you faced in 1963, Father, when Grandfather died, and what you faced in 1926, Grandfather. I am just the latest son to grieve his father while taking over. I know this is part of life, but that doesn't mean it doesn't hurt. It does, more than I've let anyone know. I can't let them know. They're hurting, too, so how can I dump my pain on them? I can't do that.*

Eric sat in that old leather chair and cried for nearly six hours, until his tear ducts dried. He had no tears left. He took several deep breaths, straightened his tie, combed his hair with his fingers, and unlocked the door.

Roger had understood when he heard the door close and lock that his best friend needed the time alone. He had rerouted the King's telephone calls to his office, and had left Eric in quiet. Peace would come later, after the grieving process. He knew that from his own father's death from a sudden heart attack.

Eric stepped to Roger's office. "Roger, please reschedule all of my meetings and appointments for the next five days."

Roger's heart skipped a beat. He knew without being told that Gerard had begun dying. "Of course. Eric, is there anything else I can do?"

Eric smiled at his closest friend. "No. Let me know if anything urgent or important comes up. I want to stay with Father and Mother."

"I will. Daniel and I will do anything for you and Gerard. Just know we're here."

"I do. Thanks, Musketeer," Eric said and returned to his parents' bedroom, where he sat until 2:00 in the morning.

"I'm sorry, darling. I've neglected you lately," Eric said when he entered their bedroom and found Marisol sitting in a chair reading.

"No, you have not. Your parents need you more than ever. You should be with them. We have many years ahead for us, mi amor, many years," she said and kissed him.

369

§§§§§

"Daddy, oh Daddy. I don't want you to hurt again. Why can't I take your pain? Why?" Anglia said as she watched Eric that day, feeling his pain. "Please, God, give me his pain. Don't let him go through this again. Please." Her tears, like Eric's, lasted many hours, and filled the Angel Choir with sadness, unprecedented prior to Patrick's death.

Patrick ran to his niece and held her. He knew his words wouldn't mean much to her, but he refused to let her suffer alone.

Her wailing cut through Stefan, who had watched his son and grandson throughout Gerard's brain cancer. He never wanted them to suffer either, but he understood that suffering came with earthly life. He, like his son, believed that many of life's ills came from Satan in retaliation for belief in God and Jesus as His Son. He also knew that God did His part to lessen suffering so that no one dealt with more than they could bear at any one time.

The same applied to angels, Stefan decided. Angilia's sensitivity to her father often caused her tremendous pain. Since time didn't exist in Heaven, he had no idea how long she wailed, screaming and crying simultaneously, but from his memory he estimated six or seven hours. When other angels began crying in sympathy and sadness, he knew he had to act.

Stefan walked to Angilia and Patrick, and gently lifted her into his arms. "Come."

"Where are you taking her?" Patrick asked. "Don't be mad at her. She's hurting because Eric's hurting."

"I know. I'm not mad. I'm going to help her."

"I don't know," Patrick softly said as he looked again at his crying brother. So much pain and sadness. Life was filled with both, it seemed.

Stefan bowed before the Thrones and they let him move forward to face the Cherubim, who likewise let him pass. Finally, he stood facing the Seraphim, the highest guards in Heaven. They understood his purpose and parted for Stefan to enter. Stefan fell to his knees in front of the throne and lay Angilia at God's feet.

"You bring her here because her father's pain fills her. You want me to ease her suffering."

"Great-Grandfather, God can't help me. I am too tightly connected to Daddy," Angilia managed to say.

"Surely He can, dear."

"No," she said, crying more violently. "Daddy is too much a part of me, of my heart and soul. We are one."

"She is right, Stefan. To ease her pain, to stop it, would sever their connection, and that can never happen," God said. "Her suffering will end, just as will Eric's."

Stefan bowed and said, "As you command, my God." He picked up the crying girl and returned her to the Angel Choir. He looked sadly at Patrick and placed her in Patrick's arms.

Stefan walked away, forcing his shoulders back and his spine straight. Patrick had known this would happen. Pain is part of life. *Everyone suffers pain, even this angel,* he thought and hugged his niece close.

§§§§§

Eric sat next to his father's bed nearly every minute of the following three days, barely taking time to shower, shave, and change clothes. He didn't attend the Sunday morning church service, although he did telephone Reverend Simmons to explain why. He hardly slept, occasionally dozing off in the chair.

Matilda had not left her husband since his fall, and the stress, worry, and exhaustion clearly showed on her face. She stood at one point on the Tuesday morning and kissed her husband's cheek and lips. She leaned close to him and whispered in his ear. Gerard didn't respond, which caused Matilda to turn toward the wall and run her hands through her hair. Gerard's illness took a huge toll on her own well-being, which Eric realized.

He went to her, put his hands on her shoulders, and softly said, "Mother, lie next to him and get some sleep. I'll stay right here, and I'll wake you if anything at all happens. Please, Mother. I don't want you sick, too."

She shook her head and said, "I can't. What if he goes while I'm sleeping?"

"I'll wake you if anything changes or if he moves. I promise. Please."

Matilda's shoulders drooped, and she nodded. She walked around the bed, lay beside Gerard, and placed her hand over his heart. She stared at him until her eyes closed in sleep.

Eric took his mother's chair and wrapped his hand around his father's. Nearly three hours later, Gerard opened his eyes, seeing his son where his wife had been for days. He turned his head, and Eric saw a weak smile when Gerard saw his wife beside him.

Eric stood and reached to wake her, but Gerard managed to grab his arm and shake his head. "I promised her I'd wake her if you awoke."

"No," Gerard whispered. "Do not let her. . .see me. . .die. Please. I can't. . .die in. . .front. . .of her. This can't. . .be her. . .last memory. . .of me. I can't bear. . .her tears. I can't."

Tears filled Eric's eyes. Even in his last moments, his father's first thought focused on his treasured wife. How great their love and devotion remained! Eric held his father's hands and nodded his head. "I understand, Father. I love you."

Gerard smiled again. "I. . .love. . .you." His breathing became more labored and moister, a sign that his lungs would soon cease breathing.

Eric forced his tears and emotions deep inside him. He did not want to cry now, before his dying father. *I can't. Father cannot feel any guilt in leaving us. Please, God, help me.*

Gerard looked directly at Eric, nodded once, and took his final breath, jagged, raspy, moist. His eyes stared at Eric for nearly two minutes. His heart stopped long before the last moment, when Gerard tightly grasped his son's hands and closed his eyes.

Eric bent, kissed his father's forehead, and said, "I love you, Father."

He gently placed his father's hands on the bed, walked around the bed, and touched his mother's arm. He leaned down and softly said, "Mother."

Matilda opened her eyes and instantly saw that her husband had died. She threw herself atop him and cried, holding him tightly. After several minutes, she asked a tear-stained, "Why didn't you wake me before?"

Eric went to his mother, sat on the bed beside his parents, put his hand on her back, and said, "Father awoke for just a couple of moments. I started to wake you, but he stopped me. He managed to say that he didn't want you to see it happen, that this shouldn't be your last memory of him. I had to do as he asked, Mother. I had to."

Matilda nodded and buried her face in Gerard's chest. "Yes. I want to stay with him for a while."

Eric kissed her and left his parents alone for their last minutes together. He walked to his father's office—now his office—and turned on the computer.

Royal Statement

15 September 1992

I have the very sad task of letting you know that my father King Gerard died this afternoon at 4:13. I was with him, as was my mother, and he left this world surrounded by love. He felt your love, too, I know.

My father's state funeral shall occur on Friday, 18 September 1992 in Christ Church Valmondois.

Thank you for loving and supporting my father throughout his life. He loved you, as well. Take comfort in knowing that he never feared death, for he believes that we live eternally. My father is healed and safe in God's arms.

Eric

Eric sent the statement to Carol for immediate release. When she brought the framed copy to Roger to place on the Palace gates, his first thought went for his friend. He stepped across the hall. "Eric?" he softly said. "Are you all right?"

"Yes. Father's pain and suffering are over. His body is freed from cancer. Mother is heartbroken. I'll go back to her soon, but she wants to be alone with Father for a while. Let me have that," Eric said, reaching for the framed statement. "I'm going down there, so I can place it."

"You? But. . . . ."

"I'm going out there anyway, so I can take it," Eric said and took the frame from Roger, who instantly called Stanley that Eric was going out to the gates.

"I'm on my way," the loyal bodyguard said and ran to the front entrance, beating his charge.

"Stanley? What are you doing here?" Eric asked.

"It's my duty."

"Very well." Stanley opened the door, and Eric walked to the gate and posted the statement.

As people read the parchment, gasps and screams emanated from the crowd, which quickly grew as word spread. Eric motioned for the guards to open the gates, and as soon as he stepped through them, people engulfed him.

People cried, hugged Eric, and some even prayed. "God save King Gerard!" someone shouted. A man followed with "God save King Eric!" The chants continued for quite some time as people simultaneously mourned King Gerard and lauded King Eric.

Eric spoke with and comforted people for more than three hours as the news of his father's death spread, and people rushed to the Palace. Many recognized his exhaustion, and they knew he had fulfilled both his and his father's obligations for the past several months.

"I love you, King Eric!" a woman shouted, inspiring hundreds to repeat the sentiment until the mall resonated with the phrase. Eric motioned for them to stop, which only heightened their fervor and respect for their new King.

"We love you, King Eric! All hail King Eric! God Bless King Eric!" hundreds of people shouted as they surrounded him. For nearly another three hours, as the sky grew darker, they chanted and praised him.

Roger and Marisol watched from the second-floor windows with pride, love, and tears, knowing that Gerard looked down from Heaven with paternal love and pride. Everyone would mourn King Gerard, but they and their country would receive the most benevolent care and benefaction from his son, King Eric.

Sheilah R. Craft is an English professor, writer, blogger, poet, artist, ardent genealogist, and book lover. Born and raised in the Midwestern United States, Sheilah was born surrounded by a close family—including several educators—books, and animals. She began reading and writing very early, and has published short stories, articles, and poems. She was literally born a writer. Her series of novels centered on the lives of one family dynasty and spanning more than two centuries began in the fall of 2012 with the first volume, <u>Heart-Glow: A Novel</u>. <u>An Expected End</u> is the sixth volume in the series, meaning one volume publishes each year. Six more volumes are planned, all of which explore the lives of the DeBruce Martineau family members.

BOOKS BY SHEILAH R CRAFT

Published by STARLIGHT Books:

HEART-GLOW: A NOVEL

FIRST LOVE NEVER DIES: HEART-GLOW
VOLUME II

HEART ETERNAL: HEART-GLOW VOLUME III

LIFE ETERNAL: HEART-GLOW VOLUME IV

THE SPLENDOR OF HEAVEN: HEART-GLOW

VOLUME V

HE TOUCHED ME

MARY MAGDALENE: A MYSTERY PLAY

Published by Little Butterfly:

THE QUEST FOR PERFECTION: SHELLEY AND
THE POET-HERO

A DAY WITH TEDDY BEAR

SOULSCAPES